GOLD COAST MURDER

RON WICK

GOLD COAST MURDER
Ron Wick

a GlenEagle publication
Copyright ©2013 Ron Wick
rev 3.22.22
Printed in the United States of America

* * * * *

Disclaimer
This is a work of fiction, a product of the author's imagination. Any resemblance or similarity to any actual events or persons, living or dead, is purely coincidental. Although the author and publisher have made every effort to ensure there are no errors, inaccuracies, omissions, or inconsistencies herein, any slights or people, places, or organizations are unintentional.

* * * * *

Credits
Author photo courtesy of Linda Mismas
Cover photo courtesy Bigstock Photo
Editing and cover design by harveystanbrough.com
Formatting by Debora Lewis/deboraklewis@yahoo.com

* * * * *

ISBN-13: 978-1499623826
ISBN-10: 1499623828

To Ruth "Jon" and Casey

CHAPTER 1
Day 1: Friday

She'd gone for a bath after a heated argument about his wife, divorce and marriage. He sat naked on the edge of the bed looking at the wall. The faces of his wife and children appeared before his eyes. He walked to the bathroom door, paused, shook his head, opened the door and went into the steam-filled room. The silhouette of her body was outlined through the foggy shower curtain. His excitement of earlier returned. His blood pulsed. Pulling the curtain back, he stepped into the tub, straddling her thighs, facing her, looking down.

"We're for real," he said sliding down into the water, his knees on either side of her hips. Their arms became entwined. He looked past her to the back of the tub. "I love you. I'll tell her tonight."

"I can feel your excitement," she said, pressing against him, her flesh teased by his touch. She scanned his torso.

He ran his fingers along the sides of her neck. "Yes," he breathed.

She sighed. "Do me... do me now." She relaxed and melted into his arms. They pressed against each other, grinding in a familiar rhythm. She tried to move her legs but they were pinned under him. "I love you," she said, and bent her head back, sighing again as he kissed her throat and breasts.

He gripped her wrists and pulled them together under her chin. "Let's make today special." He leaned forward, pushing her shoulders and head down into the water. "Die bitch!" he whispered. "I won't let you hurt me... my future." Her face contorted and fear filled her eyes. She fought back, squirming, trying to move her legs. He kept her pinned.

"We had two good years... two years! And now you want me to marry you?" He pressed harder. "I came here for sex, not a divorce, and you threaten to expose me?" He laughed and shifted his weight. "Good riddance. I can't let you destroy me."

She struggled hard, striving to get her face above water, but finally she gasped and breathed water. A moment later she was staring at him, her eyes wide open, lifeless.

He shifted his weight onto her chest. As it collapsed, bubbles and a faint stream of blood escaped from her mouth and nose. Energy surged through his body. "My God," he said looking down at her face and breasts. "Even now you excite me." He shifted his weight again, pressing even harder, her half-submerged body splashing the soapy water. The limp form stared back with vacant, empty eyes. He stopped moving. "What am I doing? This is sick." He started to say her name, released his grip. She remained motionless. "This didn't need to happen." He leaned back. "What have I done?" He shook his head, his hands trembling, his body shivering. A chill ran the length of his spine. A cold sweat engulfed him as his stomach turned.

He finally stood up, looked away then looked down again at his former lover. Her face was partially blurred by soap bubbles. "You were so beautiful."

He stepped out of the tub, his image hazy in the fogged mirror, soap clinging to its arms and legs. He smiled at the image. "You're a pervert," he said, as he toweled off. He couldn't stop looking into the mirror, watching his own eyes. "I've got to clean this place and get out of here."

He glanced back at the tub, at the gold hoop earrings, a birthday gift, glistening even in the limited light. He bent to tear them free. "You were good, but not that good."

He left the bathroom, dressed, and retrieved his watch from the dresser. He stuffed the earrings into a pants pocket and surveyed the room. Taking the plastic liner from the wastebasket and filled it collecting the glasses, wine bottle, trash and her clothes and purse after making sure her cell phone was in it. He placed her lap top next to it by the door. Then he walked to a nearby convenience store and bought packing tape and a small bottle of bleach. Back in the room he wrapped the tape around his hand with the sticky side out and patted down the sheets and pillows for any hair that might have been lost. Finally he poured bleach into the bath water and rinsed the sink, then stood motionless in the room looking around, mentally checking off the things that still needed attention.

He wiped one hand over his face and mumbled, "I killed her. How could this happen? I've got to protect myself."

He took the complimentary shoeshine cloth and wiped the room clean. He left carrying two small plastic bags and the laptop, leaving the door to latch on its own.

At the elevator, he waited, tapping his left foot. "There's more fish in the sea." He pressed the down arrow a second time.

CHAPTER 2
Day 2: Saturday

Detective Michelle Santiago, an attractive four-year member of the Seattle Police Department Homicide Unit, drove the unmarked car north on 15th Northwest, an artery that feeds the Ballard community from downtown.

Her partner and mentor, Chance Stewart, a twelve-year veteran and homicide's answer to the good life, watched traffic from the passenger seat. "I hope the hobo killing doesn't interfere with my plans for the weekend. How 'bout you?" He scanned her frame.

"I have no plans, business as usual." Her eyes never left the road.

"A young beautiful woman like you? There must be someone."

"No one in particular. I'm like you... play the field, don't get too close."

The car radio crackled at 8:35 and Stewart answered. "We've got a body at the Avenue Hotel on University Way," he said replacing the microphone.

Santiago changed lanes. "Well, our John Doe investigation at Golden Gardens will have to wait a little longer. Thank God it's Saturday so we don't have to deal with the weekday rush." The rear wheels fishtailed on the metal grate of the Ballard Bridge. "Weekends are bad enough." She took a fast right on the corner of Market Street and sped up Sunset Hill, passing through the Wallingford area and crossing 45th into the U District. "Home of the Huskies," she said over the siren and flashing light on the dash. She parked in the loading zone in front of the Avenue Hotel.

"Media's already here," Stewart said looking over the heads and shoulders of the crowd beginning to collect. "Bless their hearts."

A uniformed officer met them at the elevator. "I'm Officer Jackson."

As they rode together to the fourth floor, Santiago looked at him. "You were the first to arrive on the scene?"

Jackson nodded. "Yes."

"Who's the victim?"

"We don't know. The room is rented to John Smith for the night. No woman is listed."

She took out a notepad. "Car?"

"Not on the form."

"Payment?"

"Cash."

Stewart said, "Sounds like a one night stand."

"The maid found the body in the bathtub around 8:20 on her morning rounds," Jackson said. "Her name is something or other Chey...." He thumbed through his notes. "Agnes Chey. She's a no speak. Most of the housecleaning crew is. We have some people trying to locate her now."

"Where's she from?" Santiago said.

"South Korea. She got off the boat about four months ago," Jackson said.

"We'll need an interpreter," Stewart said as they entered room 407.

Santiago was already on her cell. A moment later she joined Stewart in the bathroom. "Interpreter is on the way," she said.

Don Taber, the middle-aged supervisor of the Crime Scene Investigation Unit, worked around the three officers. "Could I have a little more space, please?" He motioned Jackson out while never taking his eyes off the half-filled tub of putrid reddish brown water; a mixture of soap, blood, and waste.

Stewart looked over his shoulder. "What've we got, Don?"

"We have a beautiful black woman, twenty-five to thirty, about five foot two, approximately a hundred pounds, very petite, and dead." Taber shook his head. "She appears to have been dead for twelve to sixteen hours. We'll know more accurately after the autopsy. It's hard to tell when the body's been immersed in water."

"Cause of death?"

"My guess right now is drowning but bruises are visible on the neck area."

Santiago said, "Gentlemen, I'd say she died at 6:07 p.m."

Stewart looked at his partner. "Why?"

"The watch crystal is broken. It stopped at 6:07."

Taber glanced over his shoulder at Santiago. "Good observation, Detective. Now, notice her ears. Both lobes have visible tissue damage."

"Earrings?" Stewart said.

"Possibly. The damage is consistent with pierced objects being torn free."

"Do you think the motive was robbery?" Santiago looked at both men.

"Possible," Stewart said. "I don't know, but I don't want the media informed of the tissue damage." He looked at Taber. "Can you keep it quiet, Don?"

"Sure. We can keep almost everything under wraps for the time being. The only ones familiar with the evidence are the three of us, Officer Jackson and my team."

"Let's withhold as much detail as possible until we get a suspect. It'll help weed out the compulsive confessors."

"What about the blood? Is she showing any wounds?" Santiago asked.

"We'll take a closer look when we get her out of the tub after the photographer's finished," Taber said. "It's possible the blood discharged from the lungs if she was drowned.

Santiago returned to the hotel room, sent Jackson into the hallway to prevent any unauthorized entries and began looking about. "The bed is a mess." She pulled back the top sheet. "Got a thick stain near the foot."

Taber walked into the room. "It's probably semen."

"Probably, but it's pretty far down in the bed."

"It could be spillage from a condom. Depends on what they were doing." Taber took a sample. "We'll know more later."

Stewart entered from the bath. "It could be a lover's quarrel, or maybe an unhappy customer. If it's semen we'll at least know what Mr. Smith was doing here."

Santiago opened the closet. "Something went wrong, that's for sure. Wait... where are her clothes? The place is cleaned out."

"Whoever it was made an effort to eliminate any evidence," Stewart said. "They took the liner from the wastebasket, glasses from the bathroom, ashtrays, everything."

"Detectives, take a look at this." Taber was on his knees by the floor-length window curtain pointing at a light-blue slip of paper. "Banquet ticket for a teacher's conference dated for Friday evening." His nose almost touched the object as he bent over. "Witherspoon Hall. We've held many conferences there over the years."

"Maybe we'll get lucky," Stewart said. "When can we get the pictures, Don?"

"It'll be a couple of hours. We've got a lot to do here. I'll call you as soon as they're ready," Taber said. "And if she's a teacher her prints ought to be on file."

Santiago looked at Stewart. "I'm going over to Witherspoon while you talk to the desk clerk. Can you get a ride back downtown and check missing persons?"

Stewart nodded and grinned. "I'll press Officer Jackson into service. While you're there, get a list of the attendees."

The detectives left the room and as they approached the lobby, Santiago paused. "Think I'll take a look around before going to Witherspoon."

"Good idea," Stewart said, then approached the desk clerk, displayed his identification to the gray-haired, pale-skinned man behind the counter while noticing his employee name badge. "Mr. Robinson, what time did John Smith check into 407 yesterday?"

"Around 11:00 a.m. when the rooms became available," Robinson said in a deep baritone voice.

"Was anyone with him?"

"No. He said he had some work to complete and needed a quiet place overnight."

"Luggage?"

"Only a thick attaché case. It was dark green or black." Robinson tilted his head far enough back to reveal large nasal openings.

"How did he pay?"

"Cash. I told the other officer."

"Is that unusual?"

"Not here, not for a $75.00 room for the Smith family," said Robinson.

"Would you recognize Mr. Smith if you saw him again?"

"Possibly, we don't get many people in here at that time of day for check-in. We're still doing check-outs."

"Good. Would you describe Mr. Smith for me?"

"Well, we were busy at the counter, but as I recall he was big, like six foot four or five, white guy, about thirty, maybe thirty-five, and looked to be in good shape. He had light-brown hair cut like a businessman, a thick mustache, and dark glasses."

"What was he wearing?"

"A yellow polo shirt, tan slacks... very casual."

"Did he have a coat?"

"A jacket was draped over his arm, the one with the attaché case."

"Jewelry?"

"A wedding ring and a large watch, one of those big southwestern numbers."

"The ring or the watch?"

"The watch."

"Which wrist, right or left?"

"The left."

"When your shift is over we'd like you to come downtown, look at some photos, maybe help a police artist create a composite sketch. I believe the manager said you're off at noon. We'll have someone pick you up and bring you back."

"Thank you," Robinson said.

Stewart noticed a security camera placed in one corner of the lobby ceiling. "Do you have any video from last night?"

"It's out of order," said Robinson.

Officer Jackson approached the counter. "Detective, your interpreter is here, but I doubt you'll get anything from the crew. They were reluctant to talk to me even through their supervisor."

"We'll see. Take the interpreter to the staff locker room. We'll be down in a minute"

* * * * *

"We didn't get much," Santiago said as the detectives left the hotel.

"Jackson said we wouldn't. Like a lot of new immigrants, they don't trust cops."

"Maybe they're illegal," she said.

"Maybe, but our job is homicide," Stewart said.

Santiago went to their car. Before she slipped in behind the wheel, she looked back at Stewart. "It's the weekend, so getting any information from the U. will be difficult at best, but who knows what's going on in the school house?"

Stewart waved back as he got into Jackson's cruiser and said, "Apparently more than meets the eye."

Officer Jackson drove downtown carefully, often quite a bit slower than the speed limit.

Stewart looked at him. "Is this your first homicide, Jackson?"

"Yes," the Afro-American officer said in a near whisper. "Please, call me Art." He paused just a moment. "How long have you and your partner been doing homicide?"

"I've been with the division eight years, Mitch the last two."

Jackson said, "She seems pretty sharp."

"She's sharp, all right. She made homicide in two years. Nobody does that."

"I meant she's really a sharp looking lady."

"That too, but I wouldn't get my hopes up," Stewart said. "She's got a guy."

"You?"

"Don't I wish," Stewart said.

Jackson's mood began to change as he loosened up. "She's a 10."

Stewart ignored Jackson's comment. "It looks messy, Art. We have a young attractive black woman who's probably single, a married white man, a wiped-clean room and one or both of the individuals involved could be teachers. Have you talked to the press?"

"No, but one lady was a real pest. Taber said to let the department handle the press through your office."

"Taber's right, but you did mention the victim being black to the clerk. Anything else?" Stewart said.

"No, and the cleaning woman had already told him the dead woman was black."

"Well, let's keep mum about the investigation. If anybody asks, refer them to Captain James, Homicide. We want to save a few surprises for the killer."

Jackson frowned. "Why do you think the dead woman is single?"

"No wedding ring."

* * * * *

By 1:30 p.m. the detectives regrouped at their fifth-floor office at 610 3rd Avenue.

Santiago handed the list to Stewart and said, "The attendee's list includes all participants at the conference. Maybe we'll get a break."

"How broken down is it?"

"Time of the dinner was 5:00 p.m., social hour, 4:00. We also have the name, address, organization and position of each."

"Ethnicity?"

"No, nothing to indicate origins."

"Well, in the spirit of sharing, the photos are back." He slid an envelope across the desktops. "A partial print was found on the banquet ticket but no numbering system. It'll be a few days before we get the autopsy report."

"Do you think she was a teacher?"

"I don't know, but it looks like at least one of them was." Stewart looked at one of the photos and shook his head. "She was a beautiful woman."

"Yes, she was. Anything from missing persons?"

"No, but she might have lived alone. If she was a teacher and lived alone she might not be missed 'til Monday when school opens."

"It doesn't help that the conference has ended and most attendees have already left."

Stewart answered the phone, nodded and hung-up. "Let's go downstairs. Robinson just finished with the sketch artist. He found nothing in our pinup file."

When they entered the cubicle Robinson was studying the sketch.

Santiago looked over his shoulder. "This guy looks like the old Marlborough Man, very rugged."

"Maybe the mustache should be a little thicker," Robinson said. "You gotta remember, I was busy with checkouts when he came in."

"We appreciate your efforts, Mr. Robinson," Stewart said. "I'm sure this sketch will help us find the killer."

Santiago looked at Bob Towne, a contract artist brought in for the task. "Thank you. We'll get this in tomorrow's papers. You do nice work."

"My pleasure, Mitch. Maybe someday I can sketch you." He smiled at her as his phone rang.

"Yeah, right, in your dreams, Bob." She chuckled and they turned to leave Towne's work area as he answered the phone.

"Hold on a minute. Chance, the call is for you," said Towne. "It's Jim Hanks in Missing Persons."

Stewart took the phone. "Jim?"

"Chance, we've got a possible identification for you. She's a thirty-one year old black woman who left home Friday morning but hasn't returned. She's single and likes to spend a lot of time in the U District. From what her father says, she's done this before. He referred to her as a wild child who heard her own drummer."

"Thanks, Jim. You may have saved our weekend." Stewart handed the receiver back to Towne then wrote down the name and address of the person who filed the report. He looked at Santiago. "Mitch, let's drive out to Northgate. We have a possible ID for our Jane Doe."

"Excellent. I don't want to handle too many more members of the Doe Family right now."

* * * * *

"When I was a kid this was a very nice area," Santiago said as they approached the door of the older home on 10th N.E. and Northgate Way. "Looks like it could use a little TLC."

Clyde Baxter answered the door on the first knock.

Stewart showed his identification. "Mr. Baxter, I'm Detective Stewart and this is my partner, Detective Santiago."

"Thank you for coming. I'm worried. Miranda, our daughter, didn't come home Friday night. Now it's late Saturday afternoon and we still haven't heard from her. The wife and I are both worried."

"Has Miranda stayed out overnight before, Mr. Baxter?" Santiago said.

"Yes, occasionally, but she always called home either that night or early the next morning. She's a free spirited child, a grown woman. I mean, God, she's thirty-one years old. The times are different than when we grew up... I mean when the wife and I were young."

"Mr. Baxter, we have a woman of approximately your daughter's age, at the King County Morgue. We need you to come with us for a possible ID."

"Oh God!" His eyes welled. Baxter looked into the sky. "Of course I'll go with you."

Mrs. Baxter came to the front door. "Clyde, what's all the noise?"

"Dear, these people are from the police. They want me to accompany them downtown to see if we can find Miranda. I'll be back later. I'll tell you all about it when I get home." He took her hand and they embraced for a brief minute. "It'll be all right, Honey." He turned to the detectives. "Let's go, officers."

After a quiet thirty minute drive they were in the morgue. The attendant slowly pulled the sheet back, revealing only the face of a young woman.

Clyde Baxter looked at the girl for several seconds, then stepped back and slowly shook his head. He pursed his lips to hide a smile. "That poor child. It's not Miranda." He took a deep breath and his eyes narrowed to slits. "Must be a lot of chemicals in here."

"We'll take you home, Mr. Baxter. Other officers will be in touch if your daughter hasn't turned up in the next day or two," Stewart said.

"My heart goes out to her parents. Somewhere that child has people who care. I just pray Miranda comes home. I don't think her mama could handle this kind of trauma even with the Lord's help. We're just not as strong as we used to be. We'll pray for that child tomorrow in the Lord's House."

CHAPTER 3
Day 3: Sunday

"Thank you very much." Stewart hung up the phone. "It's tough spending all Sunday up here on the fifth floor. How many calls do you think we've made?"

"Two hundred eighty-one to western Washington and twenty-three to the east side of the state," Santiago said, "and thirty-seven were no answers."

"Good, that'll give us something to do after grabbing a bite," Stewart said. "You hungry?"

"Getting there. Anything on her prints?"

"Not yet." Stewart leaned back in his chair, eyeing her for a moment. "On second thought, why don't we try those unanswered numbers again, then maybe we could have dinner together. We deserve a little relaxation after doing this all day."

"I think I could go for dinner, Dutch of course," she said.

He grinned. "I'd have it no other way. Thirty-seven to go, then dinner."

The phone on Santiago's desk rang and she answered it.

"Mitch? Jim Hanks in Missing Persons again. I've got another possible for you. This one is a twenty-seven year old single black woman. She was supposed to have dinner with a neighbor Friday night but didn't come home. According to the neighbor she's a teacher and was attending an education conference at the UW through Saturday."

"Who reported her missing?"

"The neighbor's name is Terry Shaw."

She took out a notepad. "Give me the address and phone. We'll talk to him right away."

Stewart perked up as he listened to her side of the conversation.

"I owe you, Jim. This could save us a ton of time. Thanks." She returned the phone to its cradle and looked at Stewart. "Partner, what say we have Mr. Shaw visit the morgue? We might get a break on one of our Does, yet."

He headed for the door and said, "I'll drive."

* * * * *

"This is a pretty fancy place," Santiago said as they approached Terry Shaw's apartment north of Seattle in Shoreline.

"Indeed." Stewart pushed the doorbell and got his identification ready.

The door opened.

"I'm Detective Stewart and this is my partner, Detective Santiago. You're Terry Shaw?"

"Yes. I've been keeping a watch for you," said the tall neighbor. "Hailey was supposed to have dinner with me Friday evening to celebrate her twenty-eighth birthday. She never showed. She—" He looked away for a moment, then back at the detectives. "She apparently found someone else of greater interest, I'm sure. She didn't come home, but she also didn't call. That's unusual."

Stewart nodded. "Mr. Shaw, we have the body of an unidentified young black woman at the county morgue. Could you come downtown with us to see whether you can identify her?"

"Of course."

On the drive downtown Shaw said, "Hailey was so impetuous. She always had a couple of men on a string. I swear the girl was a nympho." He swallowed and licked his lips and bit a nail. "I hope I'm wrong."

Stewart pulled into the city garage.

As they walked into the building and approached the viewing area Shaw snapped his fingers as though listening to a beat only he could hear. When the lab attendant revealed the girl's face, he burst into tears. "How can she be dead? Who did this to her?"

Santiago said, "Mr. Shaw, we have some questions to ask you. It would be most helpful to the investigation."

"I understand, but please, I need a restroom. I'm going to be sick."

Stewart pointed down the hall and Shaw left in a hurry.

Santiago's cell phone rang. "Hello?" She listened. "Thank you, we just got the same thing." She closed her phone and looked at Stewart. "Fingerprints identified the victim as Hailey Cashland."

"Took longer than normal," he said.

"Yeah."

A shaky pale Shaw returned from the men's room a few minutes later. They escorted him into an interview room.

When Shaw was seated, Santiago asked, "What can you tell me about Hailey Cashland?"

Shaw shook his head as he looked at the floor. "She was a beautiful woman, but you already know that. Everybody loved her. She was born in New Orleans. Her father was Navy." He looked up. "She told me once her parents divorced when she was young. She left home at seventeen because she didn't get along with her stepmother. She worked her way through college holding several menial jobs."

"What kind of jobs?" Santiago said.

"The usual... you know, waitress at pizza joints, clerking in malls, that sort of thing."

"Is that where you met her?" she said.

"No. We didn't meet until three years ago when she moved here to teach at Gold Coast Academy."

"What is it you do for a living, Mr. Shaw?" Stewart said.

"I'm an artist. I drive a delivery truck by night to pay the bills and to allow time for my work."

"Do you know where her father is now?" Santiago said.

"No Ma'am. I don't think she kept in touch with him after she left home."

"What can you tell us about her social life?"

"There were too many men in it." Shaw looked at the table, the lines around his eyes seeming to deepen.

"She always seemed to be dating, sometimes two men at a time."

"Two at a time?" Santiago said.

"Detective Santiago, I loved Hailey like a sister but her dating habits were outrageous. She had affairs with married men, enjoyed casual sex often, sometimes even had two dates on the same evening."

"Did you ever date Hailey, Mr. Shaw?" Santiago kept looking at Shaw's eyes.

"No." He blushed. "I'm... of a different persuasion. In fact, that's how we came to know each other. She always felt safe around me. She knew I wouldn't be hitting on her. Our relationship was like brother and sister."

"Did you ever meet any of her male friends?"

"Not really. I met some of the people she worked with one year at a staff Christmas party. She took me along to keep the vultures away."

"You said she had many different men. Why keep them away?"

"She liked selecting her men, not them choosing her. She once told me she could have any man she wanted."

"Did Hailey socialize with or date any of the neighbors?"

"No, she was very private. I'm the only neighbor she had any regular interaction with beyond saying hello."

Santiago said, "Did Hailey ever mention anything about someone following her or watching her?"

"No."

Stewart asked, "Do you know if anyone threatened her?"

"Not that I know of."

Santiago asked, "Did she ever bring anyone home, maybe even overnight?"

"Hailey made it a point not to bring anyone here. If she ever did, I never knew it."

Santiago said, "You took care of her mail when she was gone. Do you have a key to her apartment?"

"Yes, on my key ring. I can let you in when we get back."

"We'll take the key, Mr. Shaw. Her apartment is part of our investigation," Stewart said.

"Of course." Shaw removed it from his key ring.

Santiago slid a pen and a pad of paper across the table. "Could you write out a list of the neighbors' names and apartment numbers for us?"

Shaw nodded. "Yes, I know all of the nearby residents."

When he was finished, Santiago stood up. "I think we're finished here. We'll take you home since we are visiting her apartment."

Shaw shrugged. "Excellent."

A short while later Stewart pulled into a parking place near Hailey's apartment.

Shaw walked to Hailey's door with the officers. He said, "As you'll see when you get inside, she has—well, had—a nice place." He stood by the open door, looking in."

"Thank you, Mr. Shaw," Stewart said. "We'll take it from here. We'll be in touch if we need anything else."

He closed the door then called for a CSI crew as Shaw walked toward his own apartment.

Santiago pulled on a pair of surgical gloves. "I'll start in the living room."

Stewart went to the bedroom. "She had good taste in clothes," he said moments later. "It looks like everything is high end, some very sexy. I bet there's not a mini in here that's over sixteen inches. The brand names read like a fashion magazine: Bloomingdale's, Jacobson's, Nordstrom, Versace, Saks, Rialto. I know teachers aren't as underpaid as some people think, but hey, this stuff is big bucks."

"Chance, come out and take a look," Santiago said. "This may help with the background."

He entered the living room. "What did you find?"

"Photo albums. Looks like they go back about ten years." She handed one of the books to him.

He shook his head. "Some of these pictures look like they're from a strip club, maybe a job when she was in school?"

"Working clubs and bars is good money. A lot of coeds have earned their way through school that way."

Stewart said, "Maybe we'll find a familiar face in here. How recent do they get?"

"Who knows? Shaw told us she had several male friends, usually with more than one affair going at a time. Maybe she had a sugar daddy or two."

"Maybe she was a nympho?" Stewart said.

"Anything's possible," she said. "Our job isn't to judge and we can't diagnose."

Santiago rummaged through a closet by the front door and pulled out a garment. "Here's a Gold Coast sweatshirt. It's located in the north end."

"Gold Coast? What kind of name is that for a school?"

"We can visit tomorrow morning when they open and find out," she said.

Stewart walked to the bookcase. "She was quite a movie buff. There must be three hundred videos here."

Santiago joined him, checking the titles. "No kidding. It looks like she collected mostly chick flicks."

Stewart glanced out the front window. "Lab crew is here. Let's talk with the neighbors while they get started."

They let the lab crew in, then began interviewing the neighbors.

Ethel Jones answered on the first ring and looked at Stewart's identification for a long moment. She did not let them in. "You want to know about Hailey, don't you?"

"Yes, Ma'am," Stewart said.

"She didn't mix much with the neighbors other than Mr. Shaw. At least two or three nights a week she wouldn't get home 'til very late."

"Did she ever have guests over?" Santiago said.

"Not that I know of, but she was a party girl. We all knew that just by the way she dressed. She was private, never had any company, men or women, except Terry Shaw that I know of."

"Did you ever talk with her?"

"Only to say hello."

"Mrs. Jones, did you ever see anyone just hanging around, maybe watching her apartment?" Stewart said.

"You mean like a stalker? Heavens no! I'd have called the cops right away."

"Well, thank you for your ti—"

The woman closed the door.

Santiago glanced at the list Shaw had provided. "Mark Brothers is next." When she pressed the doorbell he answered in bare feet and well-worn jeans. Stewart greeted him. "Mr. Brothers, we're from the—"

"I know. I could hear Mrs. Jones. My kitchen window is open."

"What can you tell us about Hailey Cashland?" Stewart said.

"Not much, other than I'd like to know her better, if you get my drift." He grinned. "But she was always aloof."

"No visitors?" Santiago said.

"I was always willing. Wait... your ID card said homicide. Has something happened to her?"

"She was murdered at a hotel last Friday."

"The woman on the news?" Brothers shook his head. "What a waste."

"Did you ever talk with her?"

"Only in passing."

"Visitors?"

"Only one I know of is the artist, Shaw."

"Did you ever see anyone just hanging around, maybe watching her or the apartment?" Santiago said.

"We all watched her when we could, but always from a distance. She didn't mix with the neighbors."

Brothers' face turned red. "Ah, I've got a pan on the stove."

"I don't have any further questions at this time, but maybe later," Stewart said.

"I'm always available for the police." He looked at Santiago. "Always." He stepped inside and closed the door.

"I'm happy he's always available." Santiago glanced at his door. "He could use a lesson in subtlety."

They crossed the courtyard to the last apartment in the cluster and Santiago rang the bell.

A man opened the door.

"Mr. Todd, Lincoln Todd?" Santiago said.

"Yes."

"I'm Detective Santiago, and this is my partner Detective Stewart of the Seattle Police Department. We're seeking information about one of your neighbors."

"Hailey Cashland?"

"Yes," Santiago said with a glance toward Stewart.

"Like all the other single guys around here, I'd liked to have known her better, but I didn't have a chance."

"Did you see her often?" Santiago said.

"She hung around the pool area every day during the summer, but she kept to herself. She had her own friends unfortunately, and she didn't mix much with most of us. There's not much else to tell. None of us could figure out what she saw in that artsy fag, Shaw."

"Did she have visitors very often?"

"Only the fag, otherwise I never saw anyone visit. She went out a lot, always dressed like a club chick, but never brought anyone home."

"Did you observe anyone just hanging around, maybe watching her or the apartment?" Stewart said.

"No. Well, maybe once. He looked like a high school kid. I'm not sure whether he was looking for Hailey or an apartment."

"Would you recognize him again if you saw him," Stewart said.

"No, he was across the way, but from here he looked like a jock, muscular, fit."

"Thank you, Mr. Todd," Santiago said. "If you think of anything else, please call us at this number." She handed Todd a business card.

The two detectives walked back to their car. "The neighbors don't recall any visitors coming or going," Stewart said, "but maybe a stalker." He put his note pad away. "Let's go downtown and see what else we've got."

"Good idea. Who knows, we might even have something on our hobo John Doe."

"That would be nice but I won't take any bets on it," Stewart said.

* * * * *

Trevor Gunn drove slowly down Alki Avenue between Alki Point and the Duwamish Head to 58th S.W. looking for Bobbi Turner's apartment. "The first nice weather of the year sure brings us outside." He looked at the beach, populated by bikinis and volleyball players. "I'll bet Seattle's founding fathers

didn't anticipate this when they landed here in 1851."
He chuckled, spotted Bobbi's place and pulled off the road.

"Alki Shores, nice location." He parked in front of the complex across from the beach. "Pricey for a student." He got out of the Mustang.

Bobbi Turner opened the door on the second knock.

Gunn drank in her petite frame, which was covered only by a white string bikini. "This is my kind of place," he said. "I see you're dressed for the beach. No tan line." He smiled.

"I've been keeping an eye out for you. Come on in." She unlatched the screen door. "It's not much, but its home."

"I like it already."

"The apartment, or the beach with all those hard young bodies?"

"The hostess."

"Good answer. I thought we'd have a little picnic down on the beach if that's okay with you?"

"More than okay."

She walked to the kitchen area and picked up a small basket. "Would you grab the blanket and towels on the end of the couch?"

"Sure, but I must confess I didn't bring swim trunks."

"Wear your boxers," she said. "Trunks, boxers; they all look the same. No one will notice except me." She smiled and arched a brow.

"How'd you know I was wearing boxers?"

"Dark fabric under light fabric shows through. I'm thinking you're trolling, or something." She laughed, putting on her sunglasses as they walked out the door holding hands.

Across the street they found a comfortable semi-private space against one of the many massive driftwood logs. "Go ahead, slip off those shoes and pants. Like I said, nobody will notice." She glanced toward the volleyball players. "As long nothing pops out."

"To pop or not to pop, eh?" He slipped off his loafers, shirt and trousers.

"No socks?"

"I usually don't wear them... or underwear for that matter," he said.

"Good thing you did today," she said, propped up on her elbows, her breasts nestled in the triangles of the untied halter, looking around. "My friends would notice the lack of slacks much quicker without boxers." She patted the blanket and he stretched out beside her.

"Sun in Seattle in mid-May is a welcome treat," he said. "Would you rub a little lotion on my back?"

"I thought you'd never ask, but I'm a little more exposed, even with my tan. How about doin' me first?" She formed a small pout teasing her lips with the tip of her tongue.

"My pleasure." He spread lotion on her thighs and back, slowly rubbing her flesh. "You're smooth. I like that." He teased the waist of her bikini and slid his hand just under the fabric at the lower spine. She moaned with pleasure while he massaged the cream on the backs of her thighs. She parted her legs as his hand moved higher up her inner thigh. His fingers playfully touched and stroked the fabric of the suit bottom.

Bobbi emitted a small moan, gasped, secured her halter strap and sat up. "My turn to push some buttons." She spread lotion on Gunn's back. "My hands and fingers like to travel all over." She ran a long fingernail slowly across his back under the waistband, pausing for just a moment. "Roll over and I'll do your chest."

"I don't think I should," he whispered.

"Then I'll do the back of your legs," she said and began kneading his flesh. "Here comes that naughty fingernail again." She slid her hand into a leg of his boxers. "You feel really tense, Trev. When was the last time you scored, anyway?"

He smiled. "You're very direct."

"We're here for lunch and sex aren't we?" she said.

"Yes, between friends... lovers. It's been a few days," he said in a forced voice.

"Well, you're here with me now. We'll enjoy each other and work out this kink. We both win." Bobbi looked into his face. "So you're okay with adultery? Multiple partners? I am."

"Romance is something I practice with my wife," he said. "We have an open marriage. We've found sex with different partners keeps us alive, energetic, interesting. You have to remember we're the products of the '80s and '90s. Everybody slept with everybody. Sex was casual and acceptable."

"Casual, safe, whatever. Right now I'm thinking lunch. Don't let my looks or age fool you. I'm a diabetic," she said.

Gunn pulled the picnic basket close and opened it as a Seattle Police car passed Alki with its siren going.

Bobbi asked, "Have you heard about the woman they found dead at the Avenue Hotel?"

Gunn looked around the beach. "Yes. Terrible, isn't it...."

"They'll catch him," she said. "In my criminology class last quarter we had a guest attorney who told us people only commit murder for three reasons: sex, money or revenge."

"Interesting point of view," Gunn said. "Why do you think the killer was a man?"

"You got me there. I just assumed it. I'll have to do better than that if I'm going to be a paralegal or a chemical dependency counselor."

"Yes you will, and keep in mind they haven't said how she died either."

They finished their picnic lunch as the conversation ebbed.

"Maybe we should head back to your place." He rolled onto his side and looked at the volleyball courts. "Do you suppose they do anything else?"

"Anything they want."

"You seem to be throwing their game off."

She laughed. "They're friends of mine."

"Close?"

"Close enough." She waved and smiled at a player. "We hang out down here."

Gunn kept watching the volleyball players.

"I like experienced men," she said and touched his arm.

She leaned forward and kissed him, her tongue probing, and ran a fingernail across his belly at the waistband of the boxers.

He swallowed and shook his head.

"My mom always told me not to talk about other guys when I'm on a date."

"Your mother is wise. A smirk crossed his face. "If that suit was any smaller you'd be naked."

"From the way you're lookin' at me, I *am* naked... and sweaty."

"So you are." He nodded again toward the street.

She tossed his shirt across his lap. "I think we ought to wait a few minutes. I'm not the only one with exposed flesh." She laughed.

"Do tell." He looked at his lap. "Let me regain my composure."

"It's not your composure that's showing." Her voice was husky.

A few minutes later, he slipped his pants back on and they crossed the street, picnic basket in hand.

Bobbi held Gunn's hand as they crossed the street. "Too bad everyone can't take the time to make love like us today. No anger."

"No guilt," he said.

"No murder. It's so wrong," she said. "I can't imagine being in a hotel with a killer."

"Neither can I, but sometimes people just lose it."

"Enough talk," she said. "Let's make love."

An hour later they were naked and spent beside each other. "We're like bacchanalian buddies stretched out here," he said, their thighs touching.

"More wine?" she said finishing her glass.

"No thank you." He looked around the bedroom. "It was great, Bobbi."

"Yes, it was. I feel very satisfied. This is the only way to write a term paper, don't you think?"

"You mean the one you just aced?"

"That's the one, although I wasn't sure I'd done enough research."

"I think your effort will result in a very high mark."

"Am I a 4.0?"

"You're a 10.0."

"I think you're ready to expand my field of knowledge again," she said teasing his groin area with the tips of her fingers.

"Yes," he said, finishing the Chablis. "But first let's enjoy the beach as the falling light of day hints at romance for those who stay."

* * * * *

They returned to their fifth-floor office. "Sure is quiet here this evening, but then it is Sunday," Stewart said.

"It's probably just the calm before the storm." Santiago stretched her legs while sitting down. "I don't have anything new on the John Doe. No notes, messages, nothing. You?"

"Not a thing. This Cashland case is high profile. I expect we'll be handing the hobo off before long."

"Probably," she said. "We haven't got a lot on Cashland either, more questions than answers," Santiago said.

"I know." He looked at his watch.

She yawned. "It's getting late and I'm tired. Has the lab finished dusting the photo albums yet? I'd like to study them tonight over dinner."

"Dinner? You're going to eat tonight?"

"One of my vices." She smiled. "You should know by now this body requires food at regular intervals. Right now it's shouting at me. Remember earlier we were talking about Dutch treat? Well, I want to eat and I want to study the albums. You want to look them over too, right?"

He nodded. "I'd thought about checking them out tonight."

"It's late enough I'm having takeout rather than going to a restaurant. Want to join me? Strictly work."

"It's a plan," he said.

"Done." She looked at his physique. "We could use a clue or two." *And I want to learn a little more about you too.*

A short while later the two detectives were eating pizza and reviewing Hailey Cashland's photo albums at Santiago's apartment. Over pizza and wine they chatted briefly.

"You've got a really nice place here. Not far from Gold Coast compared to my Ballard condo." He laughed. "You have a courtyard out the front door, Jackson Golf Course for a back yard, and an indoor pool; I've got a sidewalk and a bus stop."

"We all have different priorities. You have a condo, the Locks, boats and Market Street," she said.

"I call mine child support."

"I heard you had a family, but you never mentioned it."

"My business, private." He looked across the living room. "Nice fireplace. I like the way the flames make shadows dance when the lights are low or off." He pointed. "Look at your white wine. The flame has given it a unique depth of color."

"We need more light in here if we're studying the albums," she said and flicked a three way switch on an end table. "A lot of skin seems to be showing in these pictures. Have your eyeballs popped out yet?" she said.

"Not yet, but you've got to admit Hailey was beautiful."

"No argument there," she said.

"What's a teacher doing with pictures like these?" he said.

"Like I said earlier today, we all have our baggage. The background in these looks like a lounge or club setting." *I bet there are still a few pictures of me from my days on the Strip.* Mitch pointed to a wall poster behind Hailey in one of the photos. "My bet is she worked them to pay her way through school. I know it can pay well from working vice."

"Well, I'll tell you what I don't see—one of those big southwest watches," Stewart said.

"Not so fast, Chance. Take a look at this Christmas picture from a year ago." She held out the more current album and pointed to a man's wrist in one of the pictures. "Look there."

"Could be," he said. "It sure could be. Too bad she didn't attach names to the pictures."

"Indeed. We'll take a copy with us tomorrow and ask the principal if he recognizes him. It's been a long day... a long week. I need to fold my tent before I crash."

"Me too. I'll see you downtown tomorrow. Maybe tonight I'll dream about the fresh air at Ocean Shores, my lost weekend." He paused by a small table near the entry. "Who's that with you?" He pointed at a framed photo.

"My kid sister, Jill."

"You two could almost pass for twins except for the hair."

"There's no mistaking our family origins and a woman's hair is an accessory."

"How old is she?"

"The picture was taken about six years ago. She was nineteen at the time. We gave a large portrait to our parents for their twenty-fifth anniversary."

"Your parents are fortunate to have two bright, beautiful daughters."

"I think so. Jill is a bit of a free spirit... we both are."

"What does she do?"

"Whatever moves her at the moment. She's pursuing a career in modeling. So far its calendars and boat shows... all eye candy. I hope she gets out of the fast lane one of these days." Santiago sighed.

"Where does she live?"

"Too far away for you, Redondo Beach. You know, California: sun, sand and sex." *I'm reading your mind and I don't want to talk about my kid sister.*

"Does she ever visit?"

"Only unannounced. Why, you like what you see?"

He smiled. "She's as gorgeous as you are and her line of work is dangerous, too, in its own way."

"Yes it is and I'll take the gorgeous part as a compliment, thank you." She looked at the photo and chuckled. "Besides, even with your reputation, I think she could hurt you badly." A smile crossed her face. *And so could I.*

"Like I said, I'm on my way."

"Monday, tomorrow," she said with a wave and closed the door. As she crossed to the living room couch she mumbled, "I should've offered him another glass of wine. Damn, I should've used the Hanzell Dad gave me. Next time." She sat down and returned to the photo album with the picture containing the watch. "Is he the one, Hailey? Where did you find him?"

"Fortunately we're going against traffic. This could take an hour otherwise," Stewart said as they drove to Gold Coast Academy.

"No kidding." Santiago looked up from reading a printout. "It says here the Gold Coast campus covers 110 acres overlooking Puget Sound, contains greenbelts, wetlands, an indoor swimming complex, a five-story performing arts center, and state-of-the-art science and electronic labs."

"I went to Ballard High School before it was remodeled." He turned into the entry drive. "Man, this is beyond plush by any measure."

"I went to Ingraham High, graduated about ten years ago. It was modern, but nothing like this." The shadow of the performing arts center engulfed the car. "High schools have changed."

Gold Coast did not have a principal. Jack Hartley, the school's superintendent, met the detectives at the building entry by accident. Even in heels Santiago was a head shorter than Hartley, the man in the picture at the staff party. He motioned the visitors into his office and invited them to sit down. Hartley sat behind a dark wood executive desk after telling his secretary to hold all his calls.

Stewart said, "Mr. Hartley, we received a report that Miss Hailey Cashland, one of your staff members, was missing yesterday afternoon. It was filed by a neighbor."

"Probably Terry Shaw. He keeps close tabs on Hailey. Truth be known, she attended a workshop at the UW last weekend. She's absent today and did not call in."

"Does she do this often?"

"Do you mean miss work or attend workshops?"

"Miss work without calling in."

Hartley shook his head. "Never, she's always been very reliable." He looked across the cluttered desk directly at Stewart. "She usually arrives early and leaves late."

"Mr. Hartley, how well did you know Miss Cashland?"

"She's been on our staff for almost three years. She teaches physical education, biology and swimming. She's also the coach of our cheer squad. She's very popular with the students."

"Did you know her socially?"

"I see her when the faculty has a gathering following a game or at a staff party. Away from school she has her own friends."

Stewart shifted in his chair. "That's not what I mean. Did you know her as a close friend away from campus, perhaps even intimately?"

Hartley's face reddened, and a sheepish smile formed. "Is Hailey accusing me of something, Officer?"

"Such as?"

"For the sake of argument, let's say sexual harassment."

"No, she's not accusing you of anything, Sir."

Hartley breathed a sigh of relief.

"Mr. Hartley, Hailey Cashland is dead."

"What?" He stared at Stewart then looked at Santiago. "No!" His eyes welled.

"We have her body at the King County Morgue. Mr. Shaw identified her late last evening." Stewart reached into his pocket and produced a photo of the dead woman. He handed it across the desk to the superintendent, who was looking white as a sheet. "Can you confirm the woman in the picture is Hailey Cashland?"

Hartley studied the photo carefully as his hands began to tremble. "Yes." A tear escaped the corner of his eye.

"Does Miss Cashland have any family in the area?" Stewart asked.

"None that I know of. She's from New Orleans. She's been on her own since her late teens." He handed the photo back. "What happened?"

"She was murdered at the Avenue Hotel," Stewart said.

"How awful! We're having a parent function this evening."

"Beg your pardon?" Santiago said.

"Several parents are, were, coming this evening for a special program. Hailey—I mean Miss Cashland—was going to assist me with the presentation." Hartley leaned forward and picked up the phone. "What time is it getting to be?" Without waiting for the officers to respond he pulled up the left sleeve of his blazer and checked the time. "9:10," he said.

"Nice watch," Stewart said looking at the bulky silver and jade timepiece.

"My wife gave it to me."

"Mr. Hartley, you're going to have to come downtown with us and answer some additional questions," Stewart said.

"Of course. I want her killer caught. I'll do anything I can to help." Into the phone he said, "Miss Webb, please prepare an announcement to send home canceling this evening's special parent program. We'll reschedule at a later date. One of our staff, Miss Cashland, was murdered over the weekend. Also, call a special emergency meeting of the department heads so they can review the action plan with Doctor Sherwood. They'll share it with staff members. Alert the counselors, too. We'll want to address any needs of the students immediately. I'll address the school over the PA system after the staff has been notified." He glanced back at the detectives and held his hand over the receiver. "I'll be more than pleased to go with you, but first let me share this sad news with the school. Gold Coast is a most prestigious institution with many influential backers. I certainly don't want to jeopardize its position within the community. Our emergency plan is already in place." Stewart nodded approval and Hartley returned to the phone. "Miss Webb, after I address the school I'll be going downtown with two detectives to assist in any way I can." He cradled the phone. "I'll be ready in ten minutes."

* * * * *

Jack Hartley and the two detectives were seated in the fifth-floor interrogation room, which was furnished with a chipped table, four well-used chairs and institutional gray walls.

Santiago began the questioning. "I know Detective Stewart asked you earlier, but again, how well did you know the victim?"

"God, this is a nightmare." He looked around the room, swallowed and took a deep breath. "We were having an affair."

Stewart interrupted the interrogation and read Hartley his Miranda rights. "Mr. Hartley, do you want an attorney?" Stewart said.

"No." His voice was weak. "What happened?"

"You tell us," Stewart said.

Captain James, Homicide Chief, entered the room and went to a far side where he leaned against the wall to observe.

"We've been close for the last three years, ever since she came to teach at Gold Coast. It began innocently enough at an after-game party. She was so beautiful, alive. The atmosphere was charged when we were together."

"Tell us about last Friday," Santiago said.

"I took a room at the Avenue Hotel. Hailey joined me shortly after registration. We made love as we have so many times. It was wonderful. Then, after showering I left for the banquet."

"Did you use a condom?" Stewart asked.

"Yes, as a protection from disease. Hailey was an active young woman. I certainly didn't want to transmit anything to my wife."

Santiago watched Hartley. *How noble of you.*

"What time did you leave her?" Stewart glanced at his partner.

"Around 2:00 p.m."

"Can anyone provide an alibi for your whereabouts?" Santiago asked.

"Yes, several colleagues at Witherspoon Hall. I was in a session with several associates at 3:00 after coffee with our board president, George Archer."

"And she was alive when you left her?" Santiago watched Hartley's eyes.

"Yes, alive and still in bed. Ours was a physical relationship. She knew I loved my wife, and Hailey had another man she was very interested in."

"Who was he?"

"I don't know. I felt she would tell me when she wanted me to know. She said they were headed toward marriage."

Stewart said, "Was this other man already married?"

"I don't know, but Hailey did have a habit of attracting married men."

"Are you aware of any conflicts Hailey had with colleagues or friends?"

"None that I know of. The Gold Coast staff liked and admired her."

"Ever hear of any threats from students, parents?" Santiago said.

"Never a complaint."

"Has anyone hung around or near the campus, maybe just watching?"

"We're a high school, Detective Santiago. We have people waiting for student dismissal every day. I've seen none that didn't appear to belong."

"Will you voluntarily give us a DNA sample, Mr. Hartley?" she said.

"Yes, of course. As I said earlier, I want the killer caught and punished. What I did was wrong, embarrassing. I let down my family, and the school down, but it's a far cry from murder. I will be as cooperative as you want. I only ask that you be as discreet as possible."

"Of course," Stewart said. "The officer outside the door will accompany you to the lab."

After Hartley had left the interrogation room with a uniformed officer, Captain James said, "Well, what do you think?"

"I'm not sure," Stewart said. "He's smart enough to know the accuracy of a DNA test. He placed himself at the scene and he admits the affair. I'm inclined to believe him when he says she was alive when he left the hotel."

"Likewise his refusal to call an attorney. He's an educated man. He knows how serious murder is," Santiago said. "I want to know more about the other man in her life, the one that hasn't even called to report her missing. Does he exist?"

"Good point," Stewart said, "and I don't believe Hartley's telling us the whole truth. He seems a little shifty to me. He's certainly a person of interest."

"My feeling exactly," said Captain James. "He's believable, but very smooth. Stick with him and keep looking. I think there's much more to his story than meets the eye."

Santiago said, "After he's provided a sample we'll take him back to Gold Coast. We want to interview some of the staff members."

"That'll probably take most of the afternoon," Stewart said.

* * * * *

Jack Hartley provided a plush conference room for the detectives while they interviewed staff members. The school secretary provided a list of staff names after she highlighted those who worked with Hailey. She also noted that Mr. Hartley had told the staff to be available during their prep-periods in case they were asked to an interview. The room had two windows with blinds, two entries, a locked filing cabinet, a video camera, an audio recorder and a plasma television set. An eight-foot conference table and six sled chairs filled the room.

"All we need now is room service," Santiago said, watching a muscular man in gym shorts and a school t-shirt approach the hallway door.

"I'm Rex Britton, PhysEd teacher," the man said as Stewart opened the door.

Stewart introduced himself and Santiago.

When the man was seated, Stewart asked, "What can you tell us about Hailey Cashland?"

"She was sexy. That's really all I can tell you. That and she attended more workshops on school days than most. This time it was just her and Hartley." He flashed a wide, bright smile. "I didn't know her very well, but I sure would've liked to."

"You didn't work with her here at the school? I thought she taught physical education along with her cheer squad and biology classes," Stewart said.

"She did one class per day, but not with me. And her cheer squad was deadly for my teams. Ever try to get a teenage boy to pay attention to anything when a bunch of bimbos are bouncing around?"

"Mr. Britton, did Hailey have any conflicts with staff members that you're aware of?"

"Not really. I didn't like the way her cheerleaders interrupted practice but that sort'a comes with the territory. We made things work, no conflict there."

"Do you know of any threats directed at her?" Stewart said.

"This is a very unique and special school. Threats don't happen here."

"I have no further questions," Santiago said. "Detective Stewart?"

"Not at this time."

Santiago said, "If we have anymore questions we'll get in touch."

Santiago watched Britton as he left the room and just shook her head. *Jerk.*

Toni Fryer was next on the list. The young teacher waited in the office area. She wore a stylish short skirt, white blouse, four-inch heels and caught the attention of Britton on his way out.

Santiago invited her into the conference room.

Stewart began the questioning. "Miss Fryer, how long have you known Hailey?"

"A little over a year, since I went to work here."

"How did you get along with her?"

"Very well. Hailey was a top-flight professional," Fryer said. "Everyone here thought the world of her, including the hormonally handicapped staff members." She paused for a moment. "All of us were curious about the man in her life. She often said she and 'the Prof' would get married. It was just a matter of when."

Santiago said, "Did you and Hailey socialize outside of school?"

"No. She was friendly with the staff at work, but I don't believe she had any contact with us outside, so to speak. There was a rumor going around that she had a thing going with a staff member, but nothing came of it." She laughed. "Probably started by Rex."

"So you didn't know who the 'Prof' was?" Santiago said.

Fryer shook her head. "No, none of us did. We even teased her about it."

Stewart asked, "Do you by any chance know where this unidentified professor taught?"

"Sunset Community College."

"Were you aware of any personal conflicts between staff members and Hailey?"

She shook her head. "None. Nobody on staff spoke badly about her, nor did parents or students. No conflicts, no threats from anywhere."

Santiago said, "Did she show any signs of stress or nervousness recently?"

"Only the jitters about the wedding. She talked a lot about the date not being set, stuff like that. She had no engagement ring so we speculated that maybe the delay was caused by a previous marriage, or maybe a nervous groom. It was all a mystery to the staff."

Santiago said, "Can you think of anything else at this time?"

"Not right now."

"If you do think of anything else we'd like to know." Santiago handed Fryer a business card.

"Will do. Right now I have a class to teach."

Stewart said. "Thank you."

Tim Aaron, a science teacher still in his white lab-coat, held the door for his co-worker and looked at the detectives. "I think I'm next."

Stewart looked at a page of names. "Mr. Aaron?"

"Yes."

"Please, come in and have a seat." Stewart motioned toward a chair. "What can you tell us about Hailey Cashland?"

"The obvious, she was good looking." He laughed. "The less obvious, she was smart."

"How long have you known Miss Cashland?" Santiago asked.

"Since she came here about three years ago. We're almost done with the third year."

"Did you know her socially?" Stewart asked.

Aaron shook his head. "Not a chance. She was like very distant when it got to getting close with any of the staff." Aaron leaned back in the chair and looked at Stewart. "You know the type... Ice Princess, untouchable."

Santiago watched Aaron's eyes. *So much for her mind.*

Stewart asked, "Did she have any conflicts with staff members or others?"

"None. It's very sad that she won't be around. She was a fun person. The kids will miss her. All of us will. She was distant but friendly."

When they excused him, Aaron left the room.

"He seems much more sincere than Mr. Britton," Stewart said.

"He does."

"They both seemed to notice you, too."

"Really," said Santiago. *I wish you would.* "Who's next?"

"Ron Drake, an English teacher," Stewart said. "That's probably him now. Stewart opened the conference room door for a middle-aged man in a three-piece gray pin-striped suit pacing outside the window. Mr. Drake?"

"Yes."

"Please," Stewart said ushering Drake to a chair while introducing himself and Santiago. After he was seated Stewart began. "How long have you known Hailey?"

"It would have been three years at the end of this term next month."

"What can you tell us about Hailey Cashland?"

"She had a sharp mind and was well thought of by most of the students and faculty."

"You said 'most,' Mr. Drake?

"Yes... specifically Mr. Britton was not very interested in Hailey as a person but often spoke in innuendos when addressing her. She simply ignored him."

"Did she socialize much with any other staff members?" Santiago said.

"Not really, other than at the pep rallies and after-game parties; then she was friendly with students, parents, staff, even our board president. Otherwise she kept to herself, very private." Drake paused for a moment. "And she was way too sharp for the likes of Britton, our gutter-level contribution to the northwest's best and brightest. You ought to talk to our school secretary, Miss Webb. She knows more about this school and its inhabitants than all the rest of us put together."

"We're talking to several staff members," Santiago said.

The English teacher looked out the conference room window, then back to the detectives. "Is that all?"

Santiago said, "No. Do you have any idea who her mystery man was?"

Drake smiled. "No, I don't know, but I hope you find him just so all of us can know who he was. It's been a long-term mystery."

"Mr. Drake, you mentioned Mr. Britton's innuendoes. Aside from that did Hailey have any conflicts with staff?" Santiago said.

"None."

"Did she ever show signs of stress?"

"No, not even with Britton. Rather, she laughed at him, sometimes mockingly."

Stewart said, "How did Britton react to her mocking him?"

"He loved what little attention it garnered from her."

Santiago said, "Can you think of anything else we should know at this time?"

"No... just be sure to talk with Miss Webb."

Stewart said, "Thank you, Mr. Drake. We'll be in touch if we need anything else."

Drake nodded, stood then left the conference room passing Miss Webb on the way out.

Stewart showed Miss Webb, an attractive middle-aged woman wearing a dark blue suit with padded shoulders, to a chair. He said, "As you know, we're here asking about Hailey."

"Obviously I know. The whole school knows. From when I first met her close to three years ago until now I always found her friendly, proactive, a shining light in this haven of spoiled brats and sacrosanct adults."

"Did you know her well socially?"

"Not at all socially, but I do know she was smart enough to avoid some of the pitfalls we have here."

Santiago said, "Pitfalls?"

Webb shrugged. "Just rumors she was seeing someone on the staff from time to time. If it were true, I'd know. She was way too smart for that."

"Any idea of who the alleged paramour was?" Santiago said.

She shook her head. "None. There are seventeen men on this staff. I only know it wouldn't be two of them for sure."

"Which two?" Stewart said.

"The Neanderthals; Britton and Aaron. She could have any man she wanted—of that I'm convinced—but she didn't seem interested in any of her colleagues. She was too smart to play in her own backyard."

Santiago said, "Did Hailey show any indications of being stressed or distracted in recent days?"

"Quite the contrary, she seemed very sure of herself."

"Working the front desk as you do, Miss Webb, did you receive or hear of any threats directed at Hailey?"

"Only complements from all: public, staff or students.

Stewart took a sip of water. "Can you tell us anything else, Miss Webb?"

"Not really. If I hear anything I can call you. Mr. Hartley gave me your card for our index file.

Santiago smiled. "Thank you."

Webb stood and left the room. A few minutes later a light knocking caught Stewart's attention as they were going over their notes. He looked up and saw a woman. He opened the door for the young teacher dressed in an above-the-knee, tight-fitting skirt, powder-blue blouse and running shoes. "Good afternoon. You're—"

"Stacey Morgan," she said.

Santiago checked her off on the list of staff members.

"Come in. I'm Detective Stewart and this is my partner Detective Santiago."

Stacey's eyes were watering. "Hailey and I were friends."

Santiago began the questioning. "How well did you know her?"

"We saw each other daily in the building and once in a while at the cafeteria depending on our schedules."

"How did the other staff members see her?" Stewart said.

"Hailey was a flirt. She'd string the poor guys on staff along 'til they were climbing a wall, especially Britton, but she always stopped short of suggesting they get together. Sometimes I wish I had her style. The women here admired her."

Santiago asked, "Did she ever mention a special man?"

"All the time but not by name. We all knew she had one, but as far as I know none of us knew who he was."

"Can you tell us anything else?" Stewart said.

"Not really."

"Did anyone ever threaten her?" Santiago asked.

"Not that I know of."

Stewart said, "Has she shown any signs of stress or appeared nervous recently?"

"Just the opposite. She was always very cool, calm."

"We appreciate your candor. If you do think of anything else, please call me at any of these numbers." Stewart handed her a business card.

More tears formed in her eyes. She stood and started to leave the room. "I just can't believe she's gone." The door closed quietly behind her.

Santiago looked across the table at Stewart. "None of her neighbors or co-workers seems to have any idea of who her personal friends were with the exception of Terry Shaw."

"Everyone seems to like her," he said. "No threats, no stress."

"Santiago said, "Britton is the only thing that keeps surfacing, and he seems minor at this point."

"True, nothing negative surfaced." Stewart tapped his notepad with a pen. "We know Shaw was angry with her. We're not sure of where the affair between Hailey and Hartley was going, and we won't be until we find the silent boyfriend. Does he really exist?"

Santiago shook her head. "We've also got a possible stalker according to Lincoln Todd, and Drake mentioned the Board President George Archer. Does he go to all the functions?"

"More questions," Stewart said.

"Chance, we're missing something. It's like she had a second secret life. We need to get into it. Everybody here knows her as a professional. Not one of them knows anything about her private life except Hartley. We need to find the man in her life."

"I know. So far all we have is Hartley and Shaw. We've got to find the mystery man in Hailey's life, the professor or whatever the hell he is," Stewart said.

Santiago glanced up. A young man in jeans and an open collared dress-shirt with the sleeves partially rolled up was waiting outside the conference room. "I think our last interview is here," she said, then stood and went to the door. "Mr. Palmer?"

"Please, take a seat," Stewart said.

"Thank you. It's a difficult day for the kids and staff."

"Mr. Palmer, you've worked with Hailey Cashland for how long?" Santiago said.

"A year and a half."

"How well did you know her?"

"We often lunched together. We'd discuss upcoming lessons and evaluate activities we'd completed, probably in much the same way you and your partner work together. We both taught biology."

"Did you have any social activities beyond lunch?"

"Not really. We'd go to dinner occasionally at Burger Bite if we had a parent meeting that evening, but it was like lunch. Officer Santiago, Hailey had her own social circle away from school. Ours was a professional friendship."

"Did she have any conflicts with staff members?"

"None."

"Did Hailey seem to be under stress recently?"

"Quite the contrary, she was very excited about her coming nuptials, whenever that would be."

"Mr. Palmer," Stewart said, "do you know if she was ever threatened by anyone?"

He shook his head. "Not that I'm aware of. Her life away from the academy was unknown to us, though. It's like she had a secret. Sometimes in the staff room we'd speculate on what type of man Hailey had hooked up with."

"And what type was that?" said Santiago.

"Hailey liked men who were rugged, in good physical condition without being body builders and a challenge."

"A challenge?"

"You know... hard to get." Palmer smiled. "Sometimes she kidded about it always being good to have a 'friend' with influence, and sometimes she joked that all the good men were married." His voice dropped to a whisper. "I liked her as a professional but I'm not sure I'd even want her as a close personal friend."

"Did she ever mention any of her male friends by name?"

"No, but there is one fellow she was more than a little connected to, an instructor at Sunset Community College. She never told me his name."

"You say connected... how?" Santiago watched Palmer's eyes.

"She often spoke of marriage. She was like a bride, blushing and bubbly like every woman caught in the nuptial circus of a pending wedding. When she talked about him she was radiant. Have you talked with him yet? He could probably help you with her social life.

The staff and students all liked her. She was well thought of in many ways."

"Can you think of anything else we should know?" Santiago said.

"No, but if I do I'll contact your office."

"Thank you Mr. Palmer," Stewart said and gave him a business card before he left.

Santiago and Stewart looked at each other. "Person of influence," she said.

"Board President," he said. "Another piece to the puzzle."

* * * * *

The detectives arrived back at their office by mid-afternoon. They had no sooner sat down than Stewart's phone rang.

"Detective Stewart, Homicide," he said looking around the half-empty office of the homicide squad.

"Detective Stewart, Terry Shaw here. Hailey and I often shared videos. We enjoyed films. It was a hobby of ours. Anyway, I borrowed a copy of *Titanic* from her a few days ago—the double tape set, not the DVD."

"Yes, Mr. Shaw," Stewart said.

"One of the tapes is not the film. It's terrible," Shaw said.

"What do you mean, Mr. Shaw?"

"It's... it's *filthy*. It's obscene," he said. "Disgusting."

"You mean Hailey had a porno film?" Stewart said.

"Oh yes... that and much more. I think you'll want to see this." Shaw's breath was short, his voice shaky. "She's in the film. Awful."

"We'll be out there in about half an hour, Mr. Shaw. Thank you for calling." Stewart hung up.

Santiago looked at him. "What's up?"

"Apparently Shaw found a dirty movie starring Hailey."

She picked up her purse. "Let's go."

Forty minutes later Shaw was looking out the window as they walked toward his apartment. When they were close he opened the door. "Come in, please. The video... it's so shocking it's gross." He doubled his fist. "I know love is supposed to be unconditional and I loved her like a sister, but this... it's too much. Oh... how can I be so angry at someone who's been murdered, drowned?"

"Where's the tape, Mr. Shaw?" Stewart said.

"In the tape player." He crossed the living room, pushed the Eject button and the tape appeared. He removed it and held it out to them. "Here... I don't want this in my home."

"What's on the tape?" Stewart said.

"Hailey dancing, stripping, having sex with a man in front of people. I'm going to be sick. It's awful, disgusting."

"You said the video was in a film sleeve," Stewart said.

"Yes, but obviously it's not the second part of the video set."

Santiago picked up the sleeve containing one video. "She apparently put it in the wrong sleeve," she said, waving the container.

"I guess so. Now I'll have to rent the film to see the other half."

"Well, thank you for your cooperation," Stewart said.

Santiago continued to look at the TV then the VCR. "You didn't make a print of the video did you? It could be used as evidence in a trial. We wouldn't want to see you get into any trouble."

"As a matter of fact I believe I was duplicating the other film. Perhaps the Record mode was still turned on during what I thought was the second half of the film when that other tape began to play." He bit a nail walking over to the VCR and ejected a video. He held up the tape in a shaky hand. "It was still running."

"We'll take that also." Stewart held out a hand.

"Of course; how foolish of me. Please destroy it when you're through with it."

"Thank you again, Mr. Shaw." Stewart said. "Are there any more copies?"

On the return trip to their office Stewart watched his partner as she drove. "Man, he was really worked up."

"Yeah, very excited, very angry. Even more than Saturday when he found out she'd been murdered," she said. "He seems to bite his nails when he lies."

"A strange man," he said as Santiago parked in the city garage.

"And like most of us, he's part voyeur. He hated the tape but he wanted a copy," she said.

"What made you ask for the print?"

"Elementary, my dear Chance—the Record light was showing on the VCR." She laughed.

"Not bad. I'm impressed." He smiled.

"It must be the result of my mentor." They laughed walking through the garage.

"Want me to move a television set into one of the interrogation rooms?" he said going into the office area.

"No point in providing a skin show for the entire floor, or whoever's left," Santiago said.

The video opened with Hailey performing an exotic striptease until she was completely nude. Then she brought a male partner into the sequence. She danced, enticing the smiling figure. He responded by licking and kissing her nude, sweating body, all the while groping and stroking her. Hailey slowly undressed the man, one garment at a time, rubbing against and touching all possible passion points the fellow had, showing or otherwise. Finally, she removed his bikini briefs. The hot sweaty couple performed oral sex with each other. Then they performed intercourse in a variety of positions, self-masturbation, and the obligatory explosion of his climax into her face, their smiles all the while indicating joy with their work.

As the tape played Santiago found herself rubbing her thighs together and feeling warm. She glanced at her partner. He was staring at the TV, his knees apart, pants stretched tight.

"This is pretty titillating stuff," she said, a touch of hoarseness in her voice. "Look, I think we may have a suspect."

"What do you mean?" His eyes never left the screen.

"Take a close look at the guy in the film. He appears to be Mr. Hartley. The hair is longer and he's younger. He's in great shape... but then he didn't look too shabby this morning in his clothes either."

"Truth is, they're both great looking, but let's take another look at 'Mr. Wonderful' and see what we've got." He pushed the freeze frame.

They both studied the frozen picture of the couple before them.

"You're dead on the money, Mitch. I think it's time for us to revisit Gold Coast and hear what Mr. Hartley has to say about this."

Santiago gathered her notepad and stood. "I'd better put the video away or everyone on the floor will watch it by the time we get back." She looked at her watch. "It's about 3:55. Do you think we ought to call first to make sure he's there?"

"No. We'll surprise him. If he's not at the office we'll find him."

Captain James called out, "Stewart, Santiago, wait a minute. We have a high school kid out there waiting to see you. He says it's about Hailey Cashland. I think you'll be more than a little interested in what he has to share."

"What's his name?" Santiago said.

"Moses Cruz. He's a jock, easy to spot. Most of our female officers have found a reason to go to the water cooler." He smiled and shook his head. "His dad sent him down here after they heard about the murder. I'll have him sent in."

CHAPTER 5

He looked at Santiago sitting at the desk across from Stewart, licked his lips and approached slowly. His line of sight was on her cleavage, which was enclosed in a silk Armani blouse with the two top buttons unfastened. "Detective Santiago, my dad told me I should talk to the police about Miss Cashland. He said I should tell everything. The guy out front said I should see you."

Santiago looked at the young man, taking note of his six-foot frame and his dark complexion. His short, semi-spiked hair complimented the rich flesh and beautiful black eyes that snapped as she looked at him. His smile was perfect for a toothpaste ad. His Gold Coast t-shirt clung to every ripple of his torso, and his Levi's fit tight. *I can see why the girls out front were getting excited. Definitely a young hunk.* She smiled and stood. "You know who I am. Who are you and how can you help us?" She glanced at her partner. "This is Detective Stewart."

"I'm Moses Cruz. I'm a senior at Gold Coast," he said, never taking his eyes off Santiago.

"And your father told you to talk to us about Miss Cashland?" she said.

"Yes."

"What does that entail?" Stewart said drawing the young man's attention away from Santiago's blouse.

"I had a thing with Hailey... Miss Cashland. She was hot." The bright smile returned. "Man, every guy in school wanted to get it on with her."

"You had a *thing?*" Santiago said, leaning back in her desk chair.

"Yes." His gaze returned to Santiago, but to her eyes. "I was like every guy on campus." He shrugged. "But I got sort of obsessive. Sometimes I followed her around."

"Followed her?" she said.

"Yes. Like, I watched her apartment sometimes, followed her to the mall. Once I even followed her to a restaurant."

"It sounds like you were stalking her," Stewart said.

"I never thought of it that way... suppose you could say I was."

Santiago leaned forward and jotted a note. "Did anything ever come of you following her?"

The phone on Stewart's desk rang. He spoke briefly and looked at Santiago. "That was Dick Turner from Ballard. He thinks he has something on our John Doe. I'll go see him if you want to continue with Moses solo."

"Not a problem. See you later." She looked back to the young man. "Sorry for the interruption. Please continue."

"Well, once we got together at an art festival. She'd been partyin' and was a little tipsy. She knew I was hot for her. Anyway, she came on to me. We ended up going to her place and doin' the deed."

"You mean you slept with her?" she said.

He grinned. "No, we didn't sleep. She was awesome. It was our secret... at least until now."

"Your father told you to tell us, right?"

"Yes, when I told him about Hailey this afternoon, about our gettin' together. He said I should come down here and tell you everything about us and the other man."

"Other man?"

"Yeah, once when I was visiting some friends at Sunset Community College. We were in the cafeteria. Hailey and this guy were sittin' at a corner table talkin', holdin' hands, a lot of smiles. When she left she kissed him. He sort of tucked his head and looked around, like checking to see if anyone saw them."

"Did she know you were there?"

"No. Kids from Gold Coast seldom go over to Sunset's campus. We're more UW types, but I know a chick doin' night classes at Sunset and I thought it was cool to hang out with the older dudes there. I mean, I look older than most seniors so it's no big deal. Most college kids think I'm just another student."

"Do you know the name of the man you saw with Miss Cashland?"

"No. One of my friends said he was her teacher in a counseling class."

"When did that take place?"

"Just before Valentine's Day. I thought I'd get her some flowers or something, but after seeing them together I figured she didn't see much in me except maybe a diversion... maybe the sort of thing you do when you're drunk. Who knows, maybe she just wanted a little young stuff?"

"Were you feeling hurt or angry?"

He shrugged. "I guess... maybe a little. But hey, I got something from her I never expected. You know, like a fantasy come true." He flashed another big smile and scanned Santiago again.

"Did you tell any of your friends about your night with Miss Cashland?"

"They all knew I had a thing for her—we all did—but if you mean did I tell 'em about bangin' her, no way. I didn't tell anyone about her tattoo, either. I don't want her to look cheap, or me to look like a fool. They wouldn't believe me even if I did tell 'em. Besides, I really loved her."

"Tattoo?"

"Down... you know." His face reddened. "Kind'a private."

Santiago nodded. "What did you feel about the professor?"

"I figured he was more her type. You know, older, like in his thirties... a big dude and he looked to be in pretty good shape."

"What did he look like?"

"A lot like Mr. Hartley, more athletic but older, too. He was big boned, about six-four, maybe six-five. He even wore a big southwestern watch like Mr. Hartley, only on his right wrist. He had a thick mustache, too.

He looked very cool, not like Mr. Hartley. He's married... he's our school superintendent."

Santiago looked at the young man and fought smiling. *If only you knew about your superintendent.* "Was the man white?"

"Yeah, but that wouldn't make any difference to Hailey. She liked guys that were buff, any age, any color. Otherwise, why me?"

"Did you say this man was her instructor in a counseling class that quarter?"

"Yeah, according to Dawn Javits, a friend of mine. She was in the same class. It was on Wednesday nights. Dawn said he was forever flirting with every hot chick in there."

"Tell me, how long have you known Miss Cashland?"

"Since I was a sophomore."

"Have you ever heard anyone at the school threaten her?"

"No way. Everybody liked her."

"Did she ever seem nervous when you saw her, either before or since your intimate encounter?"

"No. She was like always the same happy friendly lady. She never even mentioned our one-nighter."

"Where were you Friday afternoon from 2:30 until 8:00?"

"Track, then home for dinner. I had a date at 7:00."

"Her name?"

"Dixie Dahl."

A man in his fifties came into the office area from the hallway. He was distinguished looking; tall, dark skinned, with silver hair fashionably long to the ears. "Moses, I'm sorry I wasn't here when you came in." He looked at Santiago for a long moment. "I'm his father, Mike Cruz," he said extending his hand. "The officer out front said I could come in."

"Well, Mr. Cruz, your son has been very helpful today."

Stewart returned to the area, introduced himself and sat down. Moses looked at his father with a tired expression on his face.

"I've told 'em everything, Dad, even about my relationship with Miss Cashland."

"Good. I'm proud of you for doing what's right." He patted his son's shoulder. "Detectives, my son came down here of his own volition. He's shared some very personal things with you that he told me after we heard about the body being found. He's been through quite a strain."

Santiago said, "Yes he has," then looked at Moses. "Can you think of anything else we ought to know?"

"Not right off hand."

"We appreciate both of you coming to see us," Stewart said.

Mr. Cruz glanced at the floor and shook his head, then looked up at Santiago. "Sometimes it's hard to share things. It's hard to grow up."

Everyone stood. "Mr. Cruz, thank you for encouraging your son to help," Santiago said. She shifted her focus to Moses, who was doing a visual of her tight fitting Guess jeans. "Thank you, Moses. The information you gave us may be very helpful. If we need to talk again I'll be in touch. If you think of anything else, please give me a call at this number," she said handing him a business card.

Father and son exited, with Moses checking over his shoulder, smiling and nodding slightly.

"Well, what do you make of Moses, Mitch?" Stewart said.

"Hard to say. Maybe he's just a stud muffin and she was his chance to let dad know he could make it with an older woman."

Stewart said, "He could just be a kid looking for celebrity by claiming to be involved with our victim."

"Well, he did mention a tattoo."

"Then there's no question they were intimate," Stewart said. "I saw it at the morgue. It's in Tabor's notes."

Stewart stood and moved toward the exit. "So, do we head for the college or go back to Gold Coast?"

"I want to talk to Hartley first. We've certainly got some hard evidence here."

"That we do," he said holding the door. "It looks like another long day for homicide."

"Then it's the registrar's office," she said.

* * * * *

"You ask the questions this time," Stewart said as they approached Gold Coast Academy. "I want to watch Hartley's reactions. I'll take notes. If I think of something you don't touch on I'll break in, okay?"

"Sure. Applying a little pressure, are we?" she said.

"He didn't come clean to start with, so I want to make him uncomfortable."

"Works for me," she said as she parked the car. "Look who's here to greet us this late in the afternoon. Bet he's heading home to the little wife. He's got his attaché case in one hand."

Hartley waved. "I was just leaving for the day. I assume you're here to ask a few more questions. Let's go to my office." He led the way.

Once they were seated, Santiago said, "Mr. Hartley, we've found evidence that confirms you knew Hailey intimately long before what you admitted to this morning."

Hartley pursed his lips and squinted. "Evidence?"

"A video, Mr. Hartley, of the two of you having sex," she said.

"Oh God, no." He hung his head, the color drained from his face and suddenly he looked much older than thirty-one.

Stewart said, "You're aware of the tape?"

"Yes. It was made several years ago in Las Vegas."

Santiago said, "Okay, tell us about Hailey again." She placed a notepad on her lap.

"She was young, maybe eighteen. I was about twenty-one. We were both kids on our own. She wanted to make some fast money and go to college. I wanted the same thing."

"And the sex business was the ticket?" she said.

"Yes. She had worked as a waitress, minimum wage plus tips, an existence at best. When she hit eighteen she got a job as an exotic dancer. With her looks the money was good. She learned real fast, the more skin the better."

"And you?" Santiago watched his face.

"I was working the same club... had been for three years. I'm sure you're aware Las Vegas provides something for everyone. You know, keep the customer satisfied."

"You were a male dancer? A stripper?" she said.

"Yes. We formed a duo, a sex show. The crowds loved us. The tips were great. It's a short step to private shows and big bucks." Hartley took a deep breath. "This is so embarrassing." Head shaking, he cleared his throat. "We quickly learned that private parties wanted real sex, not the simulated club variety."

"Why did you perform?"

"Money, a thousand a night for each of us. We were young, hungry, and using stage names. I don't think we gave any thought to the long-term view. Who would think a decade later someone would recognize us?"

Santiago looked at Hartley. *It happens. Someday you might get a surprise on your desk. I did.*

Stewart said, "Nobody has yet, Mr. Hartley, except us. Hailey had the video. It surfaced unexpectedly when she loaned it out in a sleeve of another a film."

"Well, Mr. Hartley, it's safe to say your past has come back to haunt you even if you haven't done anything illegal," she said.

"The tape is a definite threat," Stewart said.

"Yes, it would have been a mutual threat. Neither one of us would survive our indiscreet youth, not in this profession, certainly not at prestige-conscious Gold Coast Academy. Let me be completely honest with you. As I said this morning, Hailey and I have been having an affair for the last three years. It all began in Las Vegas. Even when I graduated and moved on we kept in touch. When she got into teaching she was top flight. Three years ago the opportunity arose and I offered her a position because she was the best candidate. We both knew we would resume our relationship and looked forward to it. We weren't in love or jealous of other relationships. We have—" He wiped his eyes. "Sorry... we had an emotional and physical chemistry that was good. She said our time together was rewarding and gratifying. We both felt that way. We believed our relationship would continue even after she married the man in her life."

"Do you know who this man in her life is?" she said.

"I don't know who he was. She never shared his name. I know he was an instructor." Hartley rubbed the back of his neck. "He's one of her teachers at Sunset Community College."

Stewart said, "Tell us about last Friday again,"

"I rented the room for our meeting. She joined me after check-in. We made love and then I left. I was expected to dine with some colleagues at the banquet. She was going to get a little rest and would see me later at dinner with the others."

"And she never showed up?" Santiago said.

"No. I figured she and the college instructor got together," Hartley said.

Santiago asked, "Did your wife know about Hailey?"

"Yes, but it didn't bother her. We—" He looked from Santiago to Stewart. "We haven't had a physical relationship for several years... almost four."

Stewart asked, "Will your wife confirm that?"

"Yes... yes she will." Tears formed in Hartley's eyes. "God, I'm such a fool! I raped her."

Santiago asked, "You raped who, Mr. Hartley?"

"My wife, four years ago. She said we'd stay married for the kids... for my job." He swallowed again. "But no sex, ever. In return, she wouldn't file charges or file for divorce. Now it seems like a pact with the devil."

Santiago made a notation. "Hailey Cashland joins staff after the Hartley's agree to remain married but with no intimacy."

"Mr. Hartley, has anyone approached you seeking a payoff?" she said.

"You mean blackmail? No."

"And Hailey never mentioned anyone trying get money from her?"

"No, and she would've told me."

Stewart said, "Thank you for your candor."

"Am I still a suspect?"

"Certainly a person of interest," she said. "One of the things our process does is eliminate persons of interest and suspects."

"There are others?"

"Yes." Santiago nodded. "Mr. Hartley, I must emphasize if you remember anything else let us know."

"I'll work with you in any way I can."

"Good," Stewart said. "I'm sure we'll talk again."

The detectives stood and went to the door of Hartley's office.

"I just hope this doesn't get to the board of directors or into the media," Hartley said. He held the door. "The board would terminate me in a minute. Perhaps I deserve to be terminated, but the school's prestige would be seriously harmed. That ought not to happen because of my indiscretions if it can be avoided."

After returning to their office the detectives faced each other across their desks.

"I don't know what to make of this case," Stewart said. "Jack Hartley had the opportunity and means."

"True, but he's not our only suspect and we haven't nailed down motive," Santiago said. "Before we go too far in Hartley's direction we need to find the professor or instructor or whatever he is. I'm curious whether he really knew about Hailey's other relationships." She paused for a moment. "And if he's real, doesn't it seem odd we haven't heard from him. You'd think he's noticed his girlfriend missing even if he doesn't pay attention to the news."

"So who is the professor?" Stewart drummed his fingers. "And what about George Archer? Was he Hailey's person of influence? Or the young man that may have been a stalker? Or your idea of someone blackmailing her or both of them?"

Santiago called the registrar's office at Sunset Community College. It was closed until the next morning.

Stewart said, "Shaw must be on the road making deliveries. The warehouse isn't answering. His cell is off and nobody's answering at home."

"Okay," Santiago said. "We can see Shaw first. He's on the way to Sunset; then it's time for the professor."

* * * * *

Ginger Hartley walked into the main floor den and turned on a small lamp near the doorway. "Jack, what are you doing sitting in here like this? This is so gloomy."

"Nothing, absolutely nothing," he said. He tapped the fingertips of his right hand against the desk, turned toward his wife, and focused on her youthful face. "We've got to talk, Ginger. We've got trouble... big trouble."

"Really?" She sat down on a love seat near the lamp.

"You remember Hailey Cashland, the science teacher on my staff?"

"You mean the sexy little biology teacher who doubles as your mistress?" she said. "Obviously I remember her. She's difficult to forget, try as I may."

"Yes. Well...." He paused to wipe tears from his eyes. "She's dead Ginger... murdered."

"Oh no. What? What happened?"

"I don't know. Her body was found Saturday morning at the Avenue Hotel. Two homicide detectives came to see me this morning. I confirmed it was her from a photo they showed me."

"Her body was found Saturday, what took so long to connect her to Gold Coast?" she said.

"Her neighbor, a man named Terry Shaw, reported her missing. After the body was found he made a positive identification at the county morgue. That was yesterday. Otherwise, nobody would have missed her until today."

She shook her head. "You've had a long day. Did you tell the staff and students?"

"Of course. The detectives asked me several questions. Then they decided I needed to go downtown for further interrogation. Their demand was sudden, while I was canceling the parent program we'd scheduled for tonight. I don't know why they insisted on going to their office but I want to help in any way I can."

"So what did they ask you?"

"They wanted to know how well I knew Hailey. At first I lied."

"Why?" Ginger tilted her head.

"I was scared. After they took me downtown I told them everything about the affair we'd been having for the last three years. I also told them you knew about us, that we haven't had sex in four years."

"Did you tell them why?"

"Yes." Hartley choked on his words.

"So now what happens?"

"I don't know. I asked them to be discreet, but now I'm a suspect in a murder investigation, at least a person of interest."

"Are they going public?"

"I don't think so, not yet anyway."

"God, you sound like a pervert," she said twisting her lips. "And I *loved* you."

"I feel like one. Honey, I could lose my job and all that entails if the board of directors finds out."

"Not to be heartless, Jack, but you know our deal. If the paycheck goes, you go. Christ, I always knew your cock would get us in trouble. I should've left years ago." She was angry, her voice loud.

"Maybe you should've, but you wanted the big house and the prestige of being married to the superintendent of Gold Coast. The job opened many doors for you, too. A split would've eliminated everything we both wanted."

"It still comes back to your cock. That's why we have our deal. That's why you got to have that little slut on the side."

"She was a friend."

"Yeah, right!"

"She never did anything to you. She was a good person. If anything she helped you by pleasing me."

"She was balling you." Ginger looked around the room.

"Yes, but you weren't," he said.

She pierced him with a gaze. "Are you complaining? I could've charged you with rape. You wouldn't be at Gold Coast or anywhere else in your profession."

"If I survive this we'll both be in good shape in a few years. I'll land at a university or make a niche as a motivational speaker talking about not screwing up a career with poor decisions. We'll split and you'll become someone else's trophy, complete with the house, a bank account, stocks and support payments."

"Poor baby," she said. "You're not in jail for rape, and I doubt you'll be very marketable if it all comes out in public."

"What does that mean?"

"That maybe our kids won't get the life they deserve. I'm angry, Jack, at myself, you, and the drinking that got us to that awful night. We loved each other once. Maybe...."

He looked her directly in the eyes. "You don't think I killed her do you?"

"No, I don't. You didn't help yourself any by telling the police about the rape. I'll try to clarify that when they contact me."

"Clarify?" he said.

"Rape generates a very harsh image... too harsh." She looked at her husband for a long moment. "Jesus, this is all so wrong. I can't imagine anyone wanting to kill Hailey. She was screwing you, yes—that was your choice—but that was going to change too. All I heard about at your staff Christmas party was her getting married."

"Yes, she was," he said.

"It could have been a time of change for us too." Ginger's voice faded. "Jack, I'll do all I can to help us, our family."

"Thank you, Ginger. I know how awkward this is for you."

She looked into his face. "Awkward?" she said with a nervous laugh. "How about frightening? Have you ever thought about our future? The kids' future?" She shook her head. "Sometimes I think about what could have been. I feel so...." She waved a hand. "Empty."

"Maybe, if I get through this, just maybe we could try again," he said.

She crossed the room and put an arm around his shoulders. "Maybe." She bent and kissed his cheek, the first time in four years.

CHAPTER 6
Day 5: Tuesday

Santiago and Stewart parked in front of the Avenue Hotel again. Several other police cruisers, unmarked cars, crime scene vehicles and a fire truck were already on site.

"I don't believe it," Santiago said. "Two murders at the same location within a few days of each other. They've got to be connected."

"You sound a bit stressed," Stewart said. The pair crossed the alley behind the hotel to the body. "You ever notice how Seattle's alleys are all the same: trash, power lines, broken glass, fire escapes that run the length of the block, the smell of urine." Stewart chuckled. "I really like the endless string of dumpsters back here."

"I don't need a guided tour at 7:41 in the morning," she said.

He glanced at the familiar figure combing the crime scene and studying the body. "Taber's already on the job."

"Hopefully his night wasn't as short as mine." she said. "Strippers, porn movies, strangulation."

"Chill, Mitch. Let's see what he's got for us."

"I know. It's the Cashland case hanging over the John Doe and now this." She sighed.

They walked up behind Don Taber's kneeling figure. Without looking up he said, "She's an Asian woman, approximately forty years of age." He waved his hand over the blood-spattered body. "There appears to be several gunshot wounds to the torso and face. We won't know which one or ones could be fatal until the autopsy is complete."

"Jesus, she's a mess," Santiago said.

"Yes. My guess would be a spray of bullets, probably from an automatic weapon," Taber said. "Look here." He opened the bloodied blouse, revealing the right breast and shoulder. "These look like the kind of burn marks associated with cigarettes."

Santiago stared. "Christ! You mean she was tortured?"

"Possibly. There's more. Look around the dumpster and the area surrounding it. What do you see?"

Santiago looked around the dumpster then peered over the edge. "Garbage, dirt."

"Exactly... no blood." Taber smiled.

"So you're speculating she was dumped here after being tortured and killed somewhere else," Stewart said.

Taber nodded. "A reasonable deduction."

"Is there anything here that ties this murder to Hailey Cashland?" she asked.

"No, nothing other than general location," Taber said, "and the woman is Asian like the missing woman from housekeeping."

Bert Wagner, an undercover member of the Gang Task Force, approached. "Chance," he said. "I see you've had time to look at this." He glanced at the woman's body.

"Yes," Stewart said.

"Why are you guys here, anyway?" Wagner said.

"We were notified to come and take a look because a case we're on originated here last weekend," Santiago said.

"Oh yeah, I've heard rumblings about that one. The brass is getting squeezed a little because Gold Coast is the prep school for Seattle's wealthiest." Wagner smiled and lit a Camel.

"Precisely," Stewart said.

"For the time being this homicide is being investigated by my team according to Captain James. I don't think he wants anything interfering with your case," Wagner said.

"So it seems," Santiago said. "but we're still looking for Agnes Chey, the Asian lady from housekeeping."

"Will keep you informed." Wagner said.

* * * * *

Stewart patted the stack of file folders on the corner of his desk and looked across to Santiago. "Whatever happened to simple murder cases where the butler did it?"

"It's only 9:30 in the morning and we have two, maybe three murders to solve," Santiago said with a glance at the wall clock. "Time flies."

"Speaking of which, the captain has reassigned our Golden Gardens hobo to Strickland and Zinc. I briefed Zinc on the autopsy report early this morning before meeting you at the Avenue Hotel. The CSI report and location is about all we had for them. According to Taber's report the victim was already dead when the body was placed on the tracks. His skull was crushed before the train hit him."

"A cover-up?" she said.

He nodded. "And a murder."

"Getting information out of cross-tie-walkers won't be easy," Santiago said.

"I know they're closed mouth when it comes to talkin' with cops. Zinc told me another transient saw a red car in the boat launch parking lot late that evening. He also said the witness saw the victim around 10:00 p.m."

"Does he know the name of the victim?"

"Only as 'Shiv,' probably a reflection on his social skills."

"Great name," she said. "What about the car?"

"He said it looked like new. Had a horse on it, a metallic red color."

"Sounds like a Mustang."

"Could be. The hobo told Zinc it had a 5.0 on the side and a white drop top that was up."

"A candy-apple red convertible. Can't be too many of those registered in Seattle."

"It's not a stock color. If it's a newer model they ought to catch a break."

Santiago laughed and looked at her partner. "You know, Strickland and Zinc may have more solid clues than we do right now."

"But we get the high-end cases, Kid. I doubt the chief is tracking their case. And if you didn't know, his kids go to Gold Coast."

"Well, well," came the jovial voice of a very large detective as his boisterous greeting echoed across the half-empty office area. Santiago and Stewart looked up to see the bulky figure of Joe Zinc coming in their direction closely followed by Ted Strickland. "And how are the high-profile dicks doing today?"

"About the same as we were at 6:30 this morning," Stewart said.

"You mean when our partners were still sleeping or whatever?" Zinc grinned. "We may have another break. It seems the red car was parked next to a steel guard post, a yellow one used for hangin' chains across the launch at night."

"And?" Santiago said.

"If it's a Mustang less than four years old we only have five registered in the Seattle area with the custom color and the white rag-top. Go back five years and we have seventeen more. We're gettin' ready to visit the owners now."

"Maybe you'll get lucky," Stewart said.

"Hope so." Zinc glanced at Santiago. "If we do maybe we'll come back and help you folks solve the Cashland case, too."

"Yeah, we can't be like halibut all the time," Strickland said.

"Halibut?" Santiago repeated with a confused look.

"Yeah, Mitch, as in bottom feeders. We all know they eat shit," Strickland said as he and Zinc laughed.

The moment of levity passed when the two veteran homicide detectives departed. Santiago looked at Stewart. "You were here early today... *really* early. How come?"

"I'm always here early. Sometimes I think I need a life away from this place."

"I think you're right." She looked into his tired face then got back on task. "We were going by Shaw's place before Sunset CC anyway, but we have an even better reason for pushing the mysterious professor farther down the list."

"What?"

"Shaw said Hailey was a drowning victim when we talked to him yesterday afternoon when we got the video. I should have picked up on it then, but I missed it. Strickland's comment about fish brought it to mind."

"I missed it too, but you're right. He did say drowning. There's only one way he could know. He had to be there. Let's go," Stewart said.

"I'm glad he works graveyard for his deliveries. He ought to be just getting ready to paint or go to bed. We won't have to chase him down." Santiago followed her partner out the door after grabbing a takeout cup of coffee.

* * * * *

Stewart rang the doorbell three times before a sleepy-eyed Terry Shaw opened the door; his hair mussed, wearing swim trunks and a T-shirt. "Mr. Shaw, we need to talk with you. It's very important," Stewart said as the smell of paint came wafting out the door.

"Of course, please come in," said Shaw. "If you'd called I could've had coffee made."

"Mr. Shaw, when we talked with you yesterday you made a comment which we should have keyed in on but didn't." Santiago said.

"Oh? What did I say?" he said as the lines in his face becoming deep and dark.

"You said she drowned." Santiago looked at the artist. "You said Hailey was a drowning victim."

"Yes," he said. "So?"

"Who told you she was a drowning victim?" Stewart said.

He shrugged. "I don't know. I must'a read it in the paper. Or maybe I heard it on the radio, maybe TV," he said with a rising pitch to his voice and biting a fingernail.

Santiago said, "Mr. Shaw, the cause of Hailey's death has never been made public."

Stewart said, "Aside from a news statement about her body being found at the Avenue Hotel the only comments made to the press were that all details were being withheld."

"So how did you come to say she was a drowning victim?" Santiago said.

"I don't know, maybe a lucky guess." He raised his right hand to his forehead, pressed his temples with a thumb and middle finger. He gasped for breath and sniffed loudly. Then he turned, crossed to the dark-colored retro 70's couch in his art-studio living room, and slumped onto it. He looked up at the still standing detectives. "I knew I should've leveled with you guys."

"What do you mean?" Santiago said.

He sighed, took a deep breath and rubbed his left forearm. "I feel a bit of a chill this morning."

"What should you have told us?" Stewart said, refocusing the lone figure.

Santiago said, "Tell us. We need every bit of information we can get to find her killer."

"I was there," Shaw said. "I knew she was dead. I need the same thing you need: her killer brought to justice."

Santiago frowned. "Why were you there?"

"As I told you the other day, we were supposed to have dinner to celebrate her birthday. I knew about the conference. They always have banquets and socials. I wanted to spend that evening with her, but I had the feeling she wouldn't show, so I followed her. I was angry that she'd ditch me again for her friends or her lover."

"Tell us about Friday afternoon," Santiago said.

"It was around 5:30. I'd followed her all day, even at Witherspoon, and I was in the lobby of the Avenue Hotel when her superintendent checked in. I was still there when he left."

"What time did he leave?" Stewart said.

"Around 2:00. I was trying to figure out how to find her room when a big guy came into the lobby and used the house phone. He referred to Hailey by name and said he'd see her in five minutes, room 407. I decided to wait."

"How long was it from when Mr. Hartley left until the second man arrived?" Santiago asked.

"About forty-five minutes."

"Then what?" Stewart said.

"The second man went to her room. Then, around 4:00 he came through the lobby again. I decided I'd wait a little and see if Hailey came out. Next thing I knew the guy was back, walkin' through the lobby carrying a bag from the convenience store around the corner. I figured they were having snacks up in the room."

Stewart said, "So you sat there for all this time, from noon 'til evening?"

"Yes, except when I used the men's room."

"What did you observe next?" Stewart said.

"The man came through the lobby again on his way out. It was just over an hour later, about 5:15 or so. I waited a few minutes, and when she didn't come down I went up to the room."

Santiago asked, "What did you find when you got there?"

"I knocked on the door. It hadn't latched tight so I called her name. When I got no answer, I went in. I walked around the room, knocked on the bathroom door then pushed it, again because she didn't answer. She was in the bathtub, dead." Shaw began to sob.

"Did you touch anything?" Stewart said.

"No. All I did was get out of there. When I saw her I thought he'd be back. I didn't want him to catch me or see me." Shaw's breath became short.

"What did the big guy look like?" Stewart said.

"He was big, tall, like six-four, middle thirties, a white guy." The words shot out of Shaw's mouth staccato fashion. Tiny beads of sweat formed on his forehead, and the flesh covering the cheeks became flush. "He had a good build, great butt."

Santiago smiled at Shaw. "Could you identify him if he was in a lineup?"

"Probably."

"You'd never seen him before Friday?"

"No."

"Why didn't you report the murder?" Stewart said.

"I was afraid. I didn't want to be involved as a witness."

"Afraid of what, Mr. Shaw?" Santiago's voice was calm and soft, her face showing lines of intense focus. Stewart slid into the role of taking notes.

"The obvious," he said, almost pleadingly. "A gay man finding the body of a beautiful nude woman in a hotel room he has no business being in? People would make several interpretations of the scenario."

"Such as?" she said.

"Revenge killing, psychopath, whatever. I don't know. Nothing good."

"So why did you report her missing?" Santiago said.

"Hailey was my friend. I wanted the police to find whoever did that to her. I knew if I didn't call in, evidence could be lost while waiting for someone else to report her missing or find the body." He paused. "I think I read somewhere if a murder isn't solved in the first forty-eight hours the odds on closing the case become very long."

"That's true, Mr. Shaw. So you thought you'd help us along?" she said.

"Basically, yes." Shaw regained some of his composure.

"What about the video?" Stewart said. "Was that another helpful setup?"

"No. As I said, I'd borrowed *Titanic*. That disgusting video was in one of the sleeves."

"Thank you, Mr. Shaw," Santiago said. "You've been most helpful. Is there anything else we should know?"

"No."

"We'll be contacting you to review a photo collage in the near future. If you think of anything else, be in touch."

"I will," he said.

After they left, Stewart said, "Do you have the number of Sunset?"

"I have the general number." Santiago called the college and was put through.

"Registrar's Office—this is Mrs. Young."

"Good morning. I'm Detective Santiago of the Seattle Police Department Homicide Division."

"How may I assist you?" Young said.

"We're investigating the murder of a young woman who was a student during winter quarter. We need to talk with the instructor of her Chemical Dependency Certification Class. Her name was Hailey Cashland."

"Do you have the name of the instructor?"

"No, Ma'am, just the student's name."

"One moment please."

Santiago listened to background noise from a busy office through the receiver.

"Detective Santiago, I believe you want to talk with Trevor Gunn. Miss Cashland was in his class during the winter quarter."

"Is Mr. Gunn on campus today?"

"He is teaching a class as we speak. It won't end for another hour."

"Thank you, Mrs. Young."

As Stewart drove out of the apartment parking lot he said, "You know, if Shaw's comments are truthful, they'll clear Hartley."

"If the second man was really talking to Hailey," she said.

"That's how Shaw got the room number."

"If he's telling the truth. Shaw could have discovered the room number by some other means and gone up after Hartley." Santiago paused. "Shaw could be the killer. We know about Hailey's professor but we don't know if the second man at the hotel is him. Hailey's been quite active with multiple friends. Keep in mind Moses and possibly someone in a high place in addition to Hartley and the professor."

"Hopefully we'll have an answer shortly," Stewart said.

"If Shaw's telling the truth he clears Hartley and the second man becomes our prime suspect," she said.

"That it would," he said while pulling into the visitor parking lot of Sunset Community College. "Water and mountains, Mitch." He looked across Puget Sound and waved an arm after getting out of the car. "It's beautiful."

* * * * *

The detectives went straight to the Registrar's Office off the main lobby of the business offices.

"Mrs. Young?"

"Yes."

"I'm Detective Santiago. We spoke a few minutes ago." She showed her identification. "This is my partner, Detective Stewart."

"You said you were from Seattle?"

"Yes, but I'm sure you're aware of the reciprocal operating agreement we have with surrounding police agencies."

"Of course. As I recall you're here to talk with Mr. Gunn, but as I said earlier he's currently in class."

"We'll have to interrupt him," Santiago said.

"I see. Come with me." Mrs. Young walked around the counter and led the officers out of the building. "I hope it's nothing serious. Mr. Gunn is up for tenure this spring, and Lord knows we don't need any more negative publicity. I'm sure you've heard about our president is being bombarded because of an alleged kickback inquiry."

"We just need Mr. Gunn for background in the investigation," Stewart said. "We're not part of any other actions here."

As they approached the classroom Mrs. Young said, "Please wait here for a moment," then entered the class. Santiago and Stewart watched her speak briefly with a tall, rugged appearing man. He nodded and spoke to the class. The students packed their laptops and books, then filed out of the room past Santiago and Stewart.

Young motioned them in.

"I've been half-expecting you," said the man as he looked up from the table located at the front of the room. "I'm pleased you've come."

They held out their identification and Santiago introduced them.

"Hmm, Seattle... do I need my attorney?" he said casually.

Santiago said, "We're investigating the murder of Hailey Cashland and we have some questions to ask you. Certainly, if you wish to have your attorney present that is your privilege."

Gunn smiled. "No, that won't be necessary. I was just breaking the ice, so to speak." He flashed a broad smile and mouth full of perfect teeth as he looked toward the doorway where Mrs. Young was standing.

She left the room and quietly closed the door.

"This interview could be more than a little sensitive. My review is at the end of the quarter." He indicated a pair of chairs nearby. "Please, take a seat."

Santiago said, "You said you were expecting us. Perhaps you should have contacted our office and avoided this visit, Mr. Gunn."

"Yes, you're right, but I didn't want to be involved, what with my tenure in the balance."

Stewart said, "Mr. Gunn, how well did you know Miss Cashland?"

"I was her advisor, teacher and mentor. She was bright, beautiful, motivated."

"A friend of hers says she was having an affair with one of her teachers," Stewart said.

"She had several instructors over the last few years." He glanced at his watch. "How long is this going to take?"

"That depends, Mr. Gunn," Santiago said. She indicated his watch. "That's a beautiful piece of jewelry. Southwestern isn't it?"

"Yes," he said with another smile.

"Mr. Gunn, we have a witness who can positively identify the man who was at the Avenue Hotel with Miss Cashland on Friday afternoon."

He looked up into Santiago's eyes. Silence permeated the room. He flexed his lips and finally spoke in a faint voice. "I was at the hotel with her after Hartley left."

Stewart gave Gunn a Miranda warning.

"No, as I said earlier, that won't be necessary. I did nothing wrong with the exception of not calling your office when I read about the murder and her body being found."

Santiago said, "What did you and Hailey do last Friday?"

"We went there to have sex."

"Did you use a condom?"

"Never. She was on the pill... but we didn't have sex. We argued."

Santiago looked at Gunn for a long moment, lips pursed. "What did you argue about?"

"She decided she wanted to get married."

"The ring on your finger says you're already married, right?" she said.

"Yes." Gunn flashed a sheepish grin.

Stewart asked, "How long has this affair been going?"

"About two years. What stupidity!"

Santiago looked at him. "What stupidity are you referring to, Mr. Gunn?"

"Christ, my career could go down the toilet, closely followed by my marriage if word of our affair gets out. Lord only knows how many other guys could be ruined the same way. She was a fling, a diversion, an irresistible temptation, that's all."

Santiago wrote *insensitive* in her note pad.

Gunn took a deep breath and looked at her, but said nothing.

Stewart asked, "Have there been others?"

"Yes." Gunn swallowed. "It's a difficult business. They're young, eager to please, available and... they hit on *me*. They like me and they're legal. I can't resist." Gunn became agitated, his left foot bouncing, his eyes shifting back and forth.

"And your wife?" Stewart said. "Does she know about your fling?"

"She knows I'm a flirt," he said. He took another long look at Santiago.

"That's all?" Stewart said.

"She might suspect other women or students, but she doesn't know for sure."

"And Hailey wanted to marry you?" she said.

"Yes. Imagine me, a happily married man, and a candidate for tenure, tossing it all away just to marry that little black chick. We had a physical relationship, a good time, that's all it was for me. Others have done the same thing."

Stewart said, "So what happened after she talked about wanting to get married and you turned her down?"

"She was angry, made a threat. Then she calmed down and went to draw a bath. I dressed and left."

Santiago said, "You didn't look into the bathroom to say goodbye? Nothing?"

"There was no point. Hailey couldn't expose me. Her career was just as important to her as mine is to me. She said she sold her soul to get an education and become a teacher. We all have our skeletons in the closet. No, it was best to just leave and let things settle for both of us."

Stewart said, "So you just left?"

"She was alive when you left the room?" Santiago said.

"Of course, in the bath. I swear to you, she was alive. As you said, I'm a suspect. I understand that, but don't forget her boss."

"What time did you leave the hotel?" Santiago said.

"Around 3:30 or 4:00. I went home."

"What time did you arrive home?" Stewart asked.

"Probably around 4:30 or 5:00, you know, Friday rush-hour traffic."

Stewart asked, "Can anybody verify the time you got home?"

"My wife, Linda," he said with a long sigh, shaking his head.

Santiago said, "Do you recall Hailey saying anything about being threatened or followed?"

"No, just that she'd known her boss for some time."

"Did she ever say anything about someone watching her or following her?"

"Never, except about her neighbor. She said he was almost like a stalker."

"Do you know the neighbor's name?"

"No, but you should talk with him. He's a gay artist who drives a delivery truck. She said he was always hangin' around."

"I have no more questions for now. Mr. Gunn. I'm sure we'll be talking again. For now, thank you for your candor. If you should think of anything else we should know please call us." Stewart handed the instructor a business card.

"Officers, the content of our interview is confidential, correct?"

Stewart said, "The only people with access to our information are those involved in the investigation, not the public."

"Good," Gunn said.

When they reached the cruiser, Santiago and Stewart reflected for a moment before leaving the parking lot.

"Now we have two prime suspects," he said looking toward Puget Sound. "You know, yesterday I almost arrested Hartley. Today I want to arrest Shaw and now Gunn. We've got to be sure on this one. Where ever we go people are going to get hurt badly."

"Some of them deserve it," she said, also looking toward Puget Sound.

"And some don't," he said. "We need to sort this out."

"We're going near Gunn's apartment on the way downtown," she said.

"It's alibi time, Mitch. Let's do it."

* * * * *

Santiago and Stewart stopped at the Gunn residence on their way downtown, but nobody was home. A neighbor passing the apartment told them Linda Gunn had left a little while earlier, but didn't know where she had gone or when she would return.

They continued on to their office.

"What have we got so far?" Santiago said as they thumbed through their notes seated across from each other back in the office. "A high school teacher with two lovers; one is serious, one an old-friend-brother physically gratifying workmate of long standing."

"She was definitely an active lady," Stewart said. "Let's look at the facts. Gunn confirms she was alive when Hartley left, just as Shaw said."

"And both Gunn and Shaw admit to being at the hotel. Something doesn't fit. We're overlooking something," she said.

"We've got the kid, Moses. Maybe he was following her around the hotel on Friday, skipping school," he said.

"We know he felt some jealousy regarding Gunn," she added.

"Mitch, maybe we need to look closer at Shaw. He was at the hotel, he saw her and he's very angry."

"Good point. He thought of her as a sister, albeit a naughty one," she said.

"But he's gay," Stewart said.

"That's not a disqualification for murder," she said.

"No, it isn't," he said.

Stewart smiled and tapped his notebook. "You know, Shaw *did* find the porno tape, allegedly by accident."

"He's also manipulated this investigation," she said.

"I'm thinking obstruction. We have three suspects: Gunn, Shaw and Cruz."

"Let's see if we can confirm whether Moses was in school on Friday. I'll call the Gold Coast attendance office." She picked up the phone and dialed. When the secretary answered they spoke briefly. "This is Detective Santiago. Could you confirm whether Moses Cruz was in attendance last Friday, please?"

Stewart watched her wait. "Mitch, we're moving into evening here. How about tomorrow we do in-depth background on our two primes, depending on what you learn about Cruz?"

She nodded, said "Thank you," and replaced the phone. "The school confirms Moses was in attendance all day last Friday, including a track meet after dismissal."

"Good. Tomorrow you do Gunn and I'll take Shaw," he said. "For now, how about we finish our reports and do dinner again tonight? The weather is holding and I have a new gas BBQ I want to try."

"You're on, but first let's go by Gunn's place again. We seem to have a serious time gap between when Gunn says he left the hotel and when Shaw says he departed. I'll take my car. That way I can come by your place after swinging by home."

"Home?"

"I have a special bottle of Hanzell Chardonnay my dad gave me. I'd rather share it with you than a TV newsman at 10:00 p.m. I didn't think of it 'til after you'd left the other night."

"Sounds delicious, and I'll get dinner started."

* * * * *

Greenwood Avenue was much busier in late afternoon than earlier in the day when Santiago and Stewart had first come by. They parked near each other and walked to apartment 305 up two flights of stairs. Stewart pressed the doorbell and they waited. On the fourth ring an attractive women in her late twenties or early thirties opened the door. Her straight blond hair appeared lighter on the ends.

"Mrs. Linda Gunn?"

"Yes."

"I'm Detective Stewart," he said showing his identification. "This is my partner—"

"I know. Trevor called and said you might be contacting me."

"Did he tell you what we're investigating?" Santiago said.

"He said it was the murder of a student, Hailey Cashland. You'll have to excuse the mess. I'm baking today. Come in." An oven buzzer sounded. "Make yourselves comfortable." Mrs. Gunn went to the kitchen.

"They seem to like early American furniture, neat and clean," Santiago said looking around the living room.

"A bar in the living room?" Stewart said. "Nice touch if you entertain often. It sure dominates the room." He sat down on the couch.

Linda Gunn looked at Stewart as she returned from the kitchen and went to the bar. "May I offer you a drink?"

"No thank you, Mrs. Gunn. What time did your husband get home last Friday afternoon? We're just trying to verify time frames," Stewart said.

Santiago opened a notepad.

"Around 5:00, I think," she said in a shaky voice as she moved toward the couch, drink in hand. She pulled a tissue from the tiny apron pocket and wiped her brow.

"That's quite a bruise on your forearm, Mrs. Gunn. How did you get it?" he said.

"I ran into the kitchen counter top in the dark one night when I was getting a drink of water. Sometimes I'm so clumsy."

"You say your husband got home around 5:00. Are you sure?" he said.

"Yes. The news was just beginning."

"I see," he said.

Santiago looked at the woman for a moment and then asked, "Mrs. Gunn, when you ran into the counter did you bump the side of your face on anything?"

"Oh," gasped the woman as she rubbed her hands together and glanced back and forth between the two detectives. The skin around her eyes tightened as the color of crimson crept to her ears. "I guess I did. I have a little bruise, nothing serious."

Santiago looked into the woman's face. Linda Gunn's hands were trembling. "Are you feeling all right?"

"A chill came in when I opened the door." The oven buzzer sounded again. "Oh dear, excuse me. I don't want to burn the cookies," she said going back to the kitchen.

"I count one photo of Trevor and his wife and one photo of two young boys," Stewart said as he looked around the room, "and several of Gunn doing outdoor things, all alone."

"Those are good looking kids," Santiago said as Linda Gunn returned from the kitchen.

"They're my pride and joy. They'll be home from the neighbors shortly. We take turns watching each other's kids so we can shop, bake, go to the fitness club and stuff."

"Mrs. Gunn, this is a personal question, but we need to ask it," Stewart said.

"Of course, I understand."

"Has your husband ever had any interest in another woman, maybe a student?"

"No, Detective Stewart. Like all handsome young men, Trev is attractive to women. Sometimes they flirt with him. It's not really mutual. Oh, he may give a flirtatious answer occasionally to someone he knows, but that's all."

"So he's never had an affair you're aware of?"

"Of course not," she snapped. "I... I think perhaps you should go," she said in a weak voice. "My husband is a good and faithful man."

Santiago stood. "Well, thank you for talking with us, Mrs. Gunn." She handed the woman a business card. "If you think of anything else call me at either of those numbers... and take care of that bruise."

"Yes, I shall. Now, if you'll excuse me," she said, and showed the officers to the door.

"What was that all about?" Stewart said as they walked to their cars.

"She looked like a woman who's been battered. Didn't you notice the bruise on the side of her face near her right temple?"

"I guess it didn't stand out but the bruise on her arm sure did."

"The way she had her brows groomed and the light use of bright fuchsia blush on her cheeks did give her the appearance of health."

Stewart nodded. "Maybe you'll find something through the background check tomorrow."

"I hope so. I'd really like to nail him," Santiago said.

"Isn't it strange she doesn't have a clue about his affair?"

"He's a sleaze. Enough about this. I'm hungry."

"You still want to pick up the wine?"

She nodded.

"I'll see you at my place."

"Perfect. We can finish our reports and e-mail them in," she said.

"And then you can sample my cooking."

CHAPTER 7

Jack Hartley walked into the cathedral ceiling living room and looked at his wife. She was seated on the couch facing a green mottled-marble fireplace. An oversized coffee table separated her from the hearth. The faint odor of broiled steak filled the room. He sipped amber fluid from an old fashioned glass. "I'm sorry, Ginger. I'm sorry for screwing up our lives, our future, everything." He slumped into an overstuffed chair at the far end of the couch.

"I was harsh yesterday," she said, looking into the eyes of her husband. "You're tired, Jack. We're both exhausted."

He waved his empty hand in her direction. "I was thinking before this all happened whether it was possible for us to make a fresh start. I'd been trying to figure out how to approach you without being rejected."

"Doesn't that sound silly, you trying to approach me? I've had the same feeling and fear. I've—" She choked as tears filled her eyes. "I've wanted to talk with you, too. What's happened to us? Eight years ago we had no secrets and no fears."

"I know. Our relationship was built on trust and sharing. We were really a couple."

"Yes." She smiled. "We knew where we wanted to go and how we were getting there. Almost a decade later we're...." she paused looking at the ceiling.

"Pathetic," he said completing her thought. "I know it's my fault." He looked at the glass in his hand. "The booze, the rape, the other woman."

"I'm not innocent either, Jack. I haven't had a steady companion like you, but innocent? No way. I helped drive you away with my moods, and my selfish coldness."

"You did chill out after we'd been married for a couple of years, but then came that night... you know."

"Jack, let's be honest."

"I am being honest."

"I know you are, but I haven't been... not for a long time. You're accepting guilt that belongs to both of us. I share those feelings. They're mine too."

He shook his head. "Don't blame yourself. We both know what I've done."

"Jack, we know about *you*, but not about *me*."

"You're only sin is poor judgment in marrying me."

She moved to the end of the couch closest to her husband. "I have as much, if not more guilt."

"Don't say that. Don't demean yourself to spare my feelings."

"I'm not, but I had affairs too."

He looked at her with surprise. His eyes widened and lips formed a smirk. "I don't believe it." He shook his head, and his shoulders drooped.

"It's true. Nothing long-term like you and Hailey, but if you remember, I've been taking evening art classes. I spent a few evenings sketching shadows in motels."

"That's incredible. I... I never suspected." He shook his head.

"You didn't have time to suspect anything."

"True, not with my own affair." He looked around the room and focused on the gas flame behind the glass doors. "We sound more like college kids swapping stories late at night than a man and his wife in crisis. Before this mess I wanted to talk with you, as I said. I was trying to figure out how to convince you to enter marriage counseling with me."

"Marriage counseling? I was thinking the same thing, Jack. Once, we loved each other madly. I think there's something to be saved. If not, why did we make that stupid deal rather than just splitting up? Each of us could've made it on our own."

"Do you really think we have a chance to save our marriage?"

"Yes, but when everything goes public nobody but us will believe it," she said.

"We're the only ones that count—us and the kids—when we're talking about our future," he said.

"You're a prime suspect in a major murder case. I'm sure the prosecutor would see our change of direction as a circling of the wagons for a possible defense."

He nodded. "If I'm charged with something we'd take some lumps but I believe in the system. I don't expect to be charged with anything. However, my unsavory behavior could still end up in the tabloids."

She looked into his tired face. "I just want you to know, I don't doubt your innocence, not for a moment." Her voice dropped to a whisper. "You frightened me yesterday...so many things. Now I'm embarrassed."

"You weren't alone. I'm sure the detectives had their suspicions, but the threat of exposure would have been devastating to both Hailey and me. We'd both lose, hence, no motive. They'll find the killer," he said. "I'm sure of it."

"The best thing to do is tell them everything there is to tell about you, Hailey, all of it."

"I have. I'm beyond embarrassment at this point anyway."

"*We* are," she said.

"You know, I'll have to resign from the academy to avoid breaking my contract through the morals clause even if I'm not exposed in the news."

"I know. It was my greed talking last night. We can start over, but you have to admit we've had a great ride."

"Should we begin counseling immediately?" he said.

"I'm not sure. It seems our disclosures wouldn't necessarily be confidential, not if the authorities could link our sessions to a criminal investigation," she said.

He laughed. "You sound like a lawyer."

"Jailhouse, maybe. One of my friends I shared some comfort with was a legal intern."

"I should probably get an attorney, anyway," he said again, staring at the flames.

"Probably, but how do you feel about that? You don't sound very positive."

"I just want the killer caught. The damage we encounter is my fault, not the fault of the police."

"So, do you want an attorney?"

"They're expensive."

"You make good money."

"Not for long, I fear. Besides, I've already told them everything." He sighed, took a deep breath and sipped the bourbon. "I guess that's why I told you everything." He sighed again. *Up to a point.* "There wasn't anyplace left to turn. I feel so humiliated." He blinked back tears as he spoke.

"We'll make it through this, Jack. We're not losers."

"Life isn't a game. I'll wait on the attorney."

"What about your board of directors?"

"I feel I owe them. They gave me one of the choicest jobs in the country. Most school district superintendents, much less prep-school principals or headmasters, don't make nearly what I do. Perhaps I ought to have professional advice regarding my exit." He looked at the flames and smiled. "I do have some confidential information about the board president that could help our cause."

Hartley stood, walked around the table and joined his wife on the couch. His glass remained out of arm's reach on the coffee table. They embraced.

"We've wasted so much time, Jack."

"Then we shouldn't waste anymore." They kissed, hesitantly, then with passion.

"What does tomorrow hold for us?" she said, wiping her eyes.

"Hope," he said.

* * * * *

Chance Stewart lived at the Eagles Nest Condominiums. His home overlooked the entry to the Hiram Chittendem Locks in Ballard, a longtime Scandinavian community in Seattle. He sixth-floor unit faced Market Street and an eatery-tavern that catered primarily to regulars and tourists near the locks' main entrance. The lanai overlooked the street, providing a view of the canal between Puget Sound and Lake Union.

Santiago rode the elevator up while holding the bottle of Hanzell in her left hand. At Stewart's door she paused, looking at the brass knocker with a nameplate. "Impressive," she mumbled.

He opened the door and smiled. "Well, well, well... I like what I see, Detective Santiago. You have redefined the meaning of 'men in blue' to my great satisfaction." He stood to one side of the doorway. "Welcome to my humble abode. Unlike your elegant home, mine is what I think of as modern eclectic, but this is your first visit in the two years we've worked together."

She grinned. "I know it through reputation."

"One can't always believe everything one hears, believe me. He admired the snug fit of her skinny designer jeans, and deep-tan midriff partially hidden by a white cashmere sweater. "You bring not only wine but a refreshing change."

"I thought I'd wear something comfortable," she said.

His smile acknowledged the lazy sway of her hips.

Her eyes sparkled as she looked at him. She held out the bottle of wine.

He looked at the bottle as he closed the door. "The lady has taste."

She slid off the sweater, revealing a midriff crop-top blouse of metallic blue silk with a scoop neck held together by two straining buttons and watched Stewart's reaction, a smile lighting her face. She said, "Is the grill hot?"

"Yes. Are you ready to eat or would you like a glass of wine first?"

"Wine first, but would you add some ice? It's bad form, but I like it cold."

Yes," he said, going to the kitchen with a bounce in his step.

She walked to the lanai and felt the heat of the grill. "It's getting dark. Feels like it could be a chilly evening."

Stewart walked up behind her and peered over her shoulder. "Your wine." He handed her a crystal glass while fixated on her erect nipples under the silk top. "It's definitely cooling off out here, but it's only May."

"Do you want to do the reports first and get them sent?" she asked.

"That's probably a good idea," he said with a lingering look. "We don't have much but you never know; it could get too late."

Forty-five minutes later they were looking out the view windows. "Think Captain James will buy into our reasoning for not arresting anyone yet?" she said.

"Yes. This case is so high-profile now that any mistake we make will be magnified tenfold. Reputations, careers, institutions could all be damaged beyond repair. He knows that as well as we do. Are you ready to eat?"

"In a minute." She paused and took a deep breath. "Chance, before we go much further on the Cashland case there's something you have a right to know."

"About what?"

"Me. When we were talking about personal baggage a couple of days ago I was thinking back a few years. You remember when I said I worked as a dancer?"

He nodded.

"Well, I also worked as an exotic dancer on the Sea-Tac strip." She took a sip of wine and looked across the glass-covered carved coffee table at her partner.

Stewart sat quietly in a chair and looked at her. A smile creased his ruddy face. "You were a stripper?"

"Sometimes. It's not something I'm particularly proud of or embarrassed by... until now." She crossed her legs and fidgeted on the couch. "The money was good. A lot of girls in college pay their way by working. Some are waitresses, others clerks. I was a barmaid, did cocktails, and finally worked at a strip club. I was making two to three hundred a night on table dances after expenses."

"Expenses." He laughed. "You mean for lingerie?"

"No. At most clubs the dancers are independents. They pay the house a cut or a percentage from the table dances. They also agree to do a stage dance each set at no cost to the house. It's advertising the product."

"Interesting." He gave her a look. "So you feel what, compromised?"

"No... well maybe... I guess I need you to know that as we go through Hailey's life I understand some of her motives. My concern is what effect my background might have when the case gets to court."

"None," he said. "We're doing everything by the book. Tell me, did you ever get arrested for dancing or anything else related to the business?"

"You mean vice charges? No. I've never been arrested for anything, or even warned. What I'm getting at is the sex business. Exotic dancers make their money titillating a client; the greater the arousal, the bigger the tip. Hailey and Hartley were both in the same business same as me. They just took it further than I did."

"You mean the dancing or did you do a video, too?"

"No video, Partner." She smiled at him. "No show and tell. I'm sure many people think of exotic dancing as obscene or pornographic and that live sex shows are just the next step."

"Exotic dancer, eh? I would like to have seen that." He laughed. "I think you'll find most guys have visited those clubs at least a few times."

She squirmed. "What will Captain James think?"

"He probably already knows. Have you got any idea how thorough the background checks are that we do on cadets?" It's like getting a security clearance for the FBI. It's complete. For example, we've got a guy right now working vice who was a teenage gangster." He took a sip of wine. "We've got people with a variety of backgrounds on the force, some closer to the edge than others. None of our people are convicted felons. I doubt any have ever been hired who were even charged with a felony past their teen years."

"Are you sure?"

"No, but I'm pretty sure. If anything, our backgrounds make us better cops."

"Does that explain your success at working with drug dealers early in your career?"

"Actually, yes," he said. "When I was growing up I wanted to be an astronaut even more than a jock. I think every kid did. But in high school some of my friends got really hung-up with drugs. In the late eighties recreational drug use had arrived among the hip adult scene. My best friend died from an overdose. My older brother is a burnt-out hippie, his brain fried."

"And you?" She watched his face.

He shrugged. "I just didn't fit into the scene. I guess I'd always identified with adults more than my peers. Because of my parents I have a strong work ethic. You know the old 'you get what you pay for' routine. Anyway, most of the kids I hung out with were getting into drugs one way or another. Then some joined gangs." His voice dropped to a whisper, eyes locked on some distant image only he could see. "I just faded into the background."

"So you became a cop?"

"Yeah, when another friend of mine was killed in a drive-by it was time to do something. Besides, my grades weren't going to let me be a rocket jockey. Like you, I didn't want a job in the business world. I dropped out of college and applied at the academy." He flashed another smile and held his glass of wine in a toast. "The rest is history."

"Interesting," she said.

"Not nearly as interesting as your story. Tell me, did you wear a thong?" His rich blue eyes sparkled.

"Where *is* your mind?" she said with a raised eyebrow.

"Can't you tell? I'm trying to visualize you in tassels, dancing erotically on a stage, rubbing against a chrome pole."

"You've been watching too much television."

"Well, what did you wear?"

"I usually started in a bikini or a mini over a bikini." She laughed. "I finished in what my horny boyfriend at the time called a mono-kini, bottom only." Emptying her wine glass, she set it on the coffee table. "Hell, sometimes I finished in my birthday suit." She looked at her partner and smiled. "It seems like a hundred years ago, Chance, not six or seven."

A smirk crossed his face. "And what's your most vivid memory?"

"What a shock it was every time someone opened the door during the winter. Standing around in only a blouse cover-up or dancing when the cold air hit me, it generated a lot of attention."

"I'll bet your puppies stood up."

She shrugged. "It was good for tips." She looked at her empty wine glass. "Now, let's get back to the original question. You were right. I guess what I really wanted to know is whether my background might compromise the case."

"Like I said, it won't. If you're really worried about it, talk to Captain James privately." He studied his partner's silhouette in the low light of the room.

"I'll see him tomorrow," she said. "I'm sure we're going to solve this case and I want the killer to go to prison, not walk because I was shakin' my tits as a coed."

Stewart rose and headed toward the lanai. "He'll go to prison, Mitch, no doubt about that," he said as he dropped the steaks on the grill. "Salad veggies are in the fridge, if you'd do the honors?"

"You bet," she said and headed for the kitchen.

A half-hour later they finished dinner. "It must have been pretty good on both sides of the table considering how quiet we were, she said."

"I'm still visualizing you dancing in my mind," he said. "I may not sleep tonight."

"You hold that image for me." She stood and stretched her arms high overhead. Her blue silk blouse crept upwards, revealing more than a little flesh. "It's been a long few days, Chance. I'm heading home. See you in the morning, early."

Stewart stood up. "You don't have to rush."

"Oh yes I do... and tomorrow I'd like to arrange polygraph tests for Gunn and Shaw if they'll agree. How about picking me up at 8:00 and we'll catch them on our way in?"

"Excellent plan. If they agree we could get them in tomorrow afternoon, Thursday for sure."

"Dinner was great, Chance. Thanks for having me over. Sometimes it's amazing what you can accomplish when you don't plan it."

He smiled. "It sure is. Let me walk you out." He opened the door. "Didn't you have a sweater?"

"Yes," she said and scooped it from the couch. "Even if I didn't I'd be warm. We got the reports done, shared a good wine and a great dinner, and got to know each other a little better. It's time to go home." At her car she leaned just a little forward toward Stewart and kissed him lightly on the right cheek. "Thanks, Partner."

"For what?"

"Listening." She got into her car and drove off in the night.

Shaking his head and chuckling, he walked back to the elevator. "Mitch 1, Chance 0."

* * * * *

A nervous Terry Shaw dialed and waited, watching the front window of his apartment, searching for any movement. After three rings his friend answered. "Charles, how are you?"

"Fine, Terry. It's a little early for graveyard drivers to be up isn't it?"

"Yes, but I've had a bad day. I couldn't sleep this afternoon. I tried painting and that didn't work either. I tried going back to bed and was up at 7:30 after twisting for hours. I'm calling in sick tonight. I'm gonna stay home, get some sleep."

"Relax for a moment, Terry. Catch your breath," Charles said.

"You knew my neighbor, Hailey Cashland, right?"

"Sure. She's the little gal you swap videos with all the time. We've met a couple of times."

"Well—" Shaw choked to hold back a sob. "She's dead! Murdered!"

"What?"

"Her body was found last Saturday. The tough part is, I'm a suspect," Shaw said.

"You? That's absurd!"

"No, it's not. I sure wish I'd gone to Portland with you last weekend."

"What did you do?" Charles said.

"I know it was stupid but I followed her. I wanted to know who her secret lover is. I was angry. I wanted to punish her."

"God, Terry, have you told anyone else about following her?"

"Yes, the police." He took a deep breath. "They know I was angry at her, too."

"This doesn't sound good. Do you have representation?"

"No, and right now I can't afford it. I don't want one of those charity jobs, either. Anyway, let me get back to the story. It gets worse. They know I was at the hotel the day she died. I told 'em everything I knew."

"You said you're a suspect," Charles said.

"I saw her body in the hotel room. I found her but I didn't report it. I know who the killer is because I saw him leave. Now I'm scared." Shaw gulped more air.

"Of what?" Charles said.

"The killer discovering I exist."

"You're afraid he'll come after you?"

"Absolutely terrified," Shaw said.

"You say the police suspect you, too?"

"They have several suspects, but I've got to be one of 'em," he said raising his voice.

"You sound really stressed. You said you were going to stay home tonight and sleep. Would you like me to come over tomorrow evening? I'm tied up tonight and all day tomorrow. I'll come around early evening."

"Yes, that would be nice. Maybe you could do my route with me. We could talk. I just want to feel secure, safe."

"What about your boss? Isn't the rule 'No passengers in the truck,' or something?"

"We can meet at Dawson's Grocery like before. We'll go back and get your car when we're done, then come back here."

"Okay," Charles said, "but when we get back to your place I'll be crashing. You're making tomorrow a long day and night for me."

"Fair enough. You can use the bedroom. I'll use the couch if you want it that way."

"I do. Terry, you're my friend but I still feel used by you from once before."

"I understand. We're friends now, close friends," Shaw said.

"I do care for you, Terry, and this sounds like a mess."

"It is. When this is over I'm thinking of heading south to San Francisco or maybe Las Vegas. I've had four good years here but Hailey being killed, the police lurking everywhere, a killer possibly looking for me? This is bad. A fresh start sounds like my best option."

"Vegas is nice," Charles said.

"You like it? Maybe you'd like to go along?"

"I don't think so. I'll ride with you tomorrow night, maybe hangout for a few days."

"Thanks for talking," Shaw said.

"Not a problem. You're a special friend," Charles said.

There was a long pause on the phone. "You know, I *was* angry enough to kill her. I'm so ashamed. Then to find her dead... I'm so confused."

"I'll see around 6:00 and meet at Dawson's at 9:00, right?" Charles said.

Chapter 8
Day 6: Wednesday

By 7:00 a.m. Wednesday morning Stewart was already at his desk. Santiago walked past him toward the captain's office. He looked up. "You're early. Guess I won't be picking you up at 8:00."

"Guess not," she said without stopping.

"You'll feel better after talking to the man," he said watching her approach the captain's office.

James looked up at the glass door in response to her knock. He gestured her in with a wave of the hand and watched her enter. "It's early Mitch. What can I do for you?"

"Do you have a few minutes?"

"Of course. Sit down."

She sat straight in the sled chair and looked the captain directly in the eyes. "I'm concerned about our case."

"How so?"

"This is embarrassing." She swallowed, smiled and looked around. Her voice was very soft. "It's about my personnel file." She blushed.

He forced a smile. "What about it?"

"The work I did before I came here might compromise the department if it came out in public."

"And how might that be?"

"I, ah... I was an exotic dancer on the Sea-Tac strip." She rubbed her hands together.

He shrugged. "I know that. It's in your file. You know we do background checks, right. You didn't lie on the application, did you?"

"No."

"You ever been arrested?"

"No."

"You ever been charged with a felony?"

"No."

"So what's the problem?"

She sat quietly for a moment. "You've always known?"

"Yes." He sat up in the swivel chair and placed an elbow on the desk. "I want good cops, great cops. You're one of 'em."

"It's just... I guess all this sex stuff with Cashland is taking me back in time."

"You're doing an investigation and you're following procedures. You're fine. The department is fine."

Santiago swallowed. "I think sometimes I should try a different line of work."

He smiled. "You're getting too old for dancing."

"Not that. Maybe go private or something." She relaxed.

"Private?"

"Just a thought. You know, fresh start, different city."

"Where?"

"I don't know, maybe someplace that's warm and dry all the time."

"Well, for now just concentrate on the Cashland case, okay? As I see it you have a couple of prime suspects."

"We'll be doing polygraphs today or tomorrow if they agree. We've already begun in-depth background checks." She looked out the office windows at Stewart, who was watching them. "I agree with you. We have two prime suspects. I personally think Gunn is our killer. Chance is inclined toward Shaw."

The captain stood up. "Well, get back on it. This case is a hot potato. Let's not hear any more about personal history or quitting."

She stood. "Thank you, Captain."

As she walked back to her desk, Stewart said, "So how'd it go?"

"Like you said, he already knew," she said.

"See? No problem."

"It is to me." She sat down at her desk.

"It's never been before."

"It has a few times. I've just never had it come so close in a case."

"So what did James say?"

"Get back to work."

"And so we shall. I'd rather schedule Shaw in person. Give him less chance to dodge us."

"Let's go." Santiago was up and heading for the door before Stewart was out of his chair.

* * * * *

"Good morning, officers," said a sleepy-eyed Terry Shaw when he answered his door to face Santiago and Stewart twenty minutes later. Dark circles were under bloodshot eyes, his hair was in disarray, and a partial plate was absent from his upper gum. "Come in. Pardon the mess." Wearing a wrinkled nightshirt with a palate pictured on the front, he walked across the living room. He shoved a blanket and pillows off the couch. "I slept out here last night. I'm so upset I couldn't sleep yesterday either. May as well get used to it, I guess. I have a friend, Charles Goodwin, coming over tomorrow; he'll use the bedroom."

"Mr. Shaw, we're going over many leads in the case and trying to eliminate some of them," Stewart said.

"I understand. Please, sit down," Shaw said.

"Good. We'd like you to take a polygraph test," Stewart said.

"A lie detector test, Detective Stewart? They're not admissible are they?"

"Our purpose is to give direction to our inquiries and eliminate some of the many leads we've accumulated," Stewart said.

"When do you want to do the test?" Shaw said.

"This afternoon, otherwise tomorrow morning," Stewart said.

"I'd prefer tomorrow if you don't mind. With not sleeping well and working nights, I'm really beat."

Santiago said, "Mr. Shaw, I thought you said you have company coming?"

"I do. A friend is going to stay for a few days. I'm not comfortable being here alone right now."

"Why not?" she said.

"I believe I know who the killer is. If he realizes I know, I could be in danger."

"Who do you believe is the killer?" Stewart asked.

"The second man at the hotel. I'm guessing the professor or instructor, whatever he is. She was alive when he went up and dead when I saw her. I don't have to be a rocket scientist to figure that out."

"Possible, but for all we know, you could be inventing a cover too. You've been less than candid in this investigation since day one. Does he know you were at the hotel?"

"Not that I know of, but he may have seen me."

"All the more reason to take the polygraph," Santiago said. "The results could help immensely."

"We'll call you when we have a time scheduled," Stewart said.

"How long will it take?"

"Long enough for you to meet the examiner and discuss procedures, probably not more than an hour." Stewart stood to leave.

"Thank you for your cooperation, Mr. Shaw," Santiago said.

"You're welcome. Do you think he knows I was at the hotel?" Shaw's voice got higher with each word.

"Did you have any contact with him?" Stewart asked.

"No."

"Then he probably doesn't know you were there," Stewart said, "assuming you're telling the truth."

"We could station an officer here if you'd like," Santiago said.

"Let me think about that. I'm scared," Shaw said as he closed the door.

Stewart looked at his partner. "One down, one to go."

"On to Gunn's. Let's try his apartment first since he has no class until this evening."

"Good idea."

Twenty-five minutes later Gunn opened his Greenwood apartment door to the detectives.

"Good morning, Mr. Gunn" Santiago said.

"Officers." He nodded then stepped outside. "How can I help you this morning?" He looked directly at Stewart.

"We're trying to narrow some of the leads in our investigation. We'd like you to take a polygraph test this afternoon." Stewart said.

"Are other suspects taking the test?" he said.

"Yes," Stewart said.

"It's been pretty hairy around here, but okay."

"Is Mrs. Gunn home?" Santiago said.

"Yes. She's sleeping. More accurately, she's sleeping it off." He shook his head and rolled his eyes.

"Sleeping it off?" she repeated.

"My wife is a drunk. You'd find out anyway." His voice was very soft. "I'm just trying to keep it quiet so it doesn't affect my tenure review."

"What about afterwards?" Stewart said.

"Counseling, a clinic. Who knows? We might call it quits. I'm so tired of covering for her."

Could explain the bruising. Santiago said nothing.

"I have to get back inside," he said. "Call with a time. I'll be home all day. I have class tonight." In two quick steps he turned, re-entered the apartment and closed the door.

Santiago looked at Stewart. "Do you believe it?"

"What?" he said.

"Linda Gunn is a drunk?"

"He'd be foolish to lie about it. If it's true we'd find out pretty fast." He glanced at a cloud formation.

"Still, she looked battered to me when we saw her yesterday. Let's see where our background checks lead."

* * * * *

Jack Hartley took a personal leave day so he and his wife could visit the Domestic Relations Center office on 205th overlooking Lake Ballinger. Ginger Hartley made an appointment when the Center opened the same morning. After their children were off to school they headed south on Interstate 5 to 205th, the county line.

"It was nice while it lasted, but I see we're back to crisp and damp," he said.

"It makes the air fresh," she said reaching over and patting his right leg ever so gently. "I'm excited about this morning."

"Excited or anxious? We're moving into a new stage in our relationship. I'm just nervous... maybe even scared." He said.

"It's a big step, Jack."

He sighed while making a lane change to pass a car. "Well, it's long overdue. I'm just pleased we're doing it. Wish I knew what the future holds."

"It holds whatever we make of it. Wasn't it you who said life is an adventure? Well, half the adventure is in discovering where the road leads us." Ginger watched the heavy traffic as Jack exited the freeway onto 205th west bound.

"Then the other half must be finding out how we arrive," he said. "Ah, here we are."

"Ready?" Her voice was soft. A smile crossed her face.

"Ready as I'll ever be. It sure is nice to have you at my side again." He smiled. "It's an impressive old estate house." He looked at the front of the building. "It's a nice touch setting on the shores of Lake Ballinger."

"Sure beats a strip mall. I like the way they've taken care of the grounds, placed the parking spaces around the gardens," she said. "I wonder if we can see the lake from any of the counseling rooms?"

"Maybe, but I'd bet the lake view rooms are used as offices. Let's find out," he said, getting out of the car. "They've got a golf course across the lake and another one adjacent to the east side of the property. Every room has a view of something."

"Look at the small patios scattered around the grounds. Maybe on nice days they do some outside work?"

"Could be; it's a nice setting and I'll bet the area behind the house opening onto the lake is even better," he said.

They passed through the front door, a beautifully carved piece of redwood with a large etched oval window. Hartley leaned toward his wife and whispered, "Want to see my etchings?" A smile crossed her face. She poked his ribs with an elbow as they approached the receptionist area.

"Now that is a clean desk," she said to the young man seated next to a winding stairway descending from the second floor.

"I'm Matt Crane," he said looking up and smiling. "Temporary receptionist for the day."

"We're the Hartley's. I called when your office opened this morning for appointment. I talked to someone named Misty," Ginger Hartley said.

"Our regular receptionist. She had to leave shortly after we opened. She's becoming a new mom."

Ginger smiled. "Well, the little people don't wait for anyone once they've made up their mind to enter our world."

"So it seems," Matt said and checked the appointment book. "I've buzzed Miss Rogers. She'll be down in a minute."

A slight-built red headed woman dressed in a short black skirt, stiletto heels, and a white blouse with short sleeves, the top two buttons free, appeared at the top of the stairway almost immediately and walked down. "Mr. and Mrs. Hartley, I'm Tonya Rogers," she said extending a hand. "I'll be conducting the intake interview today. We have a great view of the lake from the second floor." She led them upstairs.

As they followed her, Hartley said, "Miss Rogers, you're much younger than I... we expected. I'm sure it will be easier to talk with you than with an older person." He smiled at his wife. "Counseling will be good."

"You have a beautiful office," Ginger said, looking around the room as they entered.

A large desk that was placed against one wall and an entertainment center with doors and bookcases against another wall surrounded a coffee table in the center with four chairs. A television monitor was set into the entertainment center.

Ginger looked out the windows, viewing gardens in the backyard and the lake. "The setting is gorgeous."

"Thank you." Rogers smiled. "It's a pleasant work environment, and clients generally feel comfortable. Please," she said gesturing toward the chairs, "sit wherever you choose."

The Hartley's selected two chairs side by side. Miss Rogers sat in a chair directly across from the couple. The hem of her short skirt climbed noticeably when she sat down and crossed her legs at the knees.

Ginger patted her husband's leg. "Jack, I'll let you tell Miss Rogers why we're here."

He nodded at his wife, said "Okay babe," then looked at Tonya Rogers.

"Before you begin, Mr. Hartley, let me clarify a few things first and maybe put us all at ease. Nothing is ever easy when we talk about counseling, at least initially. I like to use first names if possible. It makes things less formal. Would that be all right with you?"

Both nodded.

"We already know we're here to help both of you explore your marital relationship. Something brought you here. As a couple you've found something lacking, a problem, maybe even several problems that make you feel uncomfortable with each other. At the sessions we'll talk about feelings, identify issues, and find solutions. I'm not here to pry into your lives or judge you. My job is to facilitate a discussion between you two. I'll act as a moderator, a guide."

"We'll be talking to each other, right?" Ginger said.

"Precisely. What we talk about is confidential, but there are some considerations to keep in mind," Rogers said. "If you tell me about something that's criminal, for example, I am required to report it to the authorities. A counselor-client relationship does not have the same confidentiality you would enjoy with an attorney."

Jack Hartley shared the events leading to their visit. He began with the murder of Hailey Cashland and the investigation, then the clandestine meeting he had with her at the Avenue Hotel. He twisted in his chair, looking frequently at his wife, his voice soft and slow. "I've already told the police all of this," he said. "They also know Hailey and I had an affair going back some three years." He looked at his wife.

"Jack, you haven't really touched on why you had the affair with the young woman," Rogers said.

He shifted in his chair, reached over, patted Ginger's arm and stroked his chin with the right hand. "You have a funny way of cutting to the chase," he said, clearing his throat and shuffling his feet. Beads of sweat appeared on his forehead. "Four years ago I did a foolish thing. It's something I'm not proud of." He paused. The silence in the room was deafening.

"It's okay, Jack," Ginger said.

"I raped Ginger one night in a drunken rage. Later we agreed to stay married for the sake of the children and our own greed. I don't know why... maybe because we couldn't get to where we wanted without each other." He paused and cleared his throat again. "We agreed that we'd have no sexual relations with each other. We were going to have a Platonic relationship, just living together."

"Did you share the same bed?" Rogers said.

"Yes, we shared the same bed, felt each other's warmth and lived together, but we never talked about the rape," Ginger said. "We agreed not to have sex or separate. Staying together was good for Jack's career and the children. In return he would continue to support us. We'd maintain our status in the community. Jack would keep his job. My role was to raise the children, put on a good front, not leave him, and not file charges. And I never will."

"Why did you really make the agreement, both of you? Explore your reasons."

"We are," Jack said. "I guess that's why we're here. Looking back I'd say we were greedy, selfish, and caught up in our yuppie existence. I didn't want to lose my career and all the earning power that goes with it because of a stupid mistake. Our lifestyle is better. We live well on my salary, better than we would if I were forced to resign because of the morals clause in my contract."

"Where do you work?"

"Jack is the superintendent of Gold Coast Academy," Ginger said. "It's on the form Misty completed over the phone this morning."

"I'm sure it is. She's having a busy day. So what happened?" Rogers said.

"As I said, I had an affair with Hailey Cashland. We'd been seeing each other for three years. Neither of us was looking for a marriage. We found physical gratification in bed together. Then someone killed her." He sighed. "I'll probably lose my job anyway, but the good thing is that in this crisis we've found each other again." He reached to touch his wife's arm.

"And you, Ginger... what's your story?" Rogers asked squinting and focusing on Mrs. Hartley.

"What Jack says is true as far as it goes. He makes everything sound like it's his fault. That's not true, perhaps in the beginning, the rape and drinking, but not later. We both made a pact with the devil. In the past couple of years I've had several brief affairs with fellow students and men I've met. Jack didn't even realize what I was doing because he was so busy with Hailey."

"You knew about Hailey?" Rogers said.

"Yes, but he was very discreet. He never threw it in my face. It was something we both accepted without discussion."

Rogers looked at Jack. "How do you feel about Ginger's infidelities?"

"I didn't believe it when she told me yesterday, but what we discovered together at home last evening is that we do love and care about each other. That's what brought us here. We talked about starting over together. We both know our lives are going to be very different."

"It sounds like you two have done quite a bit of talking in the last day or two. The more you share with each other, the better."

"We want to stay together as a family," Ginger said. "There are more important things in life than a job or social status."

"It's just a tragedy that it took the death of a young woman to make us realize our true feelings," he said.

"I still think she was a bitch," Ginger said.

"She was a nice person. She didn't do anything to you. She fulfilled a need." He looked at his wife, the lines in his face becoming deep gashes. He bit his lower lip.

"God, you still talk about her like some old friend. I don't want to think about her. I want to think about us. We both had flings and made stupid mistakes."

The couple fell silent.

"We'll get together again next week," Rogers said. "I have another client due in a few minutes, but one last thing before you leave. If either of you feel uncomfortable with me as your counselor I can arrange for a different person. If you are comfortable there is no reason to change. Keep talking with each other. Awkward moments like you just experienced will happen. The more you talk and share, the less often they will occur and the less awkward they'll become. Communicating with each other is the most important part." She stood. "You can make an appointment downstairs with Matt."

The Hartleys stood and shook hands with Rogers, then embraced each other. Ginger looked at her husband. "I wonder if the receptionist has had her baby yet? It would be nice if something really special happened on our first day of counseling."

"It would be nice," he said. "Let's go."

* * * * *

Santiago and Stewart went directly to their offices at the Public Safety Building after leaving Gunn's apartment.

She waved her notepad. "When I finish looking these over, I'm going to send a few emails off to some universities, past employers, and the FBI." She glanced through a few pages and looked at her partner. "I've got a good list of people he used as references."

"Are they local?" Stewart leaned back in his chair, tapping a pen against his lip.

"Mostly. I'll call them first. Maybe they'll talk to me." She placed the receiver on her shoulder and began dialing.

"I've got the similar mess with Shaw, though maybe not as many." He began phoning.

A short while later she hung up the phone. "That's my third request to come in person. I don't think the public trusts phone calls anymore. How are you doing?"

"About the same." He sipped the last of his coffee. "We're not gaining much background, just making appointments if you think about it."

"Let's go by Gold Coast and let Hartley know he's off the hook. We can touch base with some of these references and still be back for Gunn's polygraph at 2:00." She put her notepad back into her purse.

"That's a positive thought. Did we get a time arranged for Shaw?" Stewart said.

"Thompson will see him a 9:30 tomorrow morning." She tapped her pen on the desk. "On second thought, let's wait on Hartley 'til we're done with the polygraphs. Lord only knows what strange turn this case will take next."

"Good point. We'll wait. I'll call Shaw now while you finish your list," he said. Both detectives began punching numbers again.

"Mrs. Virginia Olson?" Santiago said.

"Yes."

"I'm Detective Santiago with the Seattle Police Department. I'm completing a background check on Trevor Gunn. He listed you as a reference on his application to Sunset Community College."

"Yes. I told Trev he could use me as a reference any time. He's brilliant."

"How did you come to know him?"

"I was a student in counselor training at Snohomish Community College," she said with enthusiasm.

Santiago wrote *gusher* on a notepad by the phone. "Did you know Mr. Gunn only as a professional, or personally as well?"

"Certainly as a professional in class, but we did become good friends off campus. I was separated from my husband at the time and Trev helped me through the experience."

I'll bet he did. Santiago swallowed. "So you knew him as a really close friend?"

"Oh yes... intimately," she said with a slight chuckle.

"Was Mr. Gunn able to help resolve the marital issues?"

"Oh, Trev helped rekindle my lost passion for my husband, Jake. I learned many ways of dealing with stress and how to share feelings. We were married too young in life, before either of us had a chance to, you know, sow our wild oats."

"Oh? When did you and Jake marry?"

"We were only eighteen, just out of high school."

"Do you still keep in contact with Mr. Gunn?"

"No, but he's a wonderful teacher and counselor. I'd recommend him to anyone. He's very understanding of a woman's point of view."

"Did Mr. Olson participate in the counseling with you?"

"No. Jake actually didn't like Trev very well. He thought Trev might be taking advantage of me... you know, getting too intimate."

"Was he?"

"As I said, Jake and I were separated at the time." She laughed. "Our personal friendship shouldn't jeopardize the reference." She paused. "I am a professional he helped train."

"Mrs. Olson, this is very important. How intimately did you know Mr. Gunn?"

"You said you were a police officer?"

"Yes. I'm investigating a homicide and Mr. Gunn is a person of interest."

"Well, I don't want to cause any problems."

"You won't, Mrs. Olson, unless you withhold evidence."

"We slept together," she paused, "often, at my apartment." She chuckled again. "I learned more about myself and how to please Jake than I ever thought possible. Trev was a great friend and teacher in *so* many ways."

"Thank you, Mrs. Olson. If I need further information I'll contact you, or you can reach me at the department."

"Our chat is confidential, isn't it?"

"We operate on a need to know basis for those involved in the investigation. Thank you again, Mrs. Olson." Santiago put the phone down and looked at her partner. "God, the Bimbo Factor is alive and well."

Stewart laughed at her comment then became serious. "I just talked to Bert Wagner. The victim behind the Avenue Hotel yesterday was our cleaning lady."

"Chey?"

"Yes, but Wagner says it's definitely a gang killing, maybe involving prostitution."

"So we're out a witness because of an unconnected crime?"

"That's about it."

"I'm beginning to hate this case. All we run into are roadblocks." She tossed her pen on the desk.

"Let's grab an early lunch. I want to talk to Lester Marzinni about Shaw before Gunn's polygraph," Stewart said.

"The art dealer?"

"One and the same. My guy seems to have a few connections beyond your guy's bimbos."

"Lunch sounds good."

* * * * *

"I'd rather have eaten at Dick's," she said. "Sit-down restaurants take too long."

"Well, I tend to spill and I don't want ketchup on this shirt or jacket," he said.

Santiago laughed. "Maybe you should get a bib. I'm not worried about spills."

"No? You'd sure make a mess of that blouse and skirt if you did. You'd probably need my help cleaning up the mess." He grinned.

"Get your brain back above your belt buckle." She paused. "We've got to move on these two characters."

Stewart smiled. "Good thing I have a date tonight. She won't pick on me." He shook his head. "Anyway, this is what I've got so far. Shaw is a Navy brat. His parents are retired in Bremerton. He likes fine dining, expensive wine, jewelry, gourmet coffee and appears to have an I-I-me-me mentality."

"He does appear to live well. The complex is nice. I mean, it isn't plush but it's not what I'd expect from a delivery man."

"Apparently it's something to do with the artist's environment." Stewart shrugged. "He's a Fine Arts graduate from the UW, considered an up and coming talent. He's also racked up one or two big-ticket sales that have kept him out of debt."

"How about a record?"

"My boy Shaw, who was angry at Cashland, has a criminal history. He was charged two years ago with assault while attending a demonstration for gay rights. The charges were later dropped. Last year he was charged with indecent exposure in the men's room at Woodland Park. That charge was dropped when it was discovered the victim was facing an assault charge for another incident involving a gay member of the community."

"So he can be violent."

"We can all be violent, Mitch."

"Anything else?"

"Yes, one of his teachers said this morning Shaw once described himself as 'an artist of the proletariat, until I get rich.' He seems to be on the Machiavellian side of practical."

"Family?"

"As I said, they live in Bremerton. Mom worked menial jobs until dad retired."

"Do his parents know his persuasion?"

"Yes. They don't much care for it. Dad refuses to communicate with him. Mother follows suit."

"Siblings?"

"An older brother, two younger sisters. None of them have much to do with Terry. However, his brother did relate an interesting incident from their adolescence. Apparently dad caught Terry reading a gay magazine under the covers with a flashlight and beat him bloody. Since then the old man has taken great delight in humiliating his son during family functions at every opportunity."

"You did a lot better than I did this morning. What kind of student was he?"

"Graduated from the UW with a 3.26. He also worked at an art gallery on 45th and Brooklyn. It's now closed. His two closest friends are Charles Goodwin, his soon to be houseguest, and Hailey. He was always a loner. He met Charles in college and Hailey when she moved into her apartment." Stewart leaned back and ordered a second cup of coffee. "What have you got on Gunn?"

She adjusted her chair. "Mr. Gunn is an interesting man. He was raised in a broken home. His parents divorced when he was six. He has a brother two years older who is Mr. Everything from high school honors and jock to student Commandant of the university ROTC for a year. Now he's a CEO in New York just rollin' in the bucks."

"In other words, little brother is competing with an over achiever." He spilled a few drops of coffee on his shirtfront. "Damn it!"

"Seems that way." She ignored the spill. "His parents are also interesting. Father was a heavy drinker and brawler. By trade he was a tugboat crewman on Puget Sound. Mother was an attractive lady, apparently a fast-lane teenager in her youth. Her ex says she was seventeen going on thirty-five when they first met, something she doesn't deny."

"Both parents are still living?" He dabbed at the coffee spill.

"Yes. Dad lives in Fremont, mom in San Diego."

"Mom liked to party?"

"Yes, she pretty much chased around. From what she says, she still does. Dad says she was a pre-flower child, did some drugs, slept with anyone. They were married in late '65 and split in '75."

"How was Gunn in school?"

"A good student. Past teachers refer to him as brilliant. A few emphasized his lack of people skills. Like Shaw, he was a loner, very self-centered, and often felt persecuted. Something we already knew, he's got an ego that won't quit. So far past employers reinforce old teachers, 'That he has zero social skills unless he wants something.' One even implied there was a direct correlation between his social skills and the rumored affairs with students. Another said his short temper probably adversely affects his search for tenure."

"How about Mrs. Gunn?"

"She has two DUI's, has been in chemical dependency counseling, and once assaulted an officer who arrested her. She pleaded guilty to her first DUI. On the second she pled guilty for the DUI and the assault charge for slapping the officer was dropped on condition she do rehab. She met Gunn as one of his students at South Sound Community College. Not only did Wonder Stud leave SSCC with a wife, but amidst allegations of sexual harassment. Why am I not surprised?" She shook her head as she studied her notes.

"So how did he end up at Sunset?" Stewart said.

"Your guess is as good as mine. He seems to have taught at several different schools. I don't know. You'd think they'd stay away from a guy with his track record of alleged womanizing, student affairs, sexual harassment, and ego mania."

"But some of this supports what he said this morning about Linda sleeping it off and yesterday when she said she fell into a counter," Stewart said.

"Yeah, but I just feel Gunn is a violent man, more than capable of killing Hailey Cashland."

"So is Terry Shaw," he said.

"I know, but Gunn is a predator. I can *feel* it, Chance. He did it. I know he did." She finished her soda. "You said you wanted to talk to the art dealer?"

"Right and maybe we can catch another interview before Gunn comes in this afternoon."

"Button the blazer and your tie will cover the spill," she said as they walked out the door.

"Thanks, smart ass," he said under his breath.

CHAPTER 9

Next door to the First Avenue Eatery the detectives entered the Twilight Gallery and approached a distinguished appearing silver-haired gentleman.

"Mr. Marzinni? I'm Detective Stewart of the Seattle Police Department. This is my partner, Detective Santiago."

"Ah, yes. You said on the phone you needed some background information on Terry Shaw. I appreciate you coming to my gallery to talk. Such things are too sensitive for the phone. One never knows who's listening these days." He guided the detectives toward a coffee bar.

"I can appreciate your concern for discretion, Mr. Marzinni," Stewart said.

"Shaw's a genius, a diamond in the rough. He's sold a few works thus far at good prices. He'll do even better in a few years. By then he'll have captured the hearts and souls of collectors."

"How well do you know him?" Stewart said.

"Why, personally of course." He waved his right hand and smiled. A faint scent of incense filled the gallery mixed with the odor of fresh coffee. "My apologies, may I get either of you a cappuccino?"

"No thank you," Santiago said looking up from her notepad.

Stewart asked, "What's he like?"

"A loner, mystical, he sees everything through the eyes of an artist." The man's voice was now in a near whisper. Marzinni smiled. "He is a most sensitive and caring man, capable of showing strong emotion in his work."

"Did he show strong emotion outside of his work?" Stewart said.

"Of course! He's an artist. He has passion, feelings, loves." Marzinni's voice held a rich timber, and he seemed excited and breathless.

"How about anger?" Stewart said.

"Anger?"

"Yes, anger, Mr. Marzinni. Does Terry Shaw show anger outside his painting?"

"Of course he shows anger, but not violent behavior. He demonstrates anger, all of his emotions, through movement, looks and sensitivity. He's not a big or strong man. He's...." Marzinni paused and began waving his hand carelessly before him while moving soundless lips, "rational but compassionate."

"Do you ever mix with Shaw socially?" Stewart said.

"No. I don't know him that well, you understand." He raised an eyebrow.

"Well, thank you, Mr. Marzinni. If you think of anything else, please call me." Stewart handed the gallery owner a business card.

Santiago said, "One more thing, Mr. Marzinni, did Terry Shaw ever mention Hailey Cashland to you?"

"Why yes, he did on a few occasions. She was a neighbor. He thought of her as a sister, albeit a very naughty sister." Marzinni laughed. "Sometimes he became very frustrated when he spoke of her."

"How so?" Santiago's attention became even more intense.

"Oh, you know, he'd make a fist; sometimes say angry things about the way she behaved with so many men. He loved her passionately, as only he could. I think he wanted desperately to protect her from herself."

"Did he ever mention anyone following or stalking Hailey?"

"No. He was just angry, perhaps frustrated with her social behavior from time to time."

"Thank you again, Mr. Marzinni," she said.

As they walked back to the car Stewart looked at the sky. "We're getting a few more clouds. Did I hear some doubt in there? Are you having second thoughts about Gunn?"

"No, but I want to make sure we don't miss anything. Let's see how Doc Thompson does."

* * * * *

Trevor Gunn arrived at the appointed time, 2:00 p.m. for the polygraph. He walked up to Mitch's desk accompanied by a uniform. "Detective Santiago, are you ready for me?" he said looking around. "Where's Detective Stewart?"

"Yes, we are," she said, looking at the man dressed in tan slacks, a forest green polo shirt and low-cut tennis shoes. "Detective Stewart stepped out for a moment. He'll join us." She stood. "Doctor Thompson has set up his equipment and is waiting for you. He'll explain everything and how it works. Afterwards, he'll go over the results with us. It's the same scenario for each individual."

"You mean suspects don't you, Detective?" Gunn said.

"Yes, suspects," she said. They walked into the isolated room and Santiago gestured toward a man in a white lab coat. "Doctor Thompson, Mr. Gunn. I'll be next door observing the activity with Detective Stewart through the one-way mirror." Santiago left the room.

"Mr. Gunn," the doctor said while extending his hand. "Come and sit down. Let me explain what we'll be doing here."

"Thank you," Gunn said.

"First, I'm going to ask you a series of eight questions as a pretest. One of the items will be an obvious lie. The reaction you have to the lie is what I'm watching for. The equipment will measure any changes in your cardiovascular, respiratory, and electro-dermal patterns. Those changes will be markedly different for the lie than the other items."

"Will a week of stress and lack of sleep affect the outcome?" Gunn said.

"Possibly, but not drastically. I'll pause for ten seconds between your response to each question and my asking of the next. Each question will require a 'yes' response. When we do the actual test all but five of the items will be from the pretest. Any questions, Mr. Gunn?"

"No, I believe I understand the process. Thank you for asking."

"Now remember, each item is to be answered 'yes' including the obvious lie."

Gunn held the arms of the wooden chair firmly in each hand and looked at the doctor. "I do have a question. What are the simple truths you're going to be asking, or is that an inappropriate question?"

"Not at all. Let me read them for you. Is your name Trevor Gunn? Is your age 31? Do you live at Puget Arms Apartments? Is your wife's name Linda? Do you have two children? Are you an instructor at Sunset Community College? Are you awaiting the tenure committee review report? Is your real name Sonny Hefner?"

"And I answer each question with a 'yes' response?"

"That's correct. The only difference will be the items I add for the actual exercise, the last five questions. Those items you will answer either 'yes' or 'no,' whatever would be appropriate for you. Okay?"

"Of course."

"Now I'm going to connect the monitoring devices to you. That's really why you must sit in the hard chair. The lines only reach so far. Are you comfortable, Mr. Gunn?"

"As comfortable as one can be under these circumstances."

"Shall we begin?"

"Yes."

From the neighboring room Santiago and Stewart observed the session. A speaker carried the dialogue from the testing room. "He's cool as a cucumber, Mitch. Look at the way he just slouches in the chair," Stewart said.

She took her eyes off the subject for a moment and looked at her partner. "I want to see how he reacts to the final five on the actual test."

Thompson asked each question slowly and clearly. After the subject responded he marked the paper running through the monitor. The pretest went as expected. After he'd answered the final question, Gunn sat up straight, looked at the mirror, and wiped his brow.

"Are you ready to take the test, Mr. Gunn?"

"Yes, but like I told the officers this morning, I don't know how accurate it will be." He shuffled his feet and straightened himself in the chair.

Santiago stared at the men in the other room, tapped her fingertips on the table as she heard each question asked and answered. She looked at Stewart. "Thompson's ten second breaks sure seem long."

"He needs them for accuracy. You just don't like Gunn. You've got to enjoy watching him twitch."

"You got that right."

Thompson finished the first seven questions then looked at the clipboard holding the actual items. "Did you know Hailey Cashland?"

"Yes."

"Did you love Hailey Cashland?"

"No."

"Did you have intimate relations with Hailey Cashland?"

"Yes."

"Did you go the Avenue Hotel to kill Hailey Cashland?"

Gunn squinted, his eyes boring in on Thompson. The lines of his tanned face became jagged shadows. Beads of moisture formed on his forehead. He made a short gasping sound and gripped his legs. "No," he said clearly.

Thompson paused the ten seconds which now seemed like minutes. Santiago was as tense as the subject. Stewart watched his partner and the subject closely, but with detachment.

Thompson checked the final question on the sheet. "Did you kill Hailey Cashland at the Avenue Hotel?"

Gunn shook his head slowly, rubbed the top of his right thigh with the palm of his hand. "No," he whispered.

Thompson marked the continuous paper, put the clipboard down and disconnected the sensors. "Thank you, Mr. Gunn. We're finished."

Stewart went to the interrogation room. "If you'd like to freshen up you'll find a rest room at the end of the hall to your right."

"Thank you." Gunn left the room.

Doc Thompson wiped sweat from his forehead.

"Are you okay, Doc?" Stewart said.

"It feels warm, stuffy in here. I probably need a breath of fresh air after the session."

"When will we get the results?" Stewart said.

"I had another test already scheduled when you squeezed your man in. I'll be about an hour." Doc took a deep breath and shook his head.

"We'll see you then," Stewart said.

Santiago was already on her way down the hallway.

"Where is Mitch going in such a hurry?" Doc said watching her. "She's always quite inspirational." He laughed.

"She'll be back in an hour with me, Doc. We're doing some in-depth backgrounds."

"I see you also have another subject scheduled for tomorrow morning." Doc said, wiped his brow again and looked up. Another detective was escorting a woman down the hall. "My next appointment," he said with a nod.

"An hour, then," said Stewart. "I've got to get upstairs."

Doc smiled at Stewart. "Yes, I can see you're a man with tough duty."

Stewart laughed. "It's a dirty job but somebody's got to do it."

Gunn returned from the rest room. "Anything else, Detective Stewart?"

"No, Mr. Gunn. Thank you for coming in."

* * * * *

Santiago looked across the desks at Stewart. "I've got a lead on a past employer of Gunn. Maybe we'll have time to follow it up after we meet with Doc. It's in Snohomish."

Stewart checked his watch. "Probably."

Captain James walked over to their desks. "Downstairs just called. Doc threw-up during a session. He won't see you 'til tomorrow."

"He's sick?" Santiago said.

"Flu or something he ate," James said.

"He was sweating like crazy after Gunn's session," Stewart said.

"Do we get Gunn's results before or after Shaw?" Santiago said.

"Depends on what time Doc gets here," James said, "assuming he comes in at all."

"Thanks for the update, Captain," Stewart said.

"Chance, now we've got time to drive over to Snohomish Community College and talk with Mark Pearce, their personnel man," Santiago said.

"Plenty of time," he said.

"Don't worry. We'll be back for your date with hot little Amber? How could I forget? Just be careful she doesn't hurt you." Santiago laughed.

They headed north on Interstate 5 as the evening rush hour neared.

He smiled. "What are you doing tonight?"

"Go home, take a swim, work out and maybe think about the case."

"You need to let go a little," Stewart said.

"Maybe I'll get Jason to take a swim with me."

"Who's Jason?" His expression showed deep lines around his tired eyes and cheeks.

"Just a neighbor," she said. "A *hunk* of a neighbor."

The detectives arrived at the Snohomish campus after a half-hour drive north on I-5 then heading east on US 2. "Not as modern as the Sunset or Gold Coast campus settings," Santiago said.

"Not even close. This place looks like something from the '40s or '50s."

Mark Pearce greeted the detectives in the outer office where he was working at a file cabinet. "I've been expecting you since Detective Santiago called a little while ago. It's a long drive from Seattle." He smiled and led them into his office.

"Mr. Pearce, we're checking the background of Trevor Gunn. He's a person of interest in an investigation," Santiago said as they sat down in front of the administrator's desk.

"I've asked one of the office girls to bring in his file," said Pearce.

A moment later there was a light knock on the door; then a young woman entered without waiting for a greeting. She handed the file to Pearce.

"Thank you, Marci." His voice was soft and friendly. He watched her for a long moment as she left the office.

Stewart looked over the top of a large picture frame on the desk as Pearce read the contents, then at his partner. "Nice office," he whispered to Santiago. "We should have furniture half as comfortable." He looked over the edge of the frame again. "So Mr. Pearce, what can you tell us about Mr. Gunn?"

"He taught here for two years but failed to receive tenure. His classes were well organized, material well-presented and the students found him friendly. However, he didn't get along well with other staff members and some unsubstantiated rumors were circulating about him having relationships with some of his students."

"So you chose not to grant tenure to him?" Santiago watched the man closely.

"It's a little more complicated than that," Pearce said, the tailored cotton shirt collar beginning to look a little tight around his neck.

"In what way?" Santiago sat back and opened her notepad.

"Our enrollment wasn't at the level anticipated. Good fortune being what it is, we were able to cut his position. He was the only non-tenured instructor within the chemical dependency program."

"How convenient," she said. "You mentioned some rumors. Was there any follow up?" Santiago said.

"No. Our insurer made a small financial arrangement with a coed to sidetrack any litigation before it got started."

"We'll need the name of the school's insurance company," Stewart said.

"And the coed," Santiago said.

"Of course." Pearce paused for a moment while he looked at Santiago. He pursed his lips then wet them with his tongue. "Have you ever considered working in the private or semiprivate sector?" he said changing the subject.

"No," she said.

"Too bad." He looked back at Stewart. "Marci will provide the information you require, but keep in mind this is a confidential personnel matter," Pearce said, attempting to dismiss the detectives.

"Let's go back to the settlement with the student for a moment," Santiago said. "It seems to presume what could be very damaging rumors about a staff member and the school true without any supporting evidence. Isn't that like hanging one of your own people out to dry?" Santiago said.

He swallowed and his face reddened. "Well, we didn't follow up, Detective Santiago, because he was not renewed. Had he been renewed or tenured staff certainly we would have investigated. It was our opinion that making a small payment to the young woman involved was a show of good faith. As I said, our numbers were declining."

"What kind of reference did you provide Gunn when asked to contact Sunset?" Stewart asked.

"A very positive professional recommendation," he said looking about the office and then at his watch. "With no substantiation of any wrong doing it wouldn't be appropriate to bring any rumors to light. I'm sure you can understand the school's position." He smiled.

Stewart said, "Mr. Pearce, thank you for your time." The detectives stood. "The young lady in the office will have the information we need?"

"Yes." Pearce picked up his phone and spoke in a hushed voice.

Marci met the detectives at the door as they exited Pearce's office. "The information you needed, Detective Stewart," she said as she handed over a typed memo.

"Thank you."

"Anytime," she said as they left the office.

"Get your mind back on the job," Santiago said as they walked to the car. "What is it about guys, anyway? Old Pearce drooling all over himself looking at the office girl when she comes in."

"Marci. Her name is Marci."

"He reminds me of Moses Cruz's dad."

"Beautiful women have an effect on men. We can't help ourselves." He laughed as they got in the car.

"I think Amber is the right date for you tonight." She smiled at her partner. *Lucky bitch.* "Isn't Charles on your list to interview?"

"Yeah," Stewart said.

"Let's stop by Shaw's. We're going through the north end on the way back."

* * * * *

Santiago and Stewart arrived at Shaw's apartment complex around 5:30. They found Charles Goodwin in the cabana shooting pool alone after finding a note for Shaw on the apartment door telling him where he was.

"Mr. Goodwin?" Stewart asked.

"Yes."

"I'm Detective Stewart and this is my partner Detective Santiago."

"How do you do? Terry has mentioned you. He's out on some errands right now."

"We've come to see you, Mr. Goodwin," Santiago said. "Shooting a little pool, eh?"

"Just passing the time. I'm scheduled for a workout at 6:00 and I came over early." He put the cue stick down and walked across the room to a lounge area near the sliders.

Santiago's eyes followed his muscular frame draped in the T-shirt and gym shorts. "We'd like to talk with you about Terry," she said.

"Sure. Please sit down." When they were settled, he said, "Terry and I met some years ago in college. He was in art and I was in political science. We met in a speech class. It was required of all freshmen."

Stewart took out a notepad. "Tell us about him, please."

"When we first met, he implied he was from a wealthy family and was trying to find his own identity. I was a basic street kid trying to make a better future for myself. We both had dysfunctional backgrounds."

"Was that your link to each other?" Stewart asked.

"No, we just enjoyed each other's company. We share our dreams, and we motivate each other. Isn't it enough to say we like each other and that we're good friends?"

"Yes, it is," Santiago said. "Have you ever been around Terry when he's angry?"

"Sure I have. We all get angry at one time or another."

"How does he handle his anger?" Stewart said.

"He shouts and curses, but usually he paints something with a lot of red and black, dark colors with jagged edges. He calls it his dark side."

Stewart said, "No acts of violence?"

"He'll throw paint at the canvas, but does he strike out at other things like pets, furniture, people? No, except verbally. He's not a physical person. His life centers on painting. His emotions and feelings are displayed for all to see through his work. He's an artist."

"Has he ever talked about Hailey with you?"

"Occasionally. He thought of her as family. Her behavior with men sometimes frustrated him."

"Angered him?" Santiago said.

"Sometimes."

"Did Terry ever say he wanted to do something about her behavior?" Stewart said.

"No. He accepted it as something he had to live with, something beyond his control."

"I have no further questions. Thank you for your time, Mr. Goodwin," Stewart said handing him a business card. "If you think of anything else, please call."

"Please, call me Chuck. Terry is always so formal." He paused for a moment, and then walked the officers to the cabana door. "You know he's frightened right now. I was surprised he even went out on errands today." He opened the door and showed the officers out.

"Yes. We offered to provide police protection but he declined," Stewart said.

"That sounds like Terry. He never wants to draw attention to himself."

"Thank you again, Mr. Goodwin," Santiago said. "I mean Chuck."

As they walked to the car, Stewart said, "It sounds like Shaw is clean. At least he doesn't come across as physically violent, but you can't always tell a book by its cover."

"Gunn is my number one suspect," Santiago said, getting into the car.

"I'm inclined to agree for the moment, but I'll wait for the polygraph. All we've really got are Gunn and Shaw disagreeing about when she died," Stewart said.

"That and what time Gunn arrived home. I still think he threatened his wife too," she said.

"She could've been drunk and not really remember when he arrived." Stewart started the engine.

"Who knows? Goodwin could be protecting his friend," she said.

"He could be. Shaw looks clean for now, but I'm patient. Who knows?"

"Hard to say. Let's go."

CHAPTER 10

Santiago arrived home around 6:30 p.m. She hung her sweater on the coat tree, tossed the mail on the coffee table and headed for the refrigerator. "It's been a long day," she said, pouring a generous glass Chardonnay. She looked at the drink then raised it. "Here's to you, Doc, and all the things you'll tell us tomorrow about Gunn." She walked to the bedroom and stopped in front of a full-length mirror, placed the glass on the dresser and took off her clothes. She tossed garments onto the bed behind her. She stood erect, turned and checked her profile. "What does Amber have that I don't?" She continued to look at the mirror. "Chance, that's what."

She walked to the shower, turned on the hot water, and let it run for a few minutes to fill the bathroom with heat and steam before stepping into the warm spray. She rejoiced at the warm fluid pouring over her body. Rivers rushed over her breasts and down her cleavage. Her flat belly was soaked. The warm streams continued down her thighs. Reaching for a sponge and soap she lathered herself. "This would be a great job for you, Chance. What would your hands feel like touching me, stroking me, exciting me?" She took her time soaping and washing, and eventually glanced at her watch. "It's only 7:15. Think I'll go for a swim."

She got out of the shower, toweled herself dry and brushed her hair, then walked to the dresser and opened the top drawer. She selected a blue French bikini. Donning a cover-up and white sandals, she walked across the courtyard to the cabana and the indoor pool, a bronze beauty on the prowl.

Jason Tolliver, her neighbor and a young grocery store manager, called to her in greeting. "Hi, Mitch. Gonna catch a few laps tonight?"

At the edge of the pool she jutted out her right hip and looked down at him. "I didn't come here for the rays. How's the water?" She glanced around the area. "Looks like I'm the only woman here."

Tolliver's gaze never left her. He grinned. "It'll be warmer when you get in."

"I hope it chills me a little." She walked to the step and entered, splashing water on her legs, arms and shoulders as she went. "It feels really great." She plunged in, swam several laps then paused at one end of the pool.

"Haven't seen you around much," Tolliver said.

"I've been working a case that just refuses to come together. At least you're in a rational business."

"A break sounds in order, Mitch. Why don't you join me for drinks, maybe a pizza? We can order in."

"That's the best offer I've had today," she said.

They stepped from the pool and walked over to the lounge chairs. "I don't believe it," she said looking at the cover-up. "I didn't bring a towel."

"Too much concentration. Let me help you." He took his towel and gently started to pat her back.

She turned to face him. "I'm okay, I'll do that," she said taking the towel.

"You can do my back too, if you'd like."

"Sure, it's your towel."

Tolliver looked deep into her sculptured face and dark brown eyes. "You're beautiful."

"Thank you. You're not bad yourself, neighbor," she said. "Now how about that drink?"

They left the pool and crossed the courtyard to a building directly across from Santiago's. Jason's apartment was furnished in Spanish Mediterranean: dark wood, heavy furniture and black wrought-iron sconces surrounding the fireplace. The couch was overstuffed chocolate brown and curved around two walls of the living room. A long red shag throw rug covered the institutional gray carpet in front of the fireplace. Unlike her larger apartment, a long counter with barstools separated the living room from the kitchen in lieu of a dining room.

"I've always wondered what the one-bedroom units were like." She smiled wistfully at the young man. "You've never asked me over even though we swim a lot. I was beginning to think there was something wrong with me." Her cover fell open.

He watched her, eyes swelling. "Trust me, there's nothing wrong with you, Mitch. How about that drink? I have red or white wine, both chilled," he said walking to the kitchen. "I like it that way." He removed a bottle from the refrigerator. "White okay?"

"Always my first choice," she said.

"I thought so. You always have it when I visit your place. I'll call for pizza."

"Let's just have some wine for now." She sat down on the red rug. "How 'bout a fire? It's cool in here after the pool."

"I thought you'd never ask." He smiled again and walked across the living room, turned on the gas and lit it. Closing the glass doors he sat down beside her.

"I hope the chlorine on our suits doesn't bleach the rug," she said.

"Lucky rug." He looked into her eyes. "Is something troubling you? You seem a little distracted."

"You're sweet. Sometimes I just wish Chance was half as aware of me, my moods, as you are." She looked around. "I don't know what I'm doing here. I should go."

"He's around you every day," Jason said. "I'm sure he knows how you feel."

"Not really. I mean, he knows me as a cop, but not as a person... a woman. I can tease him. We kid back and forth. He just sees me as a partner, like best friends."

"And you want more," said Jason.

"I think I'm in love with him, but I may never get the opportunity to find out for sure."

He took a long sip of wine. "He's a lucky man. I know a lot of guys who would like to know you better as a person. You said he teases back. Maybe it's not all kidding. Didn't you tell me once he'd been married?"

"Yes. He has a couple of kids, but he's also known as fast with the ladies at the department."

"We all have history, Mitch. The older we get the more we have. Maybe he's afraid of getting too close to a meaningful relationship. You know, fear of rejection or something."

"Maybe. You're right about baggage. The case we're working on right now deals with a teacher who was leading a double life. She had a history, baggage, just like me in some ways." Santiago laughed. "Our backgrounds come close in some respects. You know I worked the clubs when I was at the UW. I met a lot of people. Some I got to know better than others."

Jason watched a drop of sweat flow down her cleavage while she looked into the fire. "Chance doesn't know how lucky he is."

"So tell me, what do I do? You're a man and you know me."

He chuckled. "Yeah, for all the good it does me... although I admit it's probably better being a close friend than being hung up on you considering how you feel about him."

"So what do I do about Chance?"

"When the moments come, drop tidbits and hints about who you are and what you like: hobbies, favorite foods, music, reading, whatever. Let him know you're a whole person, not just a cop. I bet you'll find some crossover. Think about it. How well do you know him other than that he's a homicide dick who's fast with the ladies?"

"You'd like him," she said.

"Maybe, but I wouldn't bet on it. Tell me, what's he doing tonight while you're over here draped in a sexy bikini in front of my fire sweating and making me jealous of the carpet?"

"Having dinner with his latest conquest, Amber. He was so excited about seeing her tonight you'd think he was dating the queen of cheer leaders and he was the captain of the football team."

"Maybe he's not the big time stud you think he is. Maybe he's just a guy. Maybe, like I said, he's a little unsure of himself."

"I doubt that."

"Think about it. He has this macho rep and a partner who's the hottest cop in Seattle. Why risk being turned down and screwing up a perfect record?"

Santiago laughed, blushed and finished her wine.

"Think old school. Most people don't play in their own backyard." He smiled. "I don't date the ladies at the store but there are a few I would like to."

"I'm sure." She looked into the fire.

"It's okay to string him along a little—a guy likes that—but give him something he doesn't expect. Mitch, can I be really blunt without hurting your feelings?"

"Sure."

"Leave the vain coy chick part you're so good at behind. Much as I hate the idea, you might get to know each other really well as people. I'd bet he's as attracted to you as you are to him."

"That was honest." She glanced at her watch. "We've been talking a long time. I'd better get out of here. I've still got work to do."

"Not to worry. If things get tough you can always talk to big brother. We're still friends?"

"The best."

He laughed. "I'd even give you another glass of wine."

"Thank you." She kissed his cheek and went out the door.

"What about pizza?"

"Too late," she called back as she headed across the parking lot. "I'll call you tomorrow."

"He doesn't know how lucky he is," Tolliver said closing the door.

* * * * *

Stewart stood with a smile on his face holding the door of his Ballard condo. "Come in, dear lady. There's something about a beautiful woman in black mesh stockings, spikes, and a short skirt that warms my heart. I like the way your blouse fits, too." He stepped back. "Would you care for some white Zinfandel while I finish the sauce?"

Amber stepped through the door, kissed his cheek and said in a soft voice, "Everybody likes my work clothes. And yes, the Zin sounds great."

He went to the kitchen and returned with two glasses.

Amber accepted one. "I see why some of your pals call you the playboy cop. You're lookin' good in the white tennis shorts and polo top."

She drained the small glass.

"What can I say except I dressed for you?"

With her lips in a sexy pout and waving the empty glass she said, "More wine?"

"Of course. Would you like to go out on the lanai?"

"No. It's like 9:00 and the sun has been gone for a few hours. It's chilly out there and warm in here. We'd both get cold. I like warm."

"And getting warmer," he said.

"I think we should just kick back in the living room. Where did you put the clothes I left here last time?"

"They're in the top right-hand drawer in the bedroom."

She started walking down the narrow hallway. "I'm gonna change."

Stewart followed her with his eyes. "Only five-three and I swear, you're all legs."

Amber returned a few minutes later wearing fluorescent orange shorts and a white halter-top. Her dark complexion made her smooth flesh standout, a welcome and inviting sight.

Stewart splashed some sauce on the counter as she stopped by the couch. "You're easy on the eyes."

Standing barefoot and swaying her hips she said, "Thank you, Detective Stewart."

He laughed as he wiped up the sauce. "You're so formal."

She teased her teeth with the tip of her tongue. "I wouldn't want you to think I'm easy. Besides, I've seen how you look at your partner."

"Partner? You mean Mitch? Not to worry. Ours is a professional relationship."

Stewart joined Amber on the couch, delivering another glass of chilled wine. Their thighs touched and the electricity between them, absent for a week, was rekindled.

He said, "So where have you been?"

She snuggled and said, "Around. I haven't seen much of you this past week either."

He smiled. "Just hangin' loose?"

"Pretty much. How about you?"

"Chasin' the bad guys."

"Catch any?"

"Sure. That's what I'm paid to do."

She flashed a coy smile again. "Catch anything else?"

"Not until now, I hope."

He slid his right arm around her shoulders. She snuggled in. The stereo was playing something by the Rolling Stones.

"Don't you have something mellow?"

"Romantic?"

She nudged him in the ribs, "Romantic works for me."

He said, "How about Mancini?"

She said, "How about Harry Connick?"

"Done," he said crossing the room and switching CDs. "Is that better?"

"It's great."

He got off the couch and walked toward the kitchen. "Dinner's ready."

She crossed the room after setting her wine glass on the coffee table. He lit the candles.

She gave him a knowing glance. "Are we turned on tonight?"

"I like to think I'm a romantic at heart, but yes, at least one of us is."

She laughed. "Then two of us are."

He kissed her neck then her lips. "This is gonna be a good night."

After dinner they returned to the couch. Amber stroked his belly as her hand flowed over the front of Stewart's shirt. "You're alive tonight."

He kissed her while untying her halter-top and said, "Yes. Do you think flesh goes with orange?"

She looked into her eyes. "Do you want it to?"

His voice was soft. "For a few more minutes, maybe."

She slid his shirt off, mussing his hair. "Flesh looks good with white shorts, too, and even better with your tan. How did you get that in Seattle this winter?"

"Spray on at a salon, dear, one full of women. How else?"

He opened the zipper of her tight orange shorts. "I see why you have no revealing panty line."

They kissed as the shorts hit the floor. "No panties."

She giggled then reached for the waistband of his shorts. "A bulge of promise? No boxers, no briefs. I'm gonna like this."

His shorts landed on the back of the couch.

They explored each other's flesh with slow-moving fingertips and tiny, teasing kisses. Their flesh jumped at every touch, quivered with each caress. She whispered in his ear, "I'll stay the night."

Stewart answered in a hoarse voice, "Yes."

She said, "Arousal is a specialty of mine."

"So I've noticed."

She kissed him, bent his head to her lips, and gently nipped his earlobe.

He held her tight.

She pressed her body against his nude frame and said, "We're committed to pleasure. We please each other in the most intimate ways but we're free."

He studied Amber's face for a moment. *We're not committed to each other, not yet, but we could be. Did Hartley and Hailey ever have a discussion like this?*

Amber said, "You want me, don't you?"

He nodded his head and said, "In the worst way."

"Then take me."

He stood, picked her up and carried her to the bedroom, stretched her out on the blue comforter and joined her. Rolling to one side toward the nightstand he reached for the light switch.

"Don't, you'll waste the mirrors on the closet sliders if we're in the dark."

His urgency remained and the light stayed on. He kissed her mouth hard. "You're kinky, you know that?"

"We're all a little kinky."

He held her close and looked over her shoulder. *Amber, me, our other connections—what the hell am I doing? I hate baggage.*

She said, "Is something wrong?"

"No, no, it's just this damn case."

* * * * *

"Thanks again for the call back and coming over this afternoon," Shaw said as Charles climbed into his delivery truck at Dawson's Grocery.

"It's probably just as well. Your detective friends came by this afternoon and caught me at the clubhouse."

"You were right, Charles. I needed to work tonight and get back into my routine even though tomorrow would've worked better for you."

"I know. That's why I changed my calendar. Friends help each other," Charles said.

"I'm nervous about the professor comin' after me." He checked the roadway as he pulled into traffic.

"He's not a professor. Community colleges don't have 'em," Charles said. "Does he know who you are?"

"Don't know." Shaw shook his head. "I was there when he came down both times." He made a turn.

"So he could've seen you?" Charles said.

"Yeah. I just don't know. It's scary. He killed her. He could kill me."

"You *think* he killed her," Charles corrected.

"Well, I didn't and she was dead."

Charles looked at his friend. The evening seemed chilled as they moved along with the windows open.

"Man, I'm freezing in here," Charles said.

Shaw laughed. "I must be having hot flashes." Sweat was visible on his face.

"Are you on anything? I mean, like medication?" Charles said.

"No. Don't wanna affect my creativity. An artist must suffer."

"Then you're going to need a hell of a lot of paint." Charles rubbed his arms and hands and laughed.

"Maybe I do." Shaw joined the laughter. He lifted his eyes to the mirror and noticed a vehicle behind them. "Those are the same lights we picked up at the last stop. I think we're being followed." He nodded toward the side mirror.

"Are you sure?" Charles said.

"I think so. The road isn't crowded tonight," Shaw said.

Charles scrunched down and twisted his body in the jump seat to get a look through the side mirror. "Doesn't look like a cop car."

"Maybe it's an unmarked one?" Shaw said.

"Maybe it's a lost little old lady." Charles said.

"Maybe." Shaw gripped the steering wheel, his knuckles white.

"Terry, weren't you supposed to stop at the Pink Lady Laundry?" Charles said as they passed it.

"Nah, they're off the route now." He glanced again at the headlights behind him.

"Look out!" Charles shouted.

Shaw swerved to miss a pedestrian in the crosswalk. "I hope he didn't get the truck number."

"Why? Complaints?" Charles said.

"A few. Company doesn't like gettin' 'em. They know I'm not gonna be around for the long haul but right now I need the money."

"Got another big sale closing?"

"Yup. This one will give me enough to live on for quite awhile," Shaw said.

"You've already had a couple of big ticket sales haven't you?"

"Yeah. Most of that money went to pay my bills. Now I'm even. This one puts me ahead."

"So you're getting out of the delivery business?"

"Soon as I get the money I'll start gettin' a real gallery show together."

"Congratulations."

"If I'm still alive," Shaw said glancing in the mirror again.

"The lights still with us?"

"Yeah," Shaw said.

As they approached Aurora Avenue heading east on 105th a red traffic light loomed. "Looks like the traffic is suddenly gettin' tight." The cars in front of Shaw were slowing to a stop. "I don't like this. Maybe we can creep up and roll through. I've got a block to go. There's no way off the road. Come on light, change."

Shaw checked the side view mirror again. The car was pulling into the inside lane to pass. "Thank God," Shaw mumbled watching the side view mirror.

A head and arm appeared hanging out of the passenger side of the car as it approached the driver's side of Shaw's truck.

"My God, they're gonna' shoot us!" Shaw said.

"What?" Charles eyes bulged. He looked toward the passenger window of the car approaching on Shaw's side.

"A guy is hangin' out the window. Jesus, we're trapped," Shaw said.

The car pulled alongside. The figure hanging out the window waved frantically; empty handed, mouth opened wide.

"Hey man," he shouted, "your gas cap is off. You're splashing whenever you make a right turn."

"Gas?" Shaw said.

"It's open, man."

The light changed. Traffic began moving, the car passed them.

"Pull in here," Charles said. "I'll check it."

The van came to a halt at a corner grease and go. Terry's hands fell away from the wheel. Closing his eyes, leaning back, he licked his lips.

"I can feel the blood just shootin' through me," Shaw said. "Everything is black and brown, dark blue, deep red."

Charles got out of the truck, went around the back to the left side and secured the gas cap. Next, he approached the open driver's window and tapped Shaw's shoulder.

"Don't do that! You scared the crap out of me," Shaw said.

"Your cap is on, amigo." Charles smiled walking around to his side.

"My nerves are shot. Tomorrow I have to take that stupid lie detector test. Maybe I should skip it?" Shaw said after Charles got back in the van.

"Are you asking for advice?"

"No."

"I'm sure it's routine, but you don't have to take it," Charles said.

"I know. I just don't trust cops. They try to trick me like everyone one else does, except you. Even Hailey tricked me."

"Terry, let's get these deliveries finished so we can call it a night. There's nobody chasing you, not tonight, not last night. Let tomorrow take care of itself."

Shaw looked over at his friend. "You don't understand."

"I do. You're becoming paranoid. Tomorrow, just tell them the truth. That's all they need."

* * * * *

Santiago was back at her apartment by 10:00 p.m. digging through the box of Hailey's annuals and photo albums. She found a 5 x 7 brown leather journal. She sat down on the couch and read the entire small volume. The entries were dated from August, 2005. Hailey wrote that beginning in 2007, she and Trevor had rendezvoused at several motels, in the parking lot at Sunset and once at her apartment. Later she poured out her love for Gunn and questioned her ongoing affair with Hartley. At one point her confusion between the two men became apparent when she wrote, *I don't want to stop seeing Jack. He's so good for me, and I'm good for him.* Santiago made mental notes of the content, including how Hailey had gone to Las Vegas, worked in the sex industry to pay for school, then came to Gold Coast and met Gunn.

She dug deeper into the box of annuals and photo albums and found a second diary with a faded padded cover of spring flowers. A note was taped to the inside cover: *My Life: June, 1992 to July, 2005.* The opening pages summarized how she'd gone to Las Vegas at age seventeen:

> I'm here, crashin' at the Lucky 7 Motel because it's cheap, like $12.00 a night, a dump. Across the street is a nice place but it's very expensive. The Lucky 7 advertises rooms by the hour, day or week. A lot of traffic comes and goes. I'll have to sell my body if I can't get a job, but that's better than what went on at home.

Santiago read the tiny, aged volume. It summarized her childhood. Hailey's earliest memories of her father were of him molesting her around age three. By age six it had become routine. When her parents divorced in 1984, her mother had told her, "You have to take care of Daddy now." Hailey never knew why her parents split or why her mother left her with her father. She never saw or heard from her mother after the divorce.

When she started school she learned about bad touching. She wrote, *I told my dad about it. He always said that was for other people. Ours was good touching and it was our secret. Even after remarrying he coached me on how to fulfill his needs.*

Santiago was surprised at how blunt Hailey was in describing how her dad, on her tenth birthday, had introduced her to oral sex. *He shoved his cock in my mouth and kept it there 'til he came. He told me it was another one of our secrets.* Then on her twelfth birthday she wrote, *Today I learned how to fuck. It hurt and I bled a little, but Dad said it wouldn't hurt in the future. He was right about that, but I didn't like doin' it with him.*

Hailey went on to note, *When I tried to tell adults about my dad they told me to quit exaggerating, that he's a good man or they'd say "he's a vet" and tell me to stop acting like a slut.* To keep from being home as much, Hailey worked part time at a local burger joint until she graduated. She also wrote about learning the value of sex in her work world. *I could get the right shift, a night off, and even a bonus if I did the manager. Guys with the bucks and fast cars would take me anywhere I wanted.* And she noted, *Turning a guy on is easy and fun.*

A month before graduating from high school her dad was having a poker party with his former Navy buddies. Hailey decided to disrupt the game by strutting through the living room in tight, hip-hugger shorts and a bikini top to get a soda. She got more than she bargained for when one of dad's friends came to her room and raped her. *When I cried for help my dad said I should "put out to him like you do everyone else." I told my dad if anyone bothered me again I'd report the rape and him to the police.* Santiago made a mental note that Hailey was a survivor first and always. *The night I graduated from high school I left for Las Vegas. At least I know how to please a man.*

That closing line echoed in Santiago's mind. She closed the journal and looked blankly at the cover. *Poor kid.*

* * * * *

Linda Gunn shook her husband's shoulders. "Trev, wake up."

"What is it?" He opened his eyes, blinked and stretched his arms.

"You're having a nightmare."

"I was dreaming?" He yawned and scratched his head.

"You're covered with sweat. It's happening again, isn't it?"

"What?" Gunn said.

"The dreams about tenure, being let go."

"Yes." He sighed, took a deep swallow. "It drives me crazy. It's like I know I won't get it this time either."

She stroked his forehead. "You'll get it."

"I'm never good enough, or it's the budget...always something."

She kissed his wet cheek and looked into his tired, worn face.

"Something bad is going to happen. I just know it." He turned his head away from her.

"Take another deep breath," she said, turning on a bedside light.

"Just like yesterday. They were all staring at me. I could feel 'em."

"Who?"

"The cops, especially that bitch detective."

"You said they weren't in the room. I thought it was just you and the guy askin' questions."

"They were watching through a mirrored window."

"You have nothin' to hide."

"I know that, but they don't. They think I killed that teacher."

"You hardly knew her."

"They asked if I killed her."

"You answered no."

"Yeah, but the needle jumped. I saw it."

"You've been under a lot of pressure." She took a deep breath.

"They can't use it. What do I care? They've got nothing on me." He looked around the bedroom.

"Honey, relax. You didn't do anything." She pressed her nude body against him.

"You feel warm. God, I'm sweaty."

"I'll help ease your tension."

"You're just making me sweat more."

"Don't be angry at me, Trev. Let's have a drink. Then we can get back to sleep."

He sat up in the bed and grunted, "Okay, yes, the ultimate solution. Have a drink. I drive you to drink; you drive me into the arms of other women."

"What?" She pushed herself away. What other women? How well did you know that teacher?"

He shrugged. "I knew her as a student." He looked away. "We had a little fling. The pressure, you know."

"No, I don't know. This is crazy. God, I definitely we need a drink now!" She climbed out of the bed and left the room. Gunn stretched back out resting his head on double pillows.

Linda returned a few minutes later with two tumblers.

Without opening his eyes, he said, "What'd you do, grab an extra drink before coming back?"

"No." Her voice was soft. "Trev, you look tense just sittin' there. Your face is all shadows and gray. Here." She handed him a glass.

"I don't need that."

"Put it on the nightstand. Maybe I'll finish it."

"That's a winnable bet." He shook his head. "I don't need the hassle, the cops and all the crap happening right now, either."

She remained distant.

"A drunken bimbo and an untenured college instructor make a great couple, right?"

"Trev, don't say that. It's mean."

"The muscles in my arms and legs are tight. I feel like a spring just waiting to snap."

She leaned over him, her full breasts touching his exposed chest. "I can feel you responding," she whispered. "If we had more moments like this coeds wouldn't be so tempting."

"Sex isn't love. Those in high places seek gratification, too."

"I know." She continued to press her body against him. "You sought gratification sometimes." She stared at the ceiling. *But is it my fault?*

"Men and women need gratification. Some find it in other ways. Some just don't admit to it."

"Trev, that's crazy talk."

"Let me rest." He rolled onto a side and took a deep breath. "What does tomorrow hold?"

"I've always loved you, Trev."

"We don't have love. We have sex when you're sober. Just let me rest. Leave me alone." He licked his lips. "This is so unreal." He closed his eyes.

She reached across him, took the tumbler from the nightstand, and swallowed the contents. She looked at her husband. *What have you done?*

She stretched out beside him on her back, pulling the covers over their naked frames, and looked at the ceiling. *What's happened to us?* Tears welled in her eyes. *This is not my fault. I can't live with a man who doesn't love me, respect me, want me. The kids deserve a family. I'll call Mom and Dad tomorrow. I need help. We need help.* She turned off the nightstand lamp.

Linda continued to stare at the ceiling, as sleep refused to visit. She began to wonder about the others. *He said women. Were the late arrivals after class really caused by student conferences? Who are you, Trev? God, is a divorce in our future?* She blinked back tears in the darkness, closed her eyes, but her mind would not rest.

CHAPTER 11
Day 7: Thursday

Stewart arrived Thursday morning to find Santiago early for work again, this time preparing the polygraph for Terry Shaw down the hall with Doc Thompson. When she returned to the office area she was carrying an open box of donuts. She set them on her desk next to a small gift-wrapped package. She glanced at the package but sat down without acknowledging it.

"How's Doc feeling today?" Stewart said.

"Better than yesterday," she said. "He's here, ready for Shaw. He'll do Gunn and Shaw's analysis together because of the time."

"Good."

She flashed a mischievous grin across the desktops at her tired-eyed partner. "How was your date with Amber?"

He said in a raspy voice, "Great. I'm calm as swamp water and rarin' to go. How 'bout your night?"

"I went for a swim, took a hot shower and lounged around in front of a fireplace." She looked into his red eyes. "You say swamp water? Where did that come from? Were you and Amber listening to old Fogarty hits last night? Not very romantic."

"Me? Fogarty? No, no. We enjoyed Harry Connick." He looked at Santiago for a quiet moment. "Were you alone? You've got faint circles under your eyes."

"Trust me, I slept well. I did a lot of reading before I turned out the lights."

"Reading?"

"I went through Hailey's two diaries. They were with her old yearbooks and albums."

"Yeah, I remember the diary. The last entry was in what, 1992? She'd be about 13."

Santiago smiled and sipped her latte. "Did you read it?"

"Not yet."

"There were two diaries. The other was a little more current. I wanted to know more about her... what made her run away to Las Vegas, that sort of thing. I read them both."

"Well, I can tell you found something. You're much too smug for 7:00 a.m. You're usually not even here yet."

"Her father abused her sexually and emotionally as a child, even more after her mother divorced him in '84. From then 'til he remarried in '90 he helped Hailey bathe; washed her back, hair, and everything else. When she was ten he introduced her to oral sex. On her twelfth birthday he had intercourse with her."

He shook his head. "Jesus, what an animal!"

"It gets worse. He coached her on how to bring him comfort and fulfill his needs long after he remarried when she was fifteen. The abuse continued until she left home."

"Does she say anything about her stepmother?"

"They didn't get along. Apparently the new lady in her dad's life, Rita, viewed Hailey as a whore and referred to her as the mother reincarnate."

"Poor kid."

Santiago shared the remaining details leading up to the poker party rape. "She confronted her dad and told him if anyone bothered her again she'd report them all to the police."

Stewart said, "Bet Dad was pissed."

"She was a month away from graduation; nobody she'd gone too had ever helped her. I guess he didn't know that."

"It worked?"

Santiago nodded. "Must have for a month; she left home the night of commencement. She took only some clothes, her annuals and diaries."

Stewart said, "The possible sex charges would sure explain why dad didn't file a missing persons report on her."

"That's probably why he left her alone after he found out where she was," Santiago said.

Stewart smiled "No wonder you look tired. I had more fun."

She pushed the carton across the desk tops. "Have a donut, Mr. Tired Eyes."

Captain James approached. "What's on your schedule today, Stewart?"

"And good morning to you too, Captain. Donut?"

"Not right now. Your schedule, Chance?"

Stewart said, "We have Shaw coming in at 9:30. Doc Thompson will give us his analysis of both polygraphs afterward."

James looked at both boxes on Santiago's desk and reached for a donut. "On second thought yes, they look pretty good. When Doc is ready I want to be there. One of you call me."

"Will do," Santiago said.

The captain looked at Stewart and the wrapped box again. "Chance, don't forget you have a court appearance at 11:00. The DA's office sent a reminder. It shouldn't take long."

Stewart said, "Good."

The captain shifted his attention back to Santiago. "Mitch, after Thompson, what are you doing?"

"I have a ton of paperwork to catch up on for this damnable case, depending on what Thompson gives us."

"Okay. Hopefully we'll have a better sense of direction after Doc talks with us. At least I hope so. This case is becoming a pain in the ass. Oh, and by the way, we've located the Cashland woman's father. He's coming in tomorrow."

Stewart said, "That'll be interesting."

James gave Stewart a confused look. "The man's lost his daughter."

Stewart started to say something but his phone rang. He answered and handed it to the captain. "It's for you."

James listened briefly, hung up, and nodded at the package. "Birthday?" He left for his office.

Santiago picked up the package and smiled at Stewart. "Where'd this come from?"

Stewart returned her smile. "Maybe it's from a secret admirer. Aren't you going to open it?"

"Sure. Is it from you?"

He glanced around the office area. "No, it's not."

She opened the package carefully and removed a small card like the ones florists use. Her smile disappeared and a chill ran up her spine: *I remember you on the strip.*

Stewart watched her expression change. "What is it?"

She passed the card to him and looked around the office. "Who'd do this?"

He shook his head. "It was already here when I came in."

She took a small wrapped packet from the box and removed the tissue. "A pair of pasties. Jesus!"

Stewart said, "This is a secure area, Mitch."

"I know. The public can't walk in here unescorted."

She looked around the office while pushing the box over to Stewart. "Is anybody watching?"

A frown creased his face. "No. I don't believe it. Everyone here knows you were a cocktail waitress when you went to the U, but not the dancer part. You didn't use your own name did you?"

"No."

"Have you talked to anyone else?"

"No, just you and James. Right now I wish I'd just kept quiet."

"Whoever left this obviously knows your background. If it's a cop I'd bet the Cashland case triggered old memories, even the fantasy of a cop with a double life." He smirked at Santiago. "Who knows, maybe it's a closet fan."

"Not funny."

"Let's share this with James. He'll find out who was in early. We've got company coming this morning."

* * * * *

Jack Hartley was sleeping flat on his back wearing flannel pajamas. Ginger was on her back pressed against his right side on the threshold of waking. Her left hand rested on his thigh, fingers extended. Her hand stirred, initiating the arousal of her husband. The more aroused he became, the greater the agitation of her fingers, then her hand. Within a few moments she was wide-awake. She rolled to her left pulling her hand away from his thigh. Bracing herself on an elbow she leaned over him, brushing the hair from his face. She bent down and kissed him.

Jack embraced her, wrapped an arm around her shoulder and back. "Good morning. Nice way to wake up."

She whispered into his ear, "Good morning to you."

He pressed a palm against her back and moved her warm body close. "This feels so different... so nice."

She traced a slow outline of his cheek, mouth and chin with an index finger. "It is, isn't it, Jack?"

He kissed her finger as it passed over his lips.

She said, "It's been a long time since we touched or held each other."

"I've wanted to be near you so many times. I was afraid of being rejected," he said.

She looked into his eyes. "Me too, but not now."

"A long time ago—"

"Shh... we don't want to talk about the past anymore. We've lost four years of happiness. Hold me." She wrapped her arms around him. "We've both been wrong."

He kissed her neck and throat.

She pressed her thighs against him. "I just want you to hold me."

He rolled to one side, touched the outline of her ear with warm, silky fingertips and said, "I'll hold you forever. It's like I'm not sure of what to do next."

She sat up and pulled the baby doll top over her head. "We'll figure it out together."

He smiled. "Revealing, lithesome, enticing, and inviting."

The tip of her tongue teased her lips. "Do you like what you see?"

"Oh yes."

She laughed and sat up, watching his every move. "Well, whatever happened to If I show you mine, you'll show me yours?"

Sitting up, he unbuttoned the top of the pajamas, pulled it off and tossed it on the floor. Then he slid the bottoms free, exposing his naked erection. He laughed. "It's warm in here."

"It's going to get a lot warmer," she said, kissing his chest and stomach.

They consummated their renewed love for each other in a rush of passion.

In a post-climactic gasp, she said, "My heart's pounding!"

"I can hear it over here, echoing to mine."

"This is the nicest morning I've ever had."

"Me too. I love you." He paused as they rested. "Well, tomorrow I'll either be unemployed or on leave until the end of the school year. I've scheduled a meeting with the board president. We'll see how it goes."

She kissed his cheek. "It'll go fine. So will things with the police. After what we've been through we deserve a break."

He said, "How about seconds? I'm not going in today."

"How about after we get shower and get the kids up and gone? Then we can have each other for brunch, minus morning breath."

They laughed like they hadn't in years.

* * * * *

Santiago glanced toward the doorway just in time to see Terry Shaw and Charles Goodwin being escorted into the office area. She looked at Stewart. "Your artist is here."

Stewart looked up. "Yes, and he's looking quite sharp in his retro '70s paisley shirt and denim slacks. I feel like I'm in some kind of time warp, not interviewing a murder suspect."

Shaw said, "Good morning. I'm ready. I brought Charles along to keep me company."

Stewart looked at Goodwin. "You'll have to wait in the public area. He'll be alone with Doctor Thompson unless you're his attorney."

Charles said, "No problem. I'm just here for support."

The officers escorted Shaw to the same room used by Gunn the day before. After introducing Thompson, the detectives retired to the observation room.

Santiago sat down at the table viewing the one-way glass. "This place seems more depressing every time we come in here."

Stewart moved a chair and joined her on the same side of the table. "That's a fact. I think something beyond institutional colors would be nice. You're depressed and Shaw seems nervous. Look at the way he keeps shuffling his feet."

She said, "He's drumming his fingers a lot too."

Shaw looked around the drab room. The polygraph was set up on a wooden table, a single chair placed at one end, wires and sensors connected to the unit currently lying on a towel. Shaw looked at Thompson. "This looks like a Nazi interrogation scene from a film. So this is how the state extracts the truth, eh?" He smiled and glanced down at the wooden chair. "This chair shows more than a little age. How many secrets have been told to it?" Florescent lights illuminated the room. The only obvious windows were the reinforced glass in the door and the one-way mirror. He smiled and waved. "Are you watching, detectives?"

Thompson placed the sensors, then looked Shaw straight in the eyes.

Shaw continued to drum his fingers and rubbed the tips together. A nervous chuckle emitted as he answered the pretest questions. After a brief pause Thompson began the formal test.

Santiago looked at Stewart. "It seems like an hour has passed. Finally, here come the final five questions."

Shaw sat erect in the chair as Thompson completed the seventh and final repeat from the pretest.

Without expression Thompson waited the ten seconds, then asked, "Did you know Hailey Cashland?"

"Yes," Shaw said, "as a sister."

Thompson said, "Please, answer yes or no."

Shaw moved his hands and shuffled his feet. "Yes."

Thompson marked the paper as it ran through the unit. He looked at Shaw, again without expression. "Did you love Hailey Cashland?"

"Yes, I just told you," he said.

"Yes or no, Mr. Shaw."

"Yes."

"Did you have intimate relations with Hailey Cashland?"

Shaw pursed his lips to conceal laughter and stifled a grin. "No." He chuckled. "I'm probably one of the few men she didn't know intimately."

"Please, Mr. Shaw, just yes or no." Thompson paused and then repeated the question.

"No."

Doc marked the paper again.

Shaw watched the red pencil.

"Did you go the Avenue Hotel to kill Hailey Cashland?"

Shaw's eyes narrowed, beads of moisture formed on his upper lip.

Thompson waited without expression.

Shaw's breathing became heavy. He stiffened his back and bit a fingernail. His gaze darted around the room, coming to rest on the polygraph. He cleared his throat. "No."

Thompson marked the recording paper.

Santiago said to Stewart, "That's a lie."

"What?" Stewart said.

"Every time he's lied to us he bites his nails. When he told us he didn't know Hailey was dead, copying the porn video, talking about the drowning. He hasn't bitten his nails at any other point in our conversations."

Stewart said, "He certainly had an interesting reaction to the question. We'll see what Doc has to say."

Santiago said, "Unusual to say the least, whether I'm right or wrong."

Shaw watched Thompson read the final question. "Did you kill Hailey Cashland?"

Shaw shuffled his feet and gripped the sides of the chair, then answered in a soft voice, "No."

Thompson marked the paper one last time, disconnected the sensors from Shaw and debriefed him. Charles joined Shaw as he left the interrogation room. They passed the detectives in the hall.

Stewart said, "Thank you, Mr. Shaw. Your help in the investigation is much appreciated."

The two men left the officers without comment and walked quietly to the elevator. As they boarded Charles asked, "How'd it go?"

"A piece of cake," Shaw said and bit a nail.

* * * * *

Thompson looked at the doorway as Santiago and Stewart entered. "I'll see you in about half an hour. I want to pack the equipment and review the results first."

At 10:45 Thompson and the two detectives met in the office of Captain James. Thompson looked at his colleagues for a long moment while shuffling his notes. "The two subjects were quite interesting. If their responses to the last two items are indicative of anything, they did go to the Avenue Hotel, but for opposite purposes."

Santiago said, "What do you mean?"

"When I asked 'Did you go to the hotel to kill Hailey Cashland,' both subjects responded in the negative. However, subject number two, Mr. Shaw, lied according to the polygraph."

Santiago looked at Stewart then back to Thompson. She said, "He went there to kill her?"

Thompson nodded. "According to the polygraph."

"I knew it!" she said.

"There's more. When the subjects were asked the final question, 'Did you kill Hailey Cashland?' both again responded in the negative. But this time the polygraph indicates subject number one, Mr. Gunn, is a liar."

Captain James looked at the printout. "So you're saying both guys wanted to kill her?"

"Not exactly, Captain. I'm saying the test indicates that one subject, Mr. Shaw, went to the hotel to kill Miss Cashland. The other subject, Mr. Gunn, did not go to the hotel to kill the victim. However, the results from the last question say he did kill her."

"God," Santiago said. "She was doomed either way."

"So it appears," Stewart said. He looked at Doc. "But how accurate are the results?"

Thompson said, "I believe the test was very accurate for both subjects. However, we all know the results are not admissible as evidence."

Captain James said, "Thank you, Doctor Thompson."

Thompson smiled at the trio as he rose to leave. "My pleasure. Good seeing you again, Detective Santiago."

As the door clicked shut, James smirked. "An admirer?"

Santiago said, "If so, it's one sided."

Stewart cleared his throat. "Take away the psychobabble and we're left with Gunn."

Santiago nodded. "I told you Gunn was the killer."

James tossed his pen on the glassy, neat as a pin, desktop. "So it appears." He sighed. "What about Shaw's intentions? Apparently he went there to kill her."

Santiago repeated, "Like I said, she was doomed from the beginning."

James said, "Yes, she was. However, we can't indict someone for something they intended but didn't do. If

Gunn is really our killer as Thompson says, Shaw is clear. Can we prove Gunn is the killer?"

"Not yet," said Stewart.

"Well, let's get the proof. It sounds like the guy should have a history, if only circumstantial. Talk to his wife again. Did he get home when she says? Did he threaten her? Did he beat her? Was she drunk Friday afternoon? Knowing and proving are two different things. I think that's why the Green River Killings went unresolved for so long. Gunn's our prime, no mistake about that." Captain James retrieved his pen.

Santiago said, "We'll nail him."

Stewart looked at his two companions. "The time of death is still a puzzle. The body having been immersed in the water for so long distorts findings. Her watch stopped at 6:07. That's long after Gunn left the scene. Why?"

James looked up from his desk. "What if the watch didn't stop immediately? Maybe it was waterproof and got wet when the seal was broken then slowly ground to a halt?"

Santiago said, "Or maybe Shaw *did* touch the body and accidentally submerged the watch when he was in the bathroom. He hasn't exactly been on the up and up with us."

Stewart said, "I hate loose ends, but I agree, Gunn's gotta be the killer."

* * * * *

Santiago and Stewart returned to their desks after leaving James' office. She picked up a message slip. "Do you know anyone named Doug Watson?"

"No."

She dialed the number on the slip. "He's someone at Date Rape Intervention," she said as she waited for someone to answer. "Doug Watson, please."

"Speaking—how may I help you?"

"Detective Santiago, returning your call."

"Thank you. I have a coed as a client whom you might want to talk to." The youthful voice paused. "Carla—that's her name—said she was at Golden Gardens about a week ago, maybe two. She and her date were making out, loosening their clothes, takin' stuff off, that sort of thing, when a homeless-looking man came up and tapped on the car window."

She waved to Stewart to pick up and listen. "Maybe a hobo?"

"Could be or maybe a homeless man. The railroad tracks are nearby. Anyway, she said her date got really angry, and after he zipped up he got out of the car and went to talk with the man."

Santiago said, "The man waited?"

"Yes, he perched on a nearby picnic table and watched 'em."

"Then what happened?"

"Her date approached the man. They shouted at each other at first, then talked quietly. After a few moments she said they walked across the parking lot into the shadows."

"Did she see them in the shadows?"

"No. She said her date was gone for about fifteen minutes. When he came back he was sweaty and agitated, so they left."

"She didn't see the other man again?" said Santiago.

"No."

She glanced at Stewart, who was now listening. "Tell me, how are you involved in this?"

Watson said, "They went to her apartment. She lives alone. After they arrived he resumed foreplay, very aggressively."

"Did he rape her?" said Santiago.

"In so many words, yes. She said they were going to do it in his car anyway and they'd had sex before, but she didn't like his aggressive behavior."

"Did she tell him to stop? Did she report the rape?"

"No, and she doesn't plan to. However, where a criminal act occurs I'm obligated to report it. I have to confess, I'm not sure it's even a rape. By her own account and deeds, she consented. She just didn't like the outcome."

"Mr. Watson, we have two detectives investigating the killing of a man at Golden Gardens. I'm going to have them contact you."

"The officer answering at reception was very specific about having me talk with you, Detective Santiago," Watson said.

"Did the young woman share the name of her date?"

"Gunn... Trevor Gunn. He's her instructor at one of the local community colleges."

Santiago straightened and took a breath. Her pulse surged. "What's your client's name and address? We need to talk with her."

Watson said, "Carla Johnson."

Santiago copied down the address. "You've been most helpful, Mr. Watson." She replaced the phone to its cradle. "Chance, we've got a date rape victim to interview."

"You do. I have a court date."

"Right," she said. "I best let Zinc and Strickland know. Gunn might be involved in both killings." On a legal pad, she wrote, *According to the counselor the perpetrator's name is Trevor Gunn.*

"And the young woman puts Gunn at Golden Gardens around the time of the killing," Stewart said.

"Carla Johnson will have to verify the night they were there," Santiago said as she wrote down the details.

"This could be the break we're lookin' for," Stewart said.

Santiago's face became red, her voice raspy. "God, I can feel my blood pounding!"

Her phone rang, refocusing Santiago's attention. She answered on the third ring.

"Mitch? Jim Hanks here."

"Jim, what can I do for you?"

"I just received an e-mail from DMV for your pals, Strickland and Zinc."

"And?"

"One of the Mustang owners on their list is Trevor Gunn."

She said, "Trevor Gunn? The same Gunn that's an instructor at Sunset?"

"One and the same. Do I get a dinner date for this?"

"Absolutely," she said.

"Dessert?"

Santiago laughed into the receiver. "Now you're pushing it. That sounds almost like harassment to me."

Hanks said, "Anyway, I thought you'd like to know."

"Thanks, Jim." She hung up again and shared the news with Stewart, then added a notation to the legal pad.

Stewart looked at her, then back to the screen of his PC. "I hope you didn't guarantee dinner to Hanks for an e-mail?"

She pulled up the screen. "It's been a busy morning around here. For Jim to call he must have figured I was still busy with the debriefing." She looked at the screen and laughed as the memo about the Gunn and the Mustang appeared. "I like the way we're picking up cross references now days. We'd better take a look at Gunn's car, too."

Stewart stood and moved toward the door. "I'm sure Strickland's already on his way with a warrant to search the car. You go talk with the Johnson woman. I'll be in court."

Santiago said, "Done. I'll call as soon as I finish the interview."

CHAPTER 12

Carla Johnson lived on the east side of Green Lake, a jewel in the heart of Seattle. Santiago looked at the beach as she drove into the neighborhood. *This is nice. On sunny days I could walk across the street and enjoy this to no end.* The older home faced the eastside beach, which had been built by the Civilian Conservation Corps during the Great Depression.

The street was very busy. Santiago found a parking place and walked up to the front of the house. "Pricey neighborhood for some students... nice, but the street parking is for the birds."

She approached the basement apartment door that opened onto a side of the house and knocked. A young woman answered after a few moments.

Santiago said, "Miss Carla Johnson?"

"Yes," said the woman.

"I'm Detective Santiago of the Seattle Police Department. I need to talk with you about an incident in relation to an investigation I'm working on."

The young woman glanced at Santiago's identification and stepped back from the door. "Come in," she said, showing her to the small living room area.

Santiago said, "Great looking place you have here."

"Great location, high rent, cheap furniture. I call it my basement loft, but hey, I'm across the street from the beach. What more could I ask for, except maybe a view? Please, sit down," she said, lowering herself onto a black vinyl recliner.

Santiago took a place on the tattered gold couch across from the woman. "Carla, Mr. Watson from Date Rape Intervention contacted our office. He said you'd been the victim of a possible rape a week ago last Tuesday."

Carla shook her head. "Rape? I haven't reported any rape."

"I know, and he said you probably wouldn't. I'm here because I need some information about what happened that evening. We're investigating a murder and we have reason to believe you could be of help."

Carla looked puzzled. "We?"

"My partner, Detective Stewart, is in court right now. Otherwise he'd be with me."

Carla looked away for a moment. "I'd rather just talk with you anyway, not a man. I wasn't all that comfortable with Doug either."

"Doug?" Santiago said.

"The guy at DRI," said Carla.

"Of course."

"But I don't understand... how can I help with your investigation?"

"I'm referring to the evening you were at Golden Gardens with Trevor Gunn."

The young woman became very quiet. She touched her breastbone above the open-collared pink cotton blouse and slowly rubbed her hand up and down. She crossed her legs at the knee and placed her left hand on a thigh encased by black spandex shorts. Then she reached for a cigarette pack on the end of the table beside the battered recliner. She said, "I was with Trev. So what is this about?"

"The other man, Carla. The mangled body of a man we believe to be homeless, possibly a hobo, was found Wednesday morning of last week. We think it's the same man who approached Trevor's car."

"I see," said Carla.

"Just tell me about that evening, everything you can recall."

"We went to the Gardens, as you said. We'd been at a club on Market Street, had a few drinks. We were hot."

"Hot?" said Santiago.

"You know, we'd been playin' kiss face at the club. On the way to the beach I'd teased him, brought him up." She looked away. "God, this is embarrassing."

"It's okay. I understand."

"By the time we parked I was doin' a Lewinsky."

Santiago said, "His pants were unzipped?"

"Obviously. He was unzipped and throbbing." She blushed. "He was so excited he nicked a steel post with his car."

Carla paused and took a heavy drag, exhaling a thick cloud of smoke almost in Santiago's face.

"How did he react?" Santiago asked waving the smoke away.

"He liked what I was doin' but he was pissed about dingin' his car."

"Then what?" Santiago said.

Her face was now a steady deep crimson. "He got right back in the mood and opened my blouse. I was braless."

"I don't need to know all the details of your making out, Carla. The other man, tell me about him."

Well, this old man came up to the window on Trev's side and started tappin' on the glass. Trev got really mad, waved the guy away, told me to button up."

Santiago said, "What did Trevor do?"

"The old guy went over and sat down on a picnic table near the eatery beside the boat ramp and just stared at us. After Trev zipped up he got out of the car and walked over to the guy. At first Trev shouted at him, and then they talked a little. After a few minutes they walked across the parkin' lot and across the street, under the railroad overpass."

"Was the man being forced? Did Trevor have a hold of him?"

"No, they were beside each other. Actually it looked like Trev was getting his wallet out as they passed into the shadows."

"How long was Trevor gone?"

"I don't know... fifteen, maybe twenty minutes."

"When he came back what happened?"

"He got in the car and said we'd go to my place. Then he started the engine. He seemed a little tense to me, quiet... looking around, probably for old guys pals."

"His pals? Did he say anything about the old man?"

"Only that he wanted money to go away. Trev said he gave him ten bucks, but thought we ought to get out of there before the old guy's pals all came around lookin' for a handout too."

"So you came here?"

Carla swallowed and became quiet for a moment, then nodded. "Yes."

"What happened then?"

"Trev was still upset. I'd never seen him that way before."

"Did he rape you?"

"We had sex, but it wasn't like before when we made love. He was very physical, forceful, overpowering. I was gettin' raped—I mean screwed—by an angry man, not my lover. He was bangin' me, but his head was somewhere else."

"So, did he rape you?" said Santiago.

"No. It was just rough sex... uncaring. When he finished, he got dressed and left without a word. It was a confusing night. I don't want to call it rape. I wish now I would've skipped goin' to DRI. I don't want Trev to get in trouble because of me."

"Have you seen him since?"

"Only in class."

"You're a student of his?"

"Yes."

"Were you having sex for grades or anything like that?"

"No! We were having a relationship because we're attracted to each other." Carla rolled her eyes. "I must say that it didn't hurt my grades though. All As."

"Did you know he's married?"

She nodded. "To a drunk who doesn't love him or satisfy him. The only reason he stays with her is for the kids." Carla sat up straight and rubbed the top of each thigh. "Officer, he's not goin' to get in trouble for havin' an affair with me is he?"

"No. I think he has a bigger problem. If he contacts you, call me at any of these numbers, day or night," Santiago said, handing the coed a business card. Then she looked the young woman in the eyes. "And Carla, do *not* tell him about this conversation, understand? You could be in danger."

"I have class from him Friday morning."

"I don't think he'll be there. Again, not a word if he contacts you."

"You think Trev killed that old man?"

"He might be responsible for the deaths of two people."

Santiago stood and moved toward the door. "Carla, again, thank you. You've been most helpful and candid. Any idea where I can find Mr. Gunn?"

"He's probably at the college. His conference period is 1:00 to 3:00 p.m. on Thursdays." Carla lit another cigarette.

As soon as she left Carla Johnson, Santiago was on her cell phone to her partner.

He answered as she pulled onto the I-5 heading north. "Stewart."

"Chance, are you done in court?"

"Delayed."

"We've got Gunn. Get the warrant on him for the murder of the hobo and meet me at Sunset. Also, call Zinc and Strickland. They can cover his apartment."

"The hobo?"

"Yup. We can put him at the scene. He had motive, opportunity and means...aw, son of a bitch."

"What's wrong?" he said.

"I-5 is grinding to a halt and I'm on the inside lane."

"Great," he said.

"How was court?"

"Like you, it was delayed, but while I was hanging around here Bert Wagner called. He said the murder of Agnes Chey is now closed. It seems she was involved with a couple of Japanese importers. They were smuggling aliens into the country. Their plan was to have the women work as prostitutes, living as slave labor. The women had nowhere to turn. Chey broke away from the group after stealing some money, probably holding back. When they found her, they tortured her to make an example for the others."

"How brutal," Santiago said.

"She had nobody to help her and was afraid of being deported. That's why she disappeared when Hailey turned up dead, a real Catch 22."

"Do Wagner's people know who the Japanese gangsters are?" she said.

"Better. They're in custody and singing. The DA offered them life without parole if they'd cooperate."

"Good. I'll meet you at Sunset, but take the surface streets. I-5 has now become a parking lot. You'll probably get there before I do, but wait if you do."

"Consider it done. Our reciprocal with the county will make this easy, but I'll have a county sheriff nearby if we have a problem. Oh, one more thing. You remember the fluid at the foot of the bed? It was Hartley's semen."

"Man, we just can't seem to get anything concrete on Gunn for Cashland can we?"

"We will, Mitch. I'll get the warrant and meet you at Sunset's personnel office."

After talking with Stewart, Santiago phoned Sunset's office and identified herself to Mrs. Young's clerk.

"Yes, I remember when you and your associate were here earlier."

"Is Mr. Gunn on campus at this time?"

"Yes. Would you like to make an appointment with him?"

"No. If he's available when I get there, I'll see him. This is a confidential inquiry. Do not advise Mr. Gunn I've called."

"As you wish, Detective Santiago."

"Thank you. I'll be there shortly."

* * * * *

It took another twenty minutes before Santiago finally arrived at Sunset and approached the personnel desk. "Mrs. Young, where would I find Mr. Gunn?"

She drummed her nails on the counter as she waited for Young to check some schedules and talk with her clerk.

When she looked up over the top of her glasses she said, "He left just after you called and talked with our clerk. She said he was in a bit of a hurry."

"*After* I called?" Santiago said.

"Yes. Apparently he was near the counter when you called. Cindy, my clerk, says he left the building heading in the direction of the staff parking area shortly afterward."

Santiago punched in Captain James' number on her cell. "He's on the run. We need an APB out on him."

"Will do, Mitch." James clicked off.

Stewart approached the counter patting his coat pocket. "Got 'em."

"He's gone." She looked at Mrs. Young. "We have a warrant for his arrest and another to search his office."

Mrs. Young paused. "A warrant for Mr. Gunn's arrest?"

"Yes." Stewart held it out.

"What's the charge?"

Santiago said, "Murder."

Several students and staff conducting business at nearby counters became quiet and looked in the direction of the detectives.

"Of course," Mrs. Young said. "Come with me."

When they arrived at the staff office wing, Mrs. Young unlocked the door without a word.

"Does he share the office with anyone else?" Stewart said.

"No. She reached inside and snapped on the light. "Each member of the faculty has a private office."

"Mrs. Young, when we leave we'll seal this office. Nobody is to enter. It's part of the investigation," Santiago said.

"I understand," Young said as the detectives put on surgical gloves

Stewart stepped into the small office. "We'll take it from here. Thank you."

"We'll sign for a key at your office on our way out," Santiago said. She followed Stewart in, letting the door close behind her. It locked automatically.

"Man, this place is a mess." Stewart looked around. "It's not as big as some closets."

"Just like my old adviser's office... books and papers everywhere. I'll start with the desk," she said.

Stewart activated Gunn's computer. "I'm going to see what he has on the PC."

Santiago began looking through folders of loose papers on the desk. "Nothing much here."

She tried the drawers. She thumbed through the left hand drawer and found nothing. She went to the large file drawer below it next. "Well, well, well... take a look at these." She handed the folder to Stewart.

"His own coed pinup file," Stewart said, smiling while flipping through the pictures. "Under different circumstances I'd give him high marks for taste, but I'm with you. This guy is a predator of the worst kind."

Santiago said, "Chance, remember the tissue damage to Hailey's earlobes? Look here."

She pointed to a pair of gold hoop earrings in the pencil tray. She picked one up carefully with a pencil and held it up to catch the light. "That corrosion could be our link."

Stewart held open a small evidence bag. Santiago carefully placed them inside and he sealed the bag. "We'll have the lab check this."

An hour later she asked, "Did you find anything else?"

"Just a lot of books and papers... and this." He held up a small box from a shelf near the PC. It contained a diaphragm.

Santiago said, "He definitely did more than confer in here. I just found several condoms." She tossed the packages back into the drawer. "Are you ready to go?"

Stewart said, "Yes. On the way back let's stop at his apartment. Maybe Linda Gunn can help us."

He held the door for his partner, sealing it after they were out. Santiago called Tabor's office.

* * * * *

Trevor Gunn was standing in line in a bank located at one end of a strip mall, waiting to process a cash advance against his credit card. A few housewives and children were milling about the lobby. There was a line of business types at the commercial window. The man in front of him completed his transaction and left after taking an extra few minutes to share a story with the teller.

A loud bang echoed from the entry area.

He ducked and looked back toward the door. A small child was picking up an empty metal pie pan.

"God, lady, get your kid some decent toys," he said in a soft voice, then took a deep breath.

The teller said, "May I help you, Sir?"

"What?" he said. "Oh... I was thinking about something else. Please forgive me."

The teller waited for Gunn without expression.

Gunn's hand trembled as he reached for his wallet. "Yes, yes you can. I believe my card has a $15,000 limit." He handed a platinum card to the woman. "I'd like an advance."

She took a moment to check the card history. "I can advance you $10,181 on this account, Sir."

"Great. I would like $9,999 please, and I'm pressed for time. I don't want to rush you. I'm just under a great deal of pressure."

The teller processed his request, talked briefly on a bank handset, presented the necessary paperwork and asked for his signature.

"There you are," Gunn said pushing the forms back to the teller as a man from the back desk approached. The man spoke to the teller but Gunn couldn't hear.

What now? You can't know about me. Not yet!

The teller counted out the funds, all in hundreds, and placed it in an envelope.

"Thank you. Thank you so much. You're a lifesaver," Gunn said.

"You're welcome, Sir."

After stuffing the envelope into the inside pocket of his blazer, he left the bank and drove to the other end of the mall. As he walked into a supermarket branch bank where he kept his family checking and savings accounts, he muttered, "I'm sorry Linda, but I'm going to need this more than you will."

A cool, refreshing breeze came up the hillside from the Edmonds waterfront off Puget Sound and stimulated his senses. *I love the smell of salt air. I'll go to Canada... Vancouver maybe....* He went to the counter.

"Good afternoon," the young man said.

Gunn pushed two bankbooks across the teller's counter. "I would like to close these accounts, but it's my understanding one needs both signatures to do so. Is that correct?"

"Yes Sir."

"I'm joining my wife in California. Let's just take the checking and savings to their minimums. I'm not sure my balances are correct. How much would that give me?"

The young man accessed the information after Gunn punched in his pin number.

"Checking will give you $1,986.53 and savings $4,899.12."

"I'd like that in cash.. Fifties and hundreds."

"Cash?" said the teller.

"Yes please."

Gunn thought he could feel the breath of a person standing behind him. His hand trembled when he returned a pen to his shirt pocket. The teller turned back to him. They completed some paper work and the teller counted out the funds.

Gunn placed an envelope containing the cash into a side pocket and muttered, "Thank you."

Exiting the grocery, he cut across the parking lot to his car. Looking at the right fender he winced. "I doubt you'll ever get fixed."

An Edmonds police car cruised through the lot.

Gunn squatted to retie a shoelace. *They're all around me.* He stood and got in the car. "Take a deep breath. Smell the fresh air."

He fumbled the keys into the ignition. "Quit shaking. Just get out of here."

The engine turned over. He slid the shifter into gear and moved slowly out of the parking lot. He almost hit an elderly woman pushing a shopping cart.

The matron shouted, "Watch where you're driving, asshole!"

He looked back, waved at her.

She gave him the finger.

He chuckled. "Now that's a feisty senior citizen; too much caffeine."

* * * * *

The detectives arrived at Gunn's apartment around 2:30.

Linda Gunn answered the door on the second ring. "Detectives Stewart and Santiago, I didn't expect to see you today, not after those other two men were here. Come in." She held the door open and stepped back.

"Mrs. Gunn, have you spoken with Trevor?" Santiago said as she looked around the living room.

"No. Until the other detectives arrived I thought he was at work. They said he's wanted for the murder of a hobo?"

"That's correct," Santiago said.

"I thought he was under investigation for the Hailey Cashland murder?"

"He is," Santiago said.

"Oh, Lord," Linda Gunn said. "Two possible murders?"

A bottle of Jack Daniels and a half-full tumbler was on the living room bar. Stewart said, "This will be hard for your children too, Mrs. Gunn. They're going to need all the support you can give them."

Linda Gunn looked at Stewart and nodded. "Yes, they will."

Santiago said in a soft voice, "Is there someone you can call to come over and help?"

Linda Gunn took two more short breaths. Choking, she fought to regain her composure. "Not really. My parents live in Spokane. We might go there for a few days." The short breaths continued.

Santiago took an empty paper bag from the kitchen table. "Here, breathe into this," she said handing Linda the bag.

"Thank you," she said, and a moment later tears were flowing down her cheeks. "I don't know what to do... what to say...."

Santiago said, "You haven't heard from him at all today?"

"No."

Stewart handed her another business card. "If you hear from him we need to know."

"Linda," Santiago said, "he's been on the run for about an hour. Do you have any idea where he'd go?"

"He loves the U District." Linda paused. "He doesn't carry much money."

Santiago said, "How about checks, credit cards?"

"Yes, but he wouldn't use those, would he?"

"Hard to say. Would you call your bank where you do your checking? If the credit cards are from a different source, please call them, too," said Stewart lifting the telephone receiver and handing it to the woman.

She took the phone and looked up the number in an address book sitting beside it. She spoke in a soft voice. Her face became very pale as she listened. Next, she fumbled through her purse and found a bankcard. She dialed and again spoke in a soft voice. As she put the receiver back in its cradle she began to sob. "He's cleaned out our accounts, checking and credit, almost to its max."

Santiago looked at her without expression. "How much did he get?"

"I didn't ask. I don't know. He always took care of the money. I don't even have a credit card. He didn't trust me with it." She shook her head slowly.

"If you think of anything else, any other place, please call us. We need to find him." Stewart looked at Santiago and said, "Any other thoughts?"

"Not right now." Santiago paused for a moment then reached into her purse. "Wait a minute," she said and pulled out an evidence bag. "Have you ever seen these?" she said and held up the earrings.

Linda Gunn said, "No. Where did they come from?"

"His office desk drawer," said Santiago. "Thank you again."

Santiago returned the plastic bag to her purse. Linda Gunn never took her attention from it until it disappeared.

Stewart said, "Mrs. Gunn, we'd appreciate knowing how much money Trevor has on him. We can get the information through the banks but it will take longer. If you could contact them again it would be most helpful."

"Of course. It's so strange to spend half your life with someone and not even know him. I don't believe I didn't ask the first time I called them."

The phone rang. She answered it, then placed her hand over the receiver and looked at Stewart. "Mom."

Stewart offered a weak smile. "We'll be at our office this afternoon while we try to get a line on his whereabouts. Just call in the information. We'll get the message."

* * * * *

Trevor Gunn drove aimlessly around the north end of Seattle and Shoreline for over an hour. He even passed his apartment but left the area without contacting his wife. "She knows by now I'm wanted," he said. "I've got to find a place to lay low for the night. The commuter traffic to Kingston ought to be a good cover to let me get across the Sound tomorrow morning without being noticed."

He drove north on Greenwood and caught Highway 99 heading north at 155th through Shoreline again, then through Lynnwood into south Snohomish County.

"Motel, no tell. Motel, no tell," he hummed, continuing north on 99. "Where do I hide tonight?"

At 148th S.W. on Highway 99 he passed the Plum Tree Hideaway. The sign read, *Rooms $29.95 per night.*

"Ah, a few derelict cars, old covered carports, a classic '50s place." He turned around and drove back, pulling into the parking area near the rental office.

Gunn passed through the battered doorway and approached an Asian clerk wearing a forced smile. "Good evening," he said. "I'd like a room for the night. Oh, and is the car port included?"

"Yes," said the small man behind the clear plastic enclosed counter. "I have room." The man smiled and pushed a registration form and pen through the slot. "Please."

"Of course." Gunn filled out the form using the name Clint Hanson and pushed it back through the slot.

The clerk smiled, his brown stained teeth becoming visible. "That will be $35.03 with tax."

Gunn smiled and pushed three twenties through slot. "My wife is looking for me and I like my privacy. Does this cover it?"

The clerk smiled again and handed over the key to unit six. "Very good."

Gunn drove down the driveway to his carport and room. Pulling inside he parked, opened the trunk and took out a screwdriver. As daylight faded he removed the license plates from his Mustang. *I'll trade with somebody tonight.*

The door of unit six was battered just like the door of the office: squeaky and with visible signs of having been forced open more than once. He pushed it open, snapped on the light, and deposited the plates and screwdriver on a small round table near the door. "A little abused but clean."

He reached overhead and turned on a small television bolted to ceiling mounts. The evening news was just beginning.

A serious looking commentator was staring at the camera with a poker face. "In breaking news, Seattle Police are looking for Trevor Gunn, a Sunset Community College instructor." A staff photo of Gunn appeared on the screen. "Gunn is wanted for the murder of an indigent. The homicide took place at Golden Gardens almost two weeks ago." The newscaster read a detailed description of Gunn. "The suspect, also a person of interest in another homicide, is considered dangerous. If you see him, immediately call 911. Do not under any circumstances try to follow or approach him."

"I'll be damned... no mention of Hailey by name. How the hell did they come up with the bum? This is weird." His stomach rumbled. "I need something to eat."

He walked next door to a tavern, the collar of his jacket turned up to cover as much of his face as possible.

"What'll'ya have?" the barkeep asked.

"Two Heroes to go," Gunn said, then noticed a ballgame was on the TV.

Ten minutes later he returned to his motel room, ate in the dark and waited. He kept a vigil of the parking lot. "Come on somebody... anybody." His right foot constantly tapped the floor.

At 8:15 two men dressed like construction workers staying in unit eight walked to the tavern. Gunn watched them cross the parking lot and go into the bar. He picked up the screwdriver and license plates and crept out the door into the shadows. He worked his way to their carport, entered, and removed the rear plate, then the front. He installed his plates on the older Camaro. The crunch of gravel alerted him someone one coming.

The taller of the two men was loud. "That was a good dinner, Carl."

The shorter man had a hint of slur in his speech. "Not bad, Mike. Y'wanna go to the topless joint? It's only a mile down the road."

Mike chuckled. "Yeah. Sounds like fun."

Gunn crouched in front of their parked car. Sweat formed on his forehead and upper lip. His heart beat like a hammer, and his temples throbbed. He crouched lower in the dark shadows.

Carl walked into the carport and stood beside the driver's door. "Y'comin'?"

"I gotta piss first, too much beer," Mike said.

"I'll wait here," said Carl.

Gunn squirmed lower in front of the Camaro's grillwork.

"I need the room key, Carl."

"Here." Carl tried tossing Mike the key but it fell on the ground near a rear wheel.

"You're drunk," Mike said.

Gunn's shirt collar was wet with sweat. *Jesus, my bladder is going to burst. Go inside! Go away!*

Carl picked up the key and walked over to Mike. "Take it," he said holding out his hand.

Mike said, "Thanks."

A strong gas pain filled Gunn's belly. *Don't crap, you fool!* He passed gas.

Carl said, "I'll go with you. I gotta go too, now."

"No kiddin'. You smell like somethin' crawled up inside you and died."

"Don't blame me for your fart." Carl laughed.

"Ain't mine," Mike said.

"Well, look around. How many people do you see?"

"Come on, Carl. We don't want those couch dancers avoiding us 'cause we're surrounded by gas." The men headed into their unit.

Gunn picked up the plates and screwdriver. He moved down the side of the car as quietly as possible, stopped at the driver's window, reached in and took an old baseball cap. Returning to his room he sat in the dark again, watching out the window. "Come on guys, let's go...."

Fifteen minutes later the two men left the motel. Gunn went to his car and installed the license plates.

"Tomorrow I'll take the ferry to Kingston," he said. "Just don't spot my car. Everybody deserves a break once in a while."

CHAPTER 13
Day 8: Friday

Ginger Hartley looked across the kitchen table at her husband. He was scanning the headlines of the morning paper. She held her coffee cup in front of her mouth without sipping.

He glanced up. "You look like you're in another world."

She placed the cup on the table. "I am. Are you worried about the meeting with Archer this afternoon?"

"Not really. I know I'll be unemployed. Hopefully, I'll get a leave with pay for the remainder of the term. Working at the academy is not in the cards any longer. I've got too much dirty laundry to carry around, especially if it becomes public," he said.

She took a sip of coffee. "It's like you said, we get a fresh start. Something will come along that fits your skills."

"Maybe I'll become a consultant. I have the background in both how to run and not run a private school."

Changing the subject Ginger said, "Our first session with Miss Rogers went well."

"Yes, it did." Jack Hartley smiled.

"Making love as we did yesterday just reaffirms we've wasted too much time, too many years over foolish anger and resentment."

"You still don't know the whole truth."

The smell of fresh coffee filled the room. She inhaled deeply. "I know enough. We both know enough. Honey, we had our own histories when we met. We've added to them. Now we have each other again, and we're at peace."

"I hope the kids understand, someday," he said.

"They will, but we want them to know about all that's happened from us, not from innuendo passed along by mean spirited adults and children."

He smirked. "It could stay buried if the story doesn't come out in court. I don't think it will come out at all, if not in trial."

Ginger Hartley frowned. "What about Archer and the recommendation you won't have?"

"Well, George may be more amenable to my quiet departure than we think, even to the point of giving me a recommendation. I think he might have a few warts as well. We'll see."

"I hope so." A smile crept across her face. Ginger raised an eyebrow and changed the subject. "I noticed even in counseling your roving eye was climbing a thigh that wasn't mine."

"Guilty. Old habits do die hard. She is a looker. Maybe we should have a different counselor."

"No. As my mom told my dad, 'You can look but don't touch.' It just means you're alive."

"She's not competition, Honey. She's just easy on the eyes."

"Besides," she said, "I didn't see her checking you out. I think our first session was a huge success. Look at last night, or even right now."

"I'll try not to peek next time," he said and they both laughed.

"Tell me about Archer. Why do you think he'll soft peddle this mess? He always struck me as a hard ass."

"I'm going to tell George as much as necessary because I'm obliged—it might come out anyway—but if I'm right I can help our cause. I think old George had something going with Hailey too."

"George?"

"Yes. If nothing else, Hailey knew how to use men. I'm sure she had her hooks in George. He's the only one on the board she paid any attention to."

"He's the president."

Jack Hartley said, "Precisely. Yet anytime he visited the school he went out of his way to drop by her class. If she was in the staff room he always found time to say hello and pat her back."

"You may have a point. I noticed at the socials we attended together he always found time to stop and chat over drinks with her while only saying a few words to other staff."

"He also liked sitting with the pep squad at games," said Jack. "He said it was good for morale."

Ginger laughed. "Yeah, his."

"So I think I'm going to string him along just a little. If he bites, we'll be in good shape. If not, we're no worse for wear. My career is in the toilet anyway unless we get a break."

"You really think he had something going with her?"

"Absolutely. Hailey was smart and she knew what she was doing. Archer was security."

* * * * *

Stewart was at his desk when Santiago walked into the office area. The large pink envelope on her desk immediately caught her eye. She sat down and looked at it for a long minute. She said, "Do I really want to open this? Has my admirer visited again?"

Stewart leaned forward. "Only one way to find out. Just be careful... prints, you know."

"I know."

She opened the envelope, handling just the edges. Folding the flap back she removed a 5 x 7 glossy. "It's a photo of the Mr. Tease Cabaret entrance. There's a picture in the background of the dancers." She looked at Stewart. "I'm circled in red felt pen."

He said, "Let's send the envelope down to the lab."

"I'm sending the picture, too," she said.

He looked straight into her eyes. "Are you sure you want to do that?"

"Are my parents hippies? Is piss warm? Damn right I want to do that. Someone is making my life miserable, or worse, compromising our case. Either way I want to know who the bastard is."

"Done, but I'll send it. Just maybe our test tube buddies won't ID you in the background," he said.

"Okay, but I'm not too worried about that. If one of our counterparts is trying to soil my reputation by flaunting my background he has another thing coming."

At that moment a tired looking elderly man approached their desks. "I'm Frank Cashland... Hailey's father."

He set a battered suitcase down and pulled up a chair without being invited to join them. "The guy at the door sent me over." He motioned toward the entrance and the desk sergeant.

"Mr. Cashland, I'm Detective Santiago and this is my partner, Detective Stewart."

"We're very sorry about your loss," Stewart said. "You've obviously just arrived. Would you like a cup of coffee?"

"Yeah, black with a little sugar."

Stewart left to get the coffee. Cashland leered at Santiago. He ran his tongue over his lips and his yellow teeth. "It was a long trip."

Santiago looked at his mouth, her eyes squinting. *I'd bet you licked your lips when you violated your daughter, too.* "Where are you staying, Mr. Cashland?"

"I found a cheap motel on Aurora just north of Green Lake. I'll take a cab out there when I'm done here... unless the department wants to give me a ride?"

She said, "Of course the department will give you a lift. We want to know where you're staying in case we need you for something. Besides, cabs are expensive."

Stewart returned with the coffee. "Here you go." He handed the man a steaming paper cup.

"Do you know who killed my daughter?"

Stewart said, "We have a primary suspect. He's wanted for another murder but we believe he'll be charged with Hailey's death also."

"Is he under arrest?"

Stewart said, "Not at this time. The suspect, Trevor Gunn, took off yesterday when he found out we were looking for him."

Santiago said, "We'll get him."

Cashland coughed and cleared his throat. "I'm only gonna be here a few days. I understand a memorial service is scheduled for tomorrow, Saturday, at her school."

Stewart said, "Yes, at 11:00 a.m. I imagine most of the school's students will attend."

"While I'm here I'd like to clean out her apartment. I'll just give her stuff to charity, but I'd like to go through her things first. There might be something to save."

Santiago said, "Like her diary?"

"Of course. It would be nice if she kept one."

Stewart said, "She did, but it's evidence. In fact, her apartment is still sealed as part of the investigation. It might be a few more days before it's available to you."

"Why? She wasn't killed there was she?"

"We're still finding evidence to support our case against Mr. Gunn," he said.

"Such as?"

Santiago said. "Yearbooks, diaries, personal items that might link her to the suspect."

Cashland waved a hand. "Any personal papers? Maybe she left a will, papers identifying an executor? Maybe she had a safety deposit box?"

A greedy little man and a pervert. "Nothing but her diaries," Santiago said. "Her finances were standard young adult, paycheck to paycheck, credit cards to the max, twenty-one dollars in the bank. She's behind in her car payment by a month, and she owes big bucks to a teacher's credit union account."

Cashland said, "In other words she doesn't own much."

"So it appears," Stewart said.

"Well, at least I won't be liable for her debts. I don't have much money either."

Santiago said, "Did her stepmother make the trip?"

"We got divorced about five years ago. Even if we were together Rita wouldn't have come. They hated each other."

Santiago smiled. "According to her diary Hailey didn't think much of you, either."

Cashland blinked his eyes. "I don't understand."

Santiago's eyes bored into Cashland as Stewart sat quietly. "She wrote a great deal about how you sexually abused her. She covered everything from how you bathed her as a three-year-old child up to the night you let one of your poker pals rape her. She talks about how you taught her to perform oral sex when she was ten and introduced her to intercourse as a twelfth birthday present."

Cashland said, "She was just talkin' crazy. You know, a kid runnin' away from home, that sort'a thing."

"When we're finished with Gunn, I'm referring Hailey's diaries to the DA. I'm sure his office will refer the matter to officials in Louisiana for whatever actions would be appropriate given their state statutes. I'm equally sure the DA will be in contact with the Navy. At the very least, Mr. Cashland, people are going to know how Hailey viewed her father."

Cashland's face turned almost gray. He pursed his lips. His fists opened and closed. "I'm here to mourn my daughter."

"We all mourn her," Santiago said, "but we'll also forward the diaries and their allegations to the appropriate people."

"I don't have to put up with your innuendoes." He stood and grabbed his suitcase.

Santiago also stood.

Cashland spun on his heel and left.

Stewart said, "You were pretty rough on him."

"Not rough enough. He's not here because he cares. He just wants any money she might have left, the septic bastard." She sat down and took a deep breath. "This case is getting to me."

* * * * *

Wearing the stolen baseball cap, Gunn drove south in the late morning rush hour traffic of south Snohomish County on Highway 99 to 168th SW, then turned west and followed the street until it merged into Olympic View Drive, a winding boulevard leading into Edmonds from the north. He remained alert for police cruisers as he worked his way through downtown Edmonds to the Washington State Ferry Terminal.

Traffic going west was light. "I wish more traffic was going to Kingston. Hope waiting 'til now wasn't a mistake," he said waiting to get a ticket for car and driver at the toll booth.

The clerk said, "Drive into Lane 2, please. The boat will be loading shortly."

"Thank you," Gunn said.

Within a minute of his coming to a stop the incoming ferry entered its slip. "Come on, unload that sucker." He was tapping the steering wheel and watching.

His breathing became rapid. He checked the rearview mirror every few seconds. An eighteen-wheeler pulled up behind him. "Good, I don't need any cops seeing me sitting here from the street. I'll never have another candy apple red car." His tried breathing slowly and continued to drum his fingers on the steering wheel. He became calm during the twelve minutes it took to unload the morning commute.

Several of the passengers awaiting the Kingston run had departed their vehicles and were standing on the sides of the dock watching sea otters play in the underwater park designed for scuba divers. They rushed back to their cars as the last of the motorists departed the boat. Engines fired up in the holding lanes, brake lights flashed and attendants began waving the drivers forward onto the boat.

"Yes," he said while being directed into the center lane of the main deck and boarding. When he came to a halt he looked around. *Third from the front. Not bad. Hope I can get off fast.* Leaning back in the seat, he moved his head, stretching his neck. "Man, I hate tension."

Gunn continued to look around the deck from the driver's seat, but chose not to leave the car as most travelers did for the twenty-five minute run. *I don't see anyone watching me, but that doesn't mean they're not here.*

The ride across Puget Sound to Kingston was uneventful. A light mist had covered the windshield. Wind was whipping through the open hull. He continued to drum his fingers on the steering wheel while remaining watchful. *Canada sounds good. By now everyone's looking for me. They know I've taken off. Life's never been fair to me.*

A young woman walked between the parked cars carrying a cup. He watched her every move while sitting in his front seat. "Hello, Darlin'. It's babes like you that got me into this mess."

She stopped at a yellow Corvette and let herself in. "Why do chicks always have the great cars? It's not fair." He struck the steering wheel with the palm of his hand. "Maybe you're going to Victoria too. Now that would be fine."

The boat horn sounded as the Kingston dock loomed. The hull ground against huge pilings and nestled itself into the slip. Foot traffic gathered at the bow waiting for the attendant to remove the blocking line. "There you go folks. Have a great day," he said, pulling the rope to one side.

The foot passengers walked up the wet, slippery ramp to the sidewalk on the left side. Once the way was cleared, vehicles would begin to parade off the boat through the loading zone and holding area and slowly wind their way into town. Most of the exiting vehicles would head north.

Gunn was among the first to unload. As he followed the vehicle in front of him he kept looking around. There was a police car parked near the exit to the dock area. Sweat formed on his brow. "Eat your donut, fat boy. Check the plate number. Do anything you want, but don't see me, please."

Glancing at the passenger side of the windshield he saw an old stain on the visor. "How did I get that? I hate it when people eat in my car."

He looked back at the police car. The officer was watching two young women in mini-skirts walk down the sidewalk. "They'll screw your job up too, fella." Gunn took a deep breath and read a road sign: "Fifty-five miles to Port Angeles."

Exiting the lot Gunn, drove at or just below the speed limit from Kingston to Port Gamble. He passed through the town and its collection of historic homes looking at each house and their view of the water. "I could stop here for a few days, but this car would stand out like a sore thumb."

He passed through the town. "Canada is lookin' better all the time."

He continued across Hood Canal Bridge, following Highway 104 until it merged with 101, drove north to Sequim, a former farming community turned retirement mecca because of its reputation as the sunbelt of the Olympic Peninsula.

On the outskirts of the town were parks, retirement centers and plenty of traffic. He watched the car in front of him slowly work its way into town. "This guy must be from Ballard." The man's seat belt was hanging out the door, his left blinker was flashing and his head barely showed over the top of the headrest." Gunn shook his head. "Life with the silver haired set will be different."

Downtown Sequim was busy. Pedestrians bustled along sidewalks, cars were bumper to bumper and motor homes filled every lane. "Definitely Canada," he mumbled as a police car pulled out from a side road one car behind the Mustang. "Oh crap!"

Gunn looked quickly from the road to the mirror and back. "Damn, damn, damn!" he said, looking for a place to pull off.

He approached a convenience store gas station and turned into one side of the parking lot near the entrance. "Now I'll shake you."

"Oh no!" he groaned as the officer pulled up beside the driver's door. He watched the young officer walk briskly into the store.

Gunn got out of the Mustang, walked to a phone booth near the entry. *Thank God a few payphones are still around. No trace.* He looked up the number of the ferry service to Victoria. Depositing the exact change, he dialed. "What are the departure times for your boats to Victoria?" He checked his watch as he listened.

"And Sir," said the man on the phone, "just a word of caution. Apparently the Canadian authorities are in one of their periodic work slowdowns. They seem to be taking a great deal of time checking everyone's identification."

Beads of sweat ran down Gunn's face. "Why?"

"They're in labor negotiations. They've done this before. Operate very by the book, eh? It's taking longer to enter the country."

"Thank you," he said. *Great, checking ID. That means passports.*

As he hung up, a chill crawled up his spine. The same young officer was looking at the Mustang.

Gunn stepped away from the phone backwards, bumping a lady who was walking toward the door. "Excuse me," he said choking.

He was trembling as he turned and faced the policeman. He couldn't catch his breath, and his left leg was shaking at the knee. He rubbed the side of his nose. His hands were trembling. *Put them in your pockets, dummy.*

"Nice car," said the officer. "I'd love to have one of these."

"Yes," said Gunn clearing his throat. "I've enjoyed it."

"Well, have a good day, Sir." The officer returned to his car, talked briefly on the radio and headed south.

Gunn waved as the man drove off, then got in his car. "I have *got* to get the hell outta here."

He drove to Port Angeles on Highway 101, following the multilane one-way road through town on Front Street. Approaching the ferry terminal he found parking on the street and pulled off. "You've been a good little car, but you'll be the death of me." He parked and locked it. "I need a public phone."

As he walked away from the Mustang a restaurant caught his attention. Inside the smell of grilled onions, burgers and coffee attacked his senses. He licked his lips. *I'll eat later. Right now I need information.*

A battered phone booth hung on the wall inside the door. He stepped into it. "Damn, no phone book."

Gunn went to the cashier's counter. "May I borrow your phone book for a minute?"

She reached under the counter and tossed a well-fingered directory onto the counter. "Sure."

He looked up the location of a used clothing store and returned the book. "Thank you," he said and left.

Gunn walked a few blocks to Green's Second Hand Rose. His nostrils flared when he walked in. *How do people breathe in here? It's dusty and dirty and it smells bad.* He walked the aisles, picking out a pair of trousers and a flannel shirt. He found packaged underwear and socks. *Thank God they're not used.* He tried on several pairs of hiking boots until he found something that fit and had a complete sole, then went to the cashier by the front door.

"That'll be $91.37."

Gunn handed the man a hundred dollar bill. "Out of a Franklin."

The cashier held the bill up to the light, then opened the cash drawer and said, "Don't get many of these in here, but no problem, Partner."

Gunn said, "Do you have a changing room?"

"In the back. You want to change now?"

"Yes. I'm supposed to go hiking and I'm not exactly dressed for it."

The cashier nodded. "You might want to get a warm coat, too. It gets chilly around here at night."

"Thanks. I will."

The clerk motioned toward a rack of coats nearby. "Take your pick. They're twenty bucks apiece."

He gave the man another bill. "Done. You said the changing room was in the back?"

The clerk handed Gunn his change and a second bag and pointed to a curtained area along the back wall. "Go right back there."

Gunn changed and put his clothing into one of the used shopping bags. He twisted his hips. "Jesus," he said looking at his image in the cracked mirror, "these bills are sure making my boxers tight." He smiled at his image. "Trevor, you look like a semi-clean bum. This is not sartorial splendor."

A few blocks from the secondhand store he passed an old man pushing a shopping cart full of junk. Gunn paused and looked at the bearded figure. "My friend, you may have these." He handed the shopping bag full of clothes to the indigent.

"Thanks," the man said, then moved on down the street.

"He'll probably sell them at Green's." He looked around. "I just need a copy center; one with a computer and a color copier with the capacity to print photos."

He spotted a tattoo shop advertising passport pictures and stopped long enough to acquire a photo.

"You wouldn't happen to know where I could find a copy center would you?" Gunn asked while paying the clerk.

"Just around the corner is the P. A. Copy Company. They can do anything those big national outfits can do and at a better price," the proprietor said.

"Thank you."

Gunn headed out the door, turned the corner and walked to the copy center.

A middle-aged female clerk behind a counter near the entry said, "Top of the day. May I help you?"

"I'd like to buy a little time on one of your computers."

"Do you have a preference?"

He looked at the state-of-the-art units. "No."

An hour later he emerged from the center with a new driver's license, social security card, and wallet-size birth certificate. He stopped at a small tavern with only two patrons. *Stale beer always smells the same.* He took a stool at the far end of the bar away from the front door and windows.

The bartender, a large older man with a raspy voice shouted down to Gunn, "What can I get ya?"

Gunn said, "Anything on tap and a sandwich."

"We've got salami and cheese or ham and cheese."

"Salami sounds good."

The man limped the length of the counter to a refrigerated case and microwave.

Gunn called, "Do you know where the local bus depot is located?"

The bartender gestured. "Terminal's down by the Victoria Ferry on East Front Street."

"Back the way I came," Gunn said. "Thanks."

"You got it, friend."

The man limped back from the microwave with Gunn's sandwich.

Gunn watched the bartender for a few minutes. The man was wearing a flannel shirt, red suspenders emblazoned with the name of a saw company and rumpled, loose-fitting black pants. *Probably an ex-logger that got hurt. Image is everything. I've got to blend in.*

Gunn ate and headed back toward Victoria Terminal and Front Street. When he entered the Clallam Transit System building he went to the counter clerk, a woman that looked to be in her early forties, professional.

"May I help you?" she said.

"A ticket to Forks, please."

"You're in luck. The bus is due in about twenty-five minutes."

"Great." He pushed a fifty dollar bill across the counter and looked around the waiting room.

"Your change," she said holding out a hand and jarring his attention back to her.

"Thank you." He stuffed the money into a pocket without looking at it, walked over to the waiting area and sat down near an old Indian woman. The wooden bench seats were a few rows deep and were populated by a cross section of Americana.

He tapped his foot to a silent rhythm that was passing through his mind. Suddenly two police officers walked in and scanned the waiting room. They moved along each row, often referring to a picture. Gunn watched as they approached. Occasionally one spoke to a waiting passenger.

He watched the wall clock. *Twelve minutes. Come on.*

He started to move out of his seat but the officers were coming toward him. He sat back down. *Don't draw attention to yourself.* He began to sweat. His bladder felt full. *Keep calm. Look away. Ignore 'em.*

One of the officers stopped in front of the old woman seated next to Gunn, held out a photo. "Have you seen this man?"

She looked at the picture.

Gunn glanced over.

"No," she said. "Is he bad?"

The officer nodded. "He's very bad."

The picture portrayed an old bearded man with hair to his shoulders. He was bald on top.

"Looks like a burnt-out hippie," Gunn said while shaking his head.

The officers moved on down the row.

"The bus to Forks is now loading," the announcer said.

Gunn stood, stretched, and walked to the loading area.

A slight tremor passed through his arms and legs. *Christ, I'm shuddering with every step.*

CHAPTER 14

Jack Hartley looked up from the computer in his office. Standing at the desk of the academy secretary was George Archer. "Right on time," Hartley said. "You always look the part of the successful corporate attorney. Do you ever get tired of the three-piece suits?" Hartley went to the doorway and flashed a friendly smile at his guest. In a firm voice Hartley said, "Thank you for coming, George. I really appreciate it."

Archer entered the office and sat down on a small couch. Hartley took a seat in a sled chair facing Archer from the other side of a coffee table, tapped his fingers on the side of the chair and shuffled his feet.

"You said it was important, Jack. I assume it's about the murder of Miss Cashland."

Hartley said, "Yes, but what I'm going to share is also highly personal for both of us. It will be necessary for us to come up with some form of action plan before you leave."

"You're talking in mysterious ways, Jack. You know I don't make decisions for the board."

"So you say, but they've always followed your lead. Hear me out. You might choose to take a more assertive role."

Archer stared at Hartley. "Tell me what's on your mind."

Hartley took a deep breath and looked across the table at the portly, balding board president. "I'll be brief, George. First, as you already know, Miss Cashland was murdered last Friday afternoon or evening at the Avenue Hotel. Of greater significance for today is the fact I was with her earlier in the day, at the hotel."

"At the hotel?"

"Yes, at the hotel." Hartley's eyes darted around the room. "We were having an affair."

"So you met her at the hotel?"

"She joined me there, yes, as I said."

Archer's eyes became cold, his face expressionless. "How long, Jack? How long were you and Miss Cashland enjoying each other's company?"

"Three years, but there's more, George. Hailey had a history as an exotic dancer and performed in live sex shows."

Archer's face became crimson. "A teacher of ours? No!" He gulped. "I don't believe it!"

Hartley said, "Believe it."

"Jesus!" Archer loosened the knot of his tie. "This is sensitive. As I recall when we hired her you told the board the background check was thorough and that she was perfect."

"I did. I was fully aware of her past. She graduated cum laude, had outstanding recommendations to teach, no criminal record and had danced under a stage name."

Archer said, "You knew and you hired her anyway? Why?"

A quiet calm came over Hartley's demeanor. "I guess because I was with her in those days too."

Silence filled the office. The previously unnoticed hum of the air conditioning system seemed loud. Each man straightened his back.

"You mean you knew her then... personally?" said Archer.

"Oh yes, I knew her. Hailey and I have been almost like brother and sister since we first met during our college days."

"My God, man, you're talking about a long-term immoral relationship!"

"I know. We were kindred souls, George. That's all."

"All? You know there's a morals clause in your contract! It's bad enough having this murder business, but the academy can't have its superintendent banging the hired help! I've no choice but to—"

"Hold on a moment, George," Hartley said raising his left hand. "There's more. I know you want to fire me, and rest assured, I'll resign, but first let's finish the revelations."

"There's more?"

"Come off it, George. I know you and Hailey were rolling in the hay from time to time."

The board president sat up and wiped his brow. "That's not true!"

"George, Hailey was addicted to sex. She was compulsive. It was like a drug to her."

"But with me?" Archer gasped.

"I know she went for the athletic types: young, muscular, physically desirable, and usually married."

"Married? Why married?" Archer said.

"She thought married men were safe lovers. No disclosure, no threat, no 'I want to marry you' crap. She wasn't looking for a soul mate. She'd already found one, married of course."

Archer said, "Then why the affairs?"

"As I said, George, addiction. She had little or no control over her sex drive. Think of an alcoholic or drug user. It's the same type of desire."

"I can see that, but how can you think a woman who prefers young virile specimens could possibly have a relationship with me?"

"Power. Hailey was beautiful, physically overwhelming. She knew she could have almost any man she wanted regardless of how pure he pretended to be. She knew virtually every man's dominant brain wave ran directly through his groin."

"But you've implied I had an affair with her. That's not true."

Hartley looked at Archer. *You've gone too far, Jack. No backing down now.* "Affair, fling, call it what you will. It happened, George." Hartley paused for just a moment. "Oh, did I mention her diary? She's kept one for years."

Archer leaned back on the couch and looked at the table top "No," he said in a soft voice.

"She also had a video collection, including some sex scenes."

"You've watched the video?"

"Like I said, we were close." *This is going to work. I've got you, you bastard.*

Beads of sweat formed on Archer's forehead. Then a smirk crossed his face. "Power is a wonderful aphrodisiac. You said as much yourself. " He began pulling his jacket sleeve. "Do you mind?" He slipped off the coat and tossed it casually on the couch at his side, then looked the superintendent in the eyes. "What do you want from me?"

"Let me be up front with you, George. As I said, I know I'm out of a job. I would prefer to resign."

"That would best for the academy."

"I'd like to resign at the end of the term, not immediately."

"That will be difficult to sell the board if word of your relationship gets out."

Hartley ignored the comment. "I'm thinking of a leave of absence for the last month of the term: personal reasons and stress related to the murder. I'm sure you can convince the board to accept."

Archer said, "I'm sure I can in this unusual situation if charges aren't filed against you."

"Not to worry, George. The authorities have dropped me as a suspect. Haven't you been following the news? Trevor Gunn is their man. He's been all over the news. He's a Sunset CC instructor wanted for the murder of a hobo and he's a person of interest in another homicide. I don't know how you missed it. However, it's what comes out in the trial that should concern the academy. If lawyers start digging into

Hailey's background, it's anyone's guess as to how much they will discover or what's revealed."

Archer said, "But by the time they're in trial, presuming they catch Gunn and get to trial, you'd be long gone."

Hartley said, "Exactly, and if nothing came out in testimony we'd both be clean. If my relationship with Hailey became known it would just be fodder for the scandal pages for a day or two by then."

"Good point, Jack. You know, I'm sure now I can bring the board to agreement."

Hartley said, "One other thing."

"Yes?"

"I would like a letter of recommendation from you, something strong and positive. I doubt I'll return to the field of education, but a strong letter regarding my administrative skills and expertise in operating the academy would certainly look good in my resume."

"I'll write something up."

Hartley removed a letter from the desktop adjacent to his chair and handed it to Archer. "Don't bother. I've already got one for you."

Archer said, "This is blackmail."

"Not at all. I prefer to think of it as a negotiation. George, the police already know about my affair. That's why I'm willing to leave. Your status within the community, school and legal profession is secure."

Archer said, "And the documentation? The diary?"

"Everything about you is secure. Assuming I get past the trial safely, I'll be secure, too. Other than the authorities, my wife, and now you, nobody knows about me. And as far as you're concerned, I'm the only one privy to your affair."

"Ginger doesn't know?" Archer said.

"She's smart. She might suspect something, but she doesn't know about you."

"You could come back on me, blackmail me," said Archer.

"Not really. The only way the diaries or videos could become public would be if something happened to me; then I'm sure they would be found. Otherwise, their revelations wouldn't be good for either of us. Neither you nor I nor Gold Coast could afford the negative publicity. We've created something good here at Gold Coast and we want to protect it. I've always been a man of my word, George. I trust you and hope you trust me."

Archer said, "Of course... that goes without saying. Who knows, next year when my term on the board is complete I might step aside as well. You're right, Jack, we have established the ultimate prep academy."

"Yes."

Both men stood and reached across the table. They shook hands as they had done so many times in the past, but this time they were hesitant in gripping each other's hand.

Hartley looked down at the table. "The letter, George."

"I almost forgot," he said and bent over to sign the letter typed on academy stationary.

Hartley said, "Your hand felt clammy, George. Not to worry. I'll begin my leave tomorrow, right after the services for Hailey. I can be on sick leave for a few days while you settle things with the board."

"Of course, and you'll arrange for your assistant to take over?"

"As soon as we're done here." Hartley gestured toward the couch. "Don't forget your coat."

"Jack," Archer said.

"Yes."

"Before anyone else moves in here make sure custodial cleans the place. There's dust in the corner of the windowsill. We wouldn't want to be tacky."

"Certainly not. Oh, one more thing, George. I am assuming my personal leave until the end of the term is paid."

"Of course," Archer said.

"Thank you," Hartley said. "Don't look so worried. We're all friends here. Think of the law of Karma: everything you give, you receive. We've given a great deal of good to Gold Coast and we shall receive good in return."

George Archer left Hartley's office mumbling inaudibly with his coat draped over an arm.

* * * * *

Michelle Santiago arrived home Friday afternoon, frustrated following a day of failing to locate Trevor Gunn. She took a quiet moment to relax on the couch. As she did the phone rang. She picked up the cordless unit. "Hello?" she said expecting the caller to be Chance Stewart.

"Mitch? It's me, Jill. I just landed at Sea-Tac," her nomadic sister said with enthusiasm.

"Jill! What are you doing in town?"

"I'm here for the auto show at Seattle Center tomorrow. I jumped at the opportunity to come up and see you."

"I'll be down in about forty-five minutes, maybe an hour. Which gate?"

"I don't need a ride. Some hunk on the plane is being picked up by his regional office manager. He's offered to bring me out there. You're free tonight aren't you? I wouldn't want to crowd anything," said Jill.

"I'm free as a bird... too damn free." Santiago took a breath. "You're letting a stranger you met on the plane bring you out here?"

"Don't worry, Sis. I do it all the time. He's here for the show, too."

So did I, and so did Hailey. "Really, bad things can and do happen, Jill. I'll come and get you."

"My ride is pulling up. See you in a bit," Jill said.

"I'll be here. See you in about an hour," said Santiago.

"Unless we want to stop for drinks on the way," Jill said. "You know how it is."

"Yes I do. Like I said, I'll come and get you."

"Not a problem. Gotta go. They're picking me up now."

"Do tell."

Two and half hours later Santiago answered the knock at her door. Jill was standing there in the latest fashions: a black mini above mid-thigh, great legs and a red blouse open two buttons from the neck and displaying ample cleavage. A black matching jacket completed the ensemble. "You look great," Mitch said. "And really tall."

"It's the stilettos. Remember, you told me when I was in junior high nothing made a leg look better?" They hugged at the open door, then dragged two large suitcases inside.

"I thought you said you were here just for the weekend?" Santiago said motioning toward the luggage.

"A girl's got to be prepared." They both laughed. "You look great too, Mitch."

Santiago pushed the door closed with a foot. "Thank you."

Jill said, "Tell me, any new men in your life?"

"You're direct. Just the occasional encounter," she said, then started to laugh. "And the most recent of those was on the rebound, just a swim and a talk."

"You mean we're both still doing one night stands?" Jill said.

"Encounter sounds better, especially after watching Cindy Crawford ask TV audience members to raise their hand if they'd ever had a one night stand. Only one hand went up: hers."

Jill said, "The audience lied."

"You know it. You still sip white wine?"

"Yes. You taught me well."

Santiago started for the kitchen. "Good. I was just having a glass and studying some case notes. Put your stuff in the guest room and I'll get you a drink."

Jill said, "Case notes... that sounds serious."

"Just work. We've got a case that comes way to close to home in too many ways; a victim who worked the skin industry, had an inability to make a serious commitment and was living too fast. Sound familiar? She was a teacher leading a double life."

Jill said, "Sounds a little like us, but you're out of the dance business and we don't have secret lives."

Santiago said, "You could get out."

Jill said, "I don't think so. I like being a model; the life, people and action."

"And the money," said Santiago.

"I like the fast lane."

"So did the murder victim I'm working," Santiago said. "At least we weren't forced into it."

A few minutes later the sisters were in the living room chatting about their parents and catching up.

"So how's Redondo Beach these days?"

"The usual; sunny, full of studs and bikini volleyball players," Jill said.

"The auto show... is that a regular job?"

"Regular as I get. You know me: a little bit here, a little bit there. Like always, eye candy, just like you were in college. Tomorrow's like a calendar shoot or a magazine layout. I'm just a vagabond." Jill laughed. "And you're still working with Chance, right?"

"You bet."

"Have you gotten anywhere with him?"

"We work together. He's the ultimate pro. I swear, to him I'm a cop, not a woman." Santiago paused. "I think the first thing he noticed about our current victim was that she was gorgeous."

Jill said, "Sometimes we push too hard. Put a little pressure on him to let him know he has to decide what he wants to do. He might even see you as the hottie untouchable cop with a life outside the department. Let him know you're reachable."

"Jesus, yesterday my neighbor told me I'm too vain. Apparently I have an image problem."

"There's an after-hours party at the show tomorrow. Why don't you come? I'm going with one of the promoters. I'm sure he has a friend or two. Then let Chance know you were out and about, no details of course, but it would have been nice if he was there." She held out a glass in a toast. "To the Santiago sisters." They both laughed. "Come to the party. I'm sure you'd love it and I'm equally sure it'd get Chance's attention."

"I'll see. It's a big case, high profile." She yawned. Put some pressure on him. *Maybe Hailey was putting pressure on Gunn by keeping Hartley in the picture. How to prove it?* "It's not all coming together the way we'd like."

Jill said, "A break could be what the doctor ordered."

Santiago yawned again. "Sorry, I was up half the night working the case. Chance was even giving me a hard time about circles under my eyes this morning."

Jill said, "Can you drop me at the Center on your way in tomorrow?"

"Sure." She glanced at her watch. "Have you heard from Mom and Dad?"

"Not lately. You know, since they retired and moved to Arizona it's like they're teenagers again. They're always on the road," Jill said.

Santiago said, "Or at the pool or a golf course. But they're having fun and at least they've stopped trying to get me married off." Mitch raised her glass. "Here's to Mom and Dad." They both finished the wine and laughed.

"Married... easy for you to say," said Jill. "She's still bugging me to get a regular job. I think she sees me as a loose woman."

"You are, but she sees both of us as being a little too easy when it comes to men. I prefer to think of us as modern women. Just remember, Jill, when we were growing up *they* were the love generation. It's in our genes."

"No kidding. I remember Mom once describing the '70s and '80s as a time when everyone slept with everyone," said Jill.

"Ah yes, free love and the pill. Today it's safe sex and AIDS. I think then was better, at least for the intimate side of life," Mitch said. "My victim used condoms with some of the men she was doing, but not all."

"Some?" said Jill. "A busy lady."

"It's complicated," said Santiago.

Jill changed the subject. "The last I heard from Dad is they're heading for Cabo San Lucas for a couple of weeks. He wants a picture of a red Ferrari with a thong-clad babe in the foreground, autographed."

"Are you sending a self-portrait?"

"I don't think that's what he has in mind." Jill laughed. "He also says mom just wants to enjoy the resort and catch sight of some young buns."

"A lady after my own heart," Santiago said. "Maybe that's where I got the difficulty in making long-term commitments." Mitch laughed and yawned again. *Just like Hailey.*

"It must be the way the oldster set stays young." Jill yawned, too. "Hope I'm still checking buns when I'm Mom's age. Right now I think I'm ready to crash, too."

"They stood, hugged, kissed each other on the cheek and headed for the bedrooms.

Santiago lay in bed but couldn't sleep. *Hailey, Gunn, Hartley, Chance, Amber, the hobo... so many ideas. I've got to get some rest.* She rolled onto her side. *I'm letting it get too personal. Just find Gunn.*

* * * * *

The bus passed a welcome sign entering Forks from the north side of town on Highway 101, also called Forks Avenue. *Fire Danger 65%* read the warning sign, an alert for locals and campers visiting the peninsula during the dry months. *Not bad for this time of year,* Gunn thought.

The bus let him off in front of a hotel restaurant on Forks Avenue. He watched the trailing traffic for a minute or so: campers, motor homes, cars, then a sheriff's car closely followed by a city police cruiser. "This is not the place to be. La Push sounds really good right now."

Gunn walked to a phone booth outside the entry to an old hotel, looked up the number of a resort owned by the Quileute Tribe on the coast and dialed the number.

A youthful sounding male answered, "La Push Resort."

"Do you have a room available?"

"Yes, in the motel unit."

"I'd like it for two weeks. I'll be out there later this evening."

"I'll need a credit card number to hold it, Sir."

"Credit card? I don't have one. I'll pay cash."

"Okay," said the clerk, "if the room is still available when you arrive. We're always pleased when we can accommodate a traveler but keep in mind it is getting late and folk's stream in."

"Won't be a problem," said Gunn. *We're still a month away from tourist season.* "Are any restaurants open this time of year? I don't have a car."

"In Forks, Sir."

"Are the rooms still equipped for cooking?"

"Oh yes. Everything you'll need. And there's a convenience store gas station just across the road too."

"Excellent." Gunn hung up. "Now to get a beer and a ride."

He walked into the hotel lounge, a well-used emporium of after-hours rest and relaxation. The patrons, dressed in work shirts and coveralls and boots, identified the place as a hangout for locals more than tourists.

The man behind the bar watched Gunn as he came in, scanning his worn pants and coat, but said nothing.

Gunn nodded. "Barkeep, a beer, please."

"Tap?"

"That'll be fine."

The bartender placed a mug of beer on the well-worn bar. "That'll be $2.00."

Gunn put a twenty on the counter. "How can a man get to La Push from here? Any buses?"

The bartender wiped his hands on a discolored towel, took the twenty, and turned to the cash register. "Nope. Your best bet is to get a local to drive you down. Even the town cab won't go down there in the evening." He turned back to Gunn. "It's too long a drive comin' back empty." He put Gunn's change on the bar.

An old Indian man with shoulder length gray hair sitting a few stools down on Gunn's left said, "I'm going to La Push after I have a brew. You need a ride?"

"I'd appreciate it," said Gunn. "Barkeep, would you get the man another beer, please?"

Gunn looked at his new acquaintance and extended his hand. "Clint Hanson."

The old man moved closer to Gunn and spoke in a whisper, "Bobby Running Bear. That's neighborly. Thanks."

Gunn said, "My pleasure."

Running Bear said, "Do you have someplace in particular you're goin' to?"

"A lodge on the beach."

"Nice place. Not too crowded right now. It will be in few weeks."

"I didn't think so either although the clerk on the phone made it sound crowded. I'll only be there a week or so."

"He's supposed to say that." The old Indian turned to the bartender. "I'd kind'a like to take a six pack with me, Joe."

Gunn said, "I'll get that."

The bartender set the beer on the bar and reached for some of the change from Gunn's first bill. "You got more than enough here."

"Thanks," said Bobby Running Bear, looking at Gunn.

"No problem. It'd be a long walk."

Both men laughed.

Bobby said, "You alone?"

Gunn said, "Yeah, just looking for a little peace and quiet."

A young woman in tight fitting jeans passed the bar. Both men followed her with a gaze.

The old man said, "She's a pretty young thing."

"Yes she is. Maybe I'll find a little something down at the resort," Gunn said.

"Well, if you're smart you'll leave the Indian girls alone. Some of the young bucks don't like strangers messin' with the locals."

Gunn said, "So I've been told."

They finished their beers and left, then walked across the parking lot to an old Ford pickup.

The old man said, "Just a minute. I've got a pup in there that isn't real friendly 'til he hears from me."

Gunn stood at the door but didn't move.

The old man opened the door. The dog looked at Gunn standing behind his master. The old man reached across the seat and patted the head of the German Shepherd, and in a calm voice said, "Easy, Mac." He turned toward Gunn and said, "He's friendly long as you treat us right. Know what I mean?"

Gunn looked at the dog. "For sure."

The old man nodded toward the passenger seat.

Gunn climbed into the truck and held the shopping bag on his lap. His left leg was resting against the dog. Mac was quiet but showed his teeth.

For the next twelve miles the two men said very little. The old man drove very slow and drank two beers on the way down La Push Road. He offered Gunn a brew. Gunn declined. Arriving at La Push, he parked the truck at Sonny's Gas and Grocery.

The old man pointed to a driveway and a sign with a carved whale at the entry. "The park is right across the road."

Both men and Mac got out of the truck.

The old man said, "Now, I'd like to get a case of good beer. By the way, will you be needin' a ride back out?"

Gunn said, "Probably. How do I find you when I'm ready to go?"

"I fish almost every day off the docks down by the old closed up New England Fish House."

Gunn stepped toward the grocery store. "Great. Why don't you let me get you that case of good beer?"

A few minutes later Gunn walked across the road and into the resort office by the driveway. The clerk looked up as he entered.

Gunn said, "I called about a room earlier."

"Right, and we still have it," said the clerk as he looked at the somewhat rumpled appearing man carrying a shopping bag. The clerk gestured toward the nearly empty parking lot in front of an older two-story building. "In fact, we have several rooms. Would you like one on the ground floor or upstairs? The ones on top have a nice view of the ocean for only a few dollars more."

Gunn began filling out the registration form using the name Clint Hanson. "Top floor sounds fine."

The clerk said, "I have to verify all visitors using photo ID. It's tribal policy."

Gunn showed him the driver's license.

The clerk said, "Thank you. Since you're paying cash it'll be $166.33 a night, in advance."

"Here's $500.00 for the first three days. Assuming I choose to stay I'll pay another three days then."

"Excellent," the clerk said, taking the bills and holding them to the light. Then he looked over the registration desk at the unshaved man's shopping bag. "Any other luggage?"

"I travel light."

The clerk scanned the registration form. "Your occupation, Sir?"

"I'm a writer. I want to work and not be disturbed. If anyone asks for me or anyone who looks like me, I'm not here." Gunn looked at the young man. "Sometimes I write under a different name."

"Understand," said the clerk.

"It's worth a hundred-dollar bonus to you, half now and half when my two weeks or so is up."

You won't be disturbed, Mr. Hanson."

Gunn smiled, reached into his pocket and pulled out another hundred dollar bill. "You take care of me, I take care of you." Gunn slowly tore the bill in two and handed half to the young clerk. "You get the other half when I leave." He smiled and walked out, waving the room key casually in his hand.

The clerk put the half-torn bill in his pocket. "Jerk, all writers can't be that weird. Who cares? He's got money." He watched Gunn cross the lot. "The driver's license looked phony, too."

As Gunn approached the open door of his room he called out, "Anybody here?"

A young Indian woman came to the door carrying a tote tray with rags, cleansers and individual soaps. She spoke in a warm and gentle voice. "Housekeeping... I've just finished. Excuse me."

She passed Gunn in the doorway, her eyes downcast. After placing the tray on a cart she moved on to the next room. He watched until she disappeared, then went in and closed the door. He rubbed his eyes. "Things are looking up."

He went to the window located along the back wall of the room in the kitchen dining area. Beach 1 was large, dotted by huge driftwood logs and a few boulders. The Pacific rolled onto the sand, its foaming white caps splashing the driftwood barrier that separated the resort from the beach. "Good place for a fire, maybe a cleaning lady."

Gunn surveyed the room. "Uncle Robert, thank you for bringing me to La Push all those years ago. No cops, no prying eyes. This is good... so big and beautiful. What now?"

Gunn walked to the store. He selected a frozen pizza and a few other groceries. The clerk watched the clock while tapping the counter.

He brought the items to the register. "I just got enough for tonight. I'll be back tomorrow when we have more time. Oh, and do you have an evening paper?"

"Afternoon edition is gone, won't get anymore 'til tomorrow. Sorry."

"Not a problem. I do need some tape and writing paper."

The clerk pointed and said, "Around the corner is a shelf with some stationary and stuff."

After making his purchases Gunn walked back to the resort and locked himself in for the night. Before cooking he removed the hundred dollar bills from his socks and shorts, made them into a few small stacks, wrapped paper around the stacks and taped them to the underside of a dresser drawer.

He turned on the television set bolted to the dresser top while he ate. It buzzed while presenting only a snow image. "I wish everyone received the same picture tonight, but there are too many satellite dishes around here."

He went to the front window and checked the parking lot. "Nothing suspicious looking down there."

The resort office had only a night light showing. "I hope you keep your word, Kid, and be quiet about the money."

He turned and looked at his reflection in the window across the room. "Maybe tearing the bill was a little too dramatic."

He darkened the room and watched the phosphorous reflection from the waves. "I need to reinvent myself," he said and closed the curtains.

* * * * *

Chance Stewart paced the living room of his Ballard condo. "Where is that son of a bitch?" There had been no word from anyone in the U District, or anywhere else.

He reheated a cup of coffee in the microwave and sipped. "Christ, I could chew this stuff!" He dumped it down the sink, opened a beer and checked the time. "6:35."

He went into the bedroom. One of Amber's blouses and a pair of shorts were draped over a chair. "I've got to get my shit together. I'm as screwed up as Cashland in my own way."

He took an empty laundry bag from the closet and picked up her blouse and shorts. Moving to the dresser he opened her drawer and added the contents to the bag. "I'm too old for this and you're a good person. I want more out of life than a roll in the hay and you deserve better."

He placed the bag by the front door and called the office. Strickland answered on the third ring. "Ted, anything new on Gunn?"

"Not a word. It's like the guy vanished from the face of the earth. You'd think someone would at least spot the damn car."

Stewart said, "Maybe we're looking in the wrong place."

Strickland said, "Could be. Captain says it's your case now. We've been reassigned."

"Makes sense."

Strickland said, "How's your partner doing?"

"Just fine. What kind of question is that?" Stewart said.

"No special reason. You know, Cashland is a headline grabbin' case."

"Well, Ted, nothing personal, but that's why we got it. Captain James has every confidence in her and us. Why?"

Strickland chuckled. "Nothing. Zinc was just mentioned it could be a tough case. Guess they all are."

Stewart paused for a moment. "Seems that way."

"Sorry, Chance. Gotta roll. We've got a DB in an alley behind Second and Pine."

Stewart said, "Have a good one, Ted. Keep a stiff upper lip."

Strickland laughed. "That's about the only stiff thing I have anymore. Think I'm ready to join the blue pill set."

Stewart waited a moment, then dialed the captain's home phone.

"James."

"Captain, its Chance. Did Zinc ever work in personnel?"

James said, "That's a strange question. Why?"

Stewart said, "You know why. We both do."

"Mitch told you about the letters and gifts?"

"I was with her when they arrived." He took a breath. "It might be nothing, but I was just talking with Strickland. He wanted to know if she's a good cop. I asked why. He said it was nothing special, just that Zinc had wondered aloud."

James said, "Could be because it's such a high profile case. She's only been working homicide a few years."

"True."

"Could be jealousy because you two are the best at closing and all of 'em know it."

Stewart said. "I thought of that, too."

James said, "You think he's the sender?"

"It's got to be someone in the department. We both know the public doesn't have access without escort."

"I'll look into it. Anything new on Gunn?"

"Not a damn thing, but we'll find him."

The men hung up.

Stewart walked over to the couch and flopped down. Digging through a stack of law enforcement journals he uncovered a copy of *Playgirl*. He took it to the bag by the door and tossed it in. "It's got to be yours, Amber."

By 9:00 p.m. Stewart was in the parking lot of Tracey's at Fisherman's Wharf, a restaurant, waiting for Amber to get off work. After a few minutes she came out the front door on the arm of a young big blond-haired fellow.

Stewart got out of his car and walked toward the couple carrying the bag. *He's probably a fisherman.*

Amber saw Chance and waved.

Stewart waved back. "Amber."

She said, "Hi, Chance. What brings you down here tonight?"

Stewart held out the bag. "Just came for a late dinner and thought I'd drop off some things you left at the policeman's picnic last week."

"Oh." She caught her breath. "Thank you."

She looked at her date for the night, then back to Stewart. "Chance, this is my friend, Bjorne." The men shook hands. "Do you have a minute before you go in for dinner?"

Stewart shifted his feet. "Sure. The wife and kids aren't home tonight."

She looked at Bjorne and said, "This'll just take a minute."

Amber and Stewart stepped a few paces away.

She looked into his eyes. "My stuff?"

"Yes, you deserve better than I'm giving. Who knows, maybe he's your knight?" he said, nodding toward her date. "I need some time for myself to think things through."

"We're still friends?"

"Always."

She said, "Are you going to make a move on Mitch?"

"Maybe, I don't know that she'd even have me. I know I can't go on just living like an adolescent. You're young, bright and beautiful. You deserve more, someone with commitment."

He looked at her date again.

She said, "Bjorne is an old friend of the family."

"I don't want to hurt you, Amber."

Her eyes welled. "I've never had anyone be this honest with me." She chuckled. "Wife and kids at home, huh."

He said, "I didn't want to queer your date."

They turned and walked toward Bjorne. She wiped her eyes. "Thanks for bringing my stuff over. There must be more dust out here than I thought. Damn contacts." She looked at Stewart again. "Say hello to the family for me."

"I will. Talk to you later."

Stewart began walking toward the restaurant door and called back, "You guys have fun tonight. Life's too short as it is."

She waved. "You got that right."

"Way too short," he mumbled.

Stewart noticed the headline of the evening paper in the vending machine by the door as he entered the restaurant. *Murdered Teacher's Funeral Tomorrow.*

The Gold Coast gym was packed with students, parents, staff and friends. All had come to pay their final respects to Hailey Cashland. The tables flanking the podium were draped in white linen bunting. The climbing ropes were tied off, hoops cranked to the ceiling, tumbling mats suspended from the walls and chairs in neat rows covered the floor. The spring interlude of sunny blue-sky weather had passed and the familiar blanket of Puget Sound gray augmented the setting.

Student attire ranged from the latest hip-hop fashion statement to semiformal. Staff and most parents were dressed in something more appropriate to their respective generations of mourners. Frank Cashland sat in the front row flanked by Stewart and Santiago on his left, the Hartleys on the right, and Reverend Taylor Moore to their right. George Archer had carefully positioned himself on the left of Santiago. The pep squad, in full uniform, filled the other side of the front row. Staff was located in the second and third rows.

Jack Hartley walked slowly to the podium. The audience, already quiet, became still. The faint odor of cleaning agents wafted through the facility. The automatic toilet flushers went off and few chuckles followed their punctuation. A custodian quietly closed the doors leading to the locker rooms. In a voice that began strong and gradually moved to breaking the superintendent began the service.

"We're gathered here today to celebrate the life of Hailey Cashland; beloved teacher, mentor and friend to all of us." Hartley looked over the room, which was filled with a deathly quiet. "Our loss is small compared to the loss her family is experiencing. To you, Mr. Cashland," he gestured toward Hailey's father, "we extend our most profound and heartfelt sympathy. For the community of Gold Coast I say let us forever remember Hailey Cashland and the many things she did for us."

He moistened his lips and said in a breaking voice, "We loved her, we learned from her, she inspired us and now she'll watch over us."

Quiet sobs emanated from the audience. Coughs and sniffles accompanied tissues and handkerchiefs. Terry Shaw, seated on Archer's left, fought to control his emotions. His chest heaved as he tried to regain his breath. Charles, seated next to him, gently patted Shaw's left leg for encouragement. Cashland was stoical, sweat forming on his forehead and neck.

Hartley continued. "We've invited Reverend Taylor Moore to conduct today's service. Reverend." Hartley stepped back from the podium and extended his hand as the black man approached holding a bible.

Reverend Moore began. "I came to know Hailey as a friend and child of God almost ten years ago in Las Vegas. She had traveled west as a young woman seeking a new life, opportunities, and an education. Knowing the many trials and tribulations she and Mr. Hartley experienced it is wonderful to witness the success she achieved."

Ginger whispered in Hartley's ear, "You knew her in Las Vegas?"

He patted his wife's leg. "You said you didn't want to know anymore. I'll tell you later."

"No, I don't want to know. We're on track with each other and that's all that counts." She reached over and squeezed his hand.

The memorial service was a cross between a structured event and an outpouring of grief-stricken emotion. George Archer said a few words on behalf of the board. Toni Fryer remembered Hailey on behalf of the staff. Moses Cruz said, "She gave more to the sports program at Gold Coast than any other individual. Thank you, Miss Cashland."

Dixie Dahl, a bubbly cheerleader, remembered Hailey as "our big sister. She always guided us and encouraged us to make the best and most responsible choices in life as a group and as individuals."

The school choir sang "Amazing Grace." The band played the Gold Coast fight song and a special blues number that had been a favorite of Hailey's. Through it all Frank Cashland remained stoic.

Following the service a reception took place in the gym. The grieving father was introduced to many of the attendees. All expressed their sympathy and love for his daughter. He accepted the many kind words and offered inspiring testimonial and asides about Hailey's strength and perseverance.

Cashland told one family. "She was a smart child, well behaved, responsible. After her mama left she provided love and understanding in our house. When she graduated from high school she wanted to travel on her own, see the country, get an education."

A woman said to Cashland, "She was very young when she left home on her own."

He answered, "She wanted it that way. She was a strong, older than her years."

Santiago and Stewart quietly accompanied Cashland around the room.

Stewart said, "He's the one lone figure in this mass of humanity."

Santiago's voice was soft. "Do you believe he feels any of this?"

Stewart sipped from a half-full paper coffee cup. "Knowing what we know about her childhood it seems a bit of a stretch."

Santiago said, "I'd like to think he's feeling something. I hope he realizes what a good person she was."

Stewart said, "I hope so too, but he's hard to read."

She looked around at the thinning crowd. "I know. Like yesterday, he was more interested in any money she might have left than anything else. I sincerely hope he's more than the sleaze I see."

Santiago placed a napkin on the table. Both detectives disposed of their cups.

Stewart said to Cashland, "When you're ready we'll take you back to the motel."

"Thank you. That's very kind."

The young cheerleader who had spoken earlier approached the trio. She fought to maintain her composure. "Mr. Cashland, I'm so sorry for what's happened."

Cashland, while ogling the young woman, said, "You're very kind. Thank you."

The cheerleader looked away and excused herself, blushing.

Santiago said quietly to Stewart, "I don't *believe* the way he checked that girl out, just stripping her with his eyes."

Stewart said, "He's one sick bastard. Let's get him outta here."

* * * * *

Shaw's voice was loud and fast as he spoke to his friend. "Have you heard the news?"

Charles Goodwin said, "If you mean about Gunn, sure. Who hasn't? It's been all over the TV, radio, the net since day yesterday."

"Well, I guess that lets me off the hook, don't you think?"

Charles laughed. "Probably. Does this new surge of energy and excitement mean I can go home?"

Shaw said, "You don't want to stay?"

"Not really. Terry, you asked me to stay a few days because you were afraid of Gunn coming after you. It's safe to say he's gone, done, split, out of here."

"I know, but—"

"No buts about it. He's history. I'm going to finish getting my stuff together and head for home."

Shaw said, "It's early."

"It's almost noon."

Shaw dropped his head, lips puckered. "Okay, but he might still be out there watching me."

"You know he's not around here. You never knew whether he was even lookin' for you. Even if he was, the guys got bigger fish to fry. Besides, I'm due in Las Vegas for a meeting. I've got to get back to work."

"You're leaving town?"

"Business, Terry... its business."

"You'll keep in touch?"

Charles began to laugh. "Terry, relax. We've been friends for years. Of course I'll keep in touch. Look, I'm going home, not moving. I'm going to Vegas on business. Chill."

Shaw said, "But Vegas?"

"Business, and I'll be home in a few days. Look, you've just had a monumental experience in your life. You're more nervous than I've ever seen you. God, you're even gnawing your finger nails, something you haven't done since cheating in school when you got caught and tried to lie your way out of it. You're an artist. For God's sake, paint."

"You're right."

Charles said, "The other day you described everything in colors. You're emotions are in high gear. Paint."

"Is that a command? I like being ordered to do things."

"Talent notwithstanding, you're nuts. Look, you worked all night. We rode around for two nights in that truck. Go to bed and sleep. Then let your energy surge."

"I could paint."

"You need to paint, and maybe a little professional help. Gunn is gone. I'm gone. Now is a creative moment for you. Take advantage of it."

Shaw said, "My future is now."

Charles said, "Yes, and mine is too. Besides, if I don't leave I'll get as paranoid as you are."

Shaw said, "You think the cops will find him?"

"Without a doubt. Those two could find the proverbial needle. I wouldn't want them looking for me unless I was lost."

Shaw said, "I'm tired."

"You should be. I doubt either one of us has had eight hours sleep in the last two days. Rest and paint, Terry. You'll relax when you do. Painting has always helped you calm down."

"You could help by staying longer."

Charles squinted as he looked into the sad eyes of his friend. "Terry."

Shaw's voice dropped to a whisper. "I know... I know."

"If I forget anything, I'll come by in a few days when I get back."

Shaw said, "Where will you be staying? I might need to call you."

"At the timeshare. You'll have to call their office to reach me. I won't know which unit I'm in until I arrive."

"Do I have the office number?"

He looked at Shaw's tired face. "It's in your address book from the last time I went south. My friend, get some rest."

Shaw looked away. "Yes, I need rest."

* * * * *

Gunn watched the news over a cup of steaming coffee he had picked up at the resort office. *Pastry would be nice.*

The television broadcast originating from a Seattle station was snowy. After a station break the anchor talked about more overseas threats and airport security. Gunn finished his coffee. "Enough about the terrorists. Cut the world stuff short."

A different newscaster's face appeared on screen. She said, "Police continue to hunt for Sunset Community College instructor Trevor Gunn." A photo of his face flashed on the screen.

"Gunn is wanted for the murder of a homeless man in the Ballard area almost two weeks ago and is the prime suspect in the killing of Gold Coast Academy teacher Hailey Cashland. If you have any information regarding Gunn's whereabouts, call 911 immediately. Gunn is considered dangerous."

Gunn glared at the screen. "Dangerous? Christ, all I did was hit the bum. He fell and banged his head on a track."

He hit the table top with a fist, then stroked his chin, feeling the thickening stubble, stood and walked to the mirror over the dresser. "A few more days and I'll be unrecognizable."

He glanced over his shoulder at the television. A brief collage of pictures taken during Hailey's career at Gold Coast flooded the screen as another reporter said, "In a related story, memorial services were held this morning at Gold Coast Academy for Hailey Cashland. The gym was packed with students, staff, parents and friends. Her father, Frank Cashland, described his daughter as 'a wonderful child and brilliant young woman.' It was obvious to all attending Miss Cashland was loved and will be missed."

Video of Frank Cashland appeared. "I don't know what kind of animal this man Gunn is, but I'd sure like to find him first. He snuffed my little girl, my precious daughter."

Gunn glared at the screen. "You didn't know your daughter very well, Cashland."

There was a light knock on the door. Gunn froze in his chair and watched the door handle turn. The door opened slowly.

A soft-voiced woman poked her head in cautiously. "Housekeeping."

Gunn stood and walked to the doorway. "Come on in. I'm just working on some notes for a story."

The woman from yesterday walked in carrying the tote tray of cleaning agents. A pushcart was visible on the walkway behind her. There was bedding, soaps, toilet paper, tea and towels.

Gunn said, "Any coffee on your cart?"

Yes, Sir. Do you like regular or decaf?"

"Regular. Maybe I could have a couple of extras?"

She went to the cart, got three packets and started back into the room.

He motioned to the door. "Leave it open, the salt air smells good."

"I always do. It's policy."

He watched as she completed her tasks. "Have you worked here long?"

"About a year, Sir."

He checked her left hand and saw no ring.

Gunn smiled. "Please, call me Clint."

She spoke as she worked. "The desk clerk told me you're a writer."

Gunn stepped toward her. *So much for secrecy.* "Yes. Just trying to get away from the city life and finish a project. So tell me, what does one do around here for entertainment?"

"I go to Forks with friends. There's not much here."

"So I see, but the ocean is beautiful."

She said, "So are the beaches."

"Do you walk them often?"

She looked at Gunn and smiled, her eyes sparkling. "I enjoy them when I'm with someone."

He said, "Anyone special?"

She shrugged. "Just friends."

He looked her over from head to toe. "You have beautiful eyes."

She continued to work, but said, "Alone on the beach I think too much."

Gunn paused and watched her work for a moment. "I know what you mean. I was thinking of having a fire down there this evening, maybe roasting some hot dogs. You're welcome to join me if you'd like and if you're not too busy."

The young woman reacted with a coy look that filled her face, her brown eyes cast downward. Then she looked into Gunn's face and a slight blush covered her cheeks. She smiled. "That would be nice, just to talk."

He said, "Is that a yes?"

"I'll try to come down around 7:30, but only for a short time. My day begins very early and my brother doesn't like it when I'm out alone at night."

"You won't be alone."

"It's better if he thinks I am. He worries about my reputation and...." She bit her lip. "And you're a white man."

Gunn laughed and said, "Well, I had no control over that, but I look forward to visiting. Besides, you're a young woman, not a child. How old are you?"

"Nineteen."

"A friendly voice in a strange place is soothing to the soul."

She giggled. "You sound like a romantic writer."

After completing her tasks she went to the door. Turning, she looked at Gunn. "Will your fire be in the driftwood near the trail from the motel?"

"Yes."

She moved to leave.

Gunn said, "Wait a moment, please. I don't know your name."

She smiled. "Gemma Raintree."

"See you at 7:30, Gemma Raintree. Have a good day."

The door closed.

"And maybe I'll have a good night."

* * * * *

Following the memorial service, Santiago and Stewart had dropped Frank Cashland off at his motel. When he got to his room he began looking through the phone book for a cluster of bars near the motel. He found several but not within walking distance, along with adds for escort services. As he thumbed the pages he said, "Not much use for one of those. I don't have that much money, Hailey."

He took another pull on the brown bottle of whiskey. "Clubs, gentlemen's clubs. Why don't they call 'em what they are, strip joints? That'd be an honest ad."

He looked around the sparsely furnished room and laughed. "Frank, my man, you're in the wrong neighborhood. You ought to be downtown on First."

He took another pull. "Man, I'm itchin' for a woman."

The phone rang. Cashland went to the bedside and picked up the receiver. He said in a gruff, thick-tongued voice, "Hello."

"Mr. Cashland, Detective Stewart here."

Cashland cleared his throat. "Oh, hello."

"You were asking about Hailey's property."

"Yes. I want to take care of my little girls belongings."

"I've done some checking and you can go to her apartment today if you'd like."

"That'd be nice. Can I get a ride?"

"The department doesn't provide taxi service, Mr. Cashland, but I have some free time, so I could take you out there... unless we get a lead on Gunn, of course."

"I'd appreciate it, Detective, ah...."

"Stewart."

"Yes, Stewart. Will you bring me back?"

Stewart rolled his eyes. "I'll be with you when you go through her things."

"Good. That way I'll know if everything is there."

"We both will. We wouldn't want anything to come up missing that's on the inventory."

He said again, "And you'll bring me back to my motel?"

"I said I would."

"Will your partner be there?"

"No. She's going to be busy for the next few hours or until we get a break."

"Good. I don't think she likes me."

"It's like we said yesterday, Mr. Cashland, there are many other issues that need to be addressed."

"Can I get the diaries today?"

"No. They're evidence. I can't say whether you'll ever get them. They're part of the investigation file for now, and possibly other action later as you know."

Cashland said, "Well, I should go to her place anyway. I want to see how she lived. You know, it's a dad thing."

You son of a bitch. What you really want are the diaries.
"I'll pick you up in an hour."

Both men hung up. Cashland returned to the phone book and his search for gratification.

"I need to get laid. Hell, I'll just find a hooker tonight: quick, easy, and cheap. Might even stiff her if she don't have a pimp. Ain't like she can call the cops."

He laughed at his one-sided conversation, the sound muffled in the drab room, and then he took another pull from the brown bottle.

* * * * *

After Stewart hung up he turned toward Santiago in the dining room of her apartment. He picked up a sandwich and said, "I think he's drinking his lunch. He's going out to her place with me."

Santiago said, "I heard. Why are you doing this? You don't like him any better than I do."

"I'm not sure. Maybe I'm just trying to give him a break and somebody's got to be there with him."

She said, "I know."

Stewart changed the subject. "It was a nice memorial, Mitch."

"Yes it was. I really want to believe Hartley and Moses meant what they said. She did give a great deal of herself to the school and the students."

Stewart smirked. "Perhaps too much, but I think their comments were genuine."

She said, "It's got to be so hard for kids to deal with death, to say nothing of murder. If something like that happened to my sister I'd be devastated. So would my parents."

Stewart shook his head. "I've got twelve years on homicide, and I've always been professional. But this case? It just seems to be hitting near home. I don't know what it is, but it's making me rethink a few things."

Santiago looked at him across the dining room table. "Really? It must be affecting your appetite as well. You're holding a sandwich but you haven't taken a bite."

He looked at the sandwich and then the empty plate on the table. "I know. It's sure not the weekend I planned, either. First it's the murder and now Frank Cashland."

Santiago said, "No, it's not the weekend you planned, but on the bright side Jill flew in last night. That's probably what made me relate her to the case."

"Your sister?"

"She's doing the auto show at the Center." Santiago laughed. "She's worried about my social life. She even invited me to the after-hours party."

"That was thoughtful."

"It's probably the only way I'd get to be around her for any length of time, but it would be all party. She wants me to meet some of the promoters and have a change of scenery, so to speak. She'll be doing her thing and contact is limited to the male gender in her world."

Stewart smiled. "And as a serious detective, you're different?"

"I've done my partying and chasing, and I've had my fill of one night stands if that's what you mean. I was lucky enough to survive those days without any permanent damage until the package came."

Stewart said, "I know what you mean. It's like Hailey's life exaggerates in many ways some of my own faulty values. Last night I even collected Amber's stuff from my condo and took it down to her at the restaurant."

Santiago said, "You took it to her?"

"She's a friend, but I'm tired of being a cop with an ever-building reputation of juvenile behavior. I think I'd like to... I don't know, have a greater sense of *belonging*. The stud thing is for younger guys. I'm past it. I want something better in the future. My dad always said each of us grows up at his own speed."

Santiago said, "Same with me. Good or bad, Hailey Cashland has made me realize my fling days are over. I want people to know me as a person, not just a cop or an ex-party girl. My old psych professor always talked about Maslow's Hierarchy of Needs. Now I just want to move up the scale, get beyond the physiological and security levels. I think maybe that's where Hailey was going. She just picked the wrong guy."

Stewart said, "And you?"

"Me what?"

"Have you found the right guy?"

"I think so. I'm not sure, yet. He's a lot like me, unsettled, non-committal."

"How does he feel about you?"

Santiago looked directly into Stewart's face. "I'm not sure of that either. Sometimes he seems caught up in lust, sometimes he's serious. He's easily distracted by other women, and he's a workaholic."

"You can't trust a guy with a wandering eye, Mitch. Take it from me, I know."

She said, "People change. Look at us. Would we be here talking about stuff like this if it weren't for the case?"

"You sound like a psychologist."

"In our business we meet more than enough jailhouse lawyers and psychologists. I'm just on the other side of the bars."

"I hope it works out for you, but if he's grazing, he's not for you. You deserve the best. Lucky bastard probably doesn't have a clue as to what he's got."

"We'll see. My mom always told us if a man stops looking, he's dead."

Stewart said, "You mean look but don't touch... smart mom."

"Exactly."

"When do I get to meet him?"

A knock on the door interrupted their conversation. "Excuse me."

She went to the door. "Jason, come on in. Chance and I were just going over some details from the case we're working and having lunch."

She introduced the two men.

Jason eyed Chance, "Mitch, I don't want to bother you or anything. We got some fresh peaches in today and the distributor gave us a couple of cases extra for promotion. I don't eat them but I thought you'd enjoy some."

He handed her a plastic produce bag.

She said, "Well, thank you."

Jason stepped toward the door. "Don't mention it. I've got to get going. I have a date tonight for the auto show."

Stewart said, "Nice meeting you."

Jason said, "Likewise."

Santiago returned to the kitchen after Jason had left.

Stewart said, "Mr. Wonderful?"

"No. He's a good neighbor, friend, swimming buddy."

"That's all? He's good looking."

She waved the bag of oranges and said, "He's a grocery store manager. Sometimes we date."

"Well, he's a lucky guy and doing better than some of us this weekend."

She returned to her chair. "Maybe. He's still into hustle. Now, where were we?"

Stewart laughed. "Lunch, probing our psyches. We've never chatted like this, not in the two years we've worked together. Now seriously, do you date him occasionally?"

"Occasionally, we like to hangout from time to time, not as tight as you and Amber."

"We've had an intimate friendship. It's no secret, but she's more than a date."

Santiago smirked and raised an eyebrow.

He said, "What's so funny?"

"It's true. You do tell your partner everything."

"When's the last time you spent some time with the grocer?"

"We went for a swim the last time you spent a night with Amber."

They both laughed.

Stewart said, "Where do you think he is?"

"Home getting ready for a date."

Stewart pointed at the door. "Not him, Gunn."

"I haven't a clue. He's not in the U District, that's for sure."

Stewart shook his head. "I wish somebody would do something... see him, call... something needs to happen."

Santiago said, "Let's visit Linda Gunn again. She's upset. She might have thought of another place where he could be hiding."

Stewart ignored Santiago's comment. "You'd think someone would at least spot the damn car."

Santiago's cell rang. It was Don Taber from CSI.

"Mitch, I just finished the DNA testing on the tissue samples from the earrings you and Chance brought in. It is a match to Hailey Cashland."

"Thanks, Don. That gives us a link... a strong link."

"I've copied my report to Captain James. He's been following the investigation."

"We know. Chance is with me, so I'll fill him in right now. Again, thank you." She broke the connection.

"Fill me in?"

"The tissue on the earrings matched Hailey's DNA."

Stewart said, "Finally, a break."

"Yeah."

He said, "Are you going?"

"Where?"

"To the party tonight?"

"How many conversations are we having, Chance? You're flitting all over the place."

He said, "Guilty as charged."

"No, I'm not going to the car show party."

She paused then looked Stewart in the eyes. "Do you see me as anything other than a cop?"

His voice was soft. "You're my best friend and you're a beautiful woman. How do you see me?"

She glanced down at the table. "Actually, I see a man I'd like to know and understand a whole lot better."

Stewart swallowed, bounced his foot and cleared his throat. "Why don't you visit Mrs. Gunn. I'll take care of Cashland. We're getting much too philosophical here." He rose and took the plates to the kitchen.

Santiago said, "You're right. It's time to catch the bad guy."

"It's been a long week. We're both beat. After you call on Linda Gunn, get some rest, Mitch. Your sister's in town. Enjoy yourself until we hear something."

"What about you?"

"When I'm done with Cashland I'm going home and crash for a few hours. Right now I'm dead tired."

"Okay, you go with Cashland. I'll talk with Linda. We'll compare notes later."

"We'll compare notes tomorrow unless we get a lead on Gunn. Remember, we've got to be sharp too."

"Good luck with Cashland."

"Duty calls. Your guy's a little like me, workaholic."

She didn't say a word. *You do know.*

Stewart went to the door. "Change of heart. I'll call later today."

She said, "Right."

* * * * *

Frank Cashland walked through Hailey's living room. "Nice place she had here. Looks expensive."

Stewart watched Cashland survey the apartment and the furnishings. "It's not cheap."

Cashland said, "Stuff ought to be worth something."

"According to the landlord the furniture is rental, and I imagine her car will go to finance company. Remember the debts?"

Cashland said, "How can I forget? Those vultures want everything, I'm sure."

"You're free to look around. If you find something of interest we'll need to check it against the inventory list of items being picked up Monday."

"Monday? They're coming Monday?"

"It's an apartment, Mr. Cashland. It needs to be vacated in a timely way unless you want to pay the rent."

"Vultures. I hate 'em. Who's guarding her stuff when the movers come?"

"A neighbor, Terry Shaw. They've been close friends for several years. Of course you could come back. Terry's the man who reported her missing. He had invited her to a birthday dinner and she didn't show."

Cashland said, "She'd probably been sleepin' with him, too."

"I don't think so. They're friends."

Cashland looked at Stewart. "Don't get snippy. This is a hard time for me."

Stewart said, "It was a hard time, hard life, for Hailey."

Cashland's face became flush. "We didn't have a good life; too much drinkin', movin' around, her mother leavin' and then dyin'. I made mistakes."

He walked into the bedroom. Stewart sat down on the couch and waited for Cashland to finish looking the place over. Cashland opened the refrigerator after checking the bedroom.

"Want a beer?"

Stewart said, "No thanks."

Cashland popped a tab and guzzled. Some of the contents spewed down his chin and shirtfront onto the floor. He wiped his mouth with the back of a hand. "I'll drink my inheritance. This is damn good beer. There's one left?"

Stewart said, "Go ahead, enjoy."

Cashland said, "What about pictures?"

"Other than the stuff being picked up and items of evidence you can take everything. We still have the photo albums, but eventually they'll be released except for a few pictures."

"Good. I'd like something to remember her by."

Stewart sat silently waiting for Cashland to finish.

"How about her movie collection?"

"It's yours."

"I'll take it with me. You don't have any boxes in your car, do you?"

Stewart said, "Not a one. She might have something in the pantry. I know she has plastic grocery bags in the kitchen. What are you going to do with the stuff the movers don't take?"

Cashland shrugged and sat down in a recliner. "Nothing. I'll take what I want today. Let's face it, she didn't own much other than her clothes, some costume jewelry, and household stuff. The landlord will store what's left for awhile just like they do for military guys when we move out. If I don't make arrangements it becomes theirs. They can sell it, dump it, whatever."

Stewart looked into the man's face. *Do you feel anything, Cashland? You're going through her home like a bandit.* "Have you decided when you're leaving?"

Cashland looked at his empty beer bottle and smiled. "I was gonna be outta here Monday but the folks at the school said she had a life insurance policy as part of her contract. She never named a beneficiary. I'll stick around a few more days until that's settled. They said it wouldn't be long."

Stewart looked at Cashland. *A father like you and Gunn for a lover... Hailey didn't stand a chance.*

CHAPTER 16

Gunn moved slowly as dusk turned to darkness, the light of day evaporating into a chilled black gray-green sky highlighted by the moon's sudden appearance from behind clouds and the sound of waves crashing on the beach. A few campfires, isolated among the driftwood logs, emitted harsh smoke that hung in the air. "I love the ocean but I hate the damp, cold night. Where are you, Gemma?" He looked around the area and waited. "It's almost eight o'clock, Kid. You said seven-thirty."

He continued to walk among the logs and zipped up his parka.

A soft feminine voice called from the darkness. "Clint? Clint?"

Gunn stepped into the clear. "Over here, Gemma."

The young woman came out of the darkness directly in front of him, only a few feet away.

Gunn jumped back. "Jesus, you scared me. It's really getting dark out here."

She took his hand and began walking toward flickering flames that were barely visible at ground level from behind the logs. "Let's go over by the fire. It's abandoned."

Gunn said, "I spotted it coming down the trail earlier. I thought we could enjoy it and get out of the wind. Sure beats building your own."

After sitting down on a log near the fire, which was approaching the ember stage, Gunn looked around. "I can't see a thing down here, it's so black."

She snuggled next to him. "It's getting that way, but your eyes have adjusted to the coals. Are you looking for work while you're here writing?"

"No. I'm just here for a few days at the beginning of a road trip. I'm writing a fictional account about my travel experiences. La Push is for rest and relaxation, doing some notes."

"That's good. It's hard for a white man to find work in the village... almost impossible. The tribe takes care of its own first."

He said, "Sounds fair to me. Lord knows Indians have taken it in the shorts for as long as the land has been settled."

"It was settled by us before the white man came. He just resettled it without us." She paused, then changed the subject. "Are you going to spend any time in Forks?"

He smiled. "Not if I can help it. I like it down here. Walkin' the beach is all I really need right now. No phones, news or people... except the beautiful woman I'm with now, of course."

"Where will you be next?"

He shrugged. "I'm thinking about driving through Oregon and maybe spending some time in northern

California. Are you planning on leaving the village someday?"

She pursed her lips. "If the man I marry wants to."

"No Mr. Right yet?"

She said, "Not yet, or I wouldn't be down here with you."

They talked for an hour, sharing hot dogs and a few cold beers Gunn had brought with him.

Gunn said, "I'm doing some writing while I'm here too. Would you like to take a peek?"

Gemma said nothing but snuggled closer.

A chill ran down his spine. "Would you like to go up to my room? We could warm-up and maybe play some music on the radio."

She said, "It's nice here and I have to get home in a little while."

"So early?"

"I don't want my brother looking for me, much less finding me here with you. He'd go crazy. The girls who date the Coast Guard guys catch enough flak from him and the others as it is."

Gunn wrapped an arm around her shoulder and brought her near. They kissed lightly, then with passion. "Got it."

Over the sound of the waves and wind, Gunn heard a branch break. He gripped Gemma tight and whispered, "Did you hear that?"

"What?"

"A branch broke, like someone climbing over logs or something."

"No, but others are down here, Clint."

"I know, but it sounded really close."

She said, "If it wasn't nearby you wouldn't hear it."

He wrapped his arms around her and pressed her to the ground.

"What are you doing?"

He whispered in her ear, "Shh. If it's your brother, we don't want him to find you, remember?"

Gemma nodded and kissed him again.

Two figures appeared, climbing over a large tree trunk by the fire. Gunn looked up, his body becoming rigid. Gemma tensed in his arms and looked away, hiding her face.

One of the intruders said, "Sorry, wrong fire. They must be on the other side of the logs."

The pair moved on.

Gunn stood up. "You were right, Gemma. I don't want keep you out too late tonight. There's no reason to take chances or have your brother find us, not here. Come on, I'll walk you to your car."

"No car," she said and offered her hand as he helped her up. Her lips brushed against his again as he looked about. "Maybe I *could* be a *little* later. We still have time, Clint, if you'd like to spend a few more minutes down here. I'd like that." She smiled. "Then I'll walk home."

"Not tonight. Those guys could've been your brother. We're out in the open. Maybe tomorrow we'll try again."

"Tomorrow is fine." She kissed him again.

The couple slowly walked up the trail leading back to the resort motel. The distinct smell of burning driftwood hung even thicker than before as the breeze lightened. Dark shadows of slowly moving clouds reflected eerie images against the black sky as they moved overhead across the face of the moon, Gemma and Gunn the only visible people on the trail.

Her voice was husky. "It was pleasant to talk and share a few quiet moments, Clint."

"We'll do it again tomorrow," he said, flipping the collar up on his parka.

"That will be nice." She took a few more steps. "The evenings are actually getting warmer, at least for La Push," she said.

"Would you like to come up for coffee, no strings attached?" His voice was soft, heavy with anticipation. "We wouldn't be out in the open."

"Not tonight. I really should get home or my brother will be suspicious. Tomorrow."

"Until then." He smiled and blew her a kiss.

They parted company at the corner of the building near the stairway. She walked across the parking lot and disappeared in the night. He went upstairs to the room. Within a few minutes there was a soft knock on the door.

"I hoped you'd be back," he said with a smug grin and went to the door. A second series of light knocks came. He opened the door and peered out. "Gemma?" he said softly. "I knew you'd come back." He looked into the darkness.

There was a sudden flicker of movement and a fist slammed into the right side of his jaw, snapping his head back sideways. He collapsed backward as everything ran together in a painful, psychedelic blur.

"What the hell?" he slurred trying to raise himself.

Someone kicked him, a glancing blow, in the left shoulder.

Gunn rolled over trying to regain his vision and equilibrium. Strong hands gripped the hair on the sides of his head from behind. The assailant pounded Gunn's forehead on the floor.

"You fuck with my sister, you fuck with me, big man!" said a hoarse voice.

Gunn rolled over, kicking at the blurred figure.

The man laughed. "You fight like a girl."

"I didn't fuck anyone," Gunn groaned through split lips, blood splattering on his shirt and the carpet.

The man stood and kicked his right thigh, hard. Pain shot through his leg. He tried to roll away. The man followed, breathing heavily.

"I didn't do anything," Gunn said in a weak voice, rising to his hands and knees.

His assailant grabbed him by the hair with his left hand and smashed the side of his face with a rock-hard fist. Gunn's teeth crushed together, making a sickening sound. The copper taste of blood filled his mouth as he fell back to the floor. He waited for the next blow to come, his face pressed against the dirty rug. The man continued to rant, the sounds garbled in his ears. He lay still.

A distant female voice filtered through his consciousness. "Jimmy! Leave him alone! We didn't *do* anything!"

Gunn looked up just as the stocky, blurred figure looked toward the door.

The man hissed, "Gemma! What are you doing here?"

"Trying to save two lives. We talked, Jimmy, that's all!"

"He wanted to fuck you! You're a whore!"

"You're a fool." She glared at her brother. "Help me get him on the bed."

Gunn caught his breath. His vision began to clear.

Strong hands gripped his arms under the shoulders and pulled him to his feet. Gemma came to one side and helped walk Gunn across the room. The man pushed him onto the bed.

Gemma looked at Jimmy. "Now get out of here."

Gunn looked up at the still fuzzy figures.

The man grinned. "Well, he can't do anything tonight... that's for sure." Then he turned and walked out of the room.

"The carpet smelled like urine," Gunn said in a soft voice. The room swirled and turned black.

* * * * *

Michelle Santiago had visited the Gunn apartment with the hope of getting some new insights as to where Trevor may be hiding, but Linda Gunn wasn't home. Michelle had returned home, called to leave a message with Linda Gunn, and was resting. By ten o'clock she was stretched out on the couch watching the news, trying to relax and second-guessing whether she should attend the party at the auto show. The news anchor made a comment about the show. "I'll skip it." She yawned. "Tonight I can collect myself."

The man on the screen rambled through the day's headlines, flipping sheets of paper as he went. "You guys need a TelePrompTer," she said. Then a new picture flashed on the screen and she quickly sat up.

"In a breaking story, police just announced the car of murder suspect Trevor Gunn has been found parked near the Victoria Ferry terminal in Port Angeles. The search is now centering in that area of the city and Victoria, B.C."

"Oh great... not an extradition issue, please." She reached for the phone. An answer came on the first ring. "Chance, have you heard the news?"

"About Gunn's car? I was just talking to James a few minutes ago and getting ready to call you. Why, is it on the news too?"

"A reporter got it from the cops in Port Angeles almost before we did. It would've been nice to work the area first."

"Doesn't do us any good to cry about it," he said. "Their department is canvassing the area tonight and will continue in the morning. He could be in a motel, flop house, Victoria. Who knows? I'm sure we'll be on the road tomorrow. I just don't know where to. Canada is closer than Port Angeles, but the ferries are shut down for the night." He paused. "Did you get hold of Linda Gunn?"

"No, she wasn't home. I'm going to try her again when we finish," she said.

"I figured as much when I didn't hear from you earlier."

"I'll let you know if I get anything. How's your night going?"

"Just chillin' out. It's nice to even semi-relax after this week. How about you?"

"Same thing. Tonight I'm reminding myself there's life other than work... or I was until the news. I'm exhausted." She glanced at the screen.

"Sounds like me. I'm doing a crash course in not being a workaholic." He laughed.

"It's good to hear you laugh."

"When this is over we should take a break." He paused. "I want to get to know you better as a person." There was another pause and a swallow. "The real you, y'know? Ahh... that sounded really corny, but you know what I mean."

"I'd like that too," she said, curling up her legs. "It's late but I'll call Linda Gunn right now."

"Boy, right back on task. Have a good night, Mitch. Talk to you later."

They both hung up. She was reaching for her notebook to check Linda Gunn's number when the phone rang again. She picked up the receiver. "Did you forget something, Chance?"

"Detective Santiago?"

"Oh, sorry... yes?"

"This is Linda Gunn. You said I could call you whenever I needed. I heard your message from earlier and thought I should get back to you."

"Thanks for responding. What can I do for you?"

"We both know Trev has hit the road. I've even saw his face on the news."

"Have you heard from him?"

"No, but I know you're tryin' to find him. I thought you'd like to know he's probably not in Seattle," said Linda Gunn.

"Why do you say that?"

"I know he's drained our accounts and our credit card is close to the max with a cash advance. None of our friends have seen or heard from him. He's too social not to be in circulation somewhere. He'd even ask our friends to hide him, at least some of them."

"Would they?" Santiago said.

"No. Him notwithstanding, they're good people."

"Do you have any ideas as to where he might be hiding other than Seattle?" Santiago picked up a pen and pad from an end table.

"Several," she took a deep breath. "I'm just surprised I didn't think of them before. He's always loved San Francisco and Monterey. Those are possibilities. Another, much cheaper idea would be eastern Washington."

"Eastern Washington? What area?"

"Chattaroy," said Linda Gunn.

"You mean Chattaroy north of Spokane on Highway 2?" Santiago said.

"Yes."

"Why there?"

"His grandparents have a place outside of town and a cabin at Lake Sacheen. As a kid growing up he always was close to them and went for visits during summer vacations. Even as an adult when he was studying for his orals and completing his thesis he'd go there. He always found it quiet, relaxing, safe."

He probably had a honey or two on a string there too. "That's very helpful, Linda. How are you and the kids doing?"

"Okay, considering." Her voice broke and sounds of crying came through the phone. "It's hard enough knowing about his other women, but to have my husband wanted as a suspect in two murders is just overwhelming." She sniffed. "As soon as I can I'm takin' the kids and headin' to Spokane. We'll stay with my parents for a few weeks."

"Don't forget to let me know before you leave. I'll need their address and phone number so we can reach you."

"Of course. In fact, I'll give you those now," she said and gave Santiago the information.

"Have you heard the news this evening?" Santiago asked.

"No, I've been too busy. Why?"

"Police found Trevor's car in Port Angeles."

"Really? I bet he ditched it there and went to Chattaroy on the bus or something," she said without skipping a beat. "He's always been good at deceiving people. I should know."

"No contacts in Port Angeles that you know of?" Santiago said.

"None."

"Do you have the Chattaroy address handy?"

"Yes." Linda Gunn shared it. "The kids are callin' and I have to go. Anything else?"

"Not right now. Take care of yourself and those kids."

"I will. Goodnight." Linda broke the connection.

"This is too convenient," Santiago said returning the phone to its cradle, then thumbed through her notes about Gunn's work applications but didn't find what she was looking for. She called her partner.

"Stewart," he answered in a brusque voice.

"Has your mood changed?"

"No, sorry, I was just swallowing. Was Linda Gunn home?"

"Yes. Do you trust her?"

"What do you mean?" he said.

"I didn't call her. She called me as soon as you and I hung up. She went on and on about his grandparents in Chattaroy."

"Did you ask about Port Angeles?"

"Not right away. When I mentioned his car had been found she said he didn't have any connection to PA. She went on about how he probably ditched it there to throw us off."

"Possible," he said.

"I keep thinking he had a relative on the peninsula. Didn't he use someone out there as a reference on one of his job applications?"

"You know, I think you're right. Look, I'm going downtown tonight anyway, so I'll swing by and check the file. You relax, maybe catch up with Jill at the auto show. Enjoy what's left of the evening. Tomorrow's going to be another busy day. I'll arrange a stakeout on Linda Gunn's place. Something just doesn't ring true. If he has a relative out there she might try to reach him."

"I'm thinking the same thing," she said. "Talk to you in the morning." She hung up.

* * * * *

Frank Cashland walked north along the empty sidewalk on Aurora Avenue. The lights of several older motels and restaurants created a neon jungle promising excitement, adventure and conquest. Mist provided halos around the streetlights. He saw a lone woman wearing a mini-skirt barely reaching the top of well-proportioned thighs. Her torso was wrapped in a midriff crop top made of stretch fabric. Her platinum blond hair covered her shoulders. "This looks nice... very promising," he muttered, moving closer to the woman.

Goose bumps stood out on her arms. She was smoking a cigarette, the filter covered with thick red lipstick smears. Blue eye shadow created the image of small caverns in her face. She looked him straight in the eyes as he approached. Thrusting a hip, she spread her feet to shoulder width, one knee slightly bent. "You lookin' for a good time?" She took a long drag on the cigarette and exhaled a cloud of smoke. It hung in the damp air.

"Could be." The man smiled and stopped walking, scrutinizing her from head to foot. His eyes filled with lust. There was a familiar stirring in his groin.

"I do blowjobs, hand-jobs, screw me, whatever." She dropped the butt and stepped on it with a stiletto covered foot.

"How much?"

"Depends on what you want."

"A really good time, maybe an hour or so."

"A hundred bucks. You got a hundred bucks, old man?"

He reached in his pocket and pulled out a small wad of cash. "Yeah, I got a hundred bucks. Where do we go?"

She nodded toward a motel, its flashing neon light partly burned out. "I got a room but you pay up front. No freebies."

The man handed over two twenties and showed her the remaining bills. "You get the rest when we're done." His voice was thick and raspy.

The woman reached out and took the money. "This way, Honey." She wrapped an arm around his shoulder.

They walked past a car with two men sitting in the front seat. She flashed the bills at them in passing.

The door opened behind the couple. "Hold it right there, Mister," said one of the men.

"What?" said the man turning to face the figures standing beside the car.

"You're under arrest for soliciting an act of prostitution."

The man turned to face the woman. Holding a badge in her right hand read his Miranda rights as she handed the bills to the man behind him. "That's the third one in an hour." She looked at Cashland. "Asshole."

One of the plainclothes officers cuffed the old man, turned him around and moved him toward the unmarked car.

"I was just lookin' for a little fun," Cashland said.

"Well, pal, you found something else. What's your name?"

The old man looked at the three officers standing around him. His hands shook and knees almost buckled. He wet his lips. "Cashland... Frank Cashland."

"Watch your head," said the other officer as they placed him in the back seat of the car and closed the door.

Looking at the female officer, the first man chuckled. "You go freshen up in the room. We'll be back in about ten minutes and try for number four." He looked at his partner. "Cashland... wonder if he's related to the murdered teacher?"

* * * * *

The door slammed against the wall as Jill flung it open.

Santiago sat up in bed from a sound sleep. Laughter filtered into her room followed by the muffled crash of glass breaking. "What is going on?" She climbed out of bed and slipped on a bathrobe, then walked into the living room. Her sister was passed out on the floor. Glass fragments were strewn over the floor near the entrance. A taxi driver was standing in the doorway, his eyes bulging, hands moving tentatively as he bent his knees, frozen but almost reaching out to the figure on the floor.

Santiago knelt beside her sister. "Jill... God, your lifestyle is going to kill both of us." She stroked her cheek.

Jill opened one eye to a slit. "Pay the man, will ya shish?"

Santiago stood and looked at the driver. "How much?"

"Thirty-two fifty."

She took her purse from the table near the door and gave the driver two twenties.

He looked down, nodded and disappeared.

"Come on." She took Jill under the arms, helped her stand and walked her rubber-legged sibling to the guest room. She plopped Jill onto a chair and clutched the top button of an otherwise open raincoat. "Well, at least I know how you found a cab this late, but tomorrow you'll have to find your clothes." Mitch turned back to the bed. "Here." She helped Jill take off the raincoat and put her in bed. "You're too wild for your own good." She kissed Jill's forehead and pulled the blanket up under her chin then shook her head and smiled. "I wish you'd learn to use your brain, not just your body." The blanket moved with every breath. Santiago chuckled. "I guess I'm the fire calling the kettle black." She glanced at her watch. "3:00 a.m. How I remember the days."

CHAPTER 17
Day 10: Sunday

"What's going on here, Mr. Cashland? It's Sunday morning and you call to tell me you're in jail? I thought you were here for Hailey's memorial service, not soliciting." Stewart said in a burst. Then he looked at the guard. "Could we use a prisoner's conference room, please?"

"Sure, Detective Stewart. It's not like we've got Ted Bundy here." He moved the men to a room normally used by attorneys and their clients.

"This will give us a little privacy," Stewart said.

"You got a smoke?"

"No, and you couldn't smoke in here anyway." Stewart eyes were squinted. He turned his head away, watching Cashland in his peripheral vision. "Bet you'll be glad to get cleaned up and out of those clothes. When we're done here the jailers will get you a shower and issue you some coveralls."

"Nothing wrong with my clothes, but they would get a little ripe if I stay here very long."

"Trust me, they're already way beyond ripe."

"How about the smoke?"

"Like I said, I don't have any and it's a non-smoking jail."

"How about one of your friends?"

"None of them smoke, either." Stewart leaned back in the chair. "How did you end up here?"

"I was walkin' on Aurora last night, lookin' at the sights, you know, the lights and stuff, and this lady comes on to me."

"Comes on to you, how?"

"Well, she's wearin' a really short skirt and one of those short tops stretched over her tits, showin' a lot of skin everywhere, long legs." He nodded as saliva appeared at the corner of his mouth. "Anyway, she says she'd like to have some fun with me." A smile crossed his face. "Well, it's not like I was born yesterday. I know what she's talkin' about so I ask how much. She says it depends on what I want. Well, I'm in the mood for a change of pace. I told her somethin' like one of each."

"One of each?"

"Whatever I could get for a hundred bucks in a hour."

"And what did you get for your money?"

"A pair of bracelets and a ride downtown." He grinned. "I didn't give her the whole hundred, only forty down."

"My God, the man is kin to Einstein." Stewart looked at Cashland and shook his head.

"Now I gotta go to court, I guess," Cashland said.

"That's right. The city takes prostitution seriously."

"I'm not a prostitute. She approached me."

"You're a John. It takes two to tango," Stewart said.

"I can't go to court. That costs money."

"Get off it, Cashland. You probably know the system better than I do."

"Can't you help? Maybe get them to cut me some slack? All I want to do is leave this town."

"Yesterday I felt sorry for you. I even hoped you'd realize what a well thought of person your daughter was and what she meant to those kids," Stewart said.

"I do."

"Then I watched you leering at the little cheerleader out at the school. She was expressing true feelings about your daughter and you were mentally raping her. My partner saw the same thing."

"She was a very attractive girl and she looked available."

"Cashland, you drove your daughter away from home after sexually abusing her for years, and now you come here looking for an inheritance."

"It's my right."

Stewart nodded. "So it is. Enjoy your rights. My job is to find Hailey's killer. I'm not your babysitter or your friend. You called me today because you already know Santiago finds you repulsive. She's not alone. You have to be the most loathsome person I've ever encountered." Stewart's face became flush. His eyes were fine lines, his lips pulled tight against his teeth.

"So are you gonna help me get outta here?"

"Shit man, don't you hear a goddamned word?" Stewart banged the table with his fist so hard that the jailer returned to the room. Stewart stood, shoving the wooden chair back with his legs. "You're on your own." He looked at the guard. "Take our guest back to his hole in the wall. I don't want anything else to do with him." He looked back at Cashland. "No more calls to me unless it's related to Hailey's murder." He spun on his heel and left the room.

* * * * *

"Man, I hurt all over," Gunn moaned as he opened his blinking eyes. The soft sounds of Gene Vincent singing old '50s hits filled the room. He tried to move, but his right leg was throbbing. "Ow, ow, ow!" He turned to face the soft sea breeze coming through an open window. "That feels great. Can't beat fresh ocean air."

"Good morning," Gemma said walking toward the bed. "How do you feel?"

"Like I'm stuck in the sand and can't move." He touched his jaw, the four days of stubble tickling his fingers. "Man, that hurts."

"You met my brother." She held out a cup of coffee.

"I figured as much." Gunn rolled into a sitting position on the bed. "Mean bastard, isn't he?"

"He doesn't trust me," Gemma said.

"No shit." He sipped the steaming brew. "You make good coffee. The rich flavor detracts from the pain." He swirled a mouthful several times, then swallowed another sip. "It gets the taste of blood out of my mouth too."

"Are you going to call the police?" Her voice was pregnant with concern.

"No," he said. "Did you last night?"

Gemma shook her head. "No. I don't want Jimmy in jail. It would be the end of him."

"I feel like it's the end of me. Is he coming back?"

"I don't think so."

"Good." Gunn tried to stand.

"You're moving pretty good, considering."

"Help me to a chair, please."

She took his arm.

He flinched. "No, the other one. This one hurts like crazy."

"Sorry." She helped him slowly across the room.

He lowered himself onto a chair and looked at Gemma. "I don't feel so hot."

"I don't think anything is broken," she said, touching his yellowed cheek, "but I can call a doctor if you want."

"I have some teeth that would disagree with your assessment," he said spitting out a small enamel chip over a swollen lip, "but no, a doctor isn't necessary. Did you stay all night?"

"Yes."

"Thank you." He twisted his neck and head. "I didn't feel this sore after my first car wreck."

"You probably didn't look this bad either." She smiled. "Thank you for not calling the police." Her voice was very soft.

"Not a problem, but your brother has issues with anger management. He should work on those." Gunn smiled and glanced at the mirror. "You're right, I do look a little shopworn."

"Are you hungry?" She took the now empty cup from the table.

"I ache all over. I hurt all over, but I'm not hungry. Maybe a glass of water?"

Gemma went to the bathroom and brought back a full glass. He sipped slowly.

"I think he'd have killed you if I hadn't seen him and come back," she said.

"I'm sure of it." Gunn tried to stand. "I wonder if I can make it to the bathroom on my own?"

"He's over protective."

"No, he's nuts." Gunn paused and blinked again, then rubbed his sore leg.

"I hope you don't mind. I took your pants off to check your leg. The skin was broken and the bruise is huge. I packed it in ice."

"I didn't even notice they were gone." He smiled at her while trying to keep from stretching his lips. "That's the first time someone took my pants off when I wasn't aware of it." His laugh was weak.

"I think you'll be okay in a few days, just a little worse for wear. I could shave your beard if you'd like?"

"Lord no, I wanted a beard anyway and I sure don't want a razor on my face right now." He finally struggled to his feet. "I'm going over there," he said nodding toward the bathroom.

"Need some help?" she said.

"I think I can go by myself." They both laughed as he began moving.

"It's my day off. I thought I'd stay around here at least for a while. I called my brother. I told him where I'm at and what I'm doing and that if he bothers you again I'll call the cops."

"I don't want that kind of trouble for him," Gunn said.

"You're a kind man. He's already served time twice for assault. He knows all about three-time losers. He'll stay away and so will his friends."

"Did you know the carpet smells like urine?"

"What? You said that last night, too. What kind of question is that?"

He tried to shrug. "It just does. Last night when my face was mating with the rug the odor of ammonia is what kept me from passing out. I'm serious."

"Many visitors keep dogs in the rooms, but they're supposed to do their business outside.' Gemma chuckled. "You must be feeling better if you want to piss and can't talk about nothin' but the smell of pee."

"I must be, but I'm sure tired and sore."

"Well, at least now you have something to write about."

Yeah, like I'm a writer. "Turn on the news if you can find a station. I'd rather know what's going on in the world than listen to old rock tunes." He yawned. "That fresh coffee sure is good." He yawned. "Man, am I sleepy."

"I'll find a station," she said placing a refill on the table, "but you need to rest."

"You're right," he said hobbling into the bathroom. He returned a few minutes later and went directly to the bed without help.

"Get some sleep, Clint. I'll check on you later."

"Thank you." His eyes slid shut. Only the sound of the radio invaded his privacy. He opened his eyes once when he thought he heard his name. "The smell of salt air sure beats urine," he mumbled and slipped into oblivion as darkness overtook his senses.

* * * * *

The phone seemed to ring louder than usual. Santiago mumbled, "No... I don't want to wake up." She rolled over, taking a deep breath. She blinked her eyes, trying to erase the evening fog, and peered at the clock. "8:44... it seems like 5:00." The phone blared again. She reached for the receiver. "Hello?" she said in a forced voice, her mouth and throat dry.

"Hi, Kid. How are you feelin' today?" said the chuckling, happy voice on the other end.

"Fine, Jason." Santiago yawned and sat on the edge of the bed. "Why do you ask?"

"I was up late last night. I saw you pouring out of a cab almost naked except for a raincoat." He laughed.

"Close, but not quite," she said. "That was my sister, Jill, stumbling in."

"That makes sense. We've met. You two sure look alike."

"So I've been told," she said with a sigh. "We're different, believe me. Why are you calling so early? Have a dull date?"

"I just thought, you know, you might need something at the store, whatever. You—I mean Jill—was pretty loose," he said.

"That's not the half of it. You know her, at a least a little."

"For sure. Look, I'll be washing my car later. If you'd like I can do yours."

"That'd be nice. If I'm home I'd appreciate it."

"I heard the news about your suspect's car being found. Good luck."

"Thanks. Talk to you later." She hung up.

Santiago made coffee, showered and dressed. She checked Jill's room only to find her rolled into a fetal position, blankets on the floor. She covered her, went to the living room and called Stewart's condo. There was no answer so she tried his cell phone.

"Where are you?" she said.

"Driving home. I just left Cashland."

"Cashland?"

"He's in jail. Got busted for soliciting last night."

"Couldn't happen to a more deserving guy, and I'm not surprised. Have you heard anything new on Gunn?"

"Nope." A sports car swerved in front of Stewart. "Bastard!"

"I agree," she said.

"Oh, him too, but I just had a guy try to run me off Market Street. He drives like the guys in the videos at the auto show last night."

"You were there?"

"Sure. I changed my mind after we talked. I even fantasized you might show up for the party. I didn't want you to be unescorted. Besides, it's every man's dream to have something red, fast and sexy to prowl around in."

"So I've been told. Is this the new you?"

Stewart laughed. "Change takes time."

"Well, when you get home, pack a bag."

"Why?" he said.

"I'm sure we're taking a trip. It's just a feeling, but it won't go away. I'm thinking the peninsula or Canada. Did we get the stakeout approved?"

"Our not too happy pals are sitting outside her apartment as we speak." Stewart laughed. "And yes, Gunn did have a connection on the peninsula, in Forks."

"Who?" she said.

"An uncle. Apparently he died a few years ago. Gunn used him as a family reference. You were dead on the money, Mitch."

"We should alert Zinc and Strickland to be on the lookout for a car registered in the Spokane area."

"Why?" he said.

"If Linda's going to try to reach him it wouldn't surprise me if her folks come and get the kids. She plans on spending some time with them anyway."

"Why would she want to reach him?" he said.

"The obvious answer is money. Remember, he pretty much cleaned out the accounts," she said.

"If she makes a move, we'll know." He chuckled.

"What's so funny?"

"Nothing. I was thinking of something else. I saw Jill at the show last night."

"Was she sober?"

"Yes, and very sexy."

"You should have seen her when she got home."

"I bet she was still sexy." He chuckled again, a smile spreading across his face.

"Naked, yes; sexy, no. It's been a long night. I'll tell you about it later."

"Naked? Sounds interesting."

"Except for the raincoat."

There was a long pause, and then he said, "Y'know Mitch, I'm not sure what's happening to me. Take last night for example. With so much T & A around, the sports cars were secondary, but instead of hitting on the babes I went home and hit the rack... and like I said, I went to the show just in case you showed up." He paused for a few seconds. "I wanted you to show."

"That's... sweet. Thanks for thinking of me. Now I'm going to try to wake up the sleeping nymph."

"Good luck," he said and disconnected.

Santiago went to the guest room and opened the door. She stood for a moment and watched her sister's face. It was calm and peaceful. "Flashing a bit of flesh seems to run in the family." The sheet moved with Jill's breathing. "I'll let you sleep just a little longer."

Around 10:00 Jill came out of the bedroom wearing a man's dress shirt. "I found this in the closet," she said with a thick, harsh voice.

"It looks good on you. How're you feeling?"

"Aspirin," Jill groaned with a whiskey edge. "That was a party." She shook her head, then put her hands over her temples. "Bad mistake. Don't do that, head." She blinked her bloodshot eyes and yawned. "Coffee?" she pleaded and sat down at the table.

"You lost something last night."

"My dignity," Jill said with a giggle.

"That too, but I was thinking of your clothes."

"Only a thong bikini and top. My clothes are still in the locker at the Center, or maybe in the lost and found." Jill smiled without moving her head.

"Whose raincoat?"

"The promoter's."

"Does he have a name?"

"Not that I remember, but it was fun."

"Ever thought of finding a guy interested in more than your body? Maybe one with a name?"

"Is there such a thing? You know the business I'm in," said Jill.

"I'm sure there is. Frankly it's taking me just as long to make sure."

Jill said, "My head hurts, but didn't I say something yesterday about working your partner in a way he's not accustomed to? I always remember the guys wanting to jump your bones. You ignored them and I was jealous." Jill said.

"You were fourteen, and yes, I think I have the right guy in mind."

The doorbell rang. Santiago opened it to greet Jason and handed over the car keys while he checked her over and then strained to get a peek at Jill.

"I'll be done shortly," he said waving the keys as she closed the door.

Jill said, "Jason is a hunk."

"Chance, remember? We talked about this when you got here."

"That's right." Jill shook her head, carefully. "But Jason's definitely a hunk."

"He's a nice guy. We've had our moments. We're really good friends. He offered to wash the car for me today."

"Nothing serious with him?"

"Just the occasional rebound. Like I said, I think Chance is the one." Santiago's face became flush. "We're partners, so we work together and I know he likes me. I could go for him but he's still carrying some baggage from his first marriage and he's had an eye for the ladies second only to our dad. I think he's getting better though." She smiled and said in a near whisper, "He's the genuine article."

"Um... sounds serious," said Jill.

"Well, it might be only one-sided and the department doesn't like couples working together."

"Transfer." Jill smiled, almost forgetting her throbbing head.

"Actually, I'm thinking about a career change... maybe even going private. I like what I'm doing, but I'd rather pick and choose my clients."

"Does Chance know how you feel about him?"

"I think so." She blushed. "We're awkward right now, like feeling our way along. It's hard to explain. Maybe it's like when we had crushes on guys as teens. You know, how do you tell 'em?"

Jill smiled. "Telling him how you feel shouldn't be a problem, but talking about leaving your career, that's different. I always thought homicide was your thing?"

"As far as police work goes, but the real money is in infidelity and business. I'm sure the two go hand in hand. Look at your auto show. You don't even remember who you were with last night, but I'd bet Mr. Lucky has a wife at home, maybe a sales campaign under wraps, and a deal to short circuit the competition—all valuable and sensitive information."

"Probably." Jill stood up. "My head is clearing. I'm going to clean up and go find my clothes." She started toward the guest bathroom.

"One other thing, Sis—if I'm gone when you get back go ahead and use the apartment. The suspect we're looking for may well be in another part of the state and I could be gone in a moment's notice."

Jill laughed. "Business trip with Chance, eh? Such a deal." Then she headed down the hallway.

Santiago watched her sister disappear through the bathroom door. *Could I give up my career for Chance? Putting people like Gunn away is important. Blackmail and industrial espionage are big bucks. That would be a career change to say the least and not a conflict with Chance's career.* She sighed. *But first we nail Gunn.*

* * * * *

"Damn! Another newscast about that son of a bitch! Don't they know what they're doing to these kids?" Linda Gunn's father pointed toward the bedroom door.

"They don't care, Dad. Let's just get 'em packed and on their way," she said. She rubbed her lips with the tips of her fingers. "Don't get clammy," she mumbled. "Get the kids off. Maybe one drink before heading to Forks."

"What'd y'say?"

"Nothing, Dad."

Her mother said, "Linda, the bags are in the car. We're ready but I don't like this. I don't understand why you want to talk to him."

"It's just something I have to do, mom."

Her father's voice was firm, gruff. "You ought to call the cops, that's what."

"Please, let me handle this. He's got all of our money. Maybe he did kill two people, but I want him to give up on his own for the kid's sake."

"The man's crazy or he wouldn't be in this position," her father said. "Claire, fetch the boys and let's get going." He looked at his daughter. "You're our only child. We love you, and we don't want anything bad to happen to you. Please reconsider."

"I have, Dad, over and over. The kids are going to need closure. We all are. I think he'll come in for me."

"You're sure he's in Forks?"

"Yes, either there or at La Push. He might even be camping on the beaches like in the old days. I hope not. It'll be harder to find him."

"What about the police?" her mother said.

Linda smiled. "They're poking around Chattaroy and Lake Sacheen."

"Even after his car was found in Port Angeles?" her father said.

"Yes." Linda Gunn hung her head like a naughty child. "I sort of helped them along."

"I don't like it," her father said.

"I know, but sometimes there are things we just have to do. This is one of those times."

"Well, be careful. Your father and I want to see a healthy you in a few days, and so do the boys."

"I know. I'll be fine." She looked up as the boys entered the living room. Her eyes welled. Another shiver ran down her spine. *Knees, don't buckle... please.* She motioned to the boys. "Come here." She gathered them into her arms. "Grandma and Grandpa are taking you to their house. We're going to stay with them for a little while."

"Why aren't you coming with us?" the older boy said.

"I have business to take care of then I'll join the four of you... probably in a couple of days." She embraced each boy, the youngest first. "Remember, I love you both very much. Now mind your grandparents."

"Yes, Mom," they both said.

The group walked toward the doorway. Linda's oldest son turned and looked back. "Will we ever get to see Daddy again?"

"I don't know, Sweetheart." She turned away as her eyes flooded. Her mother reached out to comfort her while Grandpa opened the door and led the boys out. She sobbed for a moment. "I'll be all right, Mom."

"I know. Here, take this," she said, pressing some bills into her daughter's hand. "It's not much but it'll get you to Forks and Spokane."

Linda Gunn took the five fifty dollar bills. "Thank you." She rolled her eyes. "It's all so hard."

"Just leave the sauce alone. Do what you have to do and come home." She stepped back from her daughter. "Your father's right. Trevor's a bum and he's crazy.

Think again before going to Forks. The police would be more than happy to make the arrest."

"I know, but I just don't want anyone else hurt. Maybe someday you and the boys will understand. Trev needs to surrender, not just get caught."

The two women hugged.

"Well, we're off." Tears were in her mother's eyes. She smiled. "It's musty in here, Linda."

"It won't be for long." She stepped toward her mother. "I love you, Mom. Now go before I fall apart completely." They hugged. "I'll call you tonight."

Linda Gunn watched her mother walk to the car, stepped out the door and waved. Two little hands from inside the dusty sedan waved back.

The older woman approached the car and got in. She sniffed as she pulled the door shut, rolled the window down and gave a final wave. "Greenwood smelled better last year. I don't like this business." She looked toward the back seat. "Okay kids, we're off." She looked at her husband as a tear ran down her left cheek.

CHAPTER 18

Jill returned to her sister's apartment around 1:30 in the afternoon. She wandered down the hallway and found Mitch packing. "Isn't that Jason washing your car? I thought he was going to do it earlier when he picked up the keys?"

"One and the same. He was called into the store for something."

Jill said, "Well that explains your micro shorts and crop top," and gave her sister an expectant glance. "He *is* gorgeous." She licked her lips. "Nice buns."

"Yes he is, but I'm just trying to take advantage of a Seattle spring day. You know 75 today and 40 with drizzle to follow," she said. "And maybe just a little teasing on the side."

Jill's smile lit up the room. "Does he always take such good care of you?"

"He's just a close friend. He lives across the way. You already know that." She continued to pack without looking up.

"I can see why he's close," Jill said.

"It's not romance."

"I was thinking physical. Your braless look isn't designed to discourage even if he's not Chance."

"Flirtation runs in the family, remember?"

"He's too good looking to just ignore," Jill said with a laugh.

"I'm sure he would let you help if you went over there." She finished packing and closed the suitcase. "Like I said last night, we've had our moments, but he's still trolling."

"Full-time friends, part-time lovers?" Jill said.

"Something like that, sort of."

"You think that's possible?" said Jill licking her lips.

"I know it is. You'd never believe the scenarios I've been working on with my current case. By the way, did you find your clothes?"

"No. There's another event going on today. One of the security guys said I might be able to find them at the lost and found tomorrow. He even offered to accompany me." She laughed. "Unfortunately I have to leave on a 6:40 flight tonight to San Francisco."

"Want me to check tomorrow or will the guard do it for you?" They both laughed.

"Sure, if you're around." Jill nodded toward her sister's travel bag. "If I don't find 'em it's no big deal. I made a lot of money on this trip."

"Why the early flight?"

"I'm doing a swimsuit shoot on Alcatraz at noon tomorrow. Time will be tight." She looked at her sister's bag again. "Where are you going?"

"Don't know yet. I'm betting on the coast unless someone finds Gunn elsewhere."

"Does Jason know?"

Santiago gave her a mischievous glance. "Jason doesn't need to know. It's the case we're on. Fact is, he's aware of the possibility. He takes care of my newspaper if I'm gone."

"Well, you said Chance was the one. Maybe this is your chance at Chance." Jill laughed.

"My chance at Chance... that has a nice ring to it. Seriously, we might get sent to Forks."

"The coast? Sounds romantic."

"We have a lead, but it might not go anywhere. Right now it depends on the suspect's wife." Mitch looked at her bag. "If we don't go, what will I do with this?"

"I'm sure you'll think of something and I'll bet you have some sexy nightwear packed just in case."

"Like you said, this might be my chance."

"You really ought to just tell him how you feel," Jill said.

"Didn't we talk about this yesterday?"

"Yes."

"Enough said then. You better call for a shuttle to Sea-Tac. I might not be around. You'll find a number in the book by the phone." Mitch closed the travel bag.

"Thanks."

"How 'bout I take you to lunch?" she said when Jill returned from making the call.

"How 'bout we order in pizza? That way we can just gab the time away," Jill said.

"I like that idea."

The phone interrupted the sister's chatter. Mitch caught it on the second ring. "Santiago."

"Are you packed?" Chance said.

"Yes."

"Good, the Spokane visitors just left Linda Gunn's with the kids. Whatever's going to happen shouldn't be long in coming."

"I'm here with Jill. Where do you want to meet?"

"Visit with Jill. I'll pick you up when we have something. Zinc and Strickland will keep me posted."

* * * * *

The Washington State Ferries Terminal at Pier 52 on Alaska Way is a large facility featuring several holding lanes for cross-water routes to Bainbridge Island, Vashon Island and Bremerton. It surprised Linda Gunn to find the lanes less than half-full on a nice spring mid-afternoon Sunday. "I'll make the 2:40 run," she said with a sigh. She looked around the parking-lot sized Colman Dock. "Probably not more than eighty cars. I wish this was a pleasure trip."

Two kids were bouncing around in the backseat of a van near her car. Inner tubes and a tent were lashed to the roof rack. *Why didn't we have that, Trev? Our kids deserved a lot more than we gave 'em.* She checked her purse and touched the unopened bottle of bourbon, then looked at her hand. "Quit shaking."

She rolled down the driver's window, allowing fresh salt air into the car and breathed deeply. Seagulls squawked as they filled the sky over the dock. *You guys must be getting lunch from the tourists today. You're so free, why not me?*

A teenage boy approached the open window carrying several Sunday papers. He bent down to face her. "Paper, lady?"

"No thank you." She looked away and he moved along. A young girl carrying another armload of papers passed along the passenger side stopping at each driver's window in the next lane over. "Enterprising... I like that."

A car horn sounded and two couples waved at each other and shared big smiles. A heavyset woman walked past her carrying two large takeout bags. *I can almost taste the fries.* She inhaled deeply and licked her lips.

A middle-aged man walked forward past the passenger side slowly, looking all around. He was dressed in rumpled slacks and a tweed blazer. A blue dress shirt was holding his girth. He paused for a moment, then moved on. "You look familiar but I can't place you. I hope you're not looking for an eatery," she said watching him continue past three or four cars before abruptly turning around. Eventually he slipped into the passenger seat of a car four spaces behind her.

Linda's hands continued to shake as she opened a highway map. Sweat dripped from her forehead onto the map. She traced 101 around Lake Crescent and into Forks. *Two hours... maybe three.* She reached again for the bottle in her purse, then withdrew. "Not today, Linda... not today."

Engines started, horns honked and people were running about. "Finally," she said as a traffic controller motioned her forward. Within a few minutes she had boarded, parked and looked around the car deck. She opened the door and went to the observation deck stairwell. On reaching the upper deck she went to the stern and looked at Seattle's slowly receding skyline.

Hundreds of small pleasure boats were in the bay. The sun reflected off the rich green surface of the water. A steady breeze bathed her face and the sweat dried. Several cargo vessels came into view as the ferry passed Harbor Island, crossing Elliott Bay. Alki Beach passed in the distance, its patrons appearing as tiny particles.

Several passengers were roaming the deck area, enjoying the unusually nice weather. Most were carrying coffee cups, even the portly man from the dock. *I wonder what it's like to commute in the winter? I'd bet it's wet and cold out here.* She walked toward the hatch. *They probably stand inside and drink coffee.*

She stopped walking the deck when some large pieces of driftwood came into view. "Hope the speedboats don't hit those," she said to a man by the rail, a shudder running up her back. She stretched her arms above her head, hands out.

A mother passed behind her, walking fast. "Casey... Casey! Take your sister's hand and come here. You know you're not supposed to run on the deck."

She turned to watch the young family. *You're a lucky lady. Your kids don't have a worry in the world.* The boy took his sister's hand and walked back to his mother, eyes sparkling and a smile on his face. Her eyes welled. *I want my kids to smile again. Children need to smile.*

The docking horn sounded as the ferry approached its birth. The passengers quickly returned to their cars.

"That was a fast fifty minutes," she said to another passenger as they made their way toward the car deck. *The rest of my drive will be a cakewalk.* She watched the heavyset man get back in his car. *Apparently the driver never got out.*

The boat shuddered as its powerful engines shifted into reverse just as she reached her car and got in. She looked into the review mirror. "It was sex, Trev. That's what brought us together. That's why we got married. Carnal lust as powerful as the engines of this boat and nothing more."

Three hours later she arrived in Forks and found lodging at Cutter's Lodge, an old motel on the southern edge of town near the airport. After checking in she went to her room and found the phone book. Thumbing through the Yellow Pages she sat back on the bed and looked at the ceiling. "My God, I didn't realize how many places there are to stay around here," she said.

She found an entry for the La Push Resort. "You're the only listing for a motel in La Push so I'll try you first." She dialed but when the resort office answered she quickly hung up. "Why bother? He isn't using his own name." She picked up her purse and headed for the door. *It's been years since we were at La Push. I'll check with the desk. Maybe I'll get lucky.*

Linda Gunn covered the twelve miles of two-lane road from Forks to La Push in good time following the directions of the desk clerk. Occasionally she saw a camper or a small group of people on the edge of the road. When she passed the 3rd Beach parking lot there were a few cars but no people. Within minutes she passed the 2nd Beach lot with the same results, except for a few hikers milling about. She chuckled. "Of course," she said looking into the rearview mirror, "The hike to 3rd Beach is quite a bit longer than the hike to 2nd Beach. If you're here, you'll be at 1st Beach and the motel. You never were an outdoorsman."

As she covered the last few miles the trees of the rain forest became dense, appearing almost solid.

The final bend in the road before entering the village revealed James Island looming out of the Pacific surrounded by cold blue water and white surf breaking against the rocks. Clouds provided a patchwork background. She slowed for a brief moment. "I remember coming here years ago, Trev. Life was different then."

She pulled into the resort parking lot. It was quiet, and very few people or cars were present. Two large buildings were side-by-side, one newer than the other, both showing the impact of ocean air. To her left were a few old cabins, some A-frames and newer units she didn't recall from prior visits. She went into the office.

"May I help you?" asked the young man behind the counter.

"Do you have any rooms available?" She looked back at the two buildings across the parking lot.

"Several. One of the buildings is still closed for painting. We're trying to get ready for the season in a few weeks. The other one has several vacancies."

"Really?" She looked back across the lot again. "I stayed here several years ago. It would be fun to stay in the same room. Which ones are vacant?"

"As of today all except 203. The weekend crowd, small as it was, has already headed home."

"You say 203 is taken?" She cast her eyes downward.

"Yes Ma'am, some writer guy." He paused and looked around. "I mean, the room's taken. You know, we can't give out information. How about another room?"

"203 is my old room. I'll have to think about a different room. Perhaps I'll walk down to the beach. I looked so forward to revisiting a place with so many good memories."

"Of course," he said motioning toward the door. "No rush. The rooms are all clean and ready to occupy."

"Thank you. I'll let you know shortly." She left the office and walked toward the beach trail, looking at the building as she passed. A rush of energy surged through her. "There's only one way to find out if you're the man in 203."

* * * * *

Santiago and Stewart arrived in Forks around 6:00 p.m. after Zinc had called in from the Bremerton Ferry dock. They had first made a brief stop in Port Angeles to talk with the officers who'd found Gunn's Mustang. When registering at the Big Tree Inn they were surprised the department had booked them into adjoining rooms. Santiago took 214, Stewart 216.

"This could be an interesting setup," she said. "Do you suppose Captain James was thinking of his secretary when he made the reservation?"

They both laughed. He said, "Who said stakeouts are boring?"

"I can hardly wait for Zinc and Strickland's reaction to our being here together," Stewart said. "I think one of them is the gift giver."

"You mean the card, pictures, tassels?"

"That's what I mean. Zinc asked the other day whether you're a good cop." Stewart paused. "I told James."

"Well," she placed a hand on her chin, "Zinc strikes me as the type that'd spend a lot of time in strip clubs. What'd James say?"

"He'll look into it."

"Will he?"

"He's good to his word. He sees the incident as sexual harassment. If it's them, or one of them, he'll nail him. The only question will be how it's handled," Stewart said.

"I don't care how. I just want whoever it is to knock it off."

"Guess I'd better call and find out where they are. We'll have to take over the stakeout soon. They've got to be beat." He retrieved his cell phone.

"I'll open a window, get a little breeze in here," she said watching Stewart. "Did you notice how good the air smelled driving along the Straits?"

"Hard to miss. You'd love Kalaloch. Some of the cabins are on a bluff overlooking the Pacific...

tremendous view." He held the phone, spoke in a quiet voice, listened for a long moment, then broke the connection. He looked at Santiago. A confused look filled his face.

"What's wrong?" she said.

"They don't know Linda's whereabouts. One of 'em went for coffee and the other fell asleep. When she left they didn't see her go. Damn, it's just like everything else in this case."

"We'd better go relieve 'em," she said and glanced at her overnight bag.

"You got that right."

When Santiago and Stewart drove into the parking lot of Cutter's Lodge, the standard issue Seattle Police unmarked cruiser was easy to spot. Its two occupants didn't pay much attention to the '98 Explorer until Stewart opened the driver's window and waved.

"How come you're driving that?" Zinc said.

"Didn't want to lose another hour going downtown. I just picked Mitch up and headed for Edmonds. Otherwise you wouldn't see us 'til 7:30, maybe 8:00. What's Linda driving?"

"Old Honda beater, dirty burgundy." Zinc gave Stewart the license number.

"Who picked up the kids?" Stewart said.

"An older couple. The car's registered to her parents in Spokane," said Zinc.

"Figures," Santiago said leaning forward so she could see into the cruiser. She gave Zinc a long look, then shifted her weight. "So what happened here?"

"I went for coffee across the highway to the convenience store." Zinc nodded toward the road. "Only took a couple of minutes. When I came back Strickland had dozed off—just for a couple of minutes you understand—and the bitch was gone."

"Has she checked out?" Stewart said.

"No," Strickland said, "and she's using her own name."

"So you don't think she made you?" Santiago said.

"No." Zinc became quiet and rubbed his eyes. "I think something from the trees around here is bothering me. My eyes are itching and burning."

Stewart said, "Why don't you two go get some rest? James booked rooms for you at Big Tree, about a mile up the road. We'll take it from here."

"Thanks, Chance." Then in a quiet whisper Zinc asked, "Do *you* have a room?"

"I heard that, Zinc," Santiago said. "We each have a room." She paused and looked straight into his face. "And they're adjoining."

Strickland started to cough and the tired pair drove off.

"What'd you tell him that for?" Stewart said.

"Why not? They'll ask the clerk anyway. Besides, if it is one of them I'd say we just got a break. I can just hear Zinc now."

"Well, I hope we get another break on Gunn... either one of 'em. For now we wait." Stewart leaned back in his seat.

"While we wait we'd better think about our report to James. Gunn's Mustang does have a ding on the right front fender with yellow paint from somewhere. We have a sample in an evidence bag. It could match the sample from the post."

"Sounds like a good start. We'll get the scraping to the lab when we get back. Right now I'm seriously concerned that Linda Gunn is in way too deep."

"I agree; she's in danger," Santiago said.

"The guy's killed two people already. I just don't like the way this is playing out."

"I know what you mean. The guys in Port Angeles didn't have much to offer either," she said.

"They had enough. We know he's dressed down, altering his appearance, trying to blend in with a backwoods logger look. I was surprised he didn't just dump his good clothes rather than give 'em to a bum. The car didn't yield anything to PA's finest, either."

"Well, I still think he's headed for Canada. The temporary delays at the border will just slow him down a little."

"Why?" he asked.

"Why else abandon the car in Port Angeles? It has different plates, and he has enough money to settle in for a while. Plus the U.S. and Canada are at odds over extraditing criminals in capital cases."

"Maybe the border slowdown did change his mind?"

"Maybe temporarily," she said. "And maybe that's why he had a Victoria Ferry time schedule written on a scrap of paper. If he changed his mind, he left that scribble as a clue to throw us off track for now, make us think he's already in Canada."

Stewart looked across the highway. "How 'bout one of us going over there and bringing something back for a non-romantic dinner?"

She grinned. "You won't fall asleep?"

"Not even a wink. Dinner with you anytime anywhere is a treat, no sleep."

"I'll go. I just hope Linda's okay wherever she is."

"You and me both. We don't need three victims."

* * * * *

A light knock came on the door. "You're not getting me with the same ploy twice, Jimmy." Gunn stood to one side and opened it slowly. The late afternoon sun against the patchy clouds framed a head. He strained for a moment to see who it was, then opened it wide as nausea rumbled through his stomach. "Linda. How did you find me?"

She looked into his battered, stubble-covered face, covered with ugly yellow and purple bruises. She gasped slightly. "Hello, Trevor." She walked in without waiting for an invite. "You look like hell."

"Thank you. I feel like hell. It's a long story. Why are you here?"

She walked to the table and sat down on one of the wooden chairs. "Aren't you going to offer a lady a cup of coffee?"

"Of course. I don't have anything stronger," he said, dripping sarcasm. He closed the door and walked into the kitchen area. "So how did you find me?"

"Remember those stories you took great pains in telling us about the La Push of your youth when we visited here?" She shrugged. "When the police found the car in Port Angeles it seemed reasonable to look out here."

"Do the police know you're here?"

"No, but your car will be a clue. I'm sure they'll figure it out."

"I've got to get moving. It won't take them long." He glanced at the door.

"Probably not, but I'm sure you have a day or two. They'll stop in Port Angeles to make inquiries and check the Mustang." She tapped the table. "Coffee?"

"I left it near the Victoria Ferry terminal. I hope they'll think I'm in Canada." He poured a cup of coffee and handed it to her.

"Thank you." She sipped the coffee. "Don't you want to know where the kids are, how they're doing?"

"I figure they must be with your parents since you're here. What I don't understand is why the visit."

"I want two things for our boys, Trev. I know you're wanted for killing two people and you're running away. But please, think what you're doing to our kids. They'll grow up knowing their daddy did bad things."

"It's a little late to worry about that."

"But you could do the right thing, give yourself up, give the boys something they can be proud of when they think of you."

"Proud because daddy's in jail or worse?"

"No, proud because after you did those bad things you realized it was wrong and didn't want to live like a fugitive until they catch up with you."

"You said two things for the boys."

"Money, Trev. You cleaned us out. I figure you have close to $16,000.00. We have nothing. I don't even have a job prospect."

"I need the money, Linda. I'm a fugitive, remember?"

She nodded, looked at the floor, then looked back up at him. "You killed that hobo, didn't you?" She watched his eyes. Fluid was seeping from his split lip. The yellow bruising gave his face a garish appearance in the stubble of his beard.

"It was an accident. I hit him, but he fell and hit his head."

"What were you doing at Golden Gardens?"

"I was with a woman."

"Was it Hailey Cashland?"

"No. It was another student."

"How many were there?"

"I didn't keep count."

"But why? Just more notches on your jockstrap?"

"What do you mean, why? You know why. You're a drunken, uncreative suburban mother. I need excitement, adventure, the chase... someone younger."

Shaking her head she looked at her husband. "I never even suspected other women."

"That's because you're a fool. Do you think seasonal sex is normal? Of course you were always wasted."

Her eyes welled. "You're a cruel man. Why did you stay married to me if I'm so useless and sexless?"

"Tenure, my dear. Once I had it you were history." He swallowed and caught his breath. "I didn't need a messy divorce to deal with as part of my portfolio."

"And now *you're* history, in my book and the public's. I need the money for the kids."

"The kids!" he shouted. "The kids be damned! They're nothing but the product of missed abortions. I never wanted them. You were a good lay at the time. That's all."

She looked at Gunn with an expressionless face. "I felt for a long time you didn't really love me. I just didn't want to admit it."

"Love is a four letter word. We grew apart a long time ago." He shook his head. "I'm not sure I ever loved you."

"What a fool I was. I loved you deeply, even after the police came. I defended you to her... to them."

"You defended your image of our family."

Linda Gunn paused and looked at the man realizing for the first time he was a complete stranger. She pushed the coffee cup away. "Why did you kill the teacher?" she asked in a quiet voice.

"She wanted to marry me. She wanted me to file for divorce right now, while the review committee was working."

"People get divorces all the time, even members of college staffs."

"Not to marry a student. I couldn't take the chance, not after so many failures."

"But to kill her?"

"She threatened me. She said she'd go public. Imagine a single teacher at one of the most prestigious prep academies in the country exposing me. I lost my head. She was in the bathtub."

"You drowned her?"

"Yes." The muscles in his face contracted and his hands began to shake. Tears formed in his eyes. "She really loved me, but she scared me. I couldn't deal with the threat... another time of being passed over...." His voice trailed off.

"You're sick, Trev! God, you killed a woman who was deeply in love with you!" She caught her breath. "You killed *two* loves. I loved you, was *devoted* to you. I don't know what made me drink. Maybe I knew about the other women and just didn't want to admit to myself."

Gunn flashed his toothpaste smile. "Hey, you win some, you lose some. Your parents will help you. Women like you always find a meal ticket."

"You uncaring bastard! We need the money!"

"Not a chance. I need it more than you do. It's hard to get work with *fugitive* on the job application."

A light knock came at the door then it slowly opened. "Clint?"

Linda looked up. Gunn shot a glance to the door.

Gemma entered just a few steps. She looked at Gunn. "I came to see how you're doing."

"I'm fine, but thank you for checking." He smiled at the woman. "I'll see you later."

"Clint?" Linda said. "Since when? Honey, he's no more a Clint than you are. His name is Trevor—"

"Smith!" he shouted.

"And he's my husband for the time being."

Gemma looked at Gunn. Her lips trembled.

"Come back in an hour and you can have him." Linda looked at her husband with disdain. "I guarantee you don't really want him."

"That's enough, Linda. She's not involved." He looked at Gemma. "Please go. I'll explain later," he said.

"There's no later. My brother was right." She turned to leave, the sound of muffled sobs filling the doorway. "It's all a lie," she murmured without looking back. "It's all a lie." She closed the door.

"Another conquest?" Linda said.

"No." He walked to the window. "Why don't you leave?"

"You don't want to kill me too?"

"No, I'm not a murderer. They were accidents, reactions."

"Give me the money and I'm gone," said Linda. "That girl doesn't know who you are, only that she met your wife."

"You won't tell the police?"

"They'll find you without me. I'm no threat and you know it. From the looks of your face the threat is much more immediate. Her brother?"

"We've met." He walked to the dresser, pulled one of the drawers open and looked at the contents. Turning, he walked slowly back to the table. *You need to be seen leaving here now that Gemma saw you.*

"Trevor, I came here for the kids. I came here because they deserve better than we've given them. Our lives are a mess, but we can do something for them."

"You're right. I need to get the money." *I need your car.*

"Where is it?"

"Here, in La Push. I can't get it 'til morning." He looked at the bed. "You could spend the night?"

"I don't think so." She shook her head. "There's too much garbage between us."

"You want the money?"

"For the boys."

"If the police find me first, they'll impound it."

"They won't find you that fast."

"If you won't stay the night, pick me up in the morning, early. We'll go from here."

"Done," she said. "I'll be back around 8:00."

"Make that 7:00."

"7:00 then."

She walked to the door.

"I'll walk you down," he said opening the door. "Shit."

Jimmy Rainwater was standing at the head of the stairs.

"Goin' somewhere white man?" he said.

"Outta here, to the parking lot." Adrenaline surged through Gunn's body. "I thought I'd walk the lady to her car."

"Not so fast." Rainwater held up his right hand.

"I don't want any trouble. Neither do you." Gunn's voice quivered.

Gemma's voice came from behind her brother. "Jimmy, let him go. He's not worth it."

"Gemma?" Jimmy said.

"He needs to answer to her." Gemma pointed at Linda Gunn, now stepping out of the doorway. "She's his wife."

Jimmy glared at Gunn. "Are you leaving?"

"Tomorrow morning."

"Don't come back." Jimmy Rainwater turned, put his arm around Gemma and walked away.

Gunn took Linda tightly by the arm. "Come on. I need to stretch my legs."

Just as they reached the bottom of the stairs a car pulled into the parking place in front of the room 103, just below Gunn's. The doors flew open and young voices filled the night air. A young family emptied out. The woman held a key in her hand and searched the door numbers. The man handed small bags to each of the children and pointed toward the woman who was now opening a door.

The Gunns watched the activity without a word. The momentary tight grip Gunn had placed on his wife's arm relaxed. "Sorry, I didn't mean to hurt you," he said.

"Do you really want to live with this much tension for the rest of your life?" she said as they approached the Honda.

"No, not really. It'll get better in time."

She opened the door and looked into his face. "I feel like I really never knew you, but I still feel something. Trev, tonight give some thought to turning yourself in." She looked at the ground. "It would be good for the boys."

"It's all so crazy. Life in prison, maybe even the death penalty?"

"Maybe manslaughter, the opportunity to be free someday. Think about it." She started to reach out in an embrace then withdrew her arms. "I'll be here in the morning. If the cops aren't in Port Angeles they're probably on a wild goose chase in eastern Washington," she said with a smile. "A bum steer."

He turned and walked back up the stairs as she left the resort. *Too bad so many people saw you here today, Linda.* He looked around and saw Gemma's brother still watching. *Stay home, Jimmy.*

CHAPTER 19

"Gets cold out here at night, doesn't it?" she said.

Stewart took a sip of tepid coffee. "We're on the coast, Mitch."

"We could be in our room... our adjoining rooms."

He smiled at her. "Yes, we could."

The Explorer smelled of cooking oil and pizza. Between the detectives sat a flat box containing the half-eaten remains and several dirty napkins.

"I've been thinking about it, and I think you're right," she said.

"About what?"

"Zinc and Strickland. I'll bet they're the ones bugging me. I doubt any woman ever enjoyed being interviewed by them. Not just interrogated, but even interviewed."

"I think so, too."

"They can't be after sex. That won't happen. I doubt either one of 'em could get it up anyway."

"Never count an old guy out. Don't forget those little blue pills. I'd use 'em before I'd give it up."

"I think they're old school. Women don't belong carrying badges, something like that."

"So they try to force you out?"

"Could be, or perhaps just some latent hazing. I don't know."

"And you won't let 'em."

"If I decide to leave, it'll be on my terms, not theirs."

Stewart looked at her for a long moment. An old car pulled into the lot and parked. They watched the driver get out.

"Well, well, looks like our heroine has arrived home for the night," he said.

"I wonder where she's been?" Santiago said.

"Let's go find out."

Linda Gunn was already inside the door by the time Santiago and Stewart were out of the Explorer. She snapped a light on and closed the door. They got out of the truck, took body armor out of a metal lock box in the bed, put them on and went to the door. They paused for a moment and listened.

Stewart whispered, "No voices."

He scanned the parking lot, then nodded to his partner and she knocked on the door. Both officers waited, guns drawn, holding their breath.

A woman called out, "Who's there?"

"Detectives Stewart and Santiago, Mrs. Gunn. Open the door, now please," he said.

The door opened slowly. Linda Gunn's eyes fixed on the drawn weapons. Santiago pushed the door open and darted past her. Stewart quickly followed. Linda Gunn closed the door.

Santiago looked at Linda Gunn through squinted eyes. "Where is he?"

"Somewhere getting our money."

Stewart said, "So you saw him?"

She walked into the room and sat down on the bed. "Yes." She motioned toward the two chairs. "I was lucky to find him. I guess you figured out he'd be here too."

The detectives remained standing. Santiago said, "We have our ways."

She smiled at Stewart. "He's considering turning himself in tomorrow."

"Really?" they said almost in unison.

Santiago said, "Why the change of heart?"

"He's frightened. He's been knocked around. Every time someone comes near him he gets really tense, jumpy."

Stewart said, "That doesn't sound like someone who's ready to give up."

"He's also thinking of the boys."

Stewart said, "He's killed two people, Linda. He's dangerous."

"Confused and scared, yes. He's not dangerous, Detective Stewart."

"Well, I disagree with you. In fact, we're both concerned about you, your personal safety. Tell us where he is and we'll arrest him," Stewart said.

"I can't, but I'll bring him to you tomorrow morning. If there's even the possibility he's as dangerous as you say I'd rather you'd arrest him here, not down there. A young family is staying in the room beneath him."

"Is he armed?" Santiago said looking out the rear window.

"I don't know. I doubt it. Trev doesn't know anything about guns or weapons."

Stewart hadn't taken his eyes off the woman. "What time are you meeting him tomorrow?"

"Around 8:30."

"Where?" Stewart asked.

"I can't tell you"

Santiago said, "You mean you won't tell us?"

"That is correct."

Santiago walked over and stood by the chairs. "You say there's a family near him?"

"Yes." Linda Gunn sat up straight on the edge of the bed. "Why don't you wait here for us? I'll tell him I have to get my stuff before heading to Seattle. He'll believe me. I'm always forgetting things. Besides, this place is empty except for me as far as I know."

Stewart said, "Will he be driving?"

"No, I don't think he can. He has an injured leg and it's quite painful for him to move."

"How did he get hurt?" Santiago said.

"He met the angry brother of a young Indian woman he was trying to seduce."

Santiago looked at Stewart, then back at Linda. "We could follow her to him and make the arrest away from where he's staying, away from the family or here."

"True," he said, giving his partner a questioning look. He turned to Linda. "We'd be with you the whole time, tailing you."

"Just make sure he doesn't see you until the last moment. If he panics, he may try to run. I don't want anyone else hurt. I told him it would be best for the boys if he surrenders," Linda Gunn said.

"That is the way you want it?" Stewart said.

"Whether he agrees to give up or not, his arrest must take place somewhere safe," Linda said.

"Tomorrow morning then, at 8:00," Santiago said.

"I won't leave until you're here."

Stewart said, "Deal, but if things go wrong, Mrs. Gunn, you could be facing some serious charges. Are you sure you won't reconsider?"

"Nothing will go wrong. Please, trust me. Is there anything else?"

"No. We'll be here at 7:30. Do you have any other questions, Chance?"

"No, not if Mrs. Gunn won't reconsider."

"It has to be my way," Linda Gunn said.

"Until morning, then," Stewart said.

Walking back to the Explorer Stewart spoke softly. "We should have arrested her for obstruction, Mitch."

"Then we wouldn't get as close. When will she try to reach him? Possibly tonight now that we've found her, or in the morning, probably before we are expected to arrive, right?"

"I'd bet on the morning and I'm convinced he's at the coast now. She kept saying 'down' when she mentioned going to him. Folks around here go down to the coast."

* * * * *

Santiago and Stewart watched Linda Gunn's hotel room from the Explorer after replacing their body armor with warm coats.

"Do you buy her intentions?" Stewart said.

"Wanting the money? Yes. Wanting him to give up? Yes. Do I think she leveled with us about the details? No. She knows where he is but she won't tell us. She wants at him first," Santiago said.

"Probably to get the money. And she's trying to steer the investigation. Why else give us the false lead to eastern Washington? Why did she forget about his uncle in Forks?" he said.

Santiago looked at the darkened office window. "Maybe surrender isn't actually something he's considering, but just something she wants him to do. She was definitely surprised to see us. Unfortunately she doesn't realize how much danger she's putting herself in."

"Maybe it's a mother instinct? Could be she still loves him in some perverse way. She might even think he still loves her. I'm beginning to think this pair is a matched set," he said.

"I don't like it," said Santiago. "Let's talk to the manager and see if he has any idea of where she went this evening."

They walked to the dark motel office and rang the night buzzer. A man in worn blue jeans and a flannel shirt came to the door after turning on the office lights.

"Hi folks, need a room?"

Stewart flashed his identification while introducing himself and Santiago. The man stepped back. "Come in. What can I do for you, officers?"

"We're here about Mrs. Gunn. After checking in today she went someplace. We're trying to verify where?"

"This is important, huh?"

"Yes," Santiago said.

"Is she a criminal?"

"No," Stewart said, "but your cooperation would be much appreciated. Do you have any idea of where she went?"

"I always cooperate with the authorities. Many years ago I was a reserve of the Forks Police."

"I'm sure you can appreciate how important details can be then," said Santiago.

"I do. She made a couple of phone calls, then came in here asking for directions to La Push. Said she hadn't been there in years and had forgotten the way. Of course, back then the road wasn't as well marked or maintained as it is now."

"La Push," Stewart said.

"She wanted to go there. Said she was goin' to a motel to visit a friend."

"Which motel?" Santiago said.

"There's only one, La Push Resort. The Quileute's own and operate it. They don't let any competition on the reservation."

"You're sure?" Stewart said.

"About the resort? Yes."

"About her going there. Do you have a record of her calls?" Santiago took out her note pad.

"Sure thing. All calls come through our system for billing purposes. Let me get a list of numbers." The man stepped to a back counter and returned a moment later.

"Here," he said, pointing to the paper with two numbers printed on it, "that's the resort. If her friend is out there, that's the only lodging available other than an RV park or campsites."

"And the other number?"

"Area code 509 is eastern Washington."

"You've been most helpful," Santiago said while walking over to a wall map of the Olympic Peninsula. She ran a finger along a curving road leading into the village and a Coast Guard Station. "Have you ever been there, Chance?"

"A few times years ago when charter fishing was still happening. My dad took me. I'm familiar with the resort."

Turning back to the manager Santiago handed him a business card. "We'd appreciate you not mentioning this discussion to Mrs. Gunn if she happens to come into the office tomorrow morning."

"I understand, Ma'am."

"Thank you for your help," Stewart said.

"Anytime," said the man and turned off the office light. The door lock clicked behind them.

They sat in the Explorer watching the dark building past midnight.

"Mitch, how would you like to spend the night at La Push?"

"I thought you'd never ask," she said as he fired up the engine.

"We'll stake the place out. Our guys and the Forks Police can cover here. I'm betting she shows at the resort. On the way out I'll call James and update the plan. He'll contact Dan Fox of the Tribal Police to coordinate with us and serve as backup. If we make the arrest on tribal land we don't want it getting choked in red tape."

"You know a tribal cop?" Santiago said.

"Yeah, Dan was in our department several years ago. I worked a homicide case with him. He and James are old pals."

"You don't want me to call while you drive?"

"I'm one of those cell phone highway hazards. You relax. I know the players. You get to call Zinc at 5:00 tomorrow morning. He always said he wanted to wake up to the sound of a beautiful woman's voice."

A half-hour later they pulled into the parking lot at La Push Resort. The office was closed and only a few lights were located throughout the park, one by the motel building.

"Do we want to alert the manager?" she said.

"We can wake him up to rent a cabin, ask about a friend we're looking for. That would explain our presence to the early morning risers and maybe we could get one located to provide a view of the motel units. Just think of it, our first night together and we'll be at the ocean."

"What a guy, a night in body armor watching for a murder suspect. I don't even have my baby doll pajamas with me."

"Baby dolls? I'll hold that image 'til morning."

After waking the night clerk they asked about a friend. They described Gunn and how he might be dressed. The night clerk advised someone like that probably couldn't afford the resort but would camp on one of the beaches. They ignored the clerk's comment and checked into a cabin between the camping area and the motel buildings.

"We're lucky it's preseason. This little place will give us all the view we need. It beats sitting in a car all night," she said.

"Now we sit in the dark and wait," he said taking a seat at the table by the door. "Good view of the motel."

"You need to work on your dating etiquette, Chance. There are a few rough edges on how you show a girl a good time."

For the next several hours they sat at the window and watched from their dark cabin. They had agreed to take turns on the hour so each could get some rest but neither left the table. They watched and visited all night. A few dogs roamed the grounds. A cat wandered onto the porch and looked in the window. At 3:30 a.m. an old man came out of the neighboring cabin, got into a battered pickup and left.

"Penny for your thoughts," she said.

"Just wondering if we have enough for a conviction on Gunn."

"In Shaw we have a witness who knows the time he left the hotel."

He nodded. "We do, but remember, Shaw's credibility could be questioned, given his lies and obstructive behavior."

"We have Moses Cruz. He saw them together. But the only concrete thing we have are the earrings. Strange that he kept them."

"I hate to say this, Mitch, but he probably thought he'd give them to another conquest."

"A confession would be nice. Maybe Linda Gunn can help. Maybe he told her something."

"Possible."

Each sat quietly in thought for a time.

"What are you thinking?" she said.

"I'm visualizing you in a baby doll outfit."

"Still?"

"I like what I see. What do you do in that outfit? I visualize this warm sensual creature, knees tucked under her, sitting on a bed, lights low, waiting in anticipation for a shining knight to arrive."

"It seems just the suggestion has you motor running."

"It does, Mitch, I admit it."

"Sounds like an erotic fantasy. Perhaps you're a victim of the species. I like to read. As for the baby doll you're visualizing, just remember what I said about the thong you were waving around at Haley's apartment. The only thing I do more of in bed than read is sleep."

Let him get to know the real you, Mitch.

"That changes my visual. What do you like to read, trashy romances?"

"That's a bit judgmental, but no. I enjoy Ayn Rand, Steinbeck, Fitzgerald, Stein, Hemingway and Kerouac. Sometimes I read the philosophers and law enforcement journals."

"Whew. Deep for a cop."

"Well, what about you? What do you do at home, sit around in your shorts and drink beer? I won't ask about bed."

"Sometimes I watch sports—mostly baseball—and I like travel narratives. I even read one of your guys, Kerouac. His *On the Road* is off the wall, some kind of trip. I like to hangout down at the Locks. I'm always amazed at the private yachts that come through. I can't even imagine how much money those things cost. I look at 'em and know I'm a bum at best, maybe a bum with a better business than the old hobo in Port Angeles, but still a bum."

"Don't knock bums and hobos. During America's Great Depression, homeless wanderers had hard lives, but some very successful people were in their ranks," she said.

"Such as?"

"Well, how about William O. Douglas, H.L. Hunt, Art Linkletter, Louis L'Amour, Eric Sevaried?"

"I'm impressed. Where do you get this stuff, anyway?"

"That came from the Smithsonian magazine. Like I said, I read a lot, the Strickland-Zinc bimbo factor notwithstanding. Last year I read a series on body language and behaviors suggested by the academy."

"Sounds interesting. Does it really help as an investigative tool?"

"Think Shaw, nail biting and lying. Mannerisms help us interpret what people share: eye movement, speech patterns, body shifts, a lot of stuff."

"I've learned through the school of hard knocks."

"Me too, but studying the science enhances application in the everyday world."

"You're definitely in the next generation of cops. But back to life, do you like to travel?"

"Sure, doesn't everyone? I'd like to travel more, see things, do things and meet new people. It's a job, time, money thing. Look at Hailey Cashland. She spent a ton of money on club clothes. All women want to look good, but she wanted to look great. Her other life was built around being attractive, coveted and satisfying an appetite."

"You push the great part sometimes too, in a good way."

"According to my sister maybe too much. I'm working on that."

"You know, thinking about Hailey's other life makes me think of a person I knew well at one time. He was the conductor of a kid's orchestra, really straight laced, and a weekend biker. He was a big guy like Gunn. Give him a three-day weekend and he was on the road. We had come to know each other at the gym. You know, workout, getting buff, all that jazz."

"To say nothing of the meat market benefits," Santiago said.

"That too. Anyway, we ran into each other one weekend down on the waterfront. I almost walked past him, didn't even recognize the guy. He stopped me and said 'Hi, Chance.' He was in torn jeans, a black leather vest, a dirty T-shirt and a headband. He had a couple days growth on his face and was sweaty as sin."

"And you didn't recognize him even a little?"

"Not even close. He was nasty looking, a bad-ass biker. I've always been curious what the kids in that orchestra would think if they knew about his other life."

"You could ask the same question about Hailey and the kids, or what will Gunn look like when we see him? Is your friend still around?"

"No. He quit a few years ago and moved to Las Vegas to sell real estate. That and test his dip stick after his wife divorced him."

"Sounds like a midlife crisis."

"Maybe, but now that I think about it, he was doing his thing with a carefree member of his staff too, kind'a like Hailey and Hartley. It was just time for him to move on."

"See? Another story about someone's baggage. It's been said each of us ought to be judged by our finest moment, not our weakest."

"I'll subscribe to that. Who said it?" he said.

"I'm not positive. I think it was Emerson."

"I've got to read more. I'm going to stretch my legs. Why don't you wake Zinc and Strickland, let 'em know what's going on. I'll be back in a minute."

He walked out the door into the morning air. Santiago dialed up the Big Tree Inn and talked to Zinc. Five minutes later Stewart returned carrying two cups.

"Mitch, have a cup of coffee."

"Thank you."

"Compliments of the early morning office lady."

"It's been a long night, but a pleasant night."

"How were our friends?"

"Asleep, unhappy to hear from me. Zinc wanted to know how our night was. I told him we spent it together in a little chalet by the ocean sharing our secrets rather than a motel parking lot."

"You're bad, you know that?"

"I can be worse."

"I believe you. We've passed an entire night sitting here talking and I'm not bored or tired."

"Anything going on out there?" she said, changing the subject.

"It's pretty quiet. I ran into a few campers, heard others moving around. I passed a few carrying towels. Ha. There goes one now."

A man walked by the cabin with a towel under his arm, carrying a shaving kit.

"Where's he going?"

"There's a shower room over there," he gestured generally toward a structure hardly visible behind some trees.

The resort area continued to wake during the next hour and a half. More campers were going to the shower, a few campfires had started, people were walking around with coffee cups, and pickup trucks were coming in and going out. Both detectives watched the bustle. Nobody came out of any of the motel rooms.

Then at 6:58 Stewart sat straight up in his chair. "Well, good morning, Mrs. Gunn."

The dirt-covered burgundy Honda pulled into a parking place near the stairs. Linda Gunn got out of the car, locked the door and walked up the stairs.

He said, "Didn't she say to meet her at 8:00?"

"Sure did, but I've got close to 7:00."

"The lady is a player," he said. "Call Zinc again and let him know where she is. Tell them to stay put. Gunn might head in their direction if we don't get him here. There aren't that many ways out of La Push. Now it's gettin' interesting." He checked his watch. It was 7:06.

A man opened the door and Linda Gunn entered.

"Was it him?" Mitch said.

"I couldn't tell, but who else would it be? How do you want to take him?"

"Let's walk over to the building and wait for them to come out."

"Good plan. I noticed this morning during my walk the stairs are open under each step. You face him off when he's got about four steps left. I'll stay underneath. Anything goes wrong I can reach through and trip him."

"Just reach through and send him tumbling, eh?"

"Why not? It'd serve him right. I don't exactly like the man."

"Is this coming from the man who thought I was making the case too personal?"

"Yes it is. Let's go."

* * * * *

Gunn looked into his wife's face, flush and moist. "Why are you crying? You came in here yesterday dripping sarcasm and demanding money." *Play her. You've got to leave together.*

"It's all so frustrating, Trev. I remember when we were in love, crazy about each other. The world was our oyster and we were going for the pearls."

"That was a long time ago. Get a tissue. There's some in the bathroom."

"Thank you."

He walked slowly toward the table. "Look at us. We're losers. For all practical purposes you're an alcoholic. I couldn't get a decent position anywhere with tenure. We have nothing, not even each other."

She was standing near the table. "It's so sad."

He stopped by the window and looked at the Pacific, then turned and faced her. "We haven't had anything for years."

"But where did it go? What happened to our dreams?"

"They went away," he said.

"Can you open the window? It's stuffy in here."

"Of course, I love salt air."

"God, I still have feelings for you and I don't even know why. How did we grow so far apart, become so different?"

"We ran away from each other. I had an affair, then another. I blamed you for my failings."

"I started drinking. Now I get the shakes when I don't."

He looked out the window. "I drove you to the bottle. Why didn't you have affairs? I remember when we slept with everyone."

"You did. I only did your friends because you wanted to do group stuff when you were in grad school. I didn't like it but you said it was turn-on, a growing experience."

"It's my fault. I can see that now. I was stupid, irresponsible," he said.

"We both were. But how did we get to this?"

"What?"

"Murder. How did we go from free spirits ten years ago to murder, running away, deserting our family?"

Gunn slowly shook his head. "I don't know. The hobo was an accident. He was. I swear it! Believe me, at least that much, please. Jesus, my leg hurts. Let's sit down for a few minutes and just talk."

"We haven't done that in years either," she said.

"Then it's about time. Linda, I don't know what I'm going to do. My whole body throbs, just surging with aimless energy. I'm scared, frightened. I know I've done something that can't be changed or forgiven."

"The breeze smells good. Have you considered turning yourself in?"

"Not really. The cops hate me. Hell, I hate me!" He looked at her. "You should hate me."

"Sometimes I hate myself," she said. "I don't know what or who I love or hate right now. I feel helpless.

Sometimes I think the kids would be better off without either one of us."

"An interesting concept, but no. They're going to need you, especially with me out of their lives. I've marked them forever."

"Then do something they can be proud of, Trev. Turn yourself in. I'll be there for you and them. Give them a shred of hope, a ray of light they can look at and someday say with pride 'In the end my dad did the right thing.' Maybe they'll reach that point when they're older. Give 'em the opportunity."

"I'd get life, maybe even the death penalty," he said.

"Truth is you've got it anyway. Look at how nervous you are every time you hear a noise. You've sentenced yourself to life already. Maybe, just maybe, when they grow up they'll have some dignity."

"I can't do that. I can't spend my life behind bars. What do I get out of it?" He paused. "You want some coffee?"

"I need something. I don't know if it's me, the booze, or what. I alternate between extremes."

"Are you cold, Linda? I'll close the window."

"No. I'm sweating too. One minute I feel like I'm going to puke and the next I'm starving."

Gunn went to the refrigerator and pulled out the remaining hot dogs. "They're cold, but they're cooked."

He slowly limped back to the table and set the plate down.

"Doesn't this take us back? Here we are facing the most serious decision of our lives and I'm gnawing on cold hot dogs." She laughed. "They're really slimy feeling."

"Bad form, Dear."

She laughed with her mouth full. "Give up, Trev. I'll go with you."

"I'm thinking about it. Did anyone see you come in, maybe that Indian?"

"Campers on the far side by some of the cabins were outside but I didn't see the Indian or anyone else around here. Why?"

"My face had been all over the news."

"We can drive back to Seattle and call the detectives," she said.

"Right. That bitch cop would love to lock me up. If I do it, I'll go alone. You should be with the kids."

"They're in Spokane."

"We'll put you on a plane."

He took a stack of bills, hundreds and fifties, out of a shopping bag. "I know this doesn't look like much in a stack, but take the money. I won't need it."

"You'll turn yourself in?"

"I only have two options. Turn myself in or get caught... well, or kill myself." Tears welled in his eyes. He shuddered. "I can't believe this has happened, all because I didn't want to hurt my family. I told her I couldn't do it."

"Well, we're beyond hurt," she said.

"Just another failure in my life. Why cause a little pain when I can do it in huge doses?" He looked across the table. Linda's mouth was moving but he didn't hear a thing she was saying. *A concrete abutment would work, hitting it at sixty or seventy straight on. Quick and painless. Get rid of both of us.*

"...still love you," she said.

He studied his wife's face. "What would become of the kids if something happened to you?"

"I don't know. My folks would try to take care of them. They're going to help a lot now, anyway. I've got to get clean to find work. Who'd've thought I'd be going home? To Spokane I mean."

"We aren't."

"You know what I mean."

"Yes, I know."

"Let's get out of here," she said. "If nothing else we can enjoy one last drive around Lake Crescent."

"What about that cup of coffee? You've been shaky and I'm hurting." *Somebody will see us leave. I need a witness that we were together in her car.*

"Actually, coffee sounds good right now, but no more hot dogs."

Gunn walked to the stove and poured two cups. "Did you leave anything in Forks?"

"Nothing I can't do without. I want this nightmare to end."

He looked at her from the stove. "And so it shall."

"It's good to see you calm again, Trev. You've always been able to relax when you've made a decision."

"Yes, I feel much better now."

"You're not even limping too much."

"Amazing what self-pity does for the body... or should I say to it?"

Linda Gunn sipped the steaming fluid and watched her husband. "What was it like when you killed her?"

Gunn looked up in surprise. "You want to know?"

"I know it sounds awful, but her death is the defining moment in our lives. Yes, I want to know."

Gunn's breath became short. He bared his teeth, thrust his hands out, then opened and closed them, watching his fingers. "It was horrible, strange. She thrashed and struggled, but not much. I held her under for a long time. Afterwards I took back the earrings I'd given her. I ripped 'em off, then cleaned the room and left. When I got home I was still excited but you were drunk. Later I told you we'd watched the news together but you slept through most of the evening thinking I was home from work at my regular time."

Linda stared at the blank expression on his face, as his lips moved and words poured out. "You're all alone now, Trev. You can't even hear me."

"And now I can end the pain and suffering. The road is the path to freedom, a truck the exit!" *You think I'm going to commit suicide. I'll stop somewhere to drop you off. We can walk into the woods to make love one last time. You'll disappear, I'll disappear, and the car will turn up in a deep part of Lake Crescent.*

"Trev, let's get going and make good on your decision."

His eyes blinked and he twisted his head. "Yes, we should get started."

"But Trev, I do need to stop at the motel in Forks after all, sorry. It's only for a minute. I forgot my overnight bag. Otherwise, I'll be a terrible sight when I arrive in Spokane."

"You don't need to go into the office?"

"No. I can just run into the room for a minute." She checked her watch.

CHAPTER 20

After putting on their body armor and loose-fitting SPD jackets, Santiago and Stewart waited beneath the resort stairs hoping at any moment the door above would open and the Gunns would descend.

"At times like this I can understand why people smoke," she said.

"I did at one time."

"What, smoke or understand?"

"Smoke, smart ass."

"Filthy habit."

He looked at his watch. "What time is it? This damn thing has stopped."

"7:17... it's like we've been here forever."

"I know. When I was a kid if I had to stand around and wait I always had to go to the bathroom."

"Careful, you know about the power of suggestion."

"Yes, Mother. They seem to be taking a lot of time up there."

"Maybe she's telling him about our visit last night."

"Could be, or maybe she's working the 'turn yourself in' line."

The smell of sausage, bacon and eggs wafted through the morning air.

"Great. Now I'm thinking about breakfast," he said.

"Me too. It smells good. I can almost taste it."

"Don't be so graphic, but I love it."

The door of 103 opened. A man in his early thirties stepped outside. "Come on, kids. Let's head down to the beach for a morning hike. We might find a Japanese float."

More noise came out the open door, closely followed by two boys in the seven to nine age range. Stewart stepped toward the man showing his identification.

"Excuse me; we're here on official business. To insure nobody gets hurt would you take your family to the beach using the trail at the far end of the building?"

"Is it dangerous?" the man said.

"Yes. We expect our work here will be completed within the next fifteen to twenty minutes. When you're ready to return from the beach just check to see if that red Explorer is still parked over there," Stewart said. "If it's gone, we're done."

The man turned toward the door and said in a firm voice, "Honey, bring the boys. We really need to go to the beach, now."

"You sure don't sound like a fun guy this morning, Dad," said the older of the boys.

"We'll have fun on the beach. Hurry, let's go."

His wife came out the door. "What is it, Dear?"

He stepped beside her and whispered in her ear, "Police business."

She turned and closed the door, then clapped her hands together over her head. "Chop, chop! Time to go."

The family moved down the sidewalk at a brisk pace and turned the corner. The man waved to the detectives.

Stewart smiled, flashed a peace sign and emitted a sigh of relief. "What time do you have now?" he asked.

"7:25... slow going, isn't it?"

"Yes. If they don't come out soon we'll go up."

A man and a woman approached from the direction of the registration office. She was an attractive Indian woman dressed in some type of uniform. The man appeared very .muscular, stocky and rugged.

"Look at his right hand... a piece of chain," Santiago said.

Stewart's nerves tensed. "Looks like trouble."

The man and woman were arguing as they approached the stairs.

"He's not worth it, Jimmy. I couldn't stand to see you in jail again."

"I'll kill that bastard!" Jimmy said.

"Let his wife. He did nothing to me. Maybe he stepped on my feelings. That's all."

Jimmy rubbed the palm of his left hand over the chain-wrapped fist and stepped on the bottom stair. "He needs to pay. They all need to pay."

Stewart stepped out from under the stairs, flashed his badge and held an index finger to his lips.

Jimmy stopped, startled by his sudden appearance.

"Quiet," Stewart said. "I'm a police officer here on official business."

Jimmy took his foot off the stair and slid his right hand behind his back.

Stewart continued. "Is the man you're angry with in 203?"

"Yes," said the woman. "My brother feels he took advantage of me."

"You're lucky. He's wanted for the murders of two people, including another young woman."

"Holy shit!" Jimmy said.

"Listen to your sister. Let my partner and me handle this. We're here to arrest him."

"Murder! Jesus!" Jimmy said. "He's not that tough."

"He was when he wanted to be. Now go and let us do our job."

"Okay, Cop." Jimmy looked through the stairs. "Your partner?"

"Yes. Now go. If you have to watch what happens do so from a distance out of danger."

The twosome turned away.

Stewart said, "By the way, you might want to put the chain away too."

Jimmy moved his right hand in front of him as he departed.

Stewart stepped back under the stairs with Santiago. "What's taking so long. What time is it now?" he muttered.

"Relax, Chance. It's 7:33."

"Is that all?"

"That's it."

He placed his arm around Santiago's shoulder. From a distance they looked like a couple of love struck newlyweds.

"You're warm, Mitch."

"So are you."

He looked into her dark eyes and kissed her, gently, softly. "Good morning, again."

"Second time is better."

They stood together for several minutes alone under the stairs. Then came the sound of a door opening above them. Both officers pulled their weapons. The voices became louder and clear.

"You left your bag in Forks? Why?"

"I'm sorry. I was just so anxious to get here."

"You mean greedy."

"I'm sorry. It's for the boys."

"Okay, okay. I'll take you back to your motel."

Gunn looked around the parking lot from the elevated walkway. His gaze shifted to the front door of the office. "Look at them sitting on a bench."

"Who?" Linda said.

"The Indian dude. We're not stopping at the entrance. In fact, I think I'll drive." *Gemma and Jimmy will attest to our leaving together.*

"But your leg?"

"Leg be damned. That guy wants my head. He's nuts."

"I can drive."

"No, I'll drive. You don't want to go where I'm going. Whatever happens today, you're better off away from me."

Below the stairs Stewart and Santiago were positioned, waiting.

Linda whispered, "We don't need a family debate."

"Amen."

"You're not going to give up are you, Trev?"

"No... not to the cops. I can't spend the rest of my life behind bars, and the thought of a dozen people watching me being strapped to a table and getting a lethal injection is even worse. They'd all be gloating, especially that bitch cop."

"Maybe you should leave me here."

"Afraid I'll take you with me? Have you ever witnessed a head-on? They're quick."

"Trev—" she said

"Quick but dirty." He smiled at his stranger wife, his eyes glazed. A cackling laugh emitted from his throat. "Maybe someplace around Lake Crescent. Maybe a logging truck."

"No, Trev. The police are—"

He pulled her by the arm. He pushed her to the head of the stairs. "Let's go. You were going to say something about the cops? I suppose they're in Forks waiting for me. I can read you like a book." He shook his head. A contorted smile crossed his face, and his deep red lips curled oddly. "My way is the highway. Just be happy if I don't take you with me. Leaving you for the boys could be my final good deed, but a truly good deed would be to free them of both of us. You have to admit, as parents *and* as humans, we're despicable."

"Please, Trev."

"I'll let you out by Lake Crescent... you and your purse full of money." *But not the way you think.*

Their footsteps echoed on the stairwell.

Santiago listened as they started down the stairs. She looked at Stewart. His eyes were focused overhead. She gripped her weapon. She could feel the pressure of Stewart's arm against the side of her body.

Stewart's lips were moving as he silently counted each step, his Glock at the ready. He looked at Santiago.

Linda's foot hit the fifth step, then the fourth. Her purse came into view, then Gunn's foot.

Stewart motioned with his hand.

Santiago stepped out from under the stairs, her weapon trained on Gunn. "Freeze!" she shouted.

Gunn looked at his wife with a cold stare. "You dirty bitch!"

"I didn't know they were here!"

Linda Gunn stumbled and fell toward Santiago, and Stewart reached through the stairs and pulled Gunn's right foot out from under him. Gunn grasped at the railing, then collapsed down the stairs. Santiago rolled away from Linda Gunn and came to her knees. She aimed her Glock at Gunn from point blank range.

"Shoot me! That's better than prison, bitch!"

Stewart moved from under the stairs and put Gunn on the ground, his knee hard between the man's shoulder blades. He jerked Gunn's right hand up and slapped a cuff on it, then pulled his left hand up and cuffed them together. Then he stood and read Gunn his Miranda rights. Santiago helped Linda Gunn to her feet.

Stewart tugged Gunn from the ground. "Get up." He sat Gunn on the stairs.

Gunn shook his head. "In an hour it would have been over for both of us."

"It's over now," Santiago said.

"No, it's just beginning. We would've disappeared, maybe dead." He began the cackling laughter again. "Now the state will have to prove I'm guilty. Am I sane? Can I stand trial? Who knows, I might walk after a few years in a hospital? Stranger things have happened."

"He's crazy, Detective Santiago," said Linda Gunn. "I knew it for sure this morning after I got here."

"You're lucky to be alive, Linda," Santiago said.

"I know."

A tribal police vehicle arrived from the direction of the cabins. A large Indian officer emerged, smiling broadly, his hand extended. "Nice work, Detective Stewart." He looked at Santiago. "This must be your partner."

"Sergeant Fox, Detective Michelle Santiago," Stewart said.

Fox glanced at Santiago for a brief moment. "It's a pleasure, Michelle." Then he addressed both officers. "I'll transport the prisoner to Forks and turn him over to the police. They'll book him and process the papers for transfer."

Santiago looked at Stewart. "It's over. We got him."

"That we did."

Fox put Gunn in the back seat of the tribal police vehicle. Gemma and Jimmy were applauding from the front of the resort office. Zinc and Strickland arrived in the SPD unmarked car and rolled to a halt, leaving the dash flasher on.

Stewart looked at Fox. "We'll let them transport the suspect back to Seattle after the paperwork is finished."

"Not a problem," Fox said. "Who's going to check the room?"

"We will," said Zinc.

"Don't look so surprised," Strickland said. "Fox called us when he saw the Gunns come out of the room. We thought you might need some backup. We were just up the road a ways."

"Check the room carefully. He should have had fifteen to sixteen thousand cash," Santiago said. *Do the right thing, Linda.*

"It's been a long night, Mitch," Stewart said.

"I'm ready for some sleep."

Gunn sat in the back seat, looking around. A small stream of saliva ran over his lower lip. "You were a dead bitch. Killers, cops, wives... we're all bad."

Linda Gunn and Santiago looked at him, their expressions confused.

Gunn began laughing again. He grinned at his wife. "You were a good lay a long time ago. Good for me, them, anyone. Lost it in a bottle, bitch. I could've ended your pain." His laughter became louder. Sweat appeared on his forehead. He tried to shake his cuffed hands.

Tears welled in Linda's eyes and her breath became short.

"Mmm," Gunn said. "Smells like breakfast is in the air. I love breakfast. I like a fresh morning filled with the scent of the coming day. I love breakfast and women. Women all day long, long, long. Me, me, me, my, my, my. I work for the government. My job is to get women ready to tease and please, oh yeah. It's government work."

"What's he saying?" Santiago said.

"Sounds like psychobabble to me," Stewart said.

Linda Gunn wiped her eyes and nose. "At first I thought he'd give himself up. Then he changed. Now he scares me. I think he wanted to kill me, maybe both of us. I'm not sure."

"Linda," Santiago said, "let your parents help you. Think about the boys."

"I'll will."

"Fuck 'em! Fuck 'em all!" Gunn shouted from the backseat.

"I've had enough of your garbage mouth." Fox stepped to the open door and slammed it. "He's nuts, man."

"Or he wants us to think he is," Stewart said.

Zinc came down the stairs from Gunn's room carrying a shopping bag. "A few clothes, a tablet, tape, not much."

"Money?" Santiago said while glancing at Linda Gunn.

"No money."

"I have it in my purse," Linda Gunn said.

Santiago looked at Stewart and nodded. *Good move.*

"For the time being we'll have to take it, Ma'am," Zinc said. "You'll get it back, but right now its evidence."

Santiago looked at her. "Contact Captain James about the money. Meanwhile, help your boys."

"Thank you again," Linda said.

Fox left first, taking Gunn to Forks for booking and processing. Strickland and Zinc left next. Linda Gunn, Stewart and Santiago watched them leave.

Santiago began laughing.

"What's so funny, Mitch?"

"Strickland. Before they left, he said, 'You two probably need some sack time after being up all night.' I told him, 'Of course, although we did spend all night in a cabin.'"

Stewart grinned. "Do tell. Well, let's call the captain with our game plan."

"I'm heading for home, I mean Spokane," Linda Gunn said. "Do you need me for anything else?"

"We don't, but those officers and the authorities in Forks will need you to make a statement," Stewart said.

"The prosecutor will need to talk with you before the trial, too, so make sure we know where to reach you," Santiago said.

"He admitted killing Hailey. He even told me how he did it." She shuddered and turned toward her car.

"I'll drive you to Forks," Stewart said. "Mitch will drive your car in so you won't need to come back out here afterwards."

"Good," she said.

Stewart looked at Mitch. "Do we have anything in the cabin?"

"Not that I can think of. We traveled light last night."

"So we did," he said.

Santiago looked up to see the father of the boys looking around the corner. "Better wave to your fan club before you leave."

Stewart waved, and he and Linda Gunn got into the Explorer, Santiago into Linda's car and they drove to the entry of the resort. Gemma and Jimmy were still on the office bench. They gave the officers a thumb up as they left.

At the Forks Police Department, Stewart escorted Linda into the office and the waiting officers after Santiago gave her the car keys.

Santiago and Stewart returned to his truck.

Stewart, with a chivalrous bow from the waist, said, "Shall we, Detective Santiago?"

"I thought you'd never ask."

"Oh yes... baby dolls and sleep. Life is good."

CHAPTER 21
Day 11: Monday

After spending the night at Big Tree Inn, Michelle Santiago and Chance Stewart reported to Captain James for a debriefing following the arrest and transfer of Gunn from Forks to Seattle.

"You two did a nice piece of work on the Cashland case. Congratulations," James said. "It's in the hands of the DA now. I hear Gunn's defense is going to be an insanity plea."

"He started his plea at La Push," Santiago said.

"I don't know where it'll go. Only about three percent are successful. We've got his wife's testimony, Terry Shaw, Moses Cruz, Carla Johnson and DNA from both the earrings and the hobo killing. I'm betting he'll want to make a deal in a few weeks, maybe a month."

The two detectives nodded. Both were informally dressed. Stewart was wearing casual slacks, an open-collared sports shirt, dark loafers and no socks. Santiago was wearing black jeans, a light print blouse, four-inch heels and aviator sunglasses.

James looked appreciatively at Santiago. "Protection from bright clouds?"

"Tired red eyes," she said.

He patted files on his desk. "Well, we can get started on something new. Some things seldom change, like homicide and the drizzle predicted for today."

"Not so fast, Captain," Santiago said. "What about Frank Cashland?"

"The DA is looking into his situation. Obviously he has the misdemeanor solicitation charge pending, but that shouldn't concern you."

"It doesn't, but the sexual abuse Hailey described in her diary at the hands of her father does."

"The DA's looking into that, too, but he can't promise anything. It's out of his hands... different state, you know, and statutes of limitations."

"By the way, did you two like the accommodations in Forks? I thought it was unusual you didn't bring the prisoner back."

"Quite satisfactory. We were really beat after the all-night visual. What did you think, Mitch?" Stewart said.

"Like you, very nice, and very accommodating."

"Well, we have other cases pending, work to do."

Mitch said, "Captain, there's still a couple of items of unfinished business."

"What?"

"The harassment issue for one, the Baxters' daughter for another."

"The culprits were Zinc and Strickland. I've turned the matter over to IA. I wouldn't want to be in their shoes right now. They'll get reprimanded, maybe early retirement. Who knows? They knew better." James paused. "Regarding the Baxters, their daughter finally called from Acapulco. Seems she ran off and married some guy she met in a bar."

"Really," Santiago said. "I guess that's good news. I expect something similar from Jill one of these days."

"At least she's alive," James said.

Santiago said, "You know, I think we both need a break too. I've got four weeks of vacation coming. What about you, Chance?"

"Three."

"And I suppose you want to take it at the same time," James said.

"Yes," they said in unison.

"That is a well-orchestrated spontaneous response," James said, laughing. "Don't forget the policy about fraternization."

"We haven't forgotten," Stewart said.

The door opened and the captain's leggy secretary sauntered in. She strolled across the office, bent slightly over the front of the desk and handed James a note. Her mini performed as directed.

James looked up at her and smiled. "I'll be there," he said in a pleasant voice. "Meet me downstairs."

She nodded, stood straight and ambled back out the door. All three sets of eyes followed her. James adjusted his tie and glasses. "Now, where were we?"

Santiago and Stewart looked at each other and laughed. "Fraternization," she said.

"And Captain," Stewart said in a low voice, "I'd be much more careful about my meetings with her in the garage."

"Yes, well... ah, I'll give each of you a week's vacation beginning now. We have too many things going to do anymore at the same time. Now I have business to take care of, things to do. And Mitch, taking a vacation, does that mean you've reconsidered the other item we talked about?"

"I'm still thinking about it. Sometimes the outside looks cleaner, less cluttered. I'll let you know."

The detectives left the captain's office and returned to their desks.

"What now, Mitch?" Stewart said.

"Let's take the video to Jack Hartley. He's paid big time for his part in all of this. If it stays here it'll resurface someday."

"That's a given. And if it comes up missing, it won't be the first time a piece of porn was misplaced," he said.

"Well, I don't want Hailey's dad getting his hands on it, either. Now, how about lunch? I'll buy."

"You're buying? What's the occasion, lady?"

"You're taking me to Kalaloch, remember? Then we're going to explore the future of our relationship."

"Are you bringing that special night wear Jill suggested?"

"Do I need to?"

"No, but it would make nice background scenery."

Zinc and Sutherland approached their desks.

"My, my, my, it's the Smut Men," she said.

"Mitch, I'm sorry," Zinc said.

Santiago looked at the rumpled figures standing next to her desk. "Guys, you have to answer to someone bigger than me. If you didn't already know it, the department was fully aware of my background when I went to work here."

"I knew. I completed most of the verifications myself," Zinc said. "You're a good cop. I hope you'll accept my apology. This could cost us our jobs!"

She watched Zinc's face turn deep red. "I accept your apology, but the rest is up to Internal Affairs. It's the price of being a professional," she said.

Both men turned and left the area. Zinc was mumbling to himself.

"That was an attempt to get me to drop the complaint, don't you think?"

"Probably. Are you going to drop it?"

"No way. In the first place, I didn't lodge it, but even if I had, I check out guy's butts and you never miss a miniskirt, but we don't demean or harass. I think most men and women are like us. We're what I think of as normal. To me, Zinc and Strickland are like the tip of an iceberg that results in a dark form of personality like Hailey's dad."

"Or the wham bam mentality that I've recently discarded?"

"Both of us have taken a step forward, Chance. Maybe it's this case. Maybe it's us coming to grips with our past. I don't know. We've taken a long time to get to know each other, maybe too long, but then again, maybe not. Even in my college years I had to have mutual respect for whomever I had a relationship with." She laughed. "Though I might have had a lapse or two."

"Don't we all? Now, how about lunch and a drive to the coast?"

"It would be a pleasure right, after our stop at Hartley's."

They left the office smiling and laughing. Their conversation was anything but police business. They arrived at the garage and got into Stewart's Explorer.

"This case was so twisted. So many lives were affected, memories stirred and poured over," she said.

"We all have our warts, Mitch. This case brought out the good and bad in all of us. What a sordid affair."

"Speaking of which, can we go by the Seattle Center? I told Jill I'd check for her clothes."

Stewart looked at Santiago with a raised eyebrow.

She grinned. "Don't go there."

~ Ends ~

In *Desert Kill*, the second title in the Santiago mystery series:

Lindsey Braun is a twenty year old going on thirty-five. She's a rich kid who has led an edgy, do-whatever-you-want lifestyle. She's even engaged in affairs with older men, including a few who were married, all with the approval of her bacchanalian father, Claude Braun, a billionaire Chandler software developer and friend to the government's highest officials. She is a student at ASU but lives off campus. She never disappears without a phone call, but no one has seen her or her car for three days

Finally, Braun's wife and Lindsey's stepmother, Nikki, calls in her dear friend, Seattle Homicide Detective Michelle Santiago. Santiago drops everything, leaving a coastal vacation in Washington with her partner and lover, Chance Stewart. She takes a leave of absence and flies into a murderous nightmare in Arizona's Valley of the Sun to find Claude and Nikki's missing daughter.

Braun believes Lindsey has been kidnapped, but he is reluctant to report her missing. Lindsey has had many flings in her short life. He doesn't want to embarrass his daughter or the company or compromise the secret government work his company does.

When the kidnapper sends Lindsey's ring finger to her father, the FBI recognize it as the signature of a serial killer who was once listed as MIA in Vietnam, and who is a CIA-type gone off the reservation. He is also a mercenary, an assassin and a stone-cold psychopath.

Santiago has become an obsession of the killer, so she works with an undercover agent posing as a long lost love interest to draw the him out. She taunts him, flaunts her flesh at the pool and teases him while bathing. But before she can do anything she must survive his life-altering plans for her.

About the Author

Ron Wick is a retired teacher, principal and poet from the Seattle area, now living in Arizona. As an educator he also worked with police and court authorities involving many criminal issues, ranging from juvenile delinquencies to suspected pedophiles. One of his students was alleged to be a Green River murder victim. He is dedicated to improving the quality of life for all humanity and will donate 10% of his royalties to Lions Clubs International Foundation, the charitable arm of the association of which he has been a member and officer for 35 years.